Pra

"*A Wi*
love i

"*Jedi*
blessi

"The
well

Pra

"A fir
comp
story

"Sch
on al

"A po
their

—

Rebecca Kertz was first introduced to the Amish when her husband took a job with an Amish construction crew. She enjoyed watching the Amish foreman's children at play and swapping recipes with his wife. Rebecca resides in Delaware with her husband and dog. She has a strong faith in God and feels blessed to have family nearby. Besides writing, she enjoys reading, doing crafts and visiting Lancaster County.

Anna Schmidt is an award-winning author of more than twenty-five works of historical and contemporary fiction. She is a three-time finalist for the coveted RITA® Award from Romance Writers of America, as well as a four-time finalist for an RT Reviewers' Choice Award. Critics have called Anna "a natural writer, spinning tales reminiscent of old favorites like *Miracle on 34th Street*." One reviewer raved, "I love Anna Schmidt's style of writing!"

REBECCA KERTZ

Loving Isaac

&

ANNA SCHMIDT

A Groom for Greta

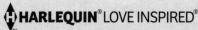

HARLEQUIN® LOVE INSPIRED®

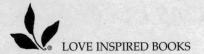

LOVE INSPIRED BOOKS

Recycling programs for this product may not exist in your area.

ISBN-13: 978-0-373-20977-4

Loving Isaac and A Groom for Greta

Copyright © 2017 by Harlequin Books S.A.

The publisher acknowledges the copyright holders of the individual works as follows:

Loving Isaac
Copyright © 2016 by Rebecca Kertz

A Groom for Greta
Copyright © 2012 by Jo Horne Schmidt

www.Harlequin.com

Printed in U.S.A.

CONTENTS

LOVING ISAAC

Rebecca Kertz

For dear friends Pat and Mike Drexel, with love

For by grace you have been saved through faith.
And this is not your own doing;
it is the gift of God.
—*Ephesians* 2:8

Chapter One

The air was rich with the scent of roses and honey-suckle as Ellen Mast walked from the house to the barn. She entered the old wooden structure to get a bucket of chicken feed, then exited to release the birds into the yard.

"Here you go! Come and get it!" She smiled as she watched the hens and chicks scurrying toward the food. The lone rooster strutted out of the enclosure last, his chest puffing up when he saw the hens.

"Red," Ellen called to him as she tossed down a handful. "Over here. Come get it!" The rooster bent and ate, his red-crested head dipping toward the feed. "That's it. You always have to make an appearance last, *ja*?" She chuckled as she threw more grain, loving how the hens followed the trail wherever it landed.

"You'd better get down, Will, or you're gonna fall!" she heard her brother Elam exclaim.

"*Nay*, I won't!"

Ellen frowned as she skirted the barn toward the sound of her younger brothers' voices. She found them near the hog pen. Will was walking barefoot along the top wooden rail of the surrounding fence while Elam watched with dismay from several feet away. A number of pigs and hogs wallowed in the mud, while others snorted and stuck their noses into the wire fencing between the rails. She approached slowly. "Will!" she called softly so as not to frighten him. "You need to get off there."

Her brother flashed a guilty look. He teetered on the rail but managed to maintain his balance.

"Now," she said sharply when he made no effort to climb down.

Will shot her a worried glance. "El, I'm trying." He wobbled, lost his balance and fell into the mud pit. The hogs grunted and squealed as her brother scrambled to his feet.

Ellen dropped her bucket and ran. According to their father, their largest sow weighed close to five hundred pounds, while the rest weighed from twenty to two hundred. Fear pumped through her as she raced to unlatch the gate. "See if you can make your way, Will. Hurry!"

Will slogged through the mud, moving as fast as he could. The hogs and pigs grunted and squealed, the big one malevolently eyeing the intruder.

Ellen kept an eye on the animals as she held open the gate. After Will was out of danger, she shut and latched it, then scowled at him.

"You know better than to climb onto that fence or to do anything near the hogs except toss scraps to them." She stood with her hands on her hips, noting the mud covering him from head to toe. She wrinkled her nose at the stench. *"Mam's* not going to be happy. You stink."

Fortunately, Will hadn't been wearing his hat and shoes or he'd have been in worse trouble with their mother.

"Ellen!" *Mam* called. Her mother waved her over to where she stood on the front porch of the farmhouse.

"Coming, *Mam*!" She hurried to put away her feed bucket, then quickly headed toward the house. Her younger brothers trailed behind—Will a sight covered in hog mud, with Elam walking some distance away, no doubt offended by the foul odor emanating from his brother.

As she drew closer, Ellen smiled at her mother. *"Ja, Mam?"*

"I need you to run an errand. The quilting bee is next week at Katie's. I'd like you to take our squares to her." *Mam* firmed her grip on the stack of colorful fabric squares as she leaned against the porch railing. "I promised to get them to her yesterday but couldn't get away—" Her mother stopped suddenly and looked past Ellen, her eyes widening. She inhaled sharply. "William Joseph Mast, what on earth have you been doing?"

"Walking the hog fence," Elam offered helpfully.

His mother frowned. "And you, Elam? What were you doing while Will was on the fence? Waiting for your turn?"

"Nay, Mam. I told him to get down but he wouldn't listen." Elam blinked up at her without worry. "And then he couldn't get down."

Her mother clicked her tongue with dismay as she turned back to Will. "Go to the outside pump and wait there, young man! You'll not be stepping into the house until you've washed and changed clothes." Her gaze didn't soften as she turned to her other son. "Elam, run upstairs and get clean garments for your *bruder*." Her lips firmed. "I'll get soap and towels."

"Mam?" Ellen asked softly. "Do you still want me to go to Katie's?"

"Ja." Her mother glanced at the fabric squares in patterns they'd stitched by hand and nodded. "Let me put them in a bag first."

Ellen left shortly afterward to the sound of Will's loud protests as *Mam* scrubbed the stinky mud from his hair and skin at the backyard water pump.

The day was clear and sunny, and the traffic on the main road was light as Ellen steered Blackie, the mare pulling her family's gray buggy, toward the Samuel Lapp farm.

Many of their women friends and neighbors would be attending the quilting bee at Katie Lapp's next week. Katie would stitch together the colorful squares that everyone had made at home. She would pin the length of stitched squares to a length of cotton with a layer of batting in between. Then she would stretch the unfinished quilt over a wooden rack from which the community women would work together, stitching carefully through all three of the layers.

Ellen enjoyed going to quilting bees. She had been taught as a young girl to make neat, even stitches and was praised often for them. After their last quilt gathering, *Mam* had confided to her on the way home that her work was much better than that of many of the seasoned quilters, who were often too busy nattering about people's doings in the community to pay much attention to their stitches. Her mother had told her once that after everyone left, Katie would tear out, then redo the worst of the stitches, especially if the quilt was meant to be given as a wedding present or sold at a community fund-raiser.

"Won't Alta know that Katie took out her stitches?" she'd asked her mother.

Mam had smiled. "*Nay*, Alta never remembers which area she quilted. She often takes credit for the beautiful work that Katie or you did, Ellen."

The memory of her *mam's* praise warmed her as Ellen drove along the paved road, enjoying the peace and beauty of the countryside.

The silence was broken when she heard the rev of an engine as a car came up too quickly from behind. A toot of a horn accompanied several young male shouts as the driver of the vehicle passed the buggy too closely without trying to slow down. Her horse balked and kicked up its pace and the buggy veered to the right. Ellen grabbed hard on the reins as the buggy swerved and bumped along the grass on the edge of the roadway.

"Easy, Blackie," she commanded, trying to steer the animal in another direction. She pulled hard on the leathers. The horse straightened, but not before the buggy's right wheels rolled into a dip along the edge of someone's property where the vehicle drew to a stop. The jerking motion caused Ellen to slide in her seat and hit the passenger door before smacking her head against the inside wall. She gasped as pain radiated from her forehead to her cheek. She raised a hand to touch the sore area as she sat, breathing hard, shaken by the accident.

"Hey, Amish girl!" a young male voice taunted. "Stop hogging the road!"

Ellen felt indignant but kept her mouth shut. She'd been driving with the awareness that if a car needed to pass her, it could. She'd stayed toward the right and left plenty of room.

She saw with mounting concern that the car had pulled over to the side of the road ahead and stopped. Four teenage English boys hung out the open windows, mocking her driving skills and the way she was dressed.

"Too afraid to wear something nice, huh?" one called.

"Why don't you let us see your pretty blond hair?"

They didn't ask, nor did they care, if she was all right. They apparently didn't worry that their actions might have caused her to be seriously hurt.

Her face throbbed and she was afraid to move. Her buggy was angled to the right, and if she shifted in the wrong way, then it might tip onto its side, causing damage to the vehicle and injuring her further.

The driver stepped out of his car. "Dunkard girl! Watch where you're going! Do I have to show you how to drive that thing?"

Ellen was suddenly afraid. What would she do if the boys came within reach of her? How could she protect herself if they surrounded her? Her heart pounded hard. She reached up to touch her face. Her forehead and cheek hurt. Her fingers burned from tugging hard on the leathers and her shoulder ached. She couldn't get out of the vehicle.

Her fear vanished and she became angry. She sent up a silent prayer for God to help her get over her anger quickly and to keep her safe from the English teenagers.

"What do you think you're doing?" a male voice called out to the *Englishers* from behind her.

That voice! Ellen recognized it immediately. He appeared next to her vehicle, confirming who it was. She frowned. Out of everyone within her church district, why did she have to be rescued by Isaac Lapp?

His heart thundered in his chest as Isaac watched the buggy bounce across uneven ground before coming to a halt in a ditch along the side of the road. The vehicle tilted at an angle and, alarmed, he raced toward the driver's side to see if he could help. He peered through the opening of the window. When he recognized Ellen Mast sitting on the far side of the front seat, he inhaled sharply. She held a hand to her forehead, and he spoke softly so as not to scare her. "Ellen? How bad are you hurt?"

She blinked pain-filled blue eyes at him. "I'm *oll recht.*"

His lips firmed; he didn't believe her. He glanced ahead toward the car and stared at the driver as another boy climbed out the front passenger side. "Ellen, hold on tight while I pull your buggy back onto the road," he said gently as, ignoring them, he turned back.

"What are you doing here, Isaac?" a boy snarled.

Silently praying for control over his anger, Isaac faced the *Englishers* he'd once regarded as friends until he'd realized how mean the boys were. The group of friends was always asking for trouble. He moved toward the front of Ellen's horse and glared at the two boys. Brad Smith had caused enough pain and heartache to last him a lifetime. Isaac wasn't about to let the *Englisher* or any of his friends hurt anyone else in his Amish community, especially Ellen, a vulnerable young girl.

"Go home, Brad," he called out. "You've done enough damage for one day."

A third youth stepped out from the car's backseat. He stared at Isaac across the distance. "I wonder what Nancy's going to say when she hears you've been hanging around that Aay-mish girl!"

Refusing to rise to their taunts, Isaac grabbed the mare's bridle and pulled the animal toward the road. The horse moved slowly with Isaac's steady pressure on the reins. Within seconds, he'd maneuvered the mare back onto the road. The buggy bucked and jerked as the right wheels rolled up the incline onto pavement. He felt Ellen's eyes on him as he calmed the animal with soft words, then returned to the driver's side of the girl's vehicle.

"Isaac!" the third boy snarled.

Isaac stiffened, then faced them. "Roy, go home—all of you! You could have caused her serious injury. If you don't want to get arrested, then you'd better go and leave us alone." Brad Smith and his friends were bullies who liked to pick on anyone who couldn't fight back. Fortunately, Brad didn't intimidate him. *I won't allow him to bully Ellen.*

"You know them?" Ellen murmured as the boys piled back into the car and left.

"Ja." He stared unhappily down the road in the direction they'd left before he turned, dismissing them.

"Who is he?" Ellen asked.

"Brad Smith. Nancy's *bruder.*"

Nancy Smith. The name filled Ellen with dread. *The girl who ruined my friendship with Isaac.* Isaac had met the English girl during his *rumspringa* and liked her so much that he'd brought her home to meet his family. He'd taken her to a community gathering and a church service. If that wasn't disturbing enough, he'd brought her to a Sunday-evening community youth singing. Having the English girl in their midst had felt awkward for her. She and Isaac had been good friends until Nancy had learned of his friendship with Ellen and proceeded to monopolize his time. Isaac had been so enamored of her that he'd allowed it. He'd forgotten about Ellen. But Nancy hadn't. She had made it clear to Ellen that Isaac was hers and he no longer would have time for her. It had been a terrible loss for Ellen, as she had fallen in love with Isaac.

Thinking to do the right thing to protect her friend, Ellen had warned Isaac that the English girl was not a nice person. But, too blinded by his infatuation with Nancy, he'd refused to believe Ellen and had become angry with her. Ellen had felt betrayed by Isaac's reaction and his lack of trust. Ellen had loved him; she wouldn't have purposely set out to hurt him. If Nancy had been the good person she'd pretended to be, if she'd been kind and genuine, someone who could have made Isaac happy, Ellen would have kept her mouth shut. She'd thought she owed it to him to tell him the truth, but the truth had backfired on her. Not only did Isaac not believe her, he'd cut off all ties of their friendship.

I don't want to think about it, Ellen thought. The incident had happened over two years ago, and she mustn't dwell on it. As far as she knew, Nancy was no longer in Isaac's life. She had gone, but she left a friendship in tatters.

Ellen was fine and she'd moved on. Hadn't she been enjoying the company of Nathaniel Peachy, their deacon's son? Her friendship with Nate was an easy one. With him, she didn't have to constantly hide her feelings. They were friends and nothing more.

Besides, she had a new plan for her life. One for which her parents hadn't given their approval, but it was something she'd begun to think of as God's calling for her. She wanted to work with special-needs Amish children, those born with genetic disorders. Her friends Rebekka and Caleb Yoder had a daughter who suffered from Crigler-Najjar syndrome, a genetic disease caused by a buildup of bilirubin—a toxic substance responsible for jaundice—in the little girl's blood. Fortunately, little Alice's condition was type 2. The child had to remain naked under a special blue LED light for ten to twelve hours a day. The treatment could be especially brutal on cold winter or hot summer days.

After visiting the Yoder home, witnessing the child's treatment, Ellen had felt something emotional shift inside her. Unlike little Alice, she'd been blessed with good health. She felt the powerful urge to help families like the Yoders with children like Alice.

The buggy suddenly jerked as it moved. Startled, she held on to the seat. She grimaced at the pain caused by the vehicle's sudden shift in movement. Soon the jerking stopped and Ellen sighed with relief as she felt the buggy wheels rolling on pavement.

She stuck her head out the window. Isaac had pulled her vehicle out of the ditch and back on the road. Fortunately, no other cars had been around to hinder the progress. As Isaac had said, the English boys were gone. She could no longer see them. She just had to get through the visit to Katie Lapp's and then she could go home.

Isaac climbed into the driver's side of her buggy. "Your wheels are out of the ditch." He stared at her, his brow furrowing. "Your head hurts," he said with concern.

"I'm fine." Ellen promptly dropped her hand and lifted her chin. The movement made her grimace with pain and she turned to stare out the passenger window. She had to be grateful for his help, but she didn't want him here. "Why are you in my buggy?"

"I'm going to drive you wherever you're going."

"There's no need. I'm fine. I just need a minute."

He remained silent as he studied her. "Where are you headed?"

"To see your *mudder*." She gestured toward the bag that had fallen to the buggy floor during the accident. "*Mam* asked me to bring those—the squares we made for the quilt we're all making."

Isaac opened the door and met her gaze. "I need to check your buggy to see if it's safe to drive."

Ellen watched as he slid out of the vehicle. Despite the rising bump on her forehead, an aching cheek, a dull throbbing in her right shoulder and some red, burning fingers, she knew she was well enough to drive her vehicle. She kept silent as she waited for Isaac to finish checking the carriage for damage.

"Looks *gut*," he said to her through the passenger window opening within inches of where she sat. "I'd suggest that Eli take a look, but I don't see anything physically wrong with the structure. Still, you may want to think about taking it to him later to be sure."

"Oll recht."

He was too close. Ellen could see the long lengths of his dark eyelashes and feel the whisper of breath across her skin. He examined her with watchful gray eyes, and she shivered in reaction to the intensity of his regard. She moved to slide across the seat. His arm on her shoulder stopped her and she had to hold a cry so he wouldn't realize that she'd hurt it when she'd been thrown against the door.

"I have to go." Ellen shifted uncomfortably when he didn't move. To her shock, he reached out to lightly stroke her cheek.

"You're going to have a bruise," he said huskily as he withdrew his touch.

Ellen was powerless to look away from the intensity of his gray eyes, the tiny smile playing about his lips. "I *need* to go—"

"You're not driving."

She gazed at him, more than a little annoyed. "'Tis a buggy, not a car. I can handle it."

"Not in your condition."

She scowled. She didn't want to ride with him, with the man who hadn't trusted her. Why should she trust him to take her anywhere? She realized that she hadn't forgiven him for the past but at the moment she didn't care.

"Ellen?" Isaac frowned. "Tell me the truth. Your head hurts, *ja*?" His tone was gentle.

She closed her eyes at his kindness, wishing that she could turn back time to before things had soured between them. Did he honestly think that she'd forgotten what he'd done? Why was he acting like her friend again when it had been two years since he'd cut off their friendship?

"Ellen?"

"*Ja*, it hurts," she admitted rudely.

"You need ice for your cheek." His voice remained kind, making Ellen feel bad. "I was on my way home. Let me drive you." He leaned in through the open window and the scent of him filled her nostrils. Memories of an earlier time rose up and slammed into her. Her eyes filled with tears. She turned away so he wouldn't see them.

"Ellen..."

She blinked rapidly before she faced him again.

He reached out to touch her forehead, his finger skimming over the lump beneath the surface of her skin. His touch was light but she couldn't help a grimace of pain. His gray eyes darkened. "I'm driving," he said in a tone that brooked no argument.

Isaac left her to skirt the vehicle. He seemed suddenly larger-than-life as he slid in next to her. She didn't want him to drive her. She didn't want him anywhere near her. The way he was making her feel made her afraid, afraid that she wasn't over him, and despite the past and the way he'd chosen Nancy over her, she might still love him. It was better to stay angry with him. It was the only way to protect her heart.

With a click of his tongue and a flick of the leathers, Isaac urged the horse forward. Ellen sat silently in her seat beside him, and she could feel his brief sideglances toward her as he drove. She ignored them.

The remaining distance to the Samuel Lapp farm wasn't far. Ellen saw the Lapp farmhouse ahead as Isaac steered the horse onto the long dirt lane that ended in the barnyard near the house. He drew on the reins carefully, easing the carriage to a halt as if he worried about hurting her. He parked the buggy near the house, then jumped down from the bench and ran to assist before she had a chance to climb out on her own. She shifted too quickly in her seat and gasped with the searing pain. Her head hurt and her right shoulder, which had slammed against the buggy wall, was throbbing. She was furious at how weak she felt. She didn't want Isaac to be right. She didn't want Isaac to be the one she had to rely on, even if just for a little while.

Isaac appeared by her side and gently clasped her arm. "Easy, now, Ellen," he murmured. "Slowly."

She winced as she swung her legs toward the door opening. She made a move to step down until, with a sympathetic murmur, Isaac released her arm to encircle her waist with his hands. He lifted her as if she weighed no more than a young child. Ellen was conscious of his nearness, his male scent and the warmth of his touch at her midsection as he held her a brief moment before he set her down. Tears filled her eyes. Her injuries hurt but so did her aching heart.

"Danki." She didn't look at him as she stood there, feeling weak. Reaction set in. The horror of what those boys could have done to her caused her body to shake. She drew deep calming breaths, hoping he didn't notice.

"Ice. You need an ice pack," he announced as he bent to retrieve her bag from the buggy floor. He tucked it under his arm, then reached for her with the other. Fortunately, Ellen had regained control. "Come. Let's get you into the house." He slipped his right arm about her waist and helped her toward the house. Ellen wanted to pull away. She felt her heart thundering in her chest and grew worried that she'd lose control of her emotions again.

Chapter Two

"Ellen?" Isaac's mother had stepped out onto the front porch of the farmhouse. She frowned as she saw Isaac leading Ellen with his arm about her waist. "What happened?"

Ellen felt the sudden tension in Isaac's shoulders. "Some *Englishers* forced her off the road. The buggy came to a stop in a ditch."

"*Ach, nay.* Poor dear." Katie eyed her with concern. "Isaac, help her into the kitchen."

Ellen wanted to insist on walking on her own, but she wasn't about to protest in front of his mother. She still wasn't feeling the best and was grateful for the assistance. Her head hurt and she felt woozy.

"Here." Katie gestured toward a chair. "Sit her here."

Isaac saw her comfortably seated, then promptly disappeared into the back room.

His mother bent to closely examine her injuries. "You hurt your cheek." She narrowed her gaze as she studied her. "And your forehead."

Ellen nodded. Her cheek throbbed and she had a

headache. She reached up to feel the sore bump on her forehead.

Isaac returned and handed his mother an ice pack.

Katie smiled at him approvingly, then pressed it gently against Ellen's forehead. "Hold it here for a few minutes and then shift it to your cheek."

"Danki." She tried to smile until the simple movement of her lips hurt. Isaac stood by the kitchen worktable, watching silently.

"The driver was reckless," Katie said.

"Ja. 'Twas Brad Smith," Isaac said darkly.

His mother shot him a glance. "You know him?"

"Ja." Isaac's scowl revealed that he wasn't pleased. "He's Nancy's *bruder.*"

Katie frowned.

"Thank the Lord that Isaac came when he did," Ellen admitted. The memory of the boys getting out of their car made her shudder.

"I'm glad I was there to help," he murmured, his expression softening.

Ellen didn't say anything as she looked away.

"You did *gut, Soohn.*" Katie regarded her son warmly.

Something flickered in Isaac's expression. "Any one of us would have helped." He smiled. "You taught us well."

Katie nodded. "I'll put on the teakettle." She turned toward the stove. "You need a cup to revive you."

As she held ice to her cheek, Ellen encountered Isaac's gaze. She shifted the bag to her forehead. Isaac frowned, left the room and returned with another ice bag. She gave a jolt when he sat down close beside her and pressed it gently against her cheek. *"Danki,"* she murmured.

He leaned forward as he kept hold of the ice. "You're *willkomm.*"

"Here we are." Katie set three cups of hot steaming tea on the table. She returned to get a coffee cake from the counter. "How about a nice slice of cinnamon cake? I made it fresh this morning."

Ellen had smelled it as soon as she'd entered the kitchen earlier. She felt her stomach rumble as if urging her to eat. Embarrassed, she nodded.

She lowered the ice pack and set it on the table. The ice was soothing to her injuries, but after a while, the cold felt too intense. Taking her cue, Isaac removed the other bag. She was aware that he watched her every moment as if he half expected her to faint or fall over… or something worse. She tried to smile reassuringly but the simple movement caused pain to radiate along the right side of her face. Without asking, Isaac quickly picked up an ice bag and held it to the painful area. Ellen welcomed the cold again, as it helped to alleviate the soreness. Disturbed by his nearness, she reached up to take control of the bag. Her fingers accidentally brushed against his; she froze as she locked gazes with him.

"I've got it," she assured him. She hated that he had the power to make her feel something besides anger, that he could still make her wish for things that she no longer wanted.

Isaac leaned back in his chair without a word as his mother sliced the coffee cake, then set the pieces within reach in the middle of the table. Katie then sat across from her and Isaac. In the ensuing silence, Ellen remained overly aware of Isaac beside her as she sipped from her teacup.

"Where's Hannah?" Isaac asked conversationally.

"At Abram's." Katie took a sip of tea. "She loves playing with Mae Anne."

Their deacon, Abram Peachy, a widower, had married Charlotte King of the Amos Kings, who lived across the road from the Lapps. When she'd married Abram, Charlotte had become mother to Abram's five children. Then a year and a half ago, Charlotte had given birth to a daughter, Mae Anne, and she had six children to mother and love. Mae Anne, a toddler, was as cute as she was bright, and her older siblings adored her. Isaac's sister, Hannah, now eight, had been drawn to the baby immediately. The youngest Lapp sibling loved spending time with babies and children younger than her, including her own nieces and nephews.

"She's *gut* with *kinner*. She'll make a fine *mudder* one day." Ellen dug her fork into the coffee cake and brought a piece to her mouth. She felt Isaac's gaze on her, met his glance and quickly looked away. She felt her heart rate accelerate, her stomach flutter as if filled with butterflies.

Isaac gazed at the girl seated at his family's kitchen table and felt his stomach tighten as he thought of the accident. When he'd learned that it was Brad and his friends in the car, he'd felt his hackles rise. These English boys were rude and nearly always up for trouble, and trouble was the last thing he needed. He'd already found it once with them, and he wasn't looking to get involved with them again. Except he'd never have known Nancy's true colors if not for them. He'd been happy when he'd met Nancy Smith, pleased when she'd wanted to meet his family. He'd found her fascinating, and after he'd spent some time with her, his fascination had grown. Dressed all in black, she'd worn heavy eye makeup and bright red lipstick. Her appearance stood out in a crowd, which wasn't the Amish way, but she'd been sweet and he'd realized after talking with her for hours that they shared a lot in common. Until he'd learned that she'd pretended to like him simply because she'd been curious about the Amish way of life.

The pain of learning the truth about her still lingered. His foolishness in getting involved with her and her unkind circle of friends bothered him. He'd given his parents cause to worry, and for that he was sincerely sorry.

As Ellen and his mother chatted, Isaac studied the young woman seated next to him. He had a clear up-close view of her features. Tendrils of blond hair had escaped from under her *kapp* during the accident. The bruise on her cheek stood out starkly against her smooth complexion. She turned, saw him staring and raised her eyebrows questioningly. He continued to watch her, unable to look away. Her cheeks turned bright pink and she averted her gaze.

It seemed impossible that they'd known each other forever, but they had. He had to admit it had been a long time since they'd spent any time together like they used to. His fault, he knew, but he couldn't undo the past. He'd chosen Nancy over Ellen.

Isaac experienced a strange tingle of awareness of Ellen that he'd never felt before. "How is your head?"

Ellen gingerly touched her forehead. "Not too painful."

He frowned, because he didn't believe her. He stood. "I'll get more ice."

"*Nay*, I'm fine." She waved at him to sit down.

He reluctantly resumed his seat. "When you're ready to go, I'll take you home."

"There's no need—"

"Let him, Ellen," *Mam* said. "You just had an accident. You shouldn't be driving home until you're certain there are no other aftereffects."

"I'll take you home," Isaac said. "Jacob can give me a ride back." It was an easy walk from Ellen's house to Zook's Blacksmithy, where his older brother Jacob worked.

"I don't want to be a bother."

"You're not, Ellen," he said, teasing her. "At least, not today." He paused. "Finish your cake. You need to keep up your strength."

She arched her eyebrows. "I don't need to eat. I'm strong enough."

"You don't like my *mam's* cake?" He laughed when he heard her inhale sharply, saw her expression fill with outrage.

She glared at him, but he could see that she fought a smile.

His mother had left the room. She returned within minutes with Ellen and her mother's quilt squares, which he'd placed on top of their hall linen chest on their way through to the kitchen. *Mam* pulled the squares out of the bag. "These are lovely, Ellen."

Ellen smiled. "I'll tell *Mam* that you said so."

"I see your work here. Your stitching is extraordinary."

Isaac was intrigued. "May I see?"

His mother chose and then handed him two squares. Isaac examined them carefully and thought he knew which one was Ellen's. "Your stitches are neat and even," he murmured and then held up the one in his right hand. "This one is yours."

Ellen seemed stunned. "How did you know?"

He shrugged. "I just did." And his mother had said that Ellen's work was extraordinary. He was unable to take his gaze off her, saw her blush. He returned the squares to his mother. "Who's getting the quilt?"

"Martha," *Mam* said. "For the baby."

Isaac smiled. His older brother Eli and his wife, Martha, were expecting their first child. "Doesn't Martha usually come to your quilting on Wednesdays?"

Mam smiled. "*Ja*, but she told me that she can't come this Wednesday. With hard work, we'll get her quilt done in one day."

He smiled knowingly. "You told Eli."

"I had to," *Mam* said defensively. "I couldn't risk that Martha would change her mind and decide to come." She rose to her feet. "I'll put these upstairs. Martha could stop by for a visit." She left with the squares and seconds later her footsteps could be heard on the stairs.

Ellen stared into her teacup.

He eyed her with concern. "You don't look well. You should see a doctor."

"Nay." She glanced up from her empty cup. "I'm fine."

He studied her with amusement. "You're too quiet."

"Quiet?" She appeared offended.

He laughed. "You *were* quiet."

She scowled, then winced as if in pain.

"Your cheek hurts." He clicked his tongue. "We have aspirin. I can get you some."

"Nay."

"Another cup of tea?" he asked.

"Nay." She shook her head and grimaced.

"You need to stop shaking your head. It hurts you." He stood. "Ellen—"

She blinked up at him. *"Ja?"* Her expression suddenly turned wary.

"You *will* let me drive you home," he said, his voice firm. He wouldn't take no for an answer.

Ellen relented. *"Oll recht,"* she said, surprising him. "After your *mudder* comes back."

He inclined his head. His *mam* returned and he waited while the women discussed refreshments for their Wednesday quilting bee. Finally, Ellen turned to him. "I'm ready to go now."

"I'll help you," he said quietly.

"I can manage on my own."

He frowned. He didn't like her coloring. She looked too pale. He exchanged meaningful glances with his mother. "*Mam*, we'll take the ice."

Mam nodded and handed the packs to Ellen.

Ellen accepted the ice bags graciously. They walked outside together until they reached the buggy.

"Ellen." Isaac extended his hand toward her. "I don't think we should take any chances." She took it reluctantly. He felt a jolt as he felt the warmth of her fingers. He helped her onto the vehicle's front passenger side. "Comfortable?" he asked huskily. He lingered, unable to withdraw his gaze.

"Despite my headache, sore cheek and throbbing shoulder?" she answered saucily. "I'm wonderful."

Her smart answer made him smile. "Shoulder?" He puckered his brow. "You hurt your shoulder and didn't tell me?"

"'Tis nothing."

He didn't believe her.

Her expression softened. "It doesn't hurt much."

Annoyed as well as concerned, Isaac rounded the vehicle, climbed in next to her, then grabbed the reins. As he drove silently down the dirt lane, then made a right onto the main road toward the Mast farm, Isaac found his thoughts fixed on the girl beside him.

Ellen stared out the side window as Isaac drove. *Why Isaac?* Why did he have to be the one who'd rescued her? She firmed her lips as she pressed the ice to her throbbing forehead. Her cheek hurt and she pressed the other bag of ice against her skin. She and Isaac had been such good friends. They'd walked often to Whittier's Store for a soda or an ice-cream cone. They'd talked about their families, their farm and their Amish community. She'd known that Isaac had looked at their relationship as just one of friendship, but Ellen had hoped that his feelings would change to become something more. She'd never told Isaac of her love for him. After what had happened with Nancy, she would have suffered the ultimate humiliation if she had.

After the accident today, she knew she could trust Isaac for help, as he'd helped her with the buggy and her injuries. But she could never trust him with her heart, not after the way he'd accused her of being mean-spirited and jealous of Nancy when she'd tried to warn him about the English girl.

Her fingers tightened on the bag of ice as she lowered it from her forehead to her lap.

She couldn't forget what she'd overheard that fateful day when Isaac, his brother and a few friends had been discussing Nancy—and her. She'd been coming around the side of the barn when she'd overheard them. She'd remained hidden, slowly dying inside as she listened to their conversation.

"Nancy is wonderful. I've never met a girl like her. I never thought I'd have a girlfriend like her."

"What about Ellen?" It had been Nate Peachy's voice.

"What about her?"

"I thought there was something special between you two."

Isaac had laughed. "*Nay*, it's not like that between us. She's like Hannah—my sister."

After hearing that, Ellen had run back the way she had come, her heart hammering within her chest, tears running down her cheeks. Thankfully, the boys hadn't seen her, hadn't witnessed the devastation she'd felt with Isaac's few simple words.

Isaac had abandoned their friendship and never looked back as he'd moved on with Nancy. Nancy had made it clear that Ellen wasn't needed in Isaac's life, and Isaac, by dismissing Ellen's fears, had agreed.

Ellen stared at the countryside as it rushed by her window. She couldn't help but remember the humiliation she'd felt the first time Isaac's friends had gazed at her with sympathy after his conversation about her with them. She hadn't wanted or needed anyone's pity. She still didn't want anyone's pity.

"You're quiet," Isaac said, interrupting her thoughts.

She met his gaze briefly. "I'm admiring the view." She paused. "I don't hear you saying much, either," she added with a lift of her eyebrows before she looked toward the window again.

He laughed. "True."

They had reached the end of the lane to her family farm. She watched as Isaac expertly made the turn onto the dirt road. As he steered into the yard, he sent her a look, his eyes briefly focused on the side of her face. "Your cheek is turning purple."

"I'll live," she said flippantly. Regretful, she drew in a sharp breath, then released it. "I'm sorry. I guess it's hurting more than I'd like to admit. I appreciate what you did for me."

His eyes softened. "I'm glad I could help." He drove the buggy close to the barn and parked. Ellen climbed out of the vehicle before Isaac had the chance to assist her.

Her mother came out of the house. "Ah, *gut*. You're back. I need help with these pies for Sunday—" She stopped when she spied Isaac. "*Hallo*, Isaac. I didn't expect to see you."

"Josie," he greeted her with a nod. "I drove Ellen home because there was an accident with the buggy."

Her mother stiffened and studied her. "Are you hurt?" She turned to Isaac. "What happened?"

"A car passed too fast and spooked Blackie. The buggy swerved off the road," Isaac said. "Ellen did a *gut* job with controlling your mare. She kept the buggy from rolling over into the drainage ditch along Ned Yoder's farm."

Ellen felt self-conscious with the two of them studying her.

"You've hurt your cheek and your forehead." *Mam* looked with approval at the bag of ice in Ellen's hands. "You iced it—*gut*. Katie was wise to give it to you."

Ellen bit her lip. "It was Isaac's idea. He gave it to me." She didn't know why she told her mother that.

Her mother gave him a half smile. "That was kind of you, Isaac."

Isaac shrugged. "I was on my way home from Eli's when I saw it happen."

Ellen noticed that he hadn't told her about the English boys who'd forced her from the road.

"I should go." His gray gaze made an assessing sweep of her head and face. "You may want to keep that iced," he said softly.

She nodded. Although she had to fight the desire to tell him that she could do without his instructions.

"Will can take you home," her mother suggested.

"Will?" Ellen said with surprise. She frowned. "*Mam*, I don't think Will should be the one to drive him home."

"I'll walk to Jacob's as planned. I've been wanting to stop in and see him." He regarded her with a crooked smile. "Take care of yourself, Ellen." He turned to her mother. "Josie, I hope those pies you mentioned are for visiting Sunday."

Mam's lips curved. "They are."

Isaac grinned. "*Gut*. Something to look forward to." His gray eyes settled on her. "Be well, Ellen." He nodded to her mother. "Josie." Then he left, departing down the dirt lane toward the main road. She watched him for several seconds before she turned toward her mother, catching a glimpse of her parent following Isaac through narrowed eyes as he walked away. Ellen couldn't help but wonder what her mother was thinking. "Is something wrong?"

Mam shook her head. "I should get back to the kitchen."

"Pies?" Ellen reminded her.

Mam seemed to shake away her thoughts. "*Ja.* I've promised to bring three pies this Sunday and I'm having trouble with them."

Ellen's lips twitched. Her mother was a good cook but for some strange reason pies weren't her strong point. Ellen's grandmother had been good at pie making and she'd taught Ellen.

Why did her mother choose to bring pies when they were clearly a chore for her? Ellen asked her.

"Alta Hershberger asked me to," she said simply, and Ellen understood. Her mother wouldn't challenge a request from the village busybody. To do so would give Alta fodder to natter about.

As she followed her mother into the kitchen, she immediately saw the mess *Mam* had made. She grinned. "How many piecrusts did you attempt to make?"

Mam looked sheepish. "One."

"Then we'd better get busy if we're going to bake three pies."

As she mixed the ingredients, then rolled out the crust dough, Ellen thought of her morning and Isaac's part in it. She frowned as she carefully lifted a rolled circle of dough and set it into a pie plate. The fact that Isaac had helped her didn't mean anything. It didn't mean he wanted them to be friends again.

Maybe it was time to go out and have some fun. She'd talk with her parents about going on *rumspringa*. Then while out and about, she could locate Dr. Westmore's medical clinic for genetic diseases. She needed to learn as much as she could to convince her parents to allow her to volunteer her time there.

Chapter Three

Sunday arrived, and Ellen climbed into the family buggy with her parents and younger brothers. The pies she'd made with her mother had come out nicely. The scent of baked apples, cherry and custard filled the vehicle, making her stomach grumble. Ellen was particularly pleased with the *snitz* and custard pies. Those were her favorite flavors, and she looked forward to enjoying a tiny sliver of each after the midday meal.

They were headed to Cousin Sarah's house. Sarah was married to Jedidiah Lapp, Isaac's oldest brother. Ellen knew that she'd probably see Isaac there, but she wasn't going to let it concern her. She'd had a couple of days to put things in perspective. She realized that it had felt odd to spend time alone with him again, the first time since before he and Nancy had begun seeing each other. *He's acted as if we've never had words over his English girlfriend.*

Now that she was on the mend, things would get back to the way they'd been before her buggy mishap. Isaac wouldn't notice her, and he'd leave her alone. Ellen looked forward to her first outing during her *rumspringa*, the running-around time during which teenagers within the Amish community were allowed the freedom to enjoy the English world. It was their parents' and the community's hope that given the choice, their young people would make the decision to join the church and stay in the community. If they chose to leave, they were free to go and return to visit as long as they hadn't joined the church first. If they joined the church and then left for the English world, they'd be shunned by their families and friends and wouldn't be allowed to return.

Ellen had every intention of joining the church, but she wanted to enjoy *rumspringa*. She'd use the opportunity to check out the Westmore Clinic for Special Children, bring home information so that she could convince her father to allow her to volunteer there. She decided that she'd talk with her friend Elizabeth to plan a trip into the city of Lancaster. They could go next Saturday. The thought of getting away for the day excited her. She hadn't spoken to her parents about it yet, but she couldn't see why it would be a problem.

They arrived at the Jedidiah Lapp farm, where *Dat* steered Blackie onto the driveway and parked in the yard on one end of a long line of familiar gray buggies.

Sarah came out of the house, carrying her son, Gideon, as Ellen climbed out of the buggy with two pies.

"Sarah!" She always enjoyed spending time with her cousin. She and Sarah had shared a room when Sarah had first come for a visit, and Ellen had loved having her stay. She'd been pleased when Sarah, originally from Kent County, Delaware, had moved permanently to their village of Happiness after she'd fallen in love and married Jedidiah Lapp.

"Ellen." Sarah beamed at her, then greeted her aunt, Ellen's mother. "Josie, 'tis *gut* to see you. We haven't had time to spend together lately."

Her mother held a pie and made to grab one from Ellen, who smiled as she shook her head. "You're looking well, Sarah," *Mam* said. "Your little one is certainly getting to be a big boy."

"*Ja*, he is. I don't know where the time has gone. It seems like only yesterday that he was a newborn and now he's three years old."

Holding two pies, Ellen asked her cousin where she wanted her to put them.

"Jedidiah is getting a table. Would you like to set them inside until the table's ready?"

"*Nay*, I'm fine," Ellen said, studying Sarah's little son, who gazed at her with a big sloppy grin. "I'll wait."

As soon as Sarah set her son down, Gideon immediately ran to Ellen for attention. Her cousin quickly grabbed Ellen's pies so that Ellen could reach for him. "Want to go for a little walk, Gid?"

"*Mam*, can I?" Gideon asked his mother in Pennsylvania Deitsch.

"*Ja*, you may walk with Cousin Ellen, but you must be a *gut* boy."

The child nodded to his mother, then to Ellen who scooped him up for a hug.

"Be careful, Ellen," Sarah warned. "My *soohn* is no lightweight."

"*Ja*, he isn't." Ellen smiled at the dark-haired child as she set him on his feet. "We'll walk side by side—*ja*, Gideon?" She extended her hand and the child grabbed it and held firm as they headed toward the back farm field.

"Where shall we go?" she asked him.

"Goats," he said.

"You want to see the goats?" When he nodded, she grinned at him. "Let's visit your goats, then."

Isaac left the house with Jedidiah, carrying the table Sarah wanted outside. He looked across the yard as they negotiated the last of the porch steps to discover his sister-in-law Sarah with Josie Mast. He glanced about but didn't see Ellen anywhere. He was strangely disappointed. He was wondering how she'd fared since the accident, whether or not the bump on her forehead had changed color like the bruise on her cheek. Then he heard a giggle and spied Gideon running from Ellen, who chuckled as she ran across the yard after him.

"Come back here, Gideon!" she called laughingly.

"Set it down a minute, Isaac," Jed said. "I need to speak with Sarah."

Isaac silently set down the table. He watched as Jed approached his wife to say a few words with her. He saw Sarah gesture toward the back lawn.

It was visiting Sunday. Community folks were milling about the yard and inside the house, family and friends of Jed and Sarah. He heard voices from near the barn, where two men whom he recognized as church elders were joined by a newcomer he didn't recognize.

The sound of a squeal made him smile and turn back to watch Ellen and his nephew as Gideon ran from Ellen, the child's shriek of laughter evidence of his enjoyment of her chase. By her expression, he could tell that Ellen was having as much fun as Gideon. She laughed as she caught up to him and snatched him into her arms. When she began to tickle the boy's ribs, Gideon burst out into childish giggles. Isaac stared, fascinated by their play, and found his lips curving in response.

Jedidiah returned and picked up the end of the table. "My son is enjoying himself. Ellen will make a *gut mudder* one day."

A *mudder*? She was too young to be a mother. Without saying a word, Isaac shot her one last quick glance. His gaze locked with Ellen's briefly as she set Gideon down, then turned away. He focused his attention on moving the table.

"Sarah wants it there," Jed said with a nod of his head.

"Close to the house, near the back door?" Isaac guessed.

"*Ja*, she says it'll be easier for the women to bring out the food."

They carried the table to the designated area. After the brothers had set the table in place, their parents arrived. Isaac followed Jedidiah to greet them. He reached for the platter of cupcakes and cookies in his mother's arms.

"Where's my *grosssoohn*?" *Mam* asked when Isaac had returned after putting the dish on the table.

"He's playing with Ellen." Jedidiah grinned as his son ran away from the young woman, who laughed as she took off after him.

Gideon saw his grandmother and raced toward her. Unaware, Ellen gave chase, looking eager to catch the little boy.

"G'mammi!" the child exclaimed as he threw himself against *Mam*.

Ellen saw Katie and halted a few feet away. "Now I know why he was running this way," she said with a grin.

"He's having a *gut* time with you, I see," *Dat* said.

"I've been having a *gut* time myself, Samuel."

"You like children," Isaac commented, unable to help himself.

She stiffened as if she'd just realized that he was there, but then he saw her relax as if she'd come to accept his presence. "*Ja*, I do."

They chatted for several minutes about Katie and Samuel's grandchildren and how much all of them had grown. Then Jedidiah picked up his son and accompanied their parents toward the house, leaving Isaac alone with Ellen.

He studied Ellen intently. "Your bruises... Your cheek looks better, but now you have one on your forehead." He paused. "You're feeling better?" he asked softly.

She nodded. "*Ja*, much better."

He looked at her approvingly. *"Gut."*

Sarah approached. "Ellen, may I talk with you for a moment?" She waved Ellen to follow and the two women moved away to chat privately.

Isaac wondered what they were discussing. He saw Ellen nod with a smile and Sarah grin, looking pleased.

"I think Sarah is asking Ellen if she'll help out after the baby comes," Jedidiah said softly as he rejoined Isaac.

Isaac glanced at his brother with surprise. "You mean Sarah's...?"

Jed beamed. *"Ja."*

"God has blessed you, *Bruder.*" Isaac was pleased for his oldest brother, who dearly loved his wife and son. "I'm happy for you."

His brother looked at him. "One day you'll have a family of your own."

Isaac shook his head. "Not anytime soon. I learned a hard lesson with Nancy."

"The *Englisher* was never like the girls in our community." Jedidiah hesitated. "We were worried from the start that she'd hurt you."

Isaac felt his stomach tighten. "I never knew you felt that way. You were all kind to her."

"And why wouldn't we be? You liked her. We hoped we were wrong, but she didn't seem as involved in your relationship as you."

Isaac sighed. If only he'd been smart enough then to realize the truth—that Nancy never cared for him. He thought of Ellen and recalled the friendship they'd once shared. Fool that he was, he'd tossed it away in favor of Nancy, believed Nancy over her when Ellen had wanted only to make him see Nancy's true nature.

Too many regrets. He didn't want to talk or even think about Nancy any more. She was gone, and he was glad. Jedidiah was an astute man and he let lie the topic of his past relationship with her.

Sarah and Ellen approached. "We're going to see to lunch. Either one of you hungry?"

"I am," Jed said.

Sarah gazed at him with affection. "You're always hungry."

"Always for your cherry pie."

"I didn't make a cherry pie for today."

"I made a cherry pie," Ellen said with a smile.

Jed's dark eyes lit up, and Isaac groaned as he shook his head. "What is it with my *bruders* and their sweets?" he groused.

Ellen raised one eyebrow. "You don't care for sweets?"

"I like them well enough, but my older *bruders* are obsessed."

"You don't like *snitz* or custard pie, I imagine," Ellen said.

"Custard pie?" Isaac asked. He enjoyed custard pie.

"Vanilla custard." She looked amused.

"I like custard pie. You made one?"

She nodded. "Too bad you don't like sweets. Fortunately, there are plenty of folk here who will be happy to eat my custard pie." She walked away with a laugh and Isaac could only stare at her. A small smile curved his lips and he chuckled. *I deserved that. But if she thinks I'll not be getting a slice of that custard pie, she is mistaken. She's yet to learn how determined I can be to get what I want.*

It wasn't long until food was put on the table that he and Jed had set in the backyard. Besides the Masts and his own family, the Kings, the Peachys, the Zooks, and Alta Hershberger and her two daughters had come to share their visiting day. This was Jed and Sarah's first gathering at the farm. Watching his sister-in-law move among her guests, Isaac felt admiration for Sarah's ease with having so many people at her home. He wondered if he'd ever have a place where he could invite family and friends and feel so comfortable with them. Ever since the night when Whittier's Store was vandalized by Nancy's brother and his friends, he hadn't known a moment's peace. He'd taken the blame for something he didn't do, not because Nancy had asked him to—although she had—but because he'd been protecting a male friend, another member of their Amish community. Other church members, he knew, now looked at him with disappointment. It bothered him that they'd never questioned whether or not he could have been guilty, but just accepted that he was. He didn't feel less in the eyes of his family. His mother and father were supportive of all of their children, but he couldn't help feeling as if he'd let them down, too.

He'd hoped that his friend Henry would come forward and confess his part in the Whittier's Store debacle. But Henry had kept silent and remained noticeably absent from the community and Isaac's life. Apparently afraid to speak up after seeing how the community reacted to Isaac's guilt, Henry must have been unable to bear what would happen if he were to admit that he was one of the guilty parties.

No one is more disappointed with me than I am, Isaac thought. By taking the blame, he had effectively lied. And that was what made it difficult for him to stay in Happiness. As hard as it would be to live out in the English world, it might be better than living here without joining the Amish church. And how could he join the church when he didn't feel worthy?

Seeing Ellen with his nephew made him think of simpler, happier times when he and she roamed the countryside together as friends. He'd made a terrible mistake when he'd taken up with Nancy, Brad and their English friends. Now he was destined to pay for it.

* * *

Ellen did what she could to help Sarah put out lunch before she went in search of her friend Elizabeth. She was eager to go *rumspringa* and she wanted Elizabeth to go with her. She found Elizabeth with a group of young people, including the Peachy siblings and Peter Zook, who had congregated near the pasture fence.

"Elizabeth," she called as she approached. Her friend's eyes brightened when she saw her. "May we talk?" Ellen asked.

Elizabeth said something to the group before she joined Ellen, who stood on the outskirts several yards away. "Is there something wrong?" her friend asked.

"*Nay*, I want to go into Lancaster next Saturday."

Her eyes gleamed. "A *rumspringa* adventure?" Elizabeth asked.

"*Ja*. Would you like to go?"

"*Ja*." Elizabeth nodded vigorously. "What should we tell our *eldre*?"

"The truth," Ellen said, hoping her parents would approve.

Her friend agreed. "What will we do?"

"Shop? Eat? See a movie?" Ellen grinned. "Whatever we want to do." *Check out the Westmore Clinic for Special Children*, she thought.

After talking with her friend, Ellen grew more excited about the trip and couldn't wait to ask her *mam* and *dat* for permission. But she decided to wait until later to approach them.

"*Dat, Mam*," Ellen said after they had returned from Jedidiah and Sarah's house and everyone had settled in at home. "I'd like to go into Lancaster with Elizabeth next Saturday."

Her father frowned as he faced her. "Why?"

Ellen felt her belly flutter with nerves. "We want to go on *rumspringa*. I'm old enough to experience the English world. We thought we'd get something to eat and wander about the outlet mall."

"I don't know if that's a *gut* idea—" *Dat* began.

"I don't see why you can't go," her mother said at the same time that her father spoke. *Mam* immediately grew silent. She wouldn't go against her father's wishes.

Ellen's spirits plummeted. Her *dat* wasn't going to allow her to go.

"She is old enough, William," *Mam* said gently, much to Ellen's shock.

Dat narrowed his gaze as he studied his daughter. "*Nay*, she can't be."

"I'm seventeen, *Dat*."

Her father looked surprised. "You are?" He firmed his lips. "You've grown up too fast."

Ellen noted his surprise with amusement. "You still have plenty of time with the boys. They are a long way from *rumspringa* age."

"Why now, *Dochter*?" he asked seriously. "Do you plan to leave our community? Are you unhappy here?"

"*Nay, Dat*. I have no plans to leave, but I want to see the English world. Just because I want to see it doesn't mean I don't want a life here…a husband and family."

"How will you get there?" *Dat* asked, looking relieved.

"May I take the pony cart? Or we can hire a driver to take us."

Her mother leaned close to whisper something in *Dat*'s ear. Her father nodded and said, "You may go next Saturday, Ellen, but I will hire a driver for you."

Ellen beamed at him. *"Danki, Dat."*

"Just come home safe and sound with no ideas of wanting to leave us," he warned. Ellen shifted uncomfortably as she thought of the clinic and her reason for visiting. Would her father and mother be upset after her return when she presented them with more information in an attempt to convince them to allow her to work there?

That night as she lay in bed, Ellen thought of the fun she'd enjoyed with her cousin Gideon and then her excitement as she and Elizabeth had discussed their Lancaster trip. She tried not to think of Isaac, with whom she'd spoken only briefly. It had been nice of him to inquire about her injuries. She'd been disturbingly aware of how he'd continually watched her.

Next Saturday, she thought with a smile, dismissing Isaac from her mind. She couldn't wait for Saturday's adventure with Elizabeth.

Chapter Four

Monday and Tuesday went by quickly as Ellen did her regular chores, including washing clothes and hanging the laundry on the line to dry. Wednesday morning she and *Mam* headed to Katie's house for their monthly quilting bee. It was a glorious day. The sun was bright in a clear azure sky and the spring blossoms looked pretty in the Amish and English yards they passed. Ellen wondered if she'd see Isaac today and decided that she wouldn't let the prospect bother her. Odds were that he would be out working with Samuel in the fields or with Jedidiah for Matt Rhoades, who had recently started his own construction company. In any event, even if she did see Isaac this morning, it wouldn't be for long. There was no reason for her to feel anxious or nervous. He had helped her last week, she had thanked him politely and she was fine. It wasn't as if she were in danger of falling for him again. The only reason they'd spent time in each other's company was that the circumstances of her accident had forced it upon them.

"How many do you think will come today?" she asked her mother.

"About ten, I suppose, as usual, with the exception of Martha."

Ellen smiled as she thought of the baby quilt they would be working on today. It wasn't large enough for a double bed. With the ten women working on it, the quilt would be completed in no time.

"*Mam*, don't you think it's going to be a bit crowded around the quilt rack if ten women show up?"

Her mother frowned as she maneuvered the buggy into a turn. "Hadn't given it any thought."

"If there are too many, I can do something else."

"*Nay*. Katie would rather have you stay than some of the others."

Driving past, Ellen waved to Annie Zook as she exited Whittier's Store. The young woman's face lit up as she acknowledged Ellen's wave with her own. She had EJ, her son, and her baby daughter, Susanna, with her.

"Are you coming to quilting?" Ellen called as *Mam* slowed the buggy and steered toward the right to allow a number of cars to pass by safely.

"*Ja*, I'll be there after I get these little ones home," Annie answered. "*Mam* said she'd stay back to watch them today."

"Why not bring them?" Ellen suggested. "Won't Hannah be there?"

"*Ja*, and Daniel," Annie said, referring to her brother-in-law. "I'll talk with *Mam*."

Once the roadway was clear, her mother drove back onto the road and continued on.

Ellen smiled as she glanced back to see Annie put her children into the buggy. "She looks happy," she murmured.

Mam flashed a smile. "*Ja*, she is. Jacob has been *gut*

for her, and I'm glad she finally understood that. He's loved her since he was a young boy."

Ellen raised her eyebrows. "He has?"

"*Ja*, and he nearly gave up. Annie fell for Jedidiah and Jacob thought that he didn't have a chance with her. Later, after Jed found Sarah, Jake hoped for another chance."

"How do you know all this?"

"Katie and Miriam, although Miriam wasn't keen on it at first."

Ellen reached up to straighten her *kapp*. "Why not?"

"That was right after Horseshoe Joe had his accident. She wanted someone who was financially able to take care of Annie. Someone like Ike King."

Ellen shuddered. "He was too old for her." She thought of Martha. "He was too old for Martha, too, but she married him anyway. She genuinely cared for him, didn't she?" She studied her mother to gauge her reaction.

"I believe she did." *Mam's* lips firmed. "'Tis too bad he passed on, but it must have been God's plan. I've never seen her as happy with Ike as she is now with Eli."

Ellen had to agree. She'd never seen such joy in Martha's brown eyes during the year she'd been married to Ike. Still, she was sorry that Ike had passed on. He'd been a nice man and Amos King's younger brother. And he'd been wonderful to Martha. They had all taken comfort that Ike was in the Lord's hands and thus resided with Him in heaven.

There were two buggies in Katie's barnyard as *Mam* pulled in and parked. No one was in the yard as they climbed out and retrieved the food dishes they'd made to share with the other women. She had made lima beans in tomato sauce and lemon chiffon cake. *Mam* had made chocolate brownies and macaroni salad. There would be plenty to eat today, more than enough to share with any of the male Lapp family members who might come in for lunch.

For a moment, Ellen's thoughts dwelled on Isaac Lapp. She wasn't alarmed that she'd thought of him; after all, this was his home.

Katie's door opened immediately after *Mam* knocked. Ellen felt her heart skip a bit as she caught a quick glance at the man who stood there. *Isaac*. The image of Isaac flittered away and she realized that it wasn't Isaac waiting patiently for them to enter. It was Joseph, the youngest brother. He was the spitting image of his older brother until she looked closer and saw the difference in eye color and the shape of his mouth. Joseph had younger, less mature features. Still, he was a handsome boy and would one day become an extremely attractive man.

"*Hallo*, Joseph," she greeted after *Mam* had gone in first.

"Ellen." He nodded. "My *mudder* and the others are in the gathering room." He glanced down at the food in her arms and finally smiled. "You've brought lemon cake."

"*Ja.*" She stepped past him and waited while he closed the door. "You like lemon chiffon cake."

"*Ja.*" His smile became a grin. "Looking forward to midday meal today." He stared at her cake plate. "I can take that for you."

"*Oll recht.*" She handed him the cake plate and Joseph disappeared into the back kitchen area. She heard someone coming down the steps from upstairs and looked up, expecting to see Katie or Hannah, her daughter. She froze. It was Isaac.

"*Hallo*, Ellen," he greeted as he approached. He narrowed his eyes as he studied her face. "Your forehead's turned a light shade of purple. Is it sore?"

"I'm fine."

"That's not what I asked you."

She sighed. "A little."

"How is your cheek? Can you smile yet without grimacing?" he teased. "Or does it still hurt?"

"What are you doing here, Isaac?" she said stiffly. She wasn't in the mood for his teasing or his questions about her health. "I thought you'd be working."

"Disappointed?"

She stared at him, wishing he would leave.

"I'm going to work soon. We've been waiting for the plumber to finish. Matt's picking Daniel and me up on his way to the job site." He glanced toward the staircase. "Daniel! Matt's going to be here any minute."

"Don't let me keep you," Ellen said tartly, and Isaac looked at her with an odd little smile.

"Ellen?" *Mam* called as she reappeared, peeking her head from a doorway. "We're ready to start. You'll want to get a good seat."

"Coming!" She turned back to Isaac. "Have a *gut* day at work, Isaac," she said, trying to be more polite.

Joseph returned from the kitchen. "I hid the cake in the back room," he confided with a grin.

"*Gut* thinking, Joseph," Ellen said with a chuckle. Isaac arched an eyebrow in question. "Lemon chiffon cake," she explained. "Apparently, it's your *bruder*'s favorite. He's protecting his fair share."

Eager to escape, she left him to join her mother in the gathering room, where Katie Lapp and several other women were seated around the quilting rack. She didn't know how long it would be before Matt Rhoades picked up Isaac and Daniel. Ellen tried not to think about Isaac at all as she greeted the other ladies in the room.

"Over here, Ellen." Katie gestured toward a seat between her and *Mam*. "I'm glad you've come."

"I enjoy quilting."

Mae King, who lived across the road, sat directly in front of her. On either side of Mae were her married daughters, Charlotte Peachy, who'd married their deacon, and Nancy Zook, who'd married Annie's brother Josiah. Ellen was pleased to see these young women, who were always pleasant and fun. She was disappointed that Elizabeth and her mother weren't here. She'd hoped to have a few private words with her friend about their outing on Saturday. She didn't know if Elizabeth's parents had agreed to let her friend go.

The six of them chatted for a while, and Katie offered them iced or hot tea. Ellen chose the iced tea, as the gleaming iced tea pitcher sitting on the table looked inviting as well as refreshing, and since it was a glorious day and the windows were open, it seemed the best choice.

"We saw Annie on our way over," she told Katie. "Coming out of Whittier's. Said she was going home to drop off EJ and Susanna and then she'd be here."

"Miriam offered to watch them," Katie said. "I wish they'd all come. Hannah is here to care for them—and Joseph."

Ellen felt her face turn red. "I'm glad you said that.

I'm afraid I may have overstepped when I suggested the same thing." She felt relieved as she saw pleasure come to Katie's expression. "I thought that Daniel would be here. I didn't think of Joseph."

"He's certainly a grown-up young man," *Mam* commented. "How old is he now?"

"Eleven."

Ellen shook her head in wonder. Would he continue to look exactly like Isaac when he got older?

Elizabeth and her mother arrived to join the quilting bee gathering, and moments later Miriam Zook came with Annie and her two children.

"You've brought them," Katie gushed. *"Gut."*

"I didn't think about Hannah and Daniel," Annie admitted. "And I wanted to spend the day with my *mudder*, too."

Miriam glanced fondly at her daughter. "Are Hannah and Daniel here?"

"Hannah is," Katie said. "And Joseph. I don't think he'll mind watching EJ." She got up and left the room, then returned with her daughter and son.

"EJ!" Joseph exclaimed, his eyes lighting up with pleasure. "Would you like to go out and play?" He shot a look to his sister-in-law, who nodded. "Come on, buddy. Let's go see the animals in the barn."

Hannah was more than happy to stay with Susanna. She spread a quilt on the floor not far from the women and sat, setting the baby next to her.

Conversation started to buzz as the women threaded their needles and got to work.

"Alta's not here?" Elizabeth's mother asked.

"She's not coming today," Miriam said. Alta Hershberger, the resident busybody, was her sister-in-law, although Alta's husband, Miriam's younger brother John, had passed on when their two daughters were nine and ten. "She said she needed to go to market with Mary."

Annie glanced at her mother with raised eyebrows but didn't comment.

The women stitched for a couple hours before Katie stood. "Let's eat."

Mae King and Miriam got up to help their hostess with the food. Ellen started to rise to join them, but Katie waved her to her seat. "Sit. We'll manage."

The work on the quilt was progressing nicely. The stitches were neat and even. Ellen knew the women hoped to get most of it done today.

Elizabeth's mother rose with *Mam* and the two went into the kitchen to help the others. Ellen slid over to the seat next to Elizabeth.

"Are you allowed to go on Saturday?"

Elizabeth frowned. "*Nay. Dat* said I wasn't ready." She sighed dramatically. "What does he mean by that? I'm old enough."

Ellen stifled her disappointment. She didn't want to make her friend feel worse. "Maybe we can try again in a couple of months." She really wanted to visit the clinic, not that she'd said anything about it to her friend.

Ellen changed the subject and the girls chatted briefly about their siblings. Soon the women had the food ready, and following Elizabeth, she went to grab a plate. After eating lunch, the women went back to work and finished up at three thirty. There'd been no sign of Isaac or Daniel, who apparently had both gone to work with their older brother Jedidiah and Matt Rhoades.

Ellen felt immense relief when she and her mother headed home. She'd spent a large part of the day at the

Samuel Lapp farm and had made it without encountering Isaac more than once. She hadn't realized that she'd been tense and worried about it until after she and her mother had climbed into their buggy and left.

Why should I care whether or not I see Isaac Lapp? She was over him. Completely. She'd moved on. But the memory of her past feelings for him lingered.

She turned her thoughts to the clinic. She didn't want to wait months until she visited the clinic, especially since her father had agreed to let her go. There must be someone who would be allowed to go. What about Barbara Zook? She'd have to think about it. Barbara was slightly older than her. There were other girls her age in her community. She had to think of one she could trust with her desire to work for the Westmore Clinic.

Isaac took off his black-banded straw hat and ran a hand through his light brown hair. It had been a good workday but he was tired. He glanced over at his younger brother Daniel and felt his lips curve upward. He wasn't as tired as Daniel. This was Daniel's first job on a construction site, and while he did hard work on the farm, he was clearly exhausted from the unaccustomed manual labor.

"Ready to go?" he asked his brother.

To his surprise, Daniel grinned at him. "*Gut* day, *ja*?"

Isaac stared at him, feeling astonished. "You like the work."

"*Ja*. Feels *gut* to see what you've accomplished in a day." Daniel glanced at the house that was currently under construction.

They had put together and set into place all the walls of the first floor of a house. It would be a large dwelling. The first floor alone was probably two thousand square feet. Isaac didn't know what the upper level would entail yet, but he was sure when the structure was done, it would be massive.

"Nice job," Matt Rhoades said as he approached with their older brother Jed.

Isaac gave a silent nod but Daniel was more effusive. "We got a lot done today."

Matt looked pleased by the boy's obvious enjoyment. Dark haired with dark eyes and a quick smile, the contractor was a favorite *Englisher* among their Amish community. "Ready to return tomorrow?"

Daniel nodded vigorously, and Isaac couldn't help but chuckle at the boy's enthusiasm.

"We should make sure that *Dat* doesn't need us on the farm tomorrow." Isaac watched Daniel's face fall. "I doubt he does, though." He made a decision, hoping that his father would agree. "We'll be here," he told Matt. "Eight o'clock sharp, as usual. Let's go home, Daniel."

As he drove their wagon home, Isaac thought of the money he'd earned today, which was his, free and clear. Until this week, everything he'd made since the Whittier's Store incident, he'd given to Bob Whittier to pay for the damages. The paint that had been splattered over the back of the building had ruined the siding. Since there was no match for the old color, all of it had been removed from the building and replaced. And Isaac had paid for it all—the material and the labor to install it—even though he wasn't the one who had been responsible for the damage.

I may as well have been, he thought. Because he'd lied when he'd taken the blame. Nancy had begged him not to tell. Her brother, Brad, had instigated the act, and she'd pleaded with him. Isaac had arrived on the scene after the deed had been done, and as he'd stared at the damage with a sick feeling of dread, the police had pulled up to the building in their cruiser and everyone had scattered into the wind, except for Isaac. Sergeant Thomas Martin, the police officer who'd questioned him, was Rick Martin's brother. Rick was a friend and neighbor, and because of Rick's connection, the officer had called Bob Whittier rather than taking him to the station immediately. Bob had refused to press charges. The officer could have pressed charges himself, but he'd let Bob handle the situation himself. Bob Whittier had said that he'd forget about the incident if Isaac would pay for the damages. So for the next couple of years, Isaac had worked hard and paid Bob Whittier every cent he'd earned until the debt was paid. He'd given Bob the last payment owed with his last paycheck.

"Isaac," Daniel said, pulling Isaac from his dark thoughts. "I did all right today, *ja*?"

Isaac nodded. "You did fine, *Bruder*."

His brother appeared relieved. "*Danki* for getting me the job."

He ran a weary hand across the back of his neck before he turned toward his brother. "You're a *gut* worker. Matt asked if I knew anyone and I did—you. Jed agreed that you were the man for the job."

Daniel looked pleased that both brothers had approved of him. "I appreciate it."

Isaac studied him. Daniel wore a blue shirt, triblend

denim pants and heavy work boots, just like he did.
His straw hat sat crookedly on his head. There was a
smudge of dirt across one cheek and sawdust on the
shirtfront, but he looked happy and content and that
was all that mattered. He wondered what his mother
would say when she saw them. "We'd better clean up
outside before we head into the house. *Mam* is bound
to take one look at us and cry out. But you can't work
and stay clean, too, *ja*?"

"Ja," Daniel agreed with a grin.

They headed toward the back of the house. As they
passed an open window, Isaac heard his mother's voice.
"Isaac, Daniel—that you?"

"Ja, Mam," they both answered.

"Just stopping to wash up at the pump."

"Hannah," he heard *Mam* call. "Get your *bruders*
some soap and towels. They're outside."

Isaac heard his little sister murmur her assent as he
pumped the handle that set forth a gush of water. "You
first," he told Daniel.

His younger brother reached in and cupped his
hands full of cold water, then splashed his face and
neck."

Hannah appeared and handed him soap. Isaac stood
by watching as Daniel lathered up his face, neck, arms
and hands while Hannah hovered nearby, waiting with
a towel. Meeting his little sister's gaze, Isaac grinned
at her.

Daniel finished up, and then Isaac took his turn.
He washed up while his brother worked the pump and
his sister looked on.

"You boys done yet?" *Mam* called out. "I need you
to do something for me."

"Coming," Isaac replied.

As the three siblings approached the back door that led to the kitchen, Isaac put a hand on his sister's shoulder. "Did you have a *gut* day, Hannah?"

"*Ja*, I got to play with Susanna. Joseph helped with EJ." She beamed up at him. "Annie came to *Mam's* quilting bee today."

Isaac nodded as he reached to open the door and waited for Daniel and Hannah to precede him. Hannah hung back as Daniel went in first. She seemed eager to talk about the day. "*Ja*, and Mae, Nancy and Charlotte came—so did Josie and Ellen," she went on. "And Elizabeth and her *mudder*, too."

"That's nice," he said. Isaac felt his belly warm at the mention of Ellen. Since her accident, he hadn't been able to get her out of his mind. Or was it because he was bothered that she'd seemed to go out of her way to avoid him since?

Mam was at the kitchen sink, washing dishes. She turned as they entered. "*Gut.*" She eyed him and Daniel, assessing their appearance. "You look clean enough," she decided.

Isaac glanced at her with raised eyebrows. "You need us for something?"

She dried her hands on a tea towel and laid it to dry over the end of the dish rack. "*Ja*. I'd like you to carry my quilt frame upstairs. Martha may stop by at any time, and I don't want her to see the baby quilt before it's done and we're ready to give it to her."

"In the sewing room," Isaac guessed.

"*Ja*, it should fit if you set it against the far wall without blocking my sewing machine." She watched approvingly as Daniel grabbed one end of the rack while Isaac picked up the other. They put it where instructed, and Daniel went back downstairs. Isaac paused a moment to admire the quilt.

Isaac changed his clothes, then returned to the kitchen. He mentioned how beautiful he thought the quilt was.

His mother looked pleased. "I think she'll like it, *ja*?"

Isaac agreed. "You had a *gut* quilting day."

"There were ten of us, and although space around the rack was limited, we worked well together." She had dried the dishes and set them on the counter. She grabbed them again and placed them on the kitchen table.

Daniel returned and appeared to have changed his clothes, as well. *Mam* looked at him, nodded approvingly. "Daniel, will you run these over to the Masts'? Josie needs them." She gestured toward the dishes and bowls on the table.

Isaac felt something shift inside him as he thought of Ellen. "I'll go."

His mother studied him silently but then nodded. Hannah walked into the room.

"I can take Hannah with me." He addressed his sister. "Hannah, would you like to take a ride to the William Masts with me?"

"Ja!" Hannah glanced at *Mam*. "May I?"

Katie's face grew soft. *"Ja*, you may go."

"You don't need me to go, then," Daniel said. "Is there something you want me to do?"

"You can feed the animals."

The boy nodded and left to do the chore.

"Hannah," *Mam* said, "go into the other room and

get the scissors and box of straight pins Ellen left behind."

As Hannah ran to do their mother's bidding, *Mam* explained, "Ellen forgot them. I know she'll need them before we can get together again. You can give them to Josie if Ellen isn't home."

His heart skipped a beat. "I will."

He and Hannah headed to the William Mast farm in the family market wagon. It was a clear day, and Isaac enjoyed the colorful countryside as he listened to his sister keep up a running dialogue of what she'd done today and what she planned to do tomorrow.

Chapter Five

"I know why Ellen forgot her pins and scissors," Hannah gushed in between relating other events that had taken place that day.

Isaac regarded his sister with good humor. "Why?"

"'Cause of Elizabeth Troyer," she said as if he'd understand.

"What does Elizabeth have to do with Ellen's forgotten pins? Did she borrow them?"

His adorable little sister made a face. "*Nay, bruder.* Ellen and Elizabeth talked with each other for a time. I know what they said. I could hear them."

He wouldn't ask. It seemed somehow wrong to ask, but Hannah was more than willing to tell, and so Isaac figured he could listen.

"*Rumspringa,*" she said. "Ellen and Elizabeth had planned a trip into Lancaster for meals and shopping, but Elizabeth wasn't allowed to go. I could tell she was disappointed. How old do I have to be before I go *rumspringa*?"

Rumspringa? he thought. *Ellen?* The idea didn't sit well with him. He knew more than anyone else how wrong things could turn in the English world if one wasn't careful. He didn't like the thought of Ellen out and about on her own. *Elizabeth can't go with her.* He breathed a sigh of relief.

"Isaac!" Hannah said sharply, and he realized that she'd been waiting for him to answer.

"Sixteen or seventeen," he said.

"*Ach*, that is a long time from now."

Not long enough, he thought.

The Mast farm loomed ahead. Isaac pulled on the reins enough to slow for the turn and once on the road that led to the farmhouse, he turned to his sister. "Why are you in a hurry to grow up, Hannah? You should enjoy being eight. 'Tis a *gut* age to be." As he pulled into the barnyard to park, he could feel his sister studying him intently. "What's wrong?" he asked, turning to her with a small smile.

"I forgot," she said soberly. "You didn't have a *gut rumspringa.*"

His smile faded. "*Nay*, I didn't."

She stared at him, refusing to look away. "She wasn't *gut* for you. Nancy," she clarified. "You need someone better."

His lips twitched. His sister rarely failed to amuse him. "I do? Like who?"

Just then, Ellen Mast exited the house, but she hesitated when she saw their buggy. He could almost feel her stiffen when she realized he was there.

"Ellen," Hannah said.

"*Ja*, that's Ellen." His heart started to thump hard, for he knew he had to find a way to apologize for the way he'd treated her after he'd met Nancy. He'd been thinking about it a lot lately. He should have said he was sorry a long time ago.

"*Nay.* That's not what I meant. I meant that Ellen Mast is the right girl for you."

Startled, he met his sister's gaze. There was a look of maturity in those blue depths that took him aback. "Ellen is a neighbor," he said. *And once a friend.*

"She can be more to you."

He shook his head. "You don't understand how things work between a man and woman."

Hannah's look turned cheeky. "Then 'tis a *gut* thing that you're not a man, nor is Ellen a woman."

"Oh?" He glanced back toward the porch in time to watch Ellen slip back into the house. Her quick exit disturbed him. How could he put things right between them? They'd been friends once. *Now she barely acknowledges me.* "At what age do you consider a boy a man and a girl a woman?" he asked Hannah, wondering with amusement how she would respond.

"A boy and girl become adults when they marry after they join the church," she said with authority.

Isaac could only nod. *She's right*, he thought. Before marriage, a boy and girl would become adult members of the church. In so doing, they'd be accepting the Amish faith and the Lord as the right path for them.

He climbed out of the vehicle with a heavy heart. He didn't know if he would ever join the church. After lying about the Whittier's Store debacle, he felt unworthy of the Lord.

He reached into the buggy to retrieve the dishes and pie plates for Josie. Hannah carried the scissors and pins as she joined him before they approached the house.

He halted. "Hannah, don't say anything about your thoughts to Ellen," he said. "She won't appreciate it."

"Because she is mad at you?"

He released a sharp breath as he struggled with the correct answer. "*Ja*, because she is mad at me."

"You could make her not mad at you," she suggested as they climbed the porch steps and reached the front door.

"Hannah," he warned.

She scowled at him, but good-naturedly. "I won't say anything."

He was so happy to hear her agree that he wanted to hug her. Instead he knocked and waited with a thundering heart for someone to answer.

Ellen's younger brother Elam opened the door and stared at them. Isaac gazed back.

"Elam," Hannah said in an extremely grown-up voice. "Is your *mam* home?"

Elam drew his gaze from Isaac to glance with surprise at the young girl. "Hannah," he murmured with a blush. He turned quickly away. "*Mam!* Someone here to see you!"

Josie appeared from the back of the house, drying her hands on a tea towel. "Isaac. Hannah." She looked at her son with raised eyebrows. "Why haven't you invited them in?"

"Sorry." Elam turned a darker shade of red and stepped aside. "Come in."

"*Mam* asked us to bring these to you," Isaac said as he extended the dishes and pie plates. "She said you'd need them before you visited again."

"And Ellen forgot these," Hannah added, holding up the scissors and pins.

"She did?" A flicker of concern entered Josie's expression before it was gone, as if Ellen's forgetfulness worried her. "Hannah, why don't you bring those upstairs? You know where her room is."

Hannah nodded and flashed him a look before Isaac watched her disappear from view. He then heard her footsteps on the stairs.

"Come into the kitchen, Isaac," Josie invited politely. "I have iced tea and cookies."

"I would enjoy some." Isaac smiled and followed her into the large kitchen at the back of the house.

She knew she shouldn't have disappeared into the house the way she had, but the last thing she wanted was to see or speak with Isaac Lapp. Ellen sat on her bed, annoyed with herself about needing to avoid him. She rose from her mattress and approached the window. The Lapp market wagon was still outside. Why was he here? Surely not to see her.

A knock on her bedroom door gave her a jolt. "Who is it?"

"Hannah Lapp," a muffled young voice said.

Ellen couldn't help her sudden smile. There was something warm and inviting about the youngest Lapp child, the only daughter in Katie and Samuel Lapp's large family household, which included seven sons. "Come in, Hannah."

The door opened immediately and the eight-year-old girl entered the room.

"What brings you here this afternoon, Hannah? Didn't we just see each other?"

Hannah nodded. "We did, but you forgot these." The

girl handed Ellen her sewing scissors and container of straight pins.

Startled, Ellen stared at the precious sewing items in her hand. She'd left her scissors and pins? What could she have been thinking? She used those scissors and pins every day. How on earth could she have left them behind?

"*Danki*, Hannah. I didn't realize I'd left them. I guess I would have known soon enough when I looked for them." She set the scissors and pins on the small table near her bed.

"I found them next to your chair."

"'Twas kind of you to bring them."

Hannah glanced about Ellen's room, noticing the neatly made bed and the slight indent in the quilt covering where Ellen had sat only moments ago.

"You're an only girl like me," she said.

"I am." Ellen murmured her agreement and had an image of Isaac downstairs waiting for his sister.

"You ever share your room?" Hannah asked.

"*Ja*, with my cousin Sarah when she first came to Happiness. Before she and Jedidiah wed."

Hannah regarded her thoughtfully a minute. She approached to where Ellen stood near the window and glanced outside. "I've never shared my room."

Ellen felt sadness radiate off the normally effervescent child. "You can stay with me sometime. I wouldn't mind." She bit her lip, wondering why she'd made the impulsive offer.

Hannah's blue eyes brightened. "*Ja?*"

Ellen felt her reservations vanish. "*Ja.*" Half expecting Hannah to set a date, she was pleasantly surprised when the girl quietly thanked her, then moved toward the door.

"I should go," she said. "Isaac is waiting for me downstairs."

"It was nice to see you again, Hannah. *Danki* for bringing my scissors and pins."

The child grinned. "I knew you'd need them." She lowered her voice to a whisper. "You're a much better quilter than a lot of them."

Ellen chuckled. "I don't know about that."

Hannah eyed her soberly, showing Ellen how serious she was. "I do." She put her hand on the doorknob. "I'll see you on Sunday, Ellen."

Ellen murmured her assent as she followed the child to the door. Hannah stepped through the opening and turned one last time. Something in her expression made Ellen reach out and embrace her. Hannah responded immediately. Placing her arms about Ellen's waist, she hugged back hard.

After Hannah left, Ellen returned to the window, waiting for her and Isaac to exit the house. But when minutes passed and there was no sign of them, Ellen worried about how long she could stay upstairs and avoid Isaac without it appearing strange.

She bit her lip and then firmed her resolve. There was no reason to avoid him. She drew a fortifying breath before she left her room and descended the stairs. As she reached the bottom landing, she heard Isaac's deep masculine voice. She froze as her breath hitched and a burning entered her stomach.

Move, she commanded herself, and she obeyed, entering the kitchen in time to see Isaac raise an iced tea glass to his lips, then swallow his last mouthful. His gaze locked with hers as he slowly lowered the glass.

"Isaac," she said.

"*Hallo*, Ellen."

"I didn't realize I'd left my pins and scissors. *Danki* for bringing them."

A troubled look entered his expression and was gone. As their gazes stayed locked, she saw him visibly relax. "Our pleasure." He turned to his little sister. "Are you ready to go?"

Hannah nodded. "*Danki* for the iced tea. I would have taken a cookie, too, but 'tis almost suppertime, and—" she turned to warmly regard her older brother "—I can't eat as much as he does."

Mam gasped out a laugh, and Ellen couldn't help snickering.

Isaac swung his attention to Ellen. The amusement and good humor in his gray gaze made her think of those earlier times when they'd been good friends. The warmth she'd felt faded as she turned her attention to Hannah, who was tugging on her brother's arm, pulling him toward the door.

Ellen realized that she must have murmured an appropriate goodbye as they left, because they were here one moment and in the next they were gone. She stood, reeling from her encounter with Isaac. She shuddered out a sigh as she headed back to her room. The man still had the power to disturb her. She wondered if she'd ever get over him.

Chapter Six

Saturday—the day she'd hoped to go to Lancaster with Elizabeth—had come and gone. That night, she'd grown sick to her stomach, and the illness, or whatever it was, lasted into the next day. She had stayed home from Sunday services, encouraged to do so by her mother. She'd rested for the entire day, eating a couple of dry crackers for breakfast, then managing a bowl of chicken soup with a few more crackers for lunch. By the time her family had returned home after church services and the midday meal, she had been feeling better. This morning, she woke up back to her normal self.

Since it was Monday, Ellen kept busy doing chores, which included the baking for the week. By late afternoon, she was done in the kitchen and had a few minutes to sit and enjoy a cup of tea before asking what else she could do to help her mother.

"Ellen," her *mam* said as she entered the kitchen. "I just went to the mailbox." She held up a letter. "We're going to have a visitor for a few days. Mary Ruth Fisher, our cousin."

Ellen was unable to place the name. "Have I met her?"

"*Nay*, she is actually my cousin Lizzie's *dochter*. Lizzie wrote a while back and said that the girl has been wonderful but that she's been working too hard. She has six siblings." Her mother paused. "I wrote back and invited Mary Ruth to come." She waved the letter. "Lizzie agreed that it would be *gut* for her daughter to spend time with family."

"How old is she?"

"Seventeen—the same age as you."

Ellen smiled. "I'll enjoy getting to know her. When will she arrive?"

"The day after tomorrow. She lives in Honeysuckle in the northern part of Lancaster County."

"How come she's never visited before?"

"The children have suffered much tragedy in their lives. First their *mudder* passed, then two years later their *vadder*. Lizzie is actually their stepmother."

"And Lizzie takes care of them all?"

"At first she did," *Mam* said. "And then Abraham's younger *bruder* came back to claim the farm. Lizzie had never met him. After Abraham, Lizzie's husband, passed on, Lizzie wrote to Zachariah to inform him of Abe's death. It took a long time for the news to reach the family. Zack's *mudder* had moved them away from the farm after her husband died. The farm rightfully belongs to Zack, the youngest. At first Lizzie was concerned that she'd lose everything—the children she loved like her own and her home."

"What happened?"

Mam smiled as she refolded the letter. "They fell

in love and later married. They are raising Abraham's seven children together."

"The Lord blessed them," Ellen said.

"*Ja.* He did." *Mam* slipped the letter back into its envelope. "Would you see to your room and then help go through the *haus* to make sure it's presentable?"

Ellen chuckled. "You know it is, but I'll go over it again if it will make you feel better." *Mam*, with her help, kept up with the housework. In fact, her chores before the baking today had included dusting, sweeping all the rooms and cleaning the bathroom.

Finished with her tea, Ellen went through the house, as promised. It was in good shape, except for Will and Elam's room. She entered her brothers' bedroom to find dirty clothes on the floor. She shook her head as she picked them up, but she really didn't mind. The boys usually kept their garments on their wall hooks and put their dirty garments in the laundry basket downstairs. She held up the shirt and pants for her inspection. Will must have dressed in a hurry for school this morning and found dirt, then quickly changed, she realized as she put the garments outside the room to take on her way down to the laundry later.

Satisfied that the room was neat, Ellen checked the rest of the upstairs. Then she retrieved the dirty garments and headed downstairs. She tossed Will's things in the washing machine and went in search of her mother. She found *Mam* outside in her vegetable garden pulling weeds.

"Everything in the house looks *gut, Mam*," she assured her as she approached. "Do you need anything from the market? I can go if you'd like."

Despite a pantry filled with food, she knew her mother would want a few special items for Mary Ruth's stay.

"*Ja*, I have a list," her mother said. They entered the house. Ellen followed her mother into the kitchen, where *Mam* gave her the list. "You can get whatever you need in Yoder's General Store."

As she drove the buggy to Yoder's, Ellen felt jumpy whenever she heard a car approach from behind. The memory of those English boys who'd run her off the road was upsetting. The store loomed ahead. Ellen put her battery-operated left blinker on before making the turn. She parked, tied up her horse and went inside.

Margaret Yoder, the owner of the store, was behind the counter as Ellen walked in. "*Hallo*, Margaret," she greeted with a smile.

"Ellen! 'Tis nice to see you. How are your *mudder* and *vadder*?"

"*Gut*. And your family—are they well? I haven't seen Henry in a long time. How is he?"

"He stays busy working in Ephrata—" she came around the counter "—for a cabinetmaker." She smiled. "What can I get for you today?"

Ellen unfolded her mother's shopping list and began to read it aloud. "Flour, sugar, cream of tartar, molasses— Do you have sorghum molasses?" She went on to tell Margaret about her *mam's* other requests.

"*Ja*. How much do you need?"

"One quart jar will be plenty."

Margaret helped Ellen find everything her mother wanted, and after Ellen had paid, the woman assisted by carrying some of the groceries to Ellen's buggy.

"Tell Josie I said *hallo*," Margaret said. "And William."

Ellen nodded. "Give my best to your Henrys." Margaret's son had been named after his father.

"I will." With a little wave, Margaret returned to her store.

Ellen drove out of the parking lot and headed for home. The rear bench in the buggy was filled with grocery bags. She wondered what her mother's plans were for all this food for when Mary Ruth arrived in two days.

Ellen murmured a silent prayer that her ride home would be as uneventful as the trip to Yoder's. When she saw an Amish woman bending over something in the middle of the road, she realized that the ride wasn't meant to be uneventful. She recognized the woman as Nell Stoltzfus, one of Arlin and Missy's five daughters and a cousin to the Lapp siblings. She pulled her buggy over to the side of the road and got out. There was no other buggy in sight, which meant that Nell must have walked here.

Ellen approached, her brow furrowing with concern when Nell looked up with tears in her eyes. "Nell, is something wrong?"

"Thanks be to *Gott*!" She appeared relieved to see her. "This puppy is badly hurt. I was walking home from Aunt Katie's when I saw a car slow ahead. Then someone threw open a door and tossed the dog out of the vehicle while it was still moving. The car sped off in a hurry after that. I saw him hit the ground," she said, gesturing toward the little dog. She sniffed. "He can't get up."

Ellen bent for a closer look. She felt the immediate sting of tears as she saw how the dog was trying valiantly to stand up but couldn't. Every time he tried, he whimpered. One or more of the animal's legs had to be injured. "What can I do to help?"

"Can you take us home—me and the puppy? I'll find someone to help him there."

"I don't know, Nell. I know you're *gut* with animals, but are you sure it's best for him if you try to help him? Maybe we should take him to that new English veterinarian in town—I think his name is James Pierce." Fortunately, there was nothing in her grocery bags that wouldn't keep until after she'd helped Nell. "It might be the best thing for him."

The young woman hesitated, then gave a nod. "I remember seeing a sign for his office, but I don't remember where. Is he far?"

"*Nay*, just past Miller's Store." Ellen studied the puppy, which responded well to Nell's soothing touch. "Can you pick him up or do we need something to carry him in?"

As if God had summoned help, Ellen and Nell heard the sound of horse hooves on pavement as a carriage approached. Ellen turned to see who it was and groaned inwardly. It was Isaac and Daniel Lapp, probably on their way home from work.

Isaac immediately parked the wagon behind Ellen's and got out. "Is everything all right?" he asked, looking concerned.

Ellen met his gaze briefly, then looked away. "Nell has an injured puppy and we've decided to take him to the vet."

"Isaac, *danki* for stopping," Nell said. "Ellen and I were trying to decide how best to move him."

Nell was Isaac's cousin. Her father, Arlin Stoltzfus, was Katie Lapp's older brother. Ellen saw her delight in seeing him and Daniel, who had climbed out of the wagon after Isaac.

Isaac's silence prompted Ellen to glance at him. Isaac appeared thoughtful, as if trying to figure out a way to help. "I have a quilt and a tarp in the wagon. Would one of them help?"

Nell nodded. "*Ja*, either one."

"We've got both in the buggy. *Mam* leaves a quilt under her seat and we've borrowed a tarp from Matt for *Dat* to use."

"Which one?" Daniel asked.

"Ellen," Isaac said, "why don't you take a look with me and help decide?"

Ellen could think of a lot of reasons why she shouldn't follow him to his vehicle, but all of them seemed uncharitable, and if truth be told, there was something about Isaac Lapp that still set her heart racing. She silently followed him to his vehicle, where a folded blue tarp lay in the back of the wagon.

"And there's the quilt," he told her, gesturing toward a folded quilt under the seat. "Ellen?" he said when she remained quiet. "What do you think? Quilt or tarp?"

She met his gaze and saw only genuine interest in her opinion. She softened toward him. "Both would work," she said quietly, "but I like the idea of using the quilt. He's just a puppy and the quilt is soft and can be washed afterward."

His features transformed as he smiled. "Quilt it is, then." He reached past her into the vehicle to retrieve it. As he silently handed it to her, he gazed at her with intense gray eyes. "Are you ever going to forget?" he murmured softly.

Ellen felt a jolt. "I—" She didn't know what to say.

"What do you mean?" But she knew. She had told him she'd forgiven him, but lately she hadn't been acting like it.

His face clouded. "Never mind." And he turned away.

She felt terrible. "Isaac—" He faced her. "I'm sorry. I—" she whispered. Her eyes started to fill, but she blinked quietly to clear them. "I can forget." She never wanted him to guess that she'd been so hurt when he'd withdrawn his friendship or that she'd once hoped to become his sweetheart. Had he guessed?

They stared at each other silently. Ellen struggled with emotion as she saw something shift in Isaac's expression.

"You always seem to be around whenever someone needs help," she said.

His lips curved crookedly. "And that's a bad thing?"

She shook her head. "*Nay*, 'tis a *gut* thing."

His eyes brightened until his effect on her had her quickly suggesting they get back to Nell. Then his gaze seemed to dim.

"Nell is *gut* with animals, but I think in this case it's better if a veterinarian sees the puppy," she said as they headed back to where Nell and Daniel were hunkered near the dog.

"*Ja*, she's always had a special way with them."

Nell sprang up when they approached, Isaac with the quilt. "That's perfect. Now to move him carefully."

"Do you want me to take you?" Isaac asked Nell.

"*Nay*. Ellen's offered. She knows where the clinic is."

Ellen feared that Isaac would change his cousin's mind, but her fears were groundless, as Isaac nodded as if in complete agreement that she should be the one to drive them to the veterinarian.

"Daniel, let's go home."

"But—" Daniel started to object.

"*Mam's* waiting," he said with a quick glance in Ellen's direction.

Ellen couldn't help it: she smiled at him, pleased by his understanding of her need to be involved.

The brothers stayed long enough to help Ellen and Nell gently shift the injured puppy onto the quilt and make sure Nell was safely settled on the front passenger side with the puppy carefully cradled in her lap. Ellen saw Isaac note the groceries on her backseat. She wondered if he might suggest a change in plans but he didn't.

"Ellen, we could take your groceries home for you," he suggested as he came around the vehicle to the driver's side, where she sat.

"There is nothing that won't keep."

"But won't it be better if we stop and tell Josie what you're doing?" he said with a beseeching smile. "We may as well take those bags with us."

She laughed at his persistence. He was right. Her mother would be worried if she took too long to get home. "*Oll recht*, Isaac." She regarded him with amusement. "*Danki.*"

He acknowledged her statement with a nod. "Daniel, help me with these."

The brothers had the groceries out of the back of the vehicle in seconds. "Go ahead, *Bruder*. I'll be right with you."

"I can carry them," Daniel said, trying to be helpful.

With good humor, Isaac handed over the rest of

the grocery bags and watched with affection as Daniel struggled to carry all of Ellen's purchases to their buggy. Ellen saw Isaac's love for his brother in his gray eyes and her heart melted toward him even more.

Isaac turned and bent close to Ellen as Nell, in her own little world, adjusted the quilt about the dog. *"Danki,"* he whispered into Ellen's ear, "for saying that you'll forget someday." His breath caressed her ear and neck before he drew back, leaving Ellen to feel off-kilter. She was speechless as her gaze followed after him as he smiled, then headed toward his vehicle.

"Isn't the clinic back the other way?" Nell asked when Ellen sat without moving for several long moments.

Jerked from her musings about Isaac Lapp, Ellen nodded and proceeded to look before pulling out onto the road until she found place to turn around. She steered her horse past Yoder's General Store and then Miller's before the veterinary clinic became visible up ahead.

"There it is." Ellen gestured toward a sign that read Pierce Veterinary Clinic.

She worried that Nell might be concerned about the cost of the puppy's veterinary care, but she had money and would insist on paying the entire bill or at least sharing the cost if Nell objected.

"Don't move yet," Ellen instructed after she'd parked in the paved lot near the building. She got out, relieved to see a hitching post, where she tied up Blackie before she went around the vehicle to help Nell. "Why don't you let me hold him until you climb out?"

"Gut idea. *Danki."*

Ellen carefully eased the blanket-wrapped dog from

Nell's lap. The animal whimpered as he was moved. "'Tis *oll recht*, little one," Ellen crooned. "Dr. Pierce is going to fix you up. Then Nell's going to take *gut* care of you."

Nell climbed out and Ellen gently placed the dog back into his new owner's arms.

The young woman behind the front desk greeted them as they entered the clinic. Ellen was relieved to find no one else in the waiting room. She listened quietly as Nell explained what had happened and why they'd come.

"Poor baby," the receptionist said as she leaned over the counter to get a closer look. She wore a nametag that read Michelle.

"James!" she called. "Will you come out front, please? Someone needs you!"

Within seconds, a man exited the back of the clinic, a stunningly handsome man with dark hair, dark eyes and a beautiful mouth that went from a smile to a concerned frown as soon as he saw Nell holding the quilt-wrapped puppy.

"Come with me," he urged gently. "What happened?"

Nell explained what she'd seen and Ellen witnessed a tightening of the man's lips as she told him about the way the puppy was tossed out of a moving car.

"Stupid people," Ellen thought she heard the vet mutter.

While she appreciated the man's good looks, she wasn't affected, but Nell, she saw, was reacting differently. The young woman had seemed stunned when Dr. Pierce came in from the back of the clinic. Ellen wondered if Nell silently was questioning the skill and experience of someone who was much younger than she'd expected.

Ellen started to hang back as Nell followed James Pierce into an exam room until Michelle at the front desk encouraged her to go with them.

Ellen was glad. She would have found it difficult waiting when she wanted to know what was happening inside. She took one of the two seats in the room while Nell settled the puppy onto the exam table and watched as the vet went to work.

Isaac pulled into the barnyard near the William Mast home and climbed out to help his brother carry in Josie's groceries. Shifting his bags, he knocked and William answered the door with Josie standing directly behind him.

"Isaac! Daniel!" Josie exclaimed, moving forward. Her gaze was wary as it glanced off Isaac to center on Daniel.

Disappointed in the reaction he often garnered since the vandalism incident at Whittier's Store for which he was blamed, Isaac spoke up, forcing the couple's attention back on him. "We've brought your groceries. Ellen is helping my cousin Nell." He explained what had happened and where their daughter was. "She didn't want you to worry, so I offered to let you know. She doesn't know how long the vet will take."

"I don't think Ellen will want to leave until she finds out how the puppy is," Daniel added.

William nodded. "*Ja*, she is kindhearted that way," he said. "As is Nell."

Isaac nodded, but William was looking at Daniel

while avoiding Isaac's gaze. Isaac tried not to feel hurt but couldn't help it.

"Danki," Josie said. He saw that she was eyeing him thoughtfully, not with censure necessarily but a look that Isaac couldn't read. "If you don't mind carrying the bags into the kitchen," she said, stepping back to invite them inside. He saw William shoot his wife a look and noticed how Josie pretended she didn't see.

Isaac set down the bags on the kitchen table. "Daniel."

Daniel nodded without Isaac's speaking.

"Say *hallo* to your *mam* and *dat*, Daniel," William said to Daniel as if purposely ignoring Isaac.

Pain radiated through his chest as Isaac headed to the front door. He was eager to leave. William's behavior toward him reminded him of how unworthy he was, how he'd messed up and no one would soon forget. Ellen said that she would someday, he thought. The notion gave him hope, although he doubted that Ellen would want to be friends with him again, not with the way her parents felt about him.

He climbed into the buggy, momentarily blinded by his inner turmoil. As Daniel climbed into the other side, Isaac gathered the strength to push the pain aside—again—and drive the rest of the way home.

Chapter Seven

Ellen thought about the wounded puppy as she hung laundry on the clothesline two days later. Dr. Pierce had been optimistic about the dog's recovery. He'd told Nell that the animal's leg wasn't broken but it was severely bruised and sprained. He taped it for support to give Jonas, the name Nell had bestowed on the little dog, time to rest and heal. The veterinarian loaned Nell a kennel to house Jonas and help curb his activities. When the time came for the vet bill, she and Nell were surprised when Dr. Pierce insisted that there was no charge for the visit. Nell started to protest until James Pierce explained to them that he'd just opened his practice. If they would spread the word about his new clinic, that would be more than enough payment for Jonas's care. He then complimented Nell on her inherent animal skills. Nell looked puzzled, probably because he'd seen her with only Jonas and none of her other animals, but Dr. Pierce said he could sense that she had a natural affinity with them simply by the way the puppy responded to her touch and soothing voice.

"Most injured dogs will strike and bite those who

try to help them, whether it's their owner or not. The fact that you picked up this little guy without incident tells me a lot. I can tell you like animals and are good to them." He paused and looked thoughtful. "I have a proposition for you—I don't want to offend you, but would you consider working here until I can hire a certified vet tech?" He smiled. "Think about it, Nell…"

"Stoltzfus," Nell supplied, apparently without thought.

"It's only a temporary position, but I could use your help."

"I don't know," Nell told him. "I'll have to ask. I can't accept without talking with my family first."

The man had nodded. "I understand, but please let me know soon. All right?"

Recalling their conversation as she continued to hang clothes, Ellen wondered whether or not Nell would accept the vet's job offer. She had a feeling that Nell wanted to work there but that the young woman was afraid of her father's disapproval. Ellen understood that fear of wanting to do something wonderful but being afraid to ask. It was the way she felt about the medical clinic…the one she had yet to visit.

Ellen had sensed an attraction between Nell and James Pierce. Would that be the reason for Nell to turn down the man's job offer? Or had she only imagined the tension between Nell and the veterinarian?

She couldn't imagine getting involved with an *Englisher. Look what happened to Isaac.* It would be worse for Nell, who had already joined the church. If a relationship occurred between her and James, there'd be only heartbreak for Nell. Their lives were too different—Nell's in the Amish community and Dr. Pierce's in the English world.

We women must guard our hearts, Ellen thought as her mind filled with the image of Isaac. She scowled as she threw a quilt over the clothesline. It was Katie Lapp's quilt, the one they'd used to carry Jonas. Once she'd brought Nell and Jonas home, she'd offered to wash the quilt and return it to Katie. The young woman had been grateful; she'd seemed to have a lot on her mind. Mostly, Ellen didn't doubt, due to Dr. Pierce's startling job offer.

Ellen knew that there was a good chance she'd encounter Isaac again when she returned his mother's quilt. So what if she did? She'd get the chance to thank him again for his help with Jonas.

She felt an infusion of warmth as she recalled the look on his face when Isaac had asked her if she'd ever forget about the mistake he'd made with their friendship. She allowed herself to wonder briefly how it might feel to have his attention the way Nancy had, to see his gaze light up whenever he laid eyes on her, to have his lips curve up in a smile that suggested she was the only woman for him.

I have to stop this! Such thoughts were dangerous. She couldn't turn back the clock to when their friendship began years ago so that Isaac could choose differently. She'd been hurt badly enough that she'd wondered if she'd ever recover. But she had recovered. But did that mean that she'd gotten over her feelings for him? She closed her eyes. *Nay.* She hugged herself with her arms. Which was all the more reason to keep her distance from him.

As she continued to hang the laundry, Ellen firmed her resolve to be pleasant to Isaac but not let her heart rule her head. She had clipped the last garment on the line when she detected the sound of a car engine and the crunch of tires on the driveway.

"Mam!" Elam cried. "She's here!"

Ellen grinned, knowing that her brother meant Mary Ruth Fisher, her cousin from Honeysuckle, a girl she hadn't known existed until two days ago when *Mam* told her about the visit. She picked up the empty wicker laundry basket and headed toward the side yard. A young woman was getting out of the backseat of a blue car. The driver was near the trunk, pulling out a suitcase, which he then handed to the girl.

"Thank you, Ted," she heard Mary Ruth say warmly. "I appreciate the ride."

"Had to come this way regardless, Mary Ruth. It was no hardship."

Mary Ruth's mouth curved. She said something, but Ellen could hear only her teasing tone. Ted's reply to her appeared to surprise and please Mary Ruth.

"I'll see you then. Thanks again." Mary Ruth watched as the man got into his car and drove away. Only then did she turn and realize that three strangers—Ellen, Elam and *Mam*, who had come out onto the porch—stood waiting to greet her.

"Sorry!" the girl gasped. She approached with a tentative smile. *"Hallo,* I'm—"

Ellen immediately rushed forward to greet her warmly. "Mary Ruth. *Hallo,* I'm your cousin Ellen."

The girl beamed at her. "Ellen, 'tis nice to meet you."

"Mary Ruth!" *Mam* descended the porch steps with Elam trailing behind. "We're so glad you could come for a visit. I'm Josie. I'm—"

Their visitor looked pleased. "You're *Mam's* first cousin."

Ellen reached toward the girl's suitcase. "May I carry your bag?"

"*Danki*, but *nay*. I can handle it. It may look small but if you knew the weight of it, you'd become nervous that I was moving in indefinitely."

Mam eyed the girl approvingly. "You're always welcome to move in and stay."

"*Ja*, Mary Ruth, there are only my two *bruders* and me. There's Elam here—" she gestured toward her younger brother "—and Will, but I have no idea where he is." Ellen glanced toward her mother. "I haven't seen Will all morning."

"He's out with your *vadder*. They went to see Samuel Lapp. Some kind of project or other."

"Come with me," Ellen invited her cousin. "You'll be staying in my room with me."

"Just the two of us?" Mary Ruth seemed pleased. "I've never slept in a room with only one other person, not since I was really little when it was just me and Hannah."

Minutes later Ellen showed Mary Ruth her room. She saw her cousin examine the space with its wooden floors and double bed with quilt coverlet and wall hooks—and wooden chest at the end of the bed.

"Nice," the girl said. "You have a lot of room. My bedroom is this size but there are two beds. Four of us shared the room at one time but not now."

"You don't mind sharing a bed?"

Mary Ruth shook her head. "*Nay*, do you?"

"Not at all," Ellen assured her. She watched as Mary Ruth set her suitcase on the floor in the corner.

"Hungry?" Ellen asked. It was near noon and she was hungry.

"I could eat."

Ellen grinned. "Let's go, then."

It seemed that *Mam* had the same idea, for her mother was putting fresh bread and a plate of ham slices and cold chicken on the table as they entered the kitchen.

"All settled in?"

Mary Ruth nodded. "*Ja.* My suitcase is upstairs." She paused. "*Danki* for having me."

"Our pleasure," *Mam* said.

After lunch the girls went back to their bedroom to chat while Mary Ruth unpacked the few garments she'd brought.

"I thought we could go into Lancaster one day," Ellen said after it occurred to her that her cousin was of an age for *rumspringa*. She didn't have to wait for Elizabeth to go while she had Mary Ruth.

"Into town?" Mary Ruth said.

"*Ja.* A big town. A city. Maybe we could go to a movie. Have you ever been?"

"*Rumspringa?*" the girl breathed. "*Nay.* With six siblings, there has never been time for running around."

"You've got time now." Ellen wiggled her eyebrows, making her cousin chuckle. "We both do. I'll have a talk with my *mudder* and *vadder*. *Dat* can hire a car for us. It will probably be our neighbor Rick Martin. He can take us and bring us home."

"Will he stay and wait for us?"

"*Nay*, he'll drop us off and then we'll call him when we want him to pick us up."

Her cousin looked excited. "When?"

"Tomorrow?"

Mary Ruth gasped. "You can arrange it that quickly?"

"*Ja*, why not? As long as *Mam* doesn't have extra chores for me to do. And if she does, then we'll go the next day."

The girl's eyes gleamed. "It sounds like fun."

"It will be. But first I need to do something. Will you come with me?" Ellen explained about Nell and the injured puppy. "I'd like to see how he's doing. Would you come with me?"

"*Ja*, I'd like to see this little dog."

After explaining about her plan to her mother, Ellen drove the buggy to the Arlin Stoltzfus residence. The short journey gave Mary Ruth a chance to catch a glimpse of their community. "When we are done at Nell's, I have a quilt to return to Nell's aunt Katie."

Meg and Charlie, Nell's younger sisters, were in the yard when Ellen pulled in and parked near the barn. Meg waved as Ellen got out. The two sisters hurried to greet them as Mary Ruth climbed out the other side. "Ellen!"

"*Hallo*, Meg." Ellen beamed at her before turning her attention to her younger sister. "Charlie." She introduced her cousin. "Mary Ruth, Meg and Charlie Stoltzfus—Nell's sisters." She waited as Mary Ruth greeted the two girls. "We've come to check on Jonas. How is he?"

"The puppy?" Charlie asked.

"*Ja*. Where is he? Is Nell with him?"

Meg inclined her head. "They're in the barn. Come and I'll show you."

Ellen waved for Mary Ruth to follow as she and Meg headed toward the barn with Charlie tagging along behind them. She immediately noted changes inside the barn. It had been some time since she'd visited last, and clearly Arlin, the girls' father, had done work to the building's interior. New stables had been constructed along the right side of the structure. There were animals housed there—no doubt brought here by Nell, who always seemed to be adding to her menagerie.

"Nell!" Meg called.

"Over here!"

"Nell," Ellen said, "I came to check on Jonas. I've brought my cousin Mary Ruth with me. She's visiting from up north."

Nell's head popped up over a stable wall as they approached. "Ellen! Come and take a look," Nell said. "He's doing much better."

As she entered the stall, Ellen saw the puppy standing on all four legs—one still bandaged. The animal was wobbly but was managing to stay up.

"Ah…how precious!" Mary Ruth gushed.

The cousins crouched low to pet the puppy, who seemed to relish the attention.

Ellen rose to her feet. "When does he go back to Dr. Pierce?"

"In two weeks."

"Have you thought about his offer?"

Nell shot a quick look behind her toward her sisters, who were within earshot.

"Nay," Nell murmured, obviously hoping her sisters wouldn't hear.

"The work would be interesting," Ellen said softly. She thought about her own desire to help special-needs children. She'd have to confide in Mary Ruth before they headed into Lancaster. Sometime during the visit, she wanted to stop and talk with the clinic doctor.

The cousins spent a half hour talking with Nell and watching Jonas move clumsily about on all four legs until Ellen suddenly realized that it was getting late. They would have just enough time for a brief stop at Katie's before heading home.

"Do you have everything you need for him?" Ellen asked. She'd be more than willing to help out with money or time.

"*Ja.* Dr. Pierce gave me everything I need until it's time for me to take him back."

"He's doing well."

"*Ja,* he is." Nell reached down and picked him up. The puppy didn't seem to mind being held by her. He snuggled against Nell as if he loved every moment in her arms. "Did you return Katie's quilt?"

"We're heading there next."

Satisfied that little Jonas was on the mend, Ellen turned to Mary Ruth. "We should go. I have one more stop to make before we go home."

Isaac couldn't stop thinking about Ellen. She'd given him hope that she would one day forget the pain he'd caused her.

Whenever he saw a buggy on the side of the road, he immediately thought of Ellen and experienced real fear. He had nightmares about Brad and his friends forcing her off the road again. *Is it any wonder I feel the need to protect her still?* He headed toward the barn to check on the animals.

The other day when he and Daniel had stopped to see what was wrong, he'd been so relieved that Ellen was well. He had understood why she and Nell were upset. The poor puppy had been injured through no fault of its own. Who could be so cruel? Brad could.

He went to old Bess's stall, and when she immediately came to lean her head over the side, he rubbed the mare's nose. He was pleased that he'd been able to help Ellen and Nell. He couldn't forget Ellen's smile when he'd given Nell the quilt for her puppy. *If only she'd smile at me all the time, the way she used to.*

The mare responded to his touch, nuzzling against his shoulder. "You like that, Bessie?" he said with a smile. He reached into his pocket and pulled out a carrot he'd snatched from the refrigerator before he'd left the house.

When had it become so important to renew his friendship with Ellen? He certainly hadn't given her much thought after he'd met Nancy. Isaac felt a burning in his stomach as he realized just how much he must have hurt her. They'd been friends, and in his infatuation with Nancy, he'd ignored her completely. He'd been a fool twice over—once when he fell for an *Englisher* and then again when he'd hurt the one person who'd been his true friend and confidante.

He left Bess to check on the other barn animals. He made sure that they all had a full day's worth of water and that certain ones were fed. Then he opened the back barn door to let the horses into the pasture, where their sheep, cows and goats already enjoyed free range. After shutting the barn door behind him, Isaac walked across the pasture toward the front fence. As he unlatched the gate, he noticed a buggy approaching the house on their dirt lane.

He experienced a knee-jerk reaction as the vehicle

parked near the barn and he saw the driver. Ellen Mast. The woman he couldn't stop thinking about. And she wasn't alone. There was another girl with her, one he'd never met before.

He hurried to the driver's side of the vehicle before Ellen had a chance to climb out. She was bent over the front seat, reaching for something in the back, her gaze turned away from him. He saw her fingers stretch toward the quilt but she couldn't quite reach it.

"May I get that for you?" he asked softly.

She stiffened and straightened. "If you must."

He smiled. "*Hallo*, Ellen." She blushed and mumbled a greeting as if realizing that she'd been less than friendly. He glanced past toward the other girl inside the vehicle. "Who's this?"

"My cousin Mary Ruth Fisher," she said stiffly. "Mary Ruth, this is Isaac Lapp."

"Isaac," the girl said with a glimmer of interest.

"Mary Ruth." He politely inclined his head. A spark of strong emotion hit him as he transferred his gaze to Ellen. He opened her door. "If you'll step out, I'll get the quilt for you."

She moved out of his way and allowed him to retrieve his mother's quilt.

His lips twitched as he fought back a smile. "I'm sure she'll be happy you've returned it."

He leaned in to smile at Mary Ruth. "Come inside," he invited. "*Mam* will be upset if you don't stop to say *hallo*."

He saw Ellen exchange looks with her cousin. "We have a few minutes. I'd like you to meet Katie," she told Mary Ruth, who then climbed out on the passenger's side.

Daniel exited the house and saw their approach. "Hey, is that Ellen Mast?"

Ellen chuckled. "Who else would be driving my *dat's* buggy?"

Daniel grinned at her before addressing Isaac. "*Dat* wants us to look in on Bess," he said, referring to their mare.

"I just checked on her."

"Oh, *gut*," Daniel said. His attention suddenly focused on Mary Ruth. "Aren't you going to introduce us, Ellen?"

"Daniel, my cousin Mary Ruth. Mary Ruth, Daniel—one of many Lapp *bruders*."

"There are seven of us," Daniel said.

"There are seven of us at home in Honeysuckle," the girl said.

"We have a sister, too. She's the youngest. Hannah is eight." Daniel smiled. "You coming in?"

Ellen nodded. "For a few minutes."

Isaac felt irritated that Ellen was so warm toward his younger brother but was cold to him. He was genuinely sorry he'd hurt her, but he didn't think she'd believe him if he tried to tell her.

Chapter Eight

Ellen followed Daniel with Mary Ruth into the house, conscious of Isaac following. She needed to gather her composure. What did it matter now if he'd chosen Nancy over her? That was two years ago. She should be well past the hurt by now.

There was no one in the kitchen as they stepped into the room.

"Mam!" Isaac called out from behind her. He was close, too close for her peace of mind. *"Mam*, we have company!"

Katie Lapp stepped into the room. "Ellen!" The woman glanced toward her cousin. "And you must be Mary Ruth. Josie told me you were coming. *Willkomm!"* She beamed at them. "I'm glad you could visit. I'm Katie Lapp." She gestured in his direction. "And these two beside you are my *soohns*." She went to the stove and put on the teakettle. "Tea? Or would you like something else to drink?"

"Danki, but *nay*, Katie," Ellen said. "We can't stay long, I'm afraid. *Mam* didn't expect us to be out this

late." She bit her lip. "We checked on Nell's puppy before we came here."

"How is Jonas doing?" Isaac asked, curious.

"He's fine," she said too politely. She spoke to Katie. "Dr. Pierce treated his injured leg and put him on an antibiotic."

"Jonas?" *Mam* asked.

"*Ja, Mam.* Nell's new puppy."

Katie's expression was warm. "My niece loves her animals. I've never seen anyone else who has such a way with them."

"She *is* special," Ellen said, drawing his glance. Isaac studied her intently, and she felt her face heat and turned away.

"We put your quilt to *gut* use, Katie, even if you didn't know."

Katie glanced at the elder of her two sons in the room. "Isaac told me when he got home."

Ellen met his gaze with raised eyebrows. "That was kind of him."

His lips curved. "I'm glad I could help."

The girls chatted a few minutes and then left soon after. Isaac walked them as far as the front porch and then watched as the girls climbed into the vehicle. Ellen picked up the leathers and glanced back toward the house. He lifted his hand in farewell. After a slight pause, Ellen raised her hand to return his wave.

"I'll see you on Sunday, Ellen," he called.

She tightened her mouth but nodded, and then with a flick of the reins, she urged her horse forward. She didn't look back as she spoke to Mary Ruth seated next to her, knowing he might be watching her as the buggy continued onto the road and disappeared from view.

* * *

Ellen sprang up out of bed, excited. This morning, Mary Ruth and she would be heading into Lancaster for the day. Her parents had given them permission, and her father had arranged for a driver, as he'd promised when she'd first thought that she'd be going with her friend Elizabeth.

"What time is it?" her cousin asked groggily.

"Five." Ellen knew because she usually got up every day at the same time, although yesterday, much to her chagrin, she'd slept a full hour later. Fortunately, *Mam* hadn't scolded her for oversleeping.

Mary Ruth bolted upright. "Time to get up! What should we do first? Feed the animals?" She climbed out of bed and immediately dressed.

"Nay." Ellen grabbed her black apron and tied it over her green dress. "We'll set the table first. I told *Mam* that I'd make breakfast."

As she got ready, Ellen didn't bother with her prayer *kapp*. She'd grab one before their driver came to pick them up at eight thirty. She had plenty of time to get her morning chores done before the driver came.

Ellen enjoyed this time of the early morning, when the birds chirped with their pleasure at the new day. She descended the stairs quietly, then entered the kitchen with Mary Ruth behind her. The two girls immediately went to work.

Mary Ruth took out plates and cups and glasses from a kitchen cabinet. While Mary set the table, Ellen placed a fresh pot of coffee on the stove to perk. While the percolator perked, she retrieved eggs, ham and cheese from the refrigerator and assembled them all into a skillet. She lit the gas oven and when it was hot, she placed the large skillet inside to bake.

"What else do you need me to do?" Mary said.

"There are muffins and biscuits in the pantry—oh, and I forgot to take out jelly and jam from the refrigerator." Her cousin nodded and left to gather the items.

The scent of ham and eggs had enveloped the kitchen as her father entered the room. "Something smells delicious."

"Dat." Ellen smiled. "Smelled the ham and eggs, *ja?"*

He inclined his head. "So did your *mudder."*

"Her *mudder* what?" *Mam* asked with a smile as she entered the room.

"Smelled breakfast."

"It does smell *gut." Mam* took a seat at the kitchen table. "Did you sleep well, Mary Ruth?"

"Like a well-fed baby." Mary Ruth laughed. "Not a newborn—they cry."

"Ja, they do." *Mam* appeared to be indulging in a fond memory.

"Dat, do you know where the boys are?" Ellen asked. "I haven't seen them."

"Outside feeding the animals."

"I would have had time to feed them," Ellen said.

"I know but this is the day of your Lancaster trip—and you've taken care of breakfast, which gave your *mudder* and me a few extra minutes of sleep."

Elam came in through the back door. "Mmm. Breakfast."

Will stepped inside after him. "I smell ham."

Ellen regarded her brothers affectionately before

she pulled the hot skillet out of the oven. "Breakfast is ready."

After an enjoyable breakfast with her family, Ellen cleaned up the kitchen with Mary Ruth's help. Then the two girls got ready for their trip into Lancaster.

Ellen was headed into town. He found out by accident when his friend Jeff Martin told him how William Mast had hired Rick, Jeff's father, to drive the girls into Lancaster. He knew what it meant. Ellen had been eager to go *rumspringa* and now she would finally have her chance.

Isaac frowned. He didn't like the idea of the two girls wandering about the city streets alone. He had a mental image of the day Brad had run Ellen off the road and attempted to bully her. What if someone tried to bother Ellen? Who would be there to help her if not him?

She wasn't alone. Her cousin Mary Ruth was with her, but what good would that do if the girls encountered trouble?

Daniel entered the bedroom. "Isaac, time for work."

"Coming." Isaac sighed. He couldn't help Ellen today. In any event, she and her cousin were probably already on their way. He sent up a silent prayer to the Lord that Ellen and her cousin stayed safe.

As he started work on Matt Rhoades's latest construction project, Isaac wondered how Ellen was managing. He'd been unable to get her out of his mind since he started work. When he asked himself why, he didn't like the answer. When they were friends, he used to think of Ellen as a sister. But Ellen seemed different now. She had matured. He found he liked this mature,

spirited version of his former friend. *Maybe too much.*
He frowned as he hammered a wooden floorboard into
place. He couldn't allow it to happen. He had to put
things back into perspective. He wanted to be friends
with her again. He wanted nothing more. He stood and
stared into space as he dug into his nail bag.

"What's wrong?" Daniel asked.

Isaac blinked and met his brother's gaze. "Nothing."

"You've been quiet, too quiet. Something must
be wrong. You haven't given me a word of advice all
morning."

Isaac arched his eyebrows. "Isn't that a *gut* thing?"

"It would be if I saw you smile at least once this
morning, but you haven't. You've been scowling since
I came to get you from your bedroom first thing."

"I have something on my mind."

Lips twitching, Daniel nodded. "What?"

"Nothing for you to concern yourself with," he replied sharply.

The morning dragged on for Isaac as he struggled
with his thoughts—and his new feelings for Ellen. He
looked around the job site. Their construction crew
had accomplished a great deal during the last few days.
Maybe he could leave and head into Lancaster.

Isaac sought out his brother just before noon. "I
think I'm going to leave for the afternoon…if Matt lets
me go. You don't have to come."

Daniel looked relieved. "I'd rather stay." He eyed
Isaac quietly. "You're going to take care of your problem." Isaac nodded. *"Gut."*

Isaac approached Matt Rhoades and asked if he
could leave work for the day. "I have something I need
to do."

Matt studied him, nodded. "Go ahead. Take care of business. Things are going well enough here. You taking Daniel with you?"

"*Nay*, he wants to stay."

"I'll give him a ride," his boss said. "You're off for the afternoon."

"If you're sure it's all right with you."

"It's fine. You'll be back tomorrow." It wasn't a question.

"I will."

"I'll see you then."

After leaving work at noon, Isaac headed right to Jeff Martin's house to see if Jeff could drive him into Lancaster to find Ellen. Jeff was bored and only too happy to take him.

"Why do you want to go?" his friend asked as he drove them into the city.

He explained about Ellen and his concerns for her safety. Jeff looked skeptical but he remained agreeable to Isaac's plan.

Rick Martin had arrived on time at eight thirty. Less than fifteen minutes later, the man had dropped her and Mary Ruth off near Target on Covered Bridge Road.

"What would you like to do first?" Mary Ruth had asked as she checked her surroundings.

At some point, Ellen hoped to locate the clinic that took care of special-needs children. "Want to go into Target?"

"*Ja,*" Mary Ruth said with a grin. "Why not?"

They passed the morning walking down the aisles of Target before moving on to a nearby Starbucks for coffee and tea. Afterward they wandered about the area. They stopped in a local PetSmart to purchase a toy and a bag of treats for Nell's puppy. By that time, the girls laughed after hearing Ellen's stomach growl with hunger. Then they went looking for a place to eat.

The restaurant they chose was empty except for the workers. They had eaten an early breakfast and so were hungry for lunch at eleven.

"What can I get you?" the girl behind the counter asked. They placed their order and chose a booth near the window where they could eat and enjoy the view outside. Ellen and her cousin grinned at each other, pleased by how their day was going.

"What would you like to do after lunch?" Mary Ruth asked after swallowing a bite of sandwich.

"I'd like to see if I can find the Westmore Clinic," Ellen said. She confessed to Mary Ruth what she wanted to do and her fear that she wouldn't be able to convince her parents, who'd objected when she'd first brought up the subject with them. "I want to stop in and see if someone will talk with me. Maybe if I give my *vadder* more information, he will change his mind. I also need to make sure that the clinic will allow me to volunteer there." Ellen worried her bottom lip with her teeth as she waited for her cousin to react.

Mary Ruth nodded solemnly but seemed to understand. "My stepmother, Lizzie—I call her *Mam* now but I wasn't always so happy to have her as my *mudder*—she has a bad leg. For years she thought she was born with hip dysplasia, a birth defect when there is a problem with the ball of the hip joint slipping from its socket. It turns out she wasn't born with the birth defect at all. She learned that she'd had an accident when she was little and there was permanent damage." The girl smiled, her eyes warming with affection as she talked about her stepmother. It was clear to Ellen how much her cousin loved the older woman. Suddenly, her face dimmed. "Ellen, I think *Mam* is going to have a baby."

Ellen brightened. "That's wonderful!"

But Mary Ruth looked worried. She glanced out the window as if deciding how best to explain. "Uncle Zack is concerned, too. Her hip—it could be a serious problem for her."

Realization dawned, and Ellen regarded her with understanding. "But you'll be happy to have a new *bruder* or *schweschter* if your *mam's* health isn't ill affected. *Ja?*"

Brown eyes shot in her direction as she nodded. Mary Ruth's lips curved up slowly. "We've known each other only a short time but already I feel like you know me."

Ellen shrugged. "You've told me about your family. I know you love them. You would be concerned."

An English family with four children entered the restaurant. A little girl looked at Ellen and Mary Ruth and tugged on her mother's shirt. "Mommy, look! Aren't they one of those people?"

The mother—a woman in her midthirties—followed the direction of her daughter's gaze. She nodded. "Yes, honey, they are Amish people."

The hostess seated the family close to the Amish cousins. The four English children continued to stare at them. A glance at Mary Ruth, and Ellen could tell that her cousin felt as uncomfortable as she did under the family's direct gazes. To her dismay, Ellen was appalled to discover all six family members were now staring at them.

"They won't stop looking at us," Ellen said in Pennsylvania *Deitsch*, the language Amish families spoke at home and within the community. They learned the English language in school so that they could do business with *Englishers*.

"Why do they wear those funny clothes, Daddy?" a young voice asked. Ellen saw a boy of about six years old and his father studying them with curiosity.

"Because they are different than us."

Ellen stood. "I've had enough."

She studied the food left on Mary Ruth's plate and sat back down. "When you're finished, we can go."

"I've had enough, too." Mary Ruth grimaced. "Let's get out of here."

They left quickly, glad to be away from the English tourists.

"I'm used to seeing tourists here in Lancaster County," Ellen said once the girls were outside. "It never occurred to me that we'd be watched as if on show for them."

"What if we weren't dressed like this?" Mary Ruth asked.

Ellen frowned. "Then they wouldn't stare at us." She knew instantly what her cousin was suggesting. But did they dare dress like the English?

Her cousin nodded. "We could go shopping."

"We could." Ellen gave it some thought. She shrugged. They were on *rumspringa*, after all. "Why not?"

She had second thoughts. *But what if someone sees us dressed in English clothes and tells Mam and Dat?* She'd simply tell her parents the truth—they'd dressed like *Englishers* to keep tourists from staring at them. "We won't be doing anything wrong," Ellen reasoned.

"Exactly." Mary Ruth was studying the businesses in the area. "We could go back to Target."

Ellen grinned. "*Oll recht.* We'll buy clothes in Target."

Less than an hour later, each girl had picked out an outfit. They were conservative by modern English teenagers' standards, but Ellen refused to wear anything too revealing. She chose a modest, midcalf skirt in a pretty blue print with a matching solid blue blouse. She studied her feet while she tried on the outfit and realized that her black shoes and dark stockings would stand out as Amish and clash with her choice of clothes. So she decided to look to purchase a simple pair of black slip-on shoes and panty hose to take the place of the black stockings. While still in the dressing room, Ellen took off her prayer *kapp* and shoved it in the pocket of her new skirt. Pockets were considered fancy in the Amish world but since she was trying to look English, she figured they were allowed this one time. She paid for a large quilted cloth purse to carry her money, Amish clothes, stockings and plain black shoes.

Mary Ruth had chosen a simple green dress. Since it was warm enough outside, she'd chosen a pair of flip-flops. She also purchased a quilted cloth bag for her belongings.

After paying for all of their new items, they hurried outside.

Ellen sighed. "We need a place to get changed."

"Look!" Mary Ruth cried. "A public restroom! We can change in there."

Later, as they left the building with their Amish

garments in their new cloth bags, the cousins studied each other's new clothes and grinned.

"Let's see if anyone stares at us," Mary Ruth suggested.

"Let's do." Ellen felt self-conscious as they walked the sidewalk together. When no one paid them any particular attention, she found herself relaxing. "Let's find that clinic," she said.

"Should we take a taxi?"

"*Ja*, that might be best."

They walked to a place where they could call a taxi. Within minutes, the taxi arrived and Ellen climbed in with Mary Ruth following.

"Do you know the Westmore Clinic?" Ellen asked.

"Yes, you want to go there?" the driver said.

"Yes, please." As the car began to move, Ellen spotted an Amish man walking along the road. The figure looked familiar. She froze. She thought he was Isaac Lapp. The thought shook her until she glanced back and realized that the man wasn't Isaac but someone she didn't know. Someone from another church district. She released a sharp breath and scolded herself for imagining things.

Within minutes, the taxi driver had pulled his car up to the curb in front of the medical clinic. Ellen got out first and waited for Mary Ruth to join her. She stared at the clinic sign and felt her heart thunder in her chest. It read Westmore Clinic for Special Children.

"It didn't take long to get here," Ellen said with great satisfaction. "And I think it's closer to home than town."

"Do you want to go in?"

Ellen wanted to, but still she felt hesitant.

"You've come for information and to inquire if they use volunteers," her cousin reminded her. "Dr. Westmore might not even be in today. There's no harm in visiting, is there? How else are you going to convince your parents?"

Ellen nodded. Her cousin had a point. "Let's go in."

The doctor wasn't in when Ellen and Mary Ruth asked to speak with him. The young woman at the front desk wasn't pleasant, a fact that upset Ellen, who worried that she was as rude with the Amish families who came to seek help for their children here.

"May I speak with a nurse?" Ellen asked politely after the receptionist had explained that Dr. Westmore would be out for the rest of the day.

The woman stared at her coldly before she headed toward the back rooms. She was gone a long time before she finally returned with an older woman dressed in white medical scrubs.

"I'm Dr. Westmore's nurse. How can I help you?"

"I'd like to ask about volunteer work."

The woman didn't look annoyed. "We don't use volunteers."

"But I know what you do here," Ellen said, "and I know I can help. Is there a better time for me to speak with Dr. Westmore?"

"Joan, please see if there is room in Dr. Westmore's schedule for—"

"Ellen Mast," Ellen supplied.

"For Miss Mast to see Dr. Westmore."

"Do I have to pay for this appointment?"

The nurse's lips firmed. "We'll schedule close to the time he usually reviews his case notes."

"Oh, but—" Ellen was silently, firmly, handed an

appointment card. She sent her cousin a silent message and they hurriedly left. She was disappointed in the lack of friendliness in the clinic staff, but she would keep the appointment with Dr. Westmore. She could only hope that the doctor was friendlier and wouldn't feel the same way.

"What now?" she asked her cousin.

"Let's see what's playing at the movies."

The prospect made Ellen smile.

Chapter Nine

The girls walked to the movie theater. As she reached the theater, Ellen saw posters in the windows and a small marquee listing the movie titles and times. She felt excitement as she and Mary Ruth read the information on the current movies.

"Look at this one! It says it's a comedy, but I wonder if it's really funny," Mary Ruth said.

"The English think differently than us. What if we don't find the movie funny like they do?"

"*Ja*, like the way they laugh when someone gets hurt."

Ellen silently agreed with her cousin. "I wonder what this one is about," she murmured as her gaze went to another title.

"Look what we have here. A couple of lonely females," someone said in a nasty male voice.

Ellen gasped and spun and, to her horror, recognized Brad Smith, the English teenager who'd driven her buggy off the road.

"You!" His eyes gleamed as they raked her from head to toe. "And you've ditched your Amish wear," he accused, looking delighted. "Hey, guys!" He called to the group of male teenagers behind her only a few yards away. "Come and see who's here! It's a couple of Amish girls pretending to be like us." He narrowed his gaze, and Ellen realized what Brad saw—she and Mary Ruth looking vastly different in their conservative outfits from a couple of English teenagers.

His predatory expression gave Ellen chills as Brad continued to stare at her. She felt the hair on her arms rise on end. Her heart began to pound harder and faster as he took several steps closer. She met her cousin's gaze, knowing that Mary Ruth would recognize her fear.

"What do you want, Brad?" she said sharply, displaying more courage than she felt.

"You know my name." The *Englisher* looked delighted as he and his friends moved closer, blocking all avenues of escape. "How?"

She raised her chin. "What does it matter? We weren't bothering you," Ellen said sharply. "Why don't you leave us alone?"

"No can do, sweetheart. I like bothering you." His gaze shifted to Mary Ruth as the other teenagers surrounded them. "You and your *friend*." He smiled darkly as he pinned Mary Ruth with his gaze. "Who are *you*?"

Mary Ruth gazed at him silently, blankly.

"What's the matter with you?" he growled, growing irritated. "Can't you talk?" He sneered. "Are you a dummy?" He laughed as he looked at his friends. "The girl is a dummy."

Mary Ruth scowled. "I can speak. I just don't want to talk with *you*!"

Fury entered Brad's features. His hands clenched

into fists at his sides and Ellen moved instinctively to shield Mary Ruth.

Brad and his friends moved to tightly box them in. Brad flashed Ellen a wicked smile and snickered as he raised his hand as if to strike.

"Get away from her!" a sharp, familiar masculine voice shouted.

Isaac! Ellen sagged with relief as she turned. Isaac approached with Jeff Martin. Both boys were furious. Ellen wondered how the situation would be resolved without a physical fight, which would go against the *Ordnung*, the Amish rules for living. She didn't think Isaac would fight, but she wasn't sure. She'd realized two years ago that she didn't know Isaac as well as she'd thought at one time. On the other hand, Jeff Martin, an *Englisher*, wouldn't be averse to tussling with the troublemakers. But it would be foolish for him to tackle the group alone. The boys outnumbered Jeff five to one. Unless Isaac decided to help Jeff. He certainly looked mad enough to fight.

Brad smirked as he gazed at Isaac. The twisted smile on his lips vanished when he realized that Isaac wasn't alone, that he and Jeff Martin were together. Ellen knew that one look at tall, well-built Jeff, who appeared as if he worked out with weights regularly, had Brad's friends backing away from a fight.

Brad cursed, angered by his cohorts' retreat. Facing the two men alone made Brad retreat a few steps.

"I think we should call the police," Jeff said to Isaac. He pulled his cell out of his pocket, ready to dial.

"Maybe we should," Isaac said, gazing at his ex-girlfriend's brother from beneath lowered lids.

Jeff addressed Brad. "My uncle is a cop. He'll arrest you for threatening and terrorizing young women."

"You can't prove that we did that."

"I'm an eyewitness." Jeff smiled thinly. "I heard what you said. So did Isaac. And the girls' testimony will add weight to what we tell them." His features turned grim. "Besides, I took a photo of you surrounding the girls with my cell phone before we approached."

"No need to get testy," Brad said. "We were just having a little fun."

"I wasn't having fun," Ellen said, able to speak freely now that Isaac had come once again to save her.

"Me neither," Mary Ruth chimed in, but her gaze wasn't on Brad and his friends. Her attention was on Jeff, and the look in her eyes was respect mingled with admiration.

"Fine!" Brad said with a hiss. "We're leaving."

"And you'll stay away from Ellen and Mary Ruth, and anyone Ellen happens to be with in the future," Isaac said with a thin smile.

"Fine." Brad cursed beneath his breath, and Ellen felt her face heat at his choice of words. "I'll leave her alone." He glared at his friends, who waited several yards away. "Let's go," he snapped and Ellen thought she heard him mutter "Cowards" as he left with his minions following him.

Ellen had never been more relieved to see anyone go.

Isaac silently seethed inside as he watched Brad Smith and his friends leave the area. He'd been stunned and more than a little worried when he'd seen Ellen and her cousin surrounded by those thugs. They were nothing more than criminals, he thought.

Why had he ever thought it a good idea to spend time with them? Nancy. He'd done it for Nancy, which had been foolish of him.

He could feel anger rising within his chest and fought it back. But he'd been terrified, and the fear hadn't gone completely away.

It was a good thing that he'd left work early. It was by the grace of God that Jeff had been available and ready to drive him. Isaac gazed at Ellen, and as his lingering fear dissipated, he became angry. She shouldn't have come into town. She didn't need to go on *rumspringa*. He knew she would join the church; he'd always known it. Ellen was happy with her life. So why would she be so foolish as to place her and her cousin in danger? He stared at their clothes. Was it just for the little thrill of pretending to be English? Ellen knew the trouble that had found him at Whittier's Store. She had watched as he'd been drawn in by an English girl and her group of English friends, and he'd suffered because of it. She had tried to warn him. The thought didn't make him feel better. It just confirmed the fact that she should have known better and stayed at home, where she belonged.

He didn't like Ellen's strange clothes. The English garments didn't look right on her. He glanced toward Mary Ruth. They didn't look right on Ellen's cousin, either. He supposed an English girl might find them pretty, but on Ellen and Mary Ruth, the outfits looked ridiculous and wrong.

He glanced in the direction that Brad and his friends had disappeared. He had the strongest urge to walk down the road to make sure that they had left and weren't just hanging around out of sight. If Brad both-

ered Ellen again, Isaac thought, he would go to the
police and confess Brad's part in the Whittier's Store
vandalism incident. He could do it without implicat-
ing Henry in the crime.

Jeff's voice filtered into his dark thoughts. He was
talking with the girls, reassuring them. Isaac looked
at Ellen standing next to Jeff, her head cocked a little
as she listened intently to what he had to say. As if
sensing his study of her, she turned and they locked
gazes. A flicker of vulnerability in her blue eyes tore
at his insides. He clenched his teeth as he relived the
past moments at the movie theater, trying but failing
not to imagine what could have happened to Ellen and
Mary Ruth if he'd decided to stay and work at the construction site.

"We should go." He addressed the girls: "We'll take
you home." He checked with Jeff, who nodded in agreement. They started to head to where Jeff had parked his
car down the street. Isaac trailed behind the two girls,
who walked with Jeff, one on each side of his friend.
He had to work to keep his emotions under control.

Ellen stepped aside and waited for him to catch up.
He didn't say anything as she started to walk alongside him. He kept having the mental image of Brad
and his friends surrounding her, felt again that awful
fear wash over him. He was determined to make sure
nothing happened to her in the future—whether or
not she liked it.

Chapter Ten

Ellen walked beside Isaac, grateful that he'd saved her. She felt disquieted by his silence. He'd barely said a word since he'd chased Brad and his cohorts away. She'd seen him glance at her English clothes earlier. He looked away when she caught him staring, but not before she glimpsed his scowl. She hated that he wouldn't talk with her. She knew he didn't approve of her clothes and the fact that she'd come to Lancaster, but she'd done nothing wrong. She'd wanted to enjoy the excursion, but mostly, she'd wanted to visit the Westmore Clinic.

"Isaac—" Ellen started to thank him for arriving in the nick of time.

"Not now," Isaac said tersely, and she flinched.

"But—"

He froze in his tracks and turned to glare at her. She gasped as she recognized anger. Irritation. *At me.*

Ellen straightened her spine, started to walk in the opposite direction, then halted. "Mary Ruth!" When her cousin turned, she waved a hand for her cousin to follow. "Let's go."

"Where do ya think you're going?" Isaac said testily.

"To finish our day in town." She narrowed her gaze, daring him to argue with her. She saw Mary Ruth smile at Jeff, then shrug before she left his side to join her.

"*Nay*, you're not," Isaac said. "You're coming home with Jeff and me. Brad and his nasty friends are still out there, and the danger from them is real."

She glared at him, refusing to look away. She fought a battle of wills with him, and she didn't want to give in, but she'd never seen Isaac act this way before. She wasn't sure what he'd do if she continued to incur his wrath.

"Fine, I'll let you!" Turning her attention to Jeff, she said, "I was supposed to call your father for a ride home. Can you let him know that we're with you?"

"Of course." Jeff gave her a slight smile after shooting a puzzled look toward Isaac. He then focused his attention on Mary Ruth. Her cousin glanced at Ellen before heading back to walk with Jeff.

"Are you all right?" Ellen heard Jeff ask Mary Ruth as they continued toward the parking lot and the *Englisher's* car.

Mary Ruth nodded. "I'm all right."

Ellen felt bad as she realized that her cousin was still shaken by their encounter with Brad Smith and his friends. What did he have against the members of the Amish community that made him bully and threaten them?

Jeff pushed a button on his car remote, and Ellen saw lights flash, identifying his car. Wanting to escape Isaac, she went to the other side of the vehicle. She waited as Jeff held open the rear door for Mary Ruth.

After her cousin got in and slid to the other side of the seat, Ellen climbed in behind her.

Isaac stood watching, brooding, from a few feet away. After Ellen was in the car, he climbed into the front passenger seat.

She could feel emotions emanating from Isaac in thick waves. She hadn't done anything wrong. Why was he acting as if she had? She firmed her lips. He'd better not tell her father. If he did, *Dat* would never allow her to go into Lancaster on her own, and she'd never be able to keep her appointment at the West-more Clinic.

Ellen wanted to ask him if he planned to tell, but she was afraid to give him the idea if it hadn't already occurred to him.

Ellen shuddered as she recalled Brad's hand on her arm, the look in his eyes that hinted at his cruel intentions. Chilled suddenly, she hugged herself with her arms.

Isaac looked back, spearing her with his gaze. A sudden heat warmed her body but did nothing for her peace of mind. Face reddening, she lifted her chin defiantly and made a big display of turning toward the window to watch the passing scenery.

The air had grown cool. She glanced ahead quickly and was relieved to discover that Isaac's attention was no longer on her. She heard him murmur something to Jeff. She couldn't make out Jeff's low mumbled answer, either. Mary Ruth had closed her eyes and she leaned her head against the back of the seat.

"Are you all right?" Ellen whispered.

Her cousin opened her eyes and gave her a barely perceptible nod.

"I'm sorry," Ellen whispered.

"Not your fault." Her lips curved into a genuine smile.

"Are you ladies hungry?" Jeff asked.

Ellen spoke without thought. *"Nay."*

Mary Ruth agreed. "I would like a drink, though," she added.

"We'll stop for drinks at a drive-through," Jeff said. "Soda or iced tea?"

"Iced tea—sweet," Mary Ruth replied as she smiled at Jeff through the rearview mirror.

"I'll have the same." Ellen quickly dug a five-dollar bill out of her new cloth bag, extended it toward the front seat. "Here."

Jeff waved his hand as he shook his head. "I've got this."

"But—"

"I'll pay," Isaac interjected, turning to face the back.

"Nay, I'll pay. I don't want your money," Ellen said, horrified by the sharpness of her words but unable to help her tone. She saw something painful move in Isaac's expression as her barb hit home and immediately felt sorry.

Jeff stopped at a traffic light, glanced toward Mary Ruth. "I'd like to pay for your drinks if you'll let me." He glanced at Ellen as if to ask permission. "All right?"

Ellen nodded. "Thank you, Jeff."

Isaac remained tensely silent. He didn't say a word as Jeff pulled into the drive-through and bought four sweet iced teas. He stayed quiet as they continued toward home and as Jeff turned onto her family driveway and parked near the front porch of the farmhouse. Eager to escape, Ellen scrambled out of the vehicle.

"Thank you, Jeff," she said softly. She settled her gaze on Isaac and immediately was sorry that things had deteriorated to this harsh tension between them. "Isaac," she murmured and then spun toward the house, fighting tears.

"Thank you, Jeff, Isaac," Mary Ruth said. "I don't know what we would have done if you both hadn't come along."

"I'm glad we did," Isaac said pleasantly. Mary Ruth clearly was not the object of his ire, Ellen realized as she heard him where she waited for her cousin a few feet away. Apparently, he blamed her for what had happened with Brad and his horrible friends. She spun toward the house and hurried to the porch steps.

"Ellen!" Isaac called after her.

She stiffened, stopped but didn't turn. She could hear his approach as his feet crunched against dirt and gravel as she stood on the bottom step.

"Ellen," he said more softly.

The entreaty in his voice had her slowly turning around. She met his gaze and blinked against tears. He made a concerned sound. Something moved in his features before his expression became unreadable. She raised her chin, determined not to be upset if he chose to scold her again. But she ruined her efforts when a tear escaped to roll down her cheek.

His features softened. He stepped closer to her. "I'm glad you are all right."

She nodded, unable to speak. She wouldn't thank him. She wouldn't allow herself to be hurt a second time, although she sensed that his anger had left him.

This sympathetic, concerned side of him stole her breath and squeezed her insides. She wanted to run inside and hide from him. To her shock, Isaac stepped closer and slowly, carefully, trailed a finger along her cheek, tracing the wet trail left by her tear. Stunned, she couldn't move as he tenderly brushed away her tear with his finger.

"I should go," she said, her throat clogged with emotion. Her sudden overwhelming rush of feeling for him terrified her.

He nodded. It seemed as if he wanted to say something but he kept silent.

Ellen shifted her gaze to where Mary Ruth chatted with Jeff Martin, a soft smile on her pretty face. She frowned, worried that her cousin and the *Englisher* appeared to like each other, maybe too much. Jeff Martin was a fine man but he was off-limits to an Amish girl like Mary Ruth.

"Ellen?"

Ellen blinked, turned her attention to Isaac. "I, ah— I've got to go." And she called, "Mary Ruth!"

Mary Ruth glanced in her direction, then said something more to Jeff before hurrying toward the house.

"Danki," Mary Ruth said to Isaac as she joined Ellen.

He smiled warmly and nodded. "You may want to stay close to home."

Mary Ruth took the advice with good humor, while Ellen narrowed her eyes as she stared at him. She wanted to say, "You can't tell me what to do." Although two years ago, she would have been eager to do whatever he wanted; she'd loved him that much.

Ellen turned then, said something she hoped was an appropriate farewell, but she wasn't certain what she had said. Her thoughts were in turmoil as she climbed the steps and went inside.

Isaac walked over to his friend, who waited by the car.

"She all right?" Jeff asked, referring to Ellen, as he opened the driver's-side door.

Isaac shrugged and then got into the vehicle beside him. "I guess so."

Jeff didn't immediately start up the car. "What is it with you and Ellen, anyway? There was definitely something heavy in the air between you two."

"Nothing," Isaac mumbled, worried that it might not be the truth. "We were friends but now we're not."

Jeff raised his eyebrows as he turned the key in the ignition. The car engine roared to life. "What happened? Or is it too personal for me to ask?"

It was personal and Isaac didn't want to tell him, didn't want to admit what he'd done to her in the past and that while he was eager to be friends with her again, he kept doing and saying the wrong things, which made things all go wrong.

"It's okay if you don't want to tell me." Jeff put his car into Reverse and backed up so that he could turn the car around.

"If I tell you, it could ruin our friendship," Isaac muttered.

"I sincerely doubt that," Jeff said, throwing the vehicle into Drive.

Isaac explained about his friendship with Ellen, about meeting Nancy and his infatuation with her. "I allowed my feelings for Nancy to ruin my friendship with Ellen." He told Jeff what happened when Ellen tried to warn him about his girlfriend. He felt something inside him jerk as he suddenly remembered the conversation in startling detail. He hadn't believed Ellen. He'd chosen to believe in Nancy instead. "It didn't take long before I saw Nancy for what she is. I should have suspected, with a brother as mean as Brad." He confided that he'd been distraught over his breakup with Nancy, which she had instigated. He hadn't had anyone close enough to tell. Ellen and he were no longer friends. He hadn't felt as if he could talk with his brothers. He'd suffered alone with his feelings. He couldn't tell Jeff everything; he'd already told him more than he'd ever expected to tell anyone.

"Bad time, man!" Jeff said with sympathy.

Isaac looked at him, understanding that his English friend was surprised and dismayed by Isaac's behavior through that difficult time.

"I've realized that I was a terrible person when Nancy and I were seeing each other." He had just now realized the awful truth.

To his amazement, Jeff laughed. "Dude, you're a guy and guys do dumb stuff sometimes. We're only human." Isaac looked at him. "We are!"

He nodded. "None of my brothers have ever acted that badly."

"Did any one of your brothers fall for someone who wasn't from the Amish community?"

Isaac blinked. "No."

Jeff looked satisfied. "Then cut yourself some slack."

"What?"

"It means to stop punishing yourself. We all mess up occasionally. Forgive yourself and move on."

Jeff must have heard that Whittier's Store had been vandalized and that he had been the one who claimed responsibility. Happiness was too small of a town for him not to have heard what had happened. Yet Jeff had never said a thing about it.

Isaac was silent a long moment. "You've given me something to think about," he admitted.

"Don't wait too long to get a clue, Isaac. You like that girl more than you're willing to admit. Mary Ruth was in danger as well as Ellen, but it's Ellen you're upset with."

"She should have known that it would be dangerous to go out alone."

"She wasn't alone. Mary Ruth was with her. You told me about Nancy and her friend Jessica. Would you have been as worried about Nancy and her friend wandering the streets of downtown Lancaster on their own?"

Isaac felt his skin grow hot and his belly burn. "Nancy is an *Englisher* like you."

"So you think harm won't come to us because we're not Amish?"

Isaac could only shake his head. "No. What makes you think that I was only worried about Ellen?" he asked, afraid to hear what his friend might say.

"Because you like her."

"Yes, we were friends."

Jeff shook his head and flashed Isaac a sad smile as he pulled onto Isaac's road. "You *like* her. Not as friends but as more." He paused. "You've fallen for her."

Isaac felt a jolt. *Nay!* He couldn't love her! But he knew his friend was right, just as he knew he had to fight his feelings to protect Ellen and his heart…but mostly Ellen. He'd already done her harm. He still hadn't made up his mind about whether he'd stay in the Amish community. He knew that someday Ellen would be joining the church happily. She'd stay among the people she'd lived with her entire life. Ellen was worthy of the Amish faith. He wasn't, but Jeff had given him something to contemplate.

If he joined the church and then decided to leave, he would be shunned by his friends and family. He wouldn't be allowed to eat with them, live with them. He would be isolated, forever punished for his refusal to adhere to his commitment to a way of life laid out by the *Ordnung*.

Struggling with his thoughts, Isaac thanked Jeff for the ride and his help this afternoon. Then, with a heavy heart, he went into the house and upstairs to his room.

He wanted to be Ellen's friend, to make amends for his behavior, for his mistrust of her when she'd told him only the truth of what she'd seen in Nancy. But he couldn't risk making another mistake. He'd have to keep his distance until he could put thoughts into the right perspective about his feelings for Ellen, about his life here in Happiness. He sat on his bed and closed his eyes and offered a prayer to the Lord.

Chapter Eleven

Mary Ruth went home the following day. Ellen was sorry to see her cousin leave.

"I've enjoyed your company," Ellen said. "I hope you'll come again to visit us."

Mary Ruth gave her a slight smile. "I'd like that, but after the baby is born, I will be busy for a while."

"*Ach*, I'm sorry. If there is any way I could help…"

Her cousin widened her smile. "Come and visit. We may not be able to take trips into Lancaster, but I'm sure we'll have some time together."

Ellen nodded. "I could help with your chores…and the baby."

"I'll write and let you know how things are."

"I'll write, too, and tell you what happens at the clinic," Ellen promised her.

"You need to tell your *mam* and *dat* about your visit to the clinic."

A frisson of apprehension ran up Ellen's spine. "I know. I will soon. If Dr. Westmore accepts my offer of volunteer work, I'll have to tell them."

Despite the way of their community, the two girls

hugged. They were in the privacy of Ellen's bedroom. Ellen's family was waiting downstairs. *Mam* had called up to them a few moments ago to tell them that Mary Ruth's ride had arrived.

"I'd better go," Mary Ruth said.

"I'll miss you."

"Not as much as I you."

Ellen eyed her cousin sadly. "But you have a house filled with family—"

"And I love every one of them, but they're not the same age as me, nor do they have as much in common with me as you do." Mary Ruth bit her lip as if wondering if she should say something. "Please thank Jeff again for me. He was…kind."

"I will." Ellen had worried that Jeff and Mary Ruth had felt something immediate for each other. Jeff had offered to take them to Lancaster the next time they went, Mary Ruth had confessed. Ellen had been alarmed when her cousin had told her. But now that Mary Ruth was heading home, there was no reason for concern.

Ellen led the way down the stairs to the main living level of the house. She carried her cousin's suitcase while Mary Ruth descended the steps more slowly.

"I had a wonderful time," she told *Mam*.

Mam regarded her with affection. "We enjoyed having you here."

"I hope we get to see each other again soon."

Her mother smiled. "I'm sure we will now that we know each other so well."

Mary Ruth sniffed. "I'll be busy helping Lizzie after…"

The baby is born, Ellen thought. She saw *Mam* nod and knew she was thinking the same thing.

Dat, Will and Elam had gone outside. They were standing near the car when the three of them exited the house.

Ellen couldn't see whom her father was talking with. *Dat* stepped back as they approached, and Ellen heard Mary Ruth cry, "Uncle Zack!"

Zachariah Fisher, Lizzie's husband and the girl's uncle, had decided to ride with the driver to pick up Mary Ruth.

Zack smiled at his niece's delight as Mary Ruth hurried forward. "You came."

"And why wouldn't I? I've missed my niece and daughter," he said, his voice laced with emotion.

"Ellen," Mary Ruth said. "Come meet my—" she looked up at Zack "—*dat*."

Ellen saw the love between them immediately. "'Tis nice to meet you. I've heard all about you and your family."

Mary stiffened as if she'd just recalled something. "How is Lizzie—? I mean *Mam*."

Zack's expression warmed. "She's well. She's eager to see you again."

"Then we should get going." Mary Ruth turned back to Ellen. *"Danki,"* she whispered, her eyes glistening.

"I'll write," Ellen reminded her.

She brightened. "It was *gut* of you all to have me."

Mam smiled while her *dat* said, "You're *willkomm* here anytime."

As her throat clogged with emotion, Ellen watched as Zack opened the car door for Mary Ruth before he got in beside her.

Ellen heard Mary Ruth cry out with surprised happiness, "Lizzie!"

Mam laughed and so did *Dat*.

"Is Lizzie in the car with them?" Ellen asked.

Her mother inclined her head. "I knew she was coming. She wasn't supposed to, but she insisted. She didn't get out, as she wanted to surprise Mary Ruth."

Ellen saw Mary Ruth wave to her through the back window, saw a pretty red-haired woman lean closer and wave to her, as well.

"Bye!" Ellen called, and then they were driving away and she felt suddenly alone. She couldn't remember ever feeling this way before...except once about two years ago.

"Come, *Dochter*," *Mam* said gently. "We've got things to do. This Sunday is church service and there is baking, cooking and housework to do."

"Housework?" Ellen echoed.

"*Ja*, didn't I tell you? The Zooks were to host, but Peter is ill, so your *dat* offered to have it here instead."

Ellen widened her eyes. "Here? In two days' time?"

Mam laughed. "We'll have help, don't *ya* worry."

"What kind of help? Elam and Will?"

Her mother shook her head. "Here comes our help now." She gestured toward the end of their road, where not one or two but three buggies headed in their direction.

Ellen beamed. It was why she loved her community so much, why the Amish life was the one life that, if she had a choice, she would choose over again.

Katie Lapp pulled her buggy into the yard and parked. While she, Hannah, and their neighbor Mae King and her daughters stepped out from the Lapp vehicle, the two other buggies pulled in and stopped. The second carriage heralded the arrival of Miriam Zook, the one who would have hosted the day if not for her son's illness. She came with her daughters Barbara and Annie, the second sister a Lapp bride. Sarah Lapp, Jedidiah's wife, and Rachel, Noah's wife, came with them. All five of them were eager to pitch in and help ready the house and property. The third vehicle had brought Alta Hershberger, her daughters Sally and Mary, and Charlotte King and two of her daughters, Mary Elizabeth and Rose Ann.

Ellen took one look at the women surrounding her and her mother and realized that she no longer felt lonely. How could she when she was in the presence of such loving family and friends?

Isaac was struggling with his thoughts as he mucked out the stables. He had released the horses into the pasture before he'd started in the stalls. Now he stuck a pitchfork into dirty straw and hefted the forkful into a wheelbarrow.

He couldn't stop thinking about Ellen. He'd acted inappropriately, but he'd been so scared. As soon as he realized that she and Mary Ruth were there at the movie theater surrounded by Brad Smith and his followers, he'd felt a terrible sickening dread. He'd been raised to be Amish. His people didn't believe in fighting but in turning the other cheek as taught in the Bible. But at that moment he'd felt like fighting. He'd wanted to grab every one of those boys and fling them away from Ellen.

Isaac paused a moment and leaned on the handle of his pitchfork. Closing his eyes, he begged the Lord for forgiveness. His feelings, his struggle, made him feel only more unworthy. He prayed that he could be as patient as his father and as kind as his mother. He prayed that he could make a decision about his future that would be best for everyone he loved.

He released an unsteady sigh and went back to work. He'd been horrible to Ellen. He'd let his fears blind him to her feelings. She must have been traumatized and then he'd gone ahead and added to her trauma by scolding and snapping at her. What kind of a man was he? He was neither ready to join the church nor ready to leave his community. He felt an ever-present gnawing pain because he still couldn't figure out what to do.

One thing I can do is to apologize to Ellen, tell her that I didn't mean to be so rude, that I'd been frightened for her, not mad. His anger was at Brad, but he'd taken it out on Ellen.

He recalled what Jeff had inferred, that he liked Ellen, not as a friend but as something more. *Love.* He loved Ellen, but he could never show her how he felt. He wasn't good enough for a nice girl like Ellen. If only he hadn't met Nancy and messed things up, then he might have had a chance with Ellen now. He wouldn't have told a lie to protect his friend. A lie that he couldn't confess to the church elders.

"Isaac." His brother stepped out of the darkness in the barn.

"Eli!" he gasped. "What are you doing here?"

"Just stopped in to see *Dat* for a minute. I'd like to add on to my house and thought he could help."

"I can help," Isaac offered immediately.

Eli regarded him with warmth. "*Danki.* You're a *gut bruder* and man."

Isaac made a sound of dismissal as the image of Ellen resurfaced to the forefront of his mind.

His brother frowned. "What's wrong?"

"Nothing," he mumbled as he stuck the pitchfork into the musty, manure-laced straw. He stopped when he felt a hand on his arm. He looked up at Eli and saw worry and concern in his brother's blue gaze.

"Tell me," Eli ordered.

Isaac shuddered. "I ruined things again."

"Ruined what?"

"Things with Ellen."

"Ellen Mast?"

Isaac nodded. He took off his hat and ran his fingers through his hair before he reseated it. "I yelled at her today." He hesitated. "I made her cry."

His brother released his arm. "What happened?"

Isaac explained about finding Ellen and her cousin surrounded by a group of *Englishers* who were threatening her. "I was scared. If anything had happened to her…"

"You were afraid for her safety. You love her."

"*Nay*, I can't." But, of course, he did.

"'Tis not something you can or can't do. We have no control over our emotions. We don't choose whom we love. God does."

Isaac experienced a fluttering within his chest. "You think the Lord chose Ellen for me?"

"I can't say that. Only time will tell. God gives us gentle hints. How we act on them is up to us."

"And we should do all we can to protect those we love," Isaac murmured.

"*Ja.*"

But he wasn't referring to his reaction after finding Ellen with Brad and his followers. What he meant was that he had to protect her from someone unworthy…himself.

"Stop worrying, Isaac. God has a way of showing us His blessings. He will help you make the right choice when the time comes."

Isaac nodded. "I hope so."

"Need any help?" Eli offered.

"You want to muck out a stall?"

His brother shrugged. "I don't have a stable this size. I don't mind getting my hands dirty for an hour or two."

Isaac beamed at him. "Is Martha angry? What did you do to her?"

"Martha's not angry."

"Oh."

"Let's get to work. I'm sure you have other things you'd rather be doing," Eli said.

He did. But he didn't have a chance of getting Ellen's forgiveness…of convincing her to spend any amount of time with him. He just had to accept that he'd made the biggest mistake of his life and go on from there.

Ellen got ready for church service on Sunday, still reeling from how quickly the house had been cleaned and the cooking and baking done. With so many women to help, it had taken only a couple of hours.

She unpinned and brushed her hair, enjoying the feeling of the nylon bristles against her scalp. Satisfied that her hair had been brushed enough, Ellen rolled and repinned it and then tugged her black prayer *kapp* over her golden tresses.

Today she would see Isaac again. She had been thinking a lot since they'd last parted, about his arrival in the nick of time, his firm stand against the *Englishers*, his anger afterward. She had come to the realization that he hadn't been angry with her. He'd just been angry at Brad and his friends, at the situation she and Mary Ruth had found themselves in. Once it had been defused, Isaac had needed an outlet and she'd been a handy target.

She felt bad at how she'd reacted, although she understood why. She'd been rude and snippy when she should have been thankful. To be truthful, she'd been more than ready to give him her thanks when he'd startled her into remaining silent when he'd yelled at her.

Later Isaac had called after her as she'd walked away. When she'd faced him, he'd been tender as he wiped away her tears. She might still be upset about the way he'd treated her when Nancy was his girlfriend, but she had to give the man credit. He'd come to her aid twice now. It was only right to apologize, to show her gratitude for what he'd done.

Yesterday she'd spent time in the kitchen baking a pie just for him. She'd made his favorite—a custard pie. She would give it to him today after service with her apology and her thanks.

"Ellen?" *Mam* called up from downstairs.

"Coming!" She knew it was getting late and the community church members would be arriving.

Ellen had dressed in her Sunday best—a light blue garment that her mother had said matched her eyes and made them look bluer. She descended the stairs slowly, anticipation running like wildfire through her veins.

"Our community is arriving for church service," her mother said.

Ellen nodded. With the community women's help,

they had cleared the gathering room of all pieces of furniture and in their place sat wooden benches in an arrangement deemed necessary for services by the church elders.

She followed her mother outside onto the front porch, watching as buggy after gray buggy pulled in and parked in a row on the grassy lawn toward the left of the barn.

Ellen saw Preacher Levi Stoltzfus get out from his buggy alone. She frowned, wondering not for the first time what had happened to the budding relationship between the good reverend and Annie Lapp's younger sister Barbara. She hadn't seen Barbara for months until the other day, when she saw hanging laundry in Horseshoe Joe's backyard.

She had to stop wondering about other people's business. She didn't want to end up alone like their resident busybody, Alta Hershberger, Annie and Barbara's aunt.

The Abram Peachys climbed out of the second buggy. Abram came around to assist his wife, Charlotte, who held their daughter Mae Ann. Their other five children jumped out of the driver's side, ribbing each other until their father turned and spoke a quiet word to them.

Ellen stifled a smile as she watched other neighbors and church members alight from their vehicles—all of the Samuel Lapps who resided at home. Isaac, Daniel, Joseph and their sister, Hannah, trailed behind their parents as they approached. Ellen allowed her gaze to rest on Isaac briefly. He stared down at his feet as he walked. As if intuitive, he glanced up, met her gaze, then promptly focused his eyes elsewhere.

Ellen stared at him. *I'm not put off by your behav-*

ior, Isaac. By the end of the day, I'll make things at least friendly between us. As friendly as she dared to be without risking her heart.

"Arlin! Missy," her mother greeted as the couple advanced with their five unmarried daughters. Arlin was Katie Lapp's brother, and Ellen liked him and every member of the Stoltzfus family. She wondered how Nell, the eldest, was making out with her puppy. As she drew near, Nell saw Ellen and headed in her direction.

"Hallo!" Ellen greeted. "How are you making out with Jonas?"

"Gut! He's no longer wearing the cast. Dr. Pierce declared him fit and Jonas has proven him correct, as the little one has been running around the barn, chasing the chickens and digging in *Mam's* flower garden."

"Oh, no!" Ellen exclaimed with a laugh.

Nell smiled. "'Tis all *gut. Dat's* not upset that he chased the chickens. Says they've been easier to manage with Jonas herding them together in the yard. *Mam* claims she didn't like those particular flowers in her garden anyway."

"So they've come to appreciate your puppy," Ellen said.

Nell smiled. *"Ja."*

Nell's other sisters joined them. "What are you talking about?" Meg asked.

"Jonas."

"Ja, what else would they be talking about?" Charlie, the youngest, teased.

"You haven't asked Ellen why church is here today and not at the Zooks?" Leah said.

"Why would Nell want to know about Peter?" Ellen said.

"Peter?" Meg asked. "What about him?

"He's sick. Hadn't you heard? Miriam canceled services at Horseshoe Joe's because of Peter's illness."

"What's wrong with him?" Leah studied her sister Meg's face with mounting curiosity.

"I hadn't heard, and I didn't want to ask," Ellen said, "but it must be serious to change service locations."

"I'm sure he's all right," Meg interjected, but she didn't appear convinced. Ellen thought the girl looked peaked herself. "You're not ill, are you?" she asked Meg.

"*Nay.*"

"She has Reuben Miller on her mind. She saw him recently and he promised to come to tonight's singing."

"I didn't think about the singing," Ellen said.

"That's because we're going to hold it in our barn," Meg said.

"*Ja*, we thought it would be fun to have it on our property, as we've never held one there before." Charlie seemed eager for tonight's youth gathering. "Are you coming?"

"I don't know," Ellen said. A lot would depend on what happened today with Isaac. If he refused to accept her apology, she wouldn't feel much like going out to have fun. If he did accept it, her attending would have everything to do with him…and only him.

"Look!" Elizabeth Stoltzfus, known as Ellie to her family and the community, pointed out. "They're gathering for service. We'd better go."

Ellen glanced back and saw that Ellie was right. Everyone was heading inside for service.

There was no sign of Isaac or any of the Lapp brothers outside. They must have gone inside. Ellen hurried with the sisters into the house, through the front room and toward the gathering area. People were filling the three areas of benches. Her father and brothers sat on the men's side. Behind them, all of the Lapp men had taken their seats. She tore her gaze away from Isaac to focus on finding a seat with the women.

After everyone was seated, the preacher started the service as usual with a hymn. After two hours of Scripture and sermon interspersed with songs from the *Ausbund*, the book of hymns, the service ended and everyone rose. The women left with their youngest children, while the older girls led their younger siblings outside. The men moved benches in the house to prepare for the midday meal, which would be served as soon as the women could bring in the food.

Ellen disappeared into the kitchen with the women. She pulled items out of the refrigerator and collected other food items that had been placed in the pantry and the back room. She took a quick peek into the gathering room, where men had finishing rearranging the church benches to form tables and seats. Ellen looked for Isaac and thought she detected him in the back of the room. She wondered how she would find time to give him his pie—and to apologize and say thanks.

The men sat down to eat first—it was the way they did things in their Amish community. While the women ensured that their men were fed, Ellen searched the Lapp table, hoping to make eye contact with Isaac. But Isaac wasn't in the room. Where was he? Should she look for him outside?

She wandered outside to check. All of the buggies were still in the yard. If she were Isaac, where would she go?

She hurried toward the barn and went inside. She heard the deep voice of someone talking to the animals, and Ellen knew she'd found him. She left before he could see her and returned to the back room off the kitchen, where she'd hidden his pie. She felt hot, then cold, a bundle of nerves as she carried her baked gift toward the barn.

She recalled Isaac's tenderness as he brushed away her tears, focused on that emotional moment to give her the strength to enter.

She entered the dark interior, waited a moment for her eyes to adjust to the light. She listened but heard nothing. Had she been wrong? Had she been mistaken when she thought she'd heard a voice just minutes earlier?

Something pulled her in the direction of the horse stalls. She smiled. Isaac was standing by Blackie, rubbing her nose as he spoke to the mare softly, praising her.

Her heart melted as she closed the distance between them. "Isaac." She didn't want to startle him, so she'd spoken quietly. She saw he grew still and tensed up as if listening. She moved closer and called him again. "Isaac."

He spun around, startled. She witnessed everything from gladness to fear in his expression before he closed it off.

"I've brought you a pie—your favorite." She rushed forward with the pie plate. "It's an apology—and a thank-you. You saved me from Brad and his friends, and I was rude and awful to you." She blinked back tears. "I don't know why I acted the way I did."

He appeared stunned. Then his expression softened as she came close enough to place the pie in his hands.

"Custard?" he asked. A smile hovered on his lips, giving her encouragement.

Her lips curved as she nodded. "*Ja.* You said it's your favorite." Nerves made her tug on her *kapp* strings, nearly jerking the covering from her head. She removed it instead, worried the fabric with nervous fingers.

"You remembered," he said as if in awe.

She shrugged. "I remember a lot about you." She paused, afraid to go on but then doing so anyway. "We used to be friends."

"Ja." He averted his glance briefly. When he looked back, his gray eyes had darkened. "I should be the one apologizing. I wasn't kind to you the other day."

"*Ja*, you were, actually." She bit her lip. "Before I went inside." She waited for him to speak but he only gazed at the pie quietly as if he was still trying to take in the fact that she'd made it for him. "Will you accept my apology?" she asked.

He was silent a long moment that made her nervous. "*Nay*, because you have nothing to be sorry for. I, on the other hand, should be the one apologizing."

"We could both say we're sorry and leave it at that," she suggested.

Isaac blinked as if stunned. *"Ja?"*

"Ja."

He sighed. "Does this mean we can try to be friends again?"

"We can try." But she was afraid. Could she trust him not to hurt her again? He wouldn't, she thought, if she kept things strictly friendly and nothing more.

Isaac seemed pleased. "We'll take it slow. See how we do." He was grinning as he said it, but there was something in his gaze that gave Ellen pause.

He stared at his pie, raised an edge of the plastic covering and took a sniff. "Smells wonderful. Will you share it with me?"

"I'll get us some plates and forks."

"Why?" he asked, and the mischievous look in his gray eyes made her chuckle. "Use your fingers and dig in." He held out the pie to her.

Ellen hesitated before inserting her fingers to grab a handful of topping, custard filling and piecrust. She bought it to her lips and tasted it. "It's not the best."

Isaac frowned and dipped in for his own taste. He ate it slowly. "What are you talking about? It tastes *gut*."

Ellen laughed, delight washing over her in huge waves. "You're the better judge. I have to be modest. I made it."

He studied her with warmth. "And for that I am grateful."

She nodded.

"Are you going to the singing tonight?" he asked.

"I hadn't thought to go."

"Want to meet me instead?"

Her heart skipped a beat. "Where?"

"The swings near the *schuulhaus*? I'll come for you. It's too far for you to go alone." He stared at her while he waited for her answer. "Well?"

She made a quick decision. "*Oll recht*, I'll go with you to the swings."

Isaac grinned, and Ellen felt good inside. "One step at a time, Ellen, and we may be friends again."

She nodded and then left to rejoin the others inside the house, but her thoughts remained with Isaac, who stayed behind in the barn.

Chapter Twelve

It was dark outside when, with flashlight in hand, Ellen tiptoed down the stairs of her family farmhouse and slipped out the front door.

The night was warm but not overly so. The stars shone in a midnight sky and the moon was a white crescent hovering above her. She wondered if Isaac would come or if he would change his mind at the last minute. She stepped off the front porch into the stillness of the night and worried that she'd have to return without spending any time in Isaac's company. She worried that she was foolish for spending time with him.

"Isaac?" She walked into the center of the yard.

"Ellen." He stepped out from behind a large bush and into the glow from her flashlight. He looked handsome, and her heart leaped. He'd kept his word, she thought, overcome with joy.

He moved forward as she approached. "You're here," she said.

"*Ja*. And why wouldn't I be?" His gray eyes sparkled in the night.

"I…" she began. "Are you ready to go?"

"I've been thinking," Isaac said. A whinny drew her attention to where he'd parked his buggy near the barn. "Why don't we just stay and walk? The swings are too far and we'd have to come back sooner, but here—" she saw his flash of teeth in the darkness "—we can take our time."

She nodded, relieved. "I don't mind staying."

He bobbed his head. "*Gut.* Let's go." He started toward her father's fields. "I finished your pie."

She gasped out her delight. "All of it?" But she knew the answer before he spoke.

"What do you think?"

"I think you liked my pie."

"*Ja*, I did."

They strolled along the width of the barn through an opening in the fence and kept going. All the animals were in for the night, so there wasn't any danger that they'd escape if they forgot to shut and lock the gate. Isaac closed and latched it, however, before they continued along the edge of the pasture and slipped out a second gate to the outside perimeter.

Walking beside Isaac in the darkness felt awkward to Ellen but wonderful at the same time. It had been a long while since they'd spent any amount of time together, and even longer since they'd been alone. Isaac didn't say a word, and Ellen wondered if he was feeling strange, too.

They made their way along the outside of the fence to the wooden bench that Ellen's father had built for his parents when they'd been alive.

Her grandfather liked to observe the animals in the pasture, and later, when he got too old to farm, he enjoyed watching the workers in the fields. Ellen as a young child had seen the sadness in his eyes and had thought he might have wanted to join *Dat* in the fields. But he'd been able to look, at least, if he wanted and he'd seemed to take comfort in that.

Ellen sat on the bench and Isaac settled down next to her.

"Do you remember when we came here to watch the lunar eclipse?" he asked.

Ellen smiled, recalling the occasion well. They had heard about the eclipse from Bob Whittier. They had both slipped out in the middle of the night to watch it. She and Isaac had talked about everything under the sun as they waited and watched as the Earth slipped between the moon and the sun, casting its shadow to turn the moon a bloodred color.

The memory gave Ellen pause as she felt herself relax. She was enjoying his company too much. She shouldn't have agreed to their meeting. Secret rendezvous were reserved for couples who were courting. She and Isaac were only friends...and friends who had been estranged. Was it wise to try to fix their friendship? After all that had happened, she'd be foolish to spend time with a man who had chosen to believe someone else over her. Could it happen again?

"Did you have any trouble getting away?" she asked politely as she clicked off her flashlight to save the batteries. An intimacy surrounded them, scaring her, and she immediately turned on the light again.

"Daniel went to the singing with John King. *Mam, Dat* and the others went to bed." Isaac shifted on the bench beside her. "*Nay*, it wasn't hard to slip away."

She saw Isaac staring straight ahead in the lamplight. His expression was unreadable. Ellen sensed that something was bothering him. Should she ask him what it was? She was afraid to ask. Did he regret meeting her?

She bit her lip as she studied him. He turned then and stared. She blinked. He'd always been a handsome boy but now as a man, he was devastating in his good looks.

Ellen felt a sliver of dread rise its way up from her midsection. She shouldn't notice such things about him. The fact that she did notice upset her. It had been a mistake to meet him.

"Isaac," she whispered when his eyes rose as if to study the moon and stars in the dark sky. "This may not be a *gut* idea—meeting like this."

He flinched but quickly got himself under control. "You may be right," he agreed too readily. But Ellen heard something in his voice that told her that something else was going on with him. Had he come to confide in her? Did he miss the way they used to talk?

She had known him well enough back then to still recognize the little changes in his expression.

"You are quiet," she improvised.

He smiled at her, a soft gentle twist of his lips. "It's peaceful out here. I was just enjoying the night."

"*Ja*, the night silence. I like this time of day, when we can enjoy the world around us as the Lord intended."

Isaac dipped his head in agreement. He paused. "Ellen, *danki* for letting me come. I know things became difficult because of me. I want you to know that I am genuinely sorry."

Ellen was silent for a long moment. "For what?" She pulled off her prayer *kapp* and placed it in her lap. For what had happened the other day? Or two years ago? She waited for him to continue.

He beamed at her, his gray eyes suddenly bright in the darkness. "We used to talk about everything, didn't we?" he said, changing the subject.

Ellen nodded. "Most everything," she agreed.

He arched an eyebrow. "Not everything?"

"Nay."

Tension cropped up between them. Ellen was hurt by it, but she didn't know how to ease the strain. The last time she'd attempted to speak to him frankly, he had ended their friendship. She tensed and stood. "I should get inside. I…have to get up early."

He froze. "I see." He got up more slowly. They silently walked back the way they'd come, stopping in the barnyard.

Isaac looked at her without expression. *"Guten nacht."* Then he turned and left her. And Ellen watched him go with tears in her eyes.

It was for the best that he'd left, for she was afraid that she wouldn't be able to control her emotions while he was around.

She heard him urge his horse forward and the sound of the animal's hooves. After Isaac's departure, Ellen returned to the house and went up to her room, glad that she was the only daughter in the house, for tonight she wanted nothing more than to be alone…and cry.

His emotions were all over the place as Isaac steered old Bess home. He'd known that he shouldn't have come to see Ellen, known the moment he'd asked her to meet him that it was a foolish thing to do.

He could still see her face when she'd called for him.

She'd seemed almost happy to see him. Her blue eyes glistened in the lamplight. She looked beautiful with the sweet curve of her lips and her pert little nose. Earlier, when she'd brought him the pie, he'd been overwhelmed. Ever since his discussion with Jeff, and then later with his brother Eli, he'd been overly aware of the depth of his feelings for Ellen. But he'd also been overwhelmingly certain that he should keep his distance, yet here he was, heading home after meeting her in secret. And Ellen must have felt the wrongness of it, too, for she'd abruptly put an end to their evening together when it had barely begun.

He understood that he'd hurt her. She'd been his friend and she'd been honest about Nancy, and he'd been shocked and too angry to listen to her. Not only did he not listen but he'd avoided her after that…at church and other community gatherings. What kind of man did that to a friend?

The road at this time of night was unusually quiet. He was ever alert for cars. They tended to race by in the darkness and the drivers could easily miss seeing an Amish buggy driver, even when the vehicle was lit up with its battery-operated lights.

Daniel would be at the singing at their *onkel* Arlin's house. Normally, the youth gathering would have been held at the Masts' residence since the event usually took place wherever church services were hosted that morning. But William and Josie had hosted because another family couldn't at the last moment. His aunt and uncle had offered to have the singing at their house so that the Masts wouldn't be burdened with two last-minute unplanned events.

Should he go to the singing or head home? Home,

he decided. He didn't feel like having fun. He'd been enjoying himself with Ellen until she'd called an abrupt halt to the evening. He should have talked with her, asked her what was wrong, but he'd been hurt.

He frowned. He could only imagine how she'd felt years ago. Perhaps she'd been worried that he'd hurt her again like he had the last time.

He had to talk with her. He could turn back now, but she would have gone to her room, and with her parents at home, he couldn't try to wake her and ask her to come outside to talk.

I should let it go. Forget about her. But he couldn't. His every waking moment was filled with thoughts of Ellen. He should have realized what he had with their friendship. They'd been good friends. Why hadn't he listened to her? Why hadn't he fallen for her instead of Nancy? Why had it taken him so long to discover that he loved her more than anything?

There had to be something he could do. But he didn't know what. The Lord was trying to tell him something. He wasn't sure how he was going to resolve things in his life. He wanted his sin to be forgiven. He wanted to court Ellen, but until he could figure out how, he'd keep his distance…and hope that he wouldn't lose her forever.

Ellen sat in the silence of her room and cried silent tears. What had she done? She had a chance of mending fences with Isaac but she'd become frightened and sent him away. So he'd hurt her years ago and she'd felt devastated. But he'd shown her that he was someone she could rely on to get her out of a difficult situation. He'd appeared whenever she needed him. That was something, wasn't it? But if he valued their friendship, why had he been so quick to leave?

She lay back on her bed, staring at the window glass where, if she looked hard enough, she could detect a track of moonlight on the white curtains.

Her appointment at the Westmore Clinic was in a few days. She needed to focus on her meeting with Dr. Westmore, be prepared to convince him that an Amish volunteer would be beneficial to his patients and their families as well as a help to him. The appointment card that Joan at the front desk had given her was tucked under her mattress. Ellen sat up, ran her hand under the mattress and located the card. She grabbed a flashlight she kept nearby in case she had to get up in the middle of the night. Shining the beam on the card, she noted the time that the receptionist had scheduled for her. Her appointment was for noon. She had to go, but what would she tell her parents? That she had to run an errand—that wouldn't be a lie. And she could tell them that she would be visiting Caleb and Rebekka Yoder. She wanted to see them after her appointment, so that afternoon would be the perfect time to stop by.

She would be driving alone, but the clinic wasn't far. She'd be fine. No one would bother her. Brad and his friends had been threatened with arrest. Surely they'd ignore her if they saw her out and about on her own.

Ellen tucked the card under the other pillow on her double bed. Then she lay back and tried to relax so she could get a restful night's sleep. She saw the mental image of Isaac's face, his smile…his concern…his anger…his tenderness.

She kept her eyes tightly closed but it didn't prevent the tears that flowed as she thought of Isaac's leaving this evening, the way she'd sent him away. She said a prayer that all would go well the next day—that she would visit the clinic and get an offer of a volunteer job—and she prayed that Isaac would find happiness again. And she couldn't help praying for the strength to accept whatever happened between her and Isaac.

Chapter Thirteen

The next morning Ellen told her mother that she was going to run some errands. When *Mam* asked where she was going, she told them about her planned visit to Rebekka and Caleb Yoder. She also mentioned that the Yoders had been taking their daughter, Alice, to the Westmore Clinic, and she thought she might stop in and visit sometime.

"Why would you want to do that?" *Dat* asked as he entered the room. He must have overheard what she'd said. They'd had this discussion before and it hadn't gone well.

"Because I'm interested. It's a terrible thing what Rebekka and Caleb's daughter, Alice, has to go through as treatment for her problem. It's awful what the Yoders are going through, what all Amish families have to go through when they have children who are sick."

"You haven't given up the notion of working there," her father accused.

"What's wrong with that? If I can make things a little easier for the families and patients—"

"You're not a trained medical professional," *Mam*

quietly pointed out. Unlike her father, who was dead set against the idea, her mother kept her expression neutral and her thoughts to herself. She wouldn't go against her father, but she seemed interested in learning more.

"The Westmore Clinic is on Old Philadelphia Pike, just a short distance away. Dr. Westmore, the English doctor there, treats only children of Amish couples. He's a geneticist who has dedicated his life to discovering ways to help his patients."

"You want to work for an *Englisher*?"

"I want to volunteer. One or two days a week at most. There are women within our community who work for the English. Ellie Stoltzfus cleans for an English family. Mary Elizabeth Peachy works at a fabric store."

"I don't like it," *Dat* groused. "God will take care of these children, not you. You, *Dochter*, should worry about finding a husband and having children."

"I'm too young to marry!" she exclaimed. She immediately softened her tone. "I'm sorry. I promise that I will join the church, marry and have children, but not right away. This is some things I would like to do first."

"I think you should get on with your chores and forget about this nonsense," her father insisted.

"*Dat*, just let me get some information," she began. "Please don't say *nay* before you know all the facts..." She went silent as she locked gazes with her mother. With tears in her eyes, she left the kitchen, where her mother and father were finishing their breakfast. Her thoughts were in turmoil as she went out to feed the chickens. Seeing the hens gobbling up their food gave her no pleasure. She didn't feel amused, as she usually did, by Red, the rooster, when he strutted out of the pen last like a king surveying his underlings. She was too blinded by tears to enjoy anything.

I will find a way. Her appointment with the clinic doctor was in two days. Her father hadn't said that she couldn't go. Of course, he didn't know about her appointment. She would keep it and get any information that might help to convince her father. If he still wouldn't allow her to work there afterward, then she would have to obey, but she wouldn't be happy.

Isaac worked beside Jedidiah to secure the four-by-eight aspenite wall sheets onto two-by-four studs. He was quiet as he hammered nails around the perimeter of the aspenite and along each stud.

"What's wrong?" his brother asked after a time.

"Nothing," Isaac said. "Why would you think something's wrong?"

"You're too quiet today."

A smile hovered on Isaac's mouth. "And that's a problem for you?"

Jedidiah grinned. "I shouldn't be complaining."

"*Ja*, you shouldn't." Isaac grabbed a nail from his leather tool bag and pounded it into place. "I've just been thinking."

"About?" Jedidiah regarded him with a serious expression.

"A lot of things. The bad choices I made in the past. The future."

"You can't do anything about the past," Jed said. He paused. "What about the future?"

He shrugged. "I'm not sure what I'll be doing."

"As if we know ahead of time," Jed murmured drily.

He was silent for a long moment as they continued to work. "Is this about joining the church or marrying?"

"I don't know that I'll join the church," Isaac admitted carefully.

"Why not?" his brother demanded.

"I've done something the Lord wouldn't approve of. I didn't live up to the ways of the *Ordnung.*"

"You haven't joined the church yet. So you made a mistake when you defaced Bob's store. You also took responsibility for the act and made restitution."

Isaac didn't agree or answer. "It doesn't feel right."

"You'll change your mind when you find the right woman, someone unlike your former girlfriend, Nancy."

Isaac grabbed one end of a piece of aspenite while Jed grabbed the other end, and the two of them set the board into place. With one hand, Jed hammered a few nails until his side was secure. Then Isaac did the same on his end of the board.

"Falling for Nancy wasn't the smartest thing I've ever done," Isaac said after he'd hammered in a few nails.

Jedidiah finished nailing a board to a two-by-four stud. He then stepped back and eyed their handiwork. "You can't help who you fall in love with, Isaac."

"I could have used better judgment."

Jed shook his head. "As if you had a choice. *Nay,* you didn't plan on liking Nancy. It just happened, and God allowed it for a reason, even if only to show you how wrong someone like her is for you."

"You didn't like her—none of our family did."

"It's not that we didn't like her. We just weren't sure she was the right girl for you. We had hoped for your sake, but we didn't want to see you hurt." He sighed. "And you were hurt—badly."

Isaac nodded as he reached for another nail. *"Ja."*

"Have faith, Isaac. God had plans for you. He will let you know in His own time. I'm sure there is a nice girl for you within our or another Amish community."

But what if I decide to leave? Isaac thought. How would he be fulfilling God's plan then? He couldn't stop the constant struggle within him. He wished he could, that he could simply confess the truth, say he was sorry and all would be right with his life and his world. But he couldn't. It wasn't about only him. It was about Henry Yoder, who had once been a close friend—not in the same way that he and Ellen had been. Henry and he had gone *rumspringa* together. Henry had been with him when he'd met Nancy. And while he was with Nancy, Henry had spent his time with Nancy's friend Jessica, another English girl.

Thoughts of Ellen rose up in his mind. Tomorrow they would spend time together, go for ice cream as they did long ago, before Nancy Smith had entered his life and made a mess of things. He'd sent Ellen a note asking her to come. To his surprise, she'd accepted his invitation as if she wanted them to be friends as much as he did.

He wished he could tell Ellen about what had happened that awful night at Whittier's Store. It wasn't that he didn't trust her, but it wasn't his secret to tell. And despite the fact that he hadn't seen Henry since the night it happened, he wouldn't betray him.

Tomorrow, he thought. *Just focus on one day at a time.* The Lord would help him find his path. Until then he could enjoy Ellen's friendship and work construction beside his oldest brother. Life could be worse. But he hoped that someday it would get better.

The next day Ellen stood at the end of the farm road, waiting for Isaac. Today would be like old times when they'd walked to Whittier's Store together, each ordering their favorite ice cream—mint chocolate chip. She'd been surprised and hopeful when he'd invited her like old times. She looked forward to spending time with him, working toward the friendship they'd had once but lost. Her thoughts switched to her appointment tomorrow with Dr. Westmore. She wished she could talk with someone else besides her parents. Could she talk with Isaac about it? She frowned. Things between them weren't like they were before Nancy. She thought of what she would say to Dr. Westmore. As she rehearsed what she had in mind, she thought of little Alice Yoder and her resolve firmed.

Ellen reached out and tugged a leaf from a tree near the edge of the property. She looked down at the green structure, the veins and edges all arranged beautifully to form the maple leaf. She ran her finger along the surface, tugged on an edge and saw the fragment splinter off to the first vein.

"You look pensive," a male voice said.

"Isaac." She looked up and smiled. "You're late."

His gray eyes gleamed with amusement as he shook his head. "*Nay*, you were early."

Her lips widened as she grinned. "I like ice cream."

"So do I." He reached for her hand and with a little inward gasp, she placed her fingers within his grasp. The warmth of his touch filled her to overflowing. She never would have thought she'd be this glad to spend time with him again. She realized that she had moved past the old hurt and was ready to start anew.

"I wasn't sure if you'd want to walk or take your family buggy," she said conversationally as they began to stroll together in the direction of their destination.

He tugged on her hand, stopped and regarded her with raised eyebrows. "You think me too old to use my legs? When did we ever not walk for ice cream?" There was a twinkle in his gray eyes.

"You may have aged overnight, found it hard to keep up with a young girl such as me."

"Woman," he said softly, making her shiver with pleasure. "There is nothing of the girl in you."

"I think I should be offended." She lifted her chin and looked down her nose at him.

Isaac laughed as he gently squeezed her hand. "You shouldn't be. It was a compliment, not a complaint."

She relaxed. "If you say so." She started to walk again and he fell into step with her. They walked in companionable silence. Ellen started to think about how and if she should tell him about the clinic. Wanting to get it over with, she opened her mouth to start but then promptly closed it. She didn't want to put a damper on the day yet. She'd feel bad if he spoke negatively about her volunteer idea like her father had. Maybe he would understand and encourage her. She wanted his friendship and his understanding of her plans. Maybe she should confide in him after ice cream. Or maybe she shouldn't.

"Do you have to be back at a certain time?" Isaac asked, hoping that she'd say no.

She shook her head. "You?"

"I've got all day." He experienced a wash of excitement and relief that they could spend the entire day together.

It was a perfect day for a walk to Whittier's Store. The warmth of the sun caressed Isaac's skin while a light breeze tousled the loose tendrils of Ellen's blond hair. She was quiet as they strolled down the main road. He chanced a peek at her and saw that her features were relaxed, happy, and he thanked God for these moments with her.

"Look!" she said. He followed the direction of her gaze and saw his cousin Nell with her puppy, Jonas. Isaac watched as Jonas ran around in circles, barking happily, his tail wagging with pleasure as he circled his mistress. "Jonas's leg is healed."

"He's doing well," Isaac murmured, pleased for Nell.

Ellen looked away from Nell to meet his gaze, her features awash with joy. "She's so good with him."

Isaac nodded. "She'd make a good veterinary assistant."

He suddenly felt Ellen stiffen beside him. "You mean that?" she asked carefully, her expression guarded.

"*Ja*, I do." Isaac looked at her with concern. "What is it? What's wrong?"

Ellen seemed as if she suddenly understood him. She relaxed and smiled. "Dr. Pierce offered her a temporary job as his vet tech."

"His assistant?" Isaac asked.

"*Ja.* I think she wants to take it but is afraid."

Isaac frowned as he gazed into Ellen's blue eyes. "Why?"

"Her father—your uncle Arlin."

"She doesn't think he'll approve?"

Ellen nodded. "Fathers often have a different idea of what is right or wrong when it comes to their *dechter*."

Isaac thought of his little sister, Hannah, and knew she was treated differently from him and his brothers, but he couldn't see his father denying Hannah something she wanted to do, not if it meant a lot to her. He knew Hannah was only eight years old, but he still thought his father would allow Hannah to work wherever she wanted as long as it was a place where she would suffer no harm.

"You think your *onkel* would let her work for Dr. Pierce? The man offered her the job until he could find a full-time certified vet tech."

"I don't see why not." Although now that he thought about it, he recalled the way his uncle had become overprotective of his cousin Meg after she'd become ill and stayed in the hospital. He probably would have felt the same if it had been his daughter—if he were married and had a daughter.

"I hope she is allowed to take the position." Ellen appeared wistful as she stared off in the distance.

"Time will tell," he said quietly. He studied Ellen, noting the changes in her features in the last two years. She had lost that baby-face look. Her eyes were large and luminous, her nose perfectly formed. Her mouth was well shaped with full lips. And her chin was slightly pointed but not much. She was quite lovely, but as he'd told her earlier, she was no longer a girl but a woman. And his feelings for her had changed, grown.

She's a friend, he thought, and he had to make sure she stayed his friend.

"I've decided to buy you an ice cream *and* a soda," he said.

She turned to him with a raised eyebrow but with a smile on her lips. His breath hitched. "Why?"

"Why not?" He looked away as she tugged on his heartstrings. He couldn't do it, fall for her and take the risk that he'd hurt her again—and himself in the process.

Suddenly, she stopped, stared at him. "What's wrong?"

He blinked. "Nothing. Why do you ask?"

"You don't seem like yourself." She was quiet a moment. "Are you sorry you asked me to come?"

"Nay."

"You're more quiet, introspective." She paused. "Is there something you want to tell me? I'm a *gut* listener. I'll be happy to help if I can."

He felt something inside him harden. *"Nay.* I'm fine." But he knew he didn't sound or feel fine. Whittier's Store loomed ahead like a lifeline. "We're here!" he announced, and with her hand still in his, he hurried forward at almost a run.

Ellen studied the man at her side and sensed he was troubled. Why wouldn't he tell her what was bothering him? Had coming here for ice cream brought back bad memories for him? Was he afraid of how Bob Whittier would act when he saw him again?

He released her hand to open the door and held it for her. His eyes gleamed at the prospect as if he was eager for their favorite treat. He didn't look upset or pensive. Had she imagined it?

"Isaac," she began as she turned to wait for him, "if you'd rather not be here…if you'd prefer to go to Miller's…"

She felt Isaac stiffen beside her. She touched his arm to offer comfort and felt the tension seep out of him.

"I'm fine with Whittier's," he said, and she realized it was true. He didn't seem upset or look as if he felt awkward.

"Oll recht," she said with a smile. "Since you're buying, I'll have a double-scoop mint chocolate chip cone."

He laughed, and the sound rippled pleasurably down her spine, making her giggle.

"And I suppose the soda needs to be the extra large?"

Ellen wrinkled her nose at him. *"Nay,* a small root beer will be just fine." She was happy to see him beam at her as his gray eyes filled with amusement.

They enjoyed their ice cream, sitting outside in the sun on a park bench. They talked about their families, their farms and the weather. Isaac told her about the current construction job the crew was working on—a large house that was progressing nicely.

"It's being insulated today, which is why I was able to take off today," he told her.

"I'm glad." She thought about telling him about the clinic now, but then she decided not to tell him until she knew whether or not her meeting with Dr. Westmore resulted in a volunteer job offer. She realized that Isaac was studying her.

"Something is bothering you."

"Nay," she said. "I just wondered how hard it was for you to get off work."

He smiled. "It wasn't a problem." He studied her thoughtfully. "Why?"

It was now or never, she thought, but still she hesitated. "I just wondered."

"You want to make plans to go somewhere tomorrow? That might be difficult since I took today off from work."

She shrugged. She paused and then admitted, "I already have plans for tomorrow. I have appointment with the Westmore Clinic."

His expression filled with concern. "Are you ill?"

"*Nay*, I want to volunteer my time there." Unable to stop, Ellen went on to explain about the Yoders' daughter, and about the other couple she'd met and how she felt the need to do something to help. "I mentioned it to *Dat*, but he didn't want to hear it. He wants me to marry and have babies, and I will…someday. I thought if I could talk with Dr. Westmore, see if he would accept my help, then I could bring home enough information to convince *Dat* to give his permission."

Isaac had been silent as he listened to her talk. She studied his features carefully, wondering what he was thinking. Would he agree with her father? Or would he understand how important this was to her?

"When is your appointment?" he asked quietly.

She blushed. "Tomorrow at noon."

"*Nay.*"

She froze. "*Nay?* You don't think I should go?"

"I think you should go, but you should change your appointment so that I can come with you."

"I don't need you to come with me, but I appreciate the offer." Her heart filled with emotion. "I don't have far to go. I won't be going into the city. The clinic is on Old Philadelphia Pike."

He narrowed his gaze. "I still think you should change your appointment and let me come. I understand how important this is to you. Are you sure you'll be safe?"

"*Ja*, I'm certain." *He understands!* Ellen exhaled on a whoosh of relief. "I was afraid that you wouldn't understand."

"You thought I wouldn't approve like your *vadder.*"

"I didn't know," she confessed softly. "I was afraid to tell you."

He didn't say anything for a minute. She shifted uncomfortably as he studied her.

"What are you looking at?" She touched her hair to see if something was out of place.

"You." He continued to study her as he took a sip from his soda, then set his cup down on the ground near his feet.

She cocked her head as her curiosity got the better of her. "Why?"

"You're different than you were."

Ellen frowned. "I'm still me."

"I'm glad of that, but it's something else." She didn't know how to respond. He stood and gazed down at her. "Will you tell me how things go with Dr. Westmore?" He looked as if he thought about insisting that he accompany her but then had thought better of it.

She nodded. "*Ja*, I may need to be consoled."

"I doubt it." He flashed a grin. They enjoyed the rest of their afternoon together. Isaac insisted on walking her home afterward. "Don't forget I'll be waiting to hear how things go tomorrow.

Ellen beamed at him. "I'll let you know. *Danki*, Isaac."

Chapter Fourteen

Ellen steered the horse-drawn buggy in the direction of the Westmore Clinic. She was nervous. So much hinged on her meeting with Dr. Westmore. If the doctor didn't use volunteers, as the employees in the office had indicated, then there was every likelihood that he would turn her away. But she had to try.

She stopped at a red light with the rest of traffic. What would she do if this didn't work out? She didn't know. She could only hope and pray that it would.

The clinic was a small brick building on Old Philadelphia Pike. Ellen recognized it immediately from her last brief visit. She turned Blackie into the lot next to the building and secured him to a hitching post. Hers was the only buggy there. The knowledge gave her confidence, although she wouldn't have minded if she had someone with her, like she did last time, when Mary Ruth had come.

The young woman at the front desk stood up as she took notice of Ellen when she walked in. "Can I help you?"

"The appointment you made for me is for today," Ellen said as she sat down in the waiting room.

Joan's gaze widened. "Miss Mast?" She looked surprised as she studied her and Ellen suddenly realized that during her last visit she'd been dressed not in her own garments but as an *Englisher*.

"*Ja*, but it's Ellen," she corrected.

"I'll tell Dr. Westmore that you're here," Joan said, sounding a little friendlier than previously.

Joan was back within seconds. "His nurse isn't here. If you come with me, I'll take you to his office," she said.

Ellen rose from her chair on shaky legs. Now that the time had come for her meeting with Dr. Westmore, she was terrified. Everything hinged on today's encounter. This would be her last chance to convince her father to give her his permission to work here.

Ellen didn't know what she expected but it wasn't the nice-looking man in his midforties who greeted her as she was escorted in. Dr. Westmore rose from behind his desk. "You must be Ellen." He gestured toward the chair. "Have a seat. I have a half hour before my next patient. I heard that you'd like to be a volunteer here."

Ellen nodded. "I believe I can be of help with your patients' families. I know how difficult life is for couples of children with special needs. I understand them. I know about their faith, their way of life… I can show them understanding and help you get through to those who are having trouble making the right decision for the children they love who are sick." She blushed. She realized that she'd been rambling on without stopping. The doctor had remained silent while she'd talked. She couldn't tell if he was receptive to the idea or if he thought her presumptuous for making the suggestion.

"How did you know about us?" he asked.

She couldn't read his expression. "Rebekka and Caleb Yoder. Their daughter, Alice, is your patient. Alice has Crigler-Najjar syndrome—type 2. I know that the little girl struggles to live a normal life, that every single day she has to lie under a blue light to keep a toxic substance called bilirubin from poisoning her."

He eyed her thoughtfully. "You've certainly done your homework." He rubbed his chin. "Why do you want to help?"

"Because I feel like I can be of service. I picture myself in the Yoders' situation and I understand their pain. I know you are doing good work here, but you're not Amish." She blushed. "I don't mean to imply that you don't know how to medically treat your patients. But do you understand what it is to be raised Amish? To live by the *Ordnung*? To be conscious of the Lord's way?" She felt a rise in confidence. "I'm not saying that I am better than anyone. I'm not trained or certified like you or your staff, but I can help if you'll let me. I honestly want to help."

"I see." He picked up a pen and turned it over, end to end in a constant fluid motion that suggested he fingered the instrument that way frequently.

"Ellen, you've given me something to think about. How often do you think you could come in to work?"

"Two days a week?" Ellen knew it wasn't much time, but she still had chores to do at home. She couldn't abandon her way of life simply because she felt the need to volunteer there. She might be able to get her father to agree to one or two days.

"I like the idea," Dr. Westmore said. "But I have to check on a few things before I can decide whether or not to accept your kind offer. Is there a way I can reach you?"

Ellen gave him the number of Bob Whittier. "Bob will see that I get your message," she said. "I can call back if you leave a phone number and time."

He nodded, looking satisfied. He rose and Ellen realized that it was her cue to leave. "Thank you for coming in, Ellen."

"I appreciate your time," she replied. "Dr. Westmore, is there literature on some of the genetic conditions that are treated here in the clinic? I'd like some information to show my parents."

"Yes, of course." He frowned. "Are there genetic disorders in your family? Do you have a special-needs sibling?"

She shook her head. "*Nay*, not as far as I am aware. We are all fortunate to be healthy."

"Your friends Rebekka and Caleb—are they happy with my care?"

"*Ja*, that's why I'm here. They are grateful that you are concerned with their daughter's illness. They appreciate that you care about our sick Amish children."

"I do what I can." He came out from behind the desk to escort her to the front reception area. "I'll be in touch," he said as they stepped into the front room.

"Thank you, Dr. Westmore."

He nodded, then turned with a smile to greet a young Amish couple who must have come in while they were in his office. They had waited patiently with their young child. Ellen saw that the little boy had a medical condition, but she didn't know what. She turned to leave.

"Ellen," Joan, the receptionist, said as Ellen started toward the door. "Dr. Westmore asked me to give you these." She handed Ellen numerous pamphlets. It was the information she'd requested.

"Thank you." She left, feeling optimistic after what had transpired during her meeting with Dr. Westmore. She suddenly had a good feeling about the job offer she wanted and about her future…until she exited the building and discovered Isaac Lapp waiting for her in the parking lot. He was leaning against her vehicle, his expression unreadable as he watched her approach.

Chapter Fifteen

"What are you doing here, Isaac?"

Isaac narrowed his gaze as he studied her. "I'm waiting for you."

"Why?"

"Because I wanted to know how you made out." He eyed her with amusement. "Did you think I followed you to make sure you were all right?"

She nodded. "You wanted to keep an eye on me, but I got here fine. If you're worried about Brad, he won't be coming back. You scared him off."

Did she really think that? "I'm afraid you're mistaken if you think he's given up being a nuisance. It's not like him to give up."

She looked suddenly uncomfortable. "I haven't seen him today. I'm not heading into the city. This is as far as I'm going. I doubt I'll encounter him on the way home."

He studied her, noting her flushed cheeks. "I didn't follow you, Ellen." He glanced across the street to the construction site where he was currently working. "I didn't follow you."

"You didn't?"

"*Nay*, I didn't have to. Once you mentioned the address, I knew exactly where you were going. So I came over."

She narrowed her gaze. "Why?"

"For you." Isaac folded his arms across his chest. "I've decided to make everything *you* do my business."

She bristled. "What are trying to do, Isaac? Upset me?"

He laughed. "I'm sorry. I'm teasing you and I shouldn't. Especially when I want us to be *gut* friends again."

She didn't understand. "Then why are you here?" She eyed him warily. "And don't say again that you wanted to know how I made out? Where did you come from?"

He grinned as he gestured toward a house under construction in the lot across the street. "I'm working over there. I had just taken my lunch break when I saw you pull in."

"That's Matt Rhoades's current project," she muttered, appearing to relax.

"Ja." He examined her closely. His gaze focused on the house across the street again before he returned his attention to Ellen. "So, how did you make out with Dr. Westmore?" From the moment she'd pulled her buggy into the lot, he'd wanted to accompany her inside to lend his support. "It went *oll recht*, I suppose"

She looked less than pleased. "He didn't offer me the position yet, but he did give me some information to give to my *mudder* and *vadder*."

"What did he say?" He sent her a look that silently begged her to confide in him.

Her expression changed as if she'd come to a decision. "That he'd think about it and get back with me."

"'Tis something, isn't it?" He glanced at the building. "I never paid attention to this place before." And now he was curious because of Ellen's interest and because of what she'd told him about the children who were helped here.

"*Ja*, 'tis something, but I was hoping for more."

"It will work out, Ellen. You just have to have faith."

"Like you have faith?" she quipped then her face turned bright red with embarrassment. "I'm sorry. That was uncalled for." To his surprise, she reached out to touch his arm. "I am sorry, Isaac. I know things have been difficult for you since…"

Her words hurt but there was truth behind what she'd implied. "I'm fine, Ellen. And, *ja*, I do have faith. That hasn't changed." It didn't mean that he felt deserving of church membership.

She looked contrite. "I'm hurt because you won't talk to me about what happened."

He felt a sudden chill. "I'm not ready to talk about it. With anyone." He glanced toward the job site to see if any of the other workers had returned from lunch. He wasn't ready for this discussion. "I hope you get your offer soon," he said softly. He couldn't be mad at her. She only wanted to know the truth and he was afraid to talk about that night at Whittier's Store. He should get back but still he lingered. "Tell me more about what is wrong with the Yoders' child. You told me she was sick with some sort of genetic disease."

"Alice has Crigler-Najjar syndrome—type 2. It's a disease where a toxic substance called bilirubin builds up in her blood, turning her yellow. Her disorder forces her to lie under a special blue light for ten to twelve hours every day."

Isaac felt compassion for the young couple. "That must be terrible for the child and her parents." He lifted himself away from her buggy. "You feel bad for them. No wonder you want to get involved." He ran fingers through his hair. "You, Ellen, have a warm and generous spirit," he said approvingly. "I think it's a wise thing you're doing. I'm sure the Lord will approve."

She blushed, apparently embarrassed by the compliment, and looked away briefly.

She sighed. "I'm glad you understand, Isaac. My *dat* doesn't. If these brochures don't help, then I have no hope of working here." She met his gaze with blue eyes filled with an emotion bordering on pleasure. "*Danki* for coming to find out how the appointment went."

"Of course I want to know. You are a *gut* person, Ellen. You care about people." His lips twisted in self-derision. "Even those who refuse to see how much you care when they should." He was referring to himself and the way she'd tried to warn him about Nancy but he'd refused to listen. He saw that she watched him closely. He gestured to the literature she held. He raised his eyebrows. "May I see the information you have to convince your *dat*?"

"*Ja.*" She handed a brochure to him. "I just hope it makes a difference."

He looked over the information and smiled. "I believe it will. I'll pray that it does."

"*Danki*, Isaac." She seemed pleased. Her expression softened as she continued to study him. "Is there anything else you'd like to talk about?"

"Can we get together again soon? Maybe go for

lunch instead of ice cream? I do have something I need to tell you, but I'd rather not discuss it here." He handed the brochure back to her.

She hesitated. "I guess we could." But she appeared reluctant.

"Just a meal, Ellen."

"*Oll recht.* When?"

"Tomorrow?" He didn't want to wait any longer. He'd already waited too long as it was.

Why hadn't he understood sooner? *Because I was too taken by Nancy to think about what I'd done to Ellen.*

After Nancy had left, he had struggled to get over the breakup and the realization that Nancy wasn't the person he'd thought she was. He should have gone to Ellen immediately, apologized and told her that she was right, but it had been months since he'd spent any time with her. And he'd been unwilling to admit that he'd done a terrible thing to Ellen by refusing to trust in what she had to say.

He waited for Ellen's answer to his request. She was quiet, reflective. "What time?"

"Eleven thirty?"

She nodded. "I will meet you at eleven thirty. Where?"

"I'll come for you." Like he used to, he thought but didn't want to say it.

"*Oll recht.*" She avoided his glance, seemed suddenly eager to leave. "I have to go."

"I'll see you tomorrow, Ellen." He watched as she threw the brochures she'd received from the doctor onto the other side of the front seat, then climbed into the buggy and picked up the leathers. He saw her give him a concerned look. "Don't worry about our discussion, Ellen. 'Tis nothing bad." At least, not for her, he hoped. But it would be difficult for him admitting that he'd been wrong, for he was afraid that by resurrecting the past, he would effectively be sending her away. He didn't know what he'd do if she wouldn't forgive him. He didn't know what he'd do if she avoided him in the future and forced him from her life.

The next morning Ellen waited for Isaac near the road on her father's farm property. She couldn't help wondering what he wanted to discuss. He'd told her she shouldn't be concerned, that it was nothing bad, but that didn't keep her from worrying.

It was a warm day. She'd finished all of her chores early. She'd told her mother that she was going out for a while. *Mam* had been too busy to ask any questions. Miriam Zook was coming to visit, and her mother was waiting for her to arrive. Fortunately, *Mam* didn't ask her to stay. She wasn't sure what she'd have told her if she had. She didn't want to bring Isaac's name into any conversation with her parents. Ever since Isaac had gotten in trouble two years ago, her mother and father had acted as if they were disappointed in him, that it bothered them that he'd never given any details of what happened.

Isaac appeared, and she watched his approach. He raised his hand in greeting, and heart thumping hard, she waved back.

He smiled as he drew closer, and her lips curved in response.

"*Hallo*, Ellen Mast," he said warmly.

She melted inside. "*Hallo.* Where are we going for lunch?"

"What would you like for lunch? A burger?" He fell in step with her as they started down the street.

"Are you buying?" It seemed for a moment that time had reversed itself and they were close friends who bantered about who would pay for their meal and what kind of soda they would order and which one tasted better. They had different opinions on soda flavors. She had liked root beer, while Isaac had liked cream soda. At one time, they'd teased each other often in this way. "*Ja,* I'm buying," he said with a twinkle in his gray eyes.

"Then I'll have soup and a sandwich."

"No burger?" He feigned momentary disappointment. Then he grinned. "Soup and sandwich it is."

They walked without speaking. Surprisingly to Ellen, the silence between them was relaxed, friendly, without the tension that had been between them when they'd chosen stargazing over their community youth singing. But their time together hadn't been long. Things had gone downhill quickly and she wasn't even sure why that night had turned sour for them.

Whittier's Store loomed ahead. They had to pass it as they walked the remaining distance to the restaurant in silence. Ellen's thoughts turned to the night that the store had been vandalized. She'd never believed that Isaac was guilty, although others had believed that he was. He wouldn't have done anything to hurt Bob Whittier, a neighbor and friend to their community. She and Isaac had enjoyed too many ice-cream cones and sodas here for her to believe that Isaac would suddenly turn on a man who was always kind to them.

Ever since it had happened, she'd been bothered by the fact that her former friend had taken the blame. Even when she'd been angry and hurt because of him, she'd still thought Isaac incapable of the crime.

They reached the restaurant. The bells clanged as Isaac opened the entrance door and gestured for Ellen to precede him.

At the sound, the hostess looked up from where she stood behind the podium. "Two today?"

Isaac nodded. Ellen felt heat rise to her cheeks as the hostess studied them a moment before going to see if there was a table available for them.

"Maybe they carry mint chocolate chip ice cream at their ice cream counter next door," Isaac said.

The hostess returned in time to hear Isaac's comment. Her eyes lit up with pleasure. "We most certainly have mint chocolate chip ice cream."

"Maybe we'll have some dessert," Isaac said, smiling at Ellen.

Ellen grinned, feeling suddenly happy. They followed the young hostess to a booth next to a window.

"Is this all right?" the young woman asked.

"It's fine. Thank you," Ellen assured her.

Ellen enjoyed a bowl of split pea with ham soup and a turkey sandwich. Isaac ordered and enjoyed his hamburger and fries. When they were done, Isaac paid the check and they rose to leave. The ice cream was sold in a glass case in the store connected to the restaurant. Ellen leaned against the glass case, eyeing the large containers of colorful ice cream that invited one to taste.

"Two mint chocolate chip ice-cream cones," Isaac

ordered. "One single scoop for me and one double for my friend Ellen here."

Ellen laughed. "*Nay*, make that two single-scoop cones," she said, flashing Isaac a teasing glance.

His expression warmed as she corrected his order. "Are you sure you don't want a double?"

She shook her head. "*Nay*, but that doesn't mean you can't have one."

He appeared to be fighting a smile. "Since I'm paying, a single scoop will be plenty."

She wrinkled up her nose at him. "You can afford a double for both of us, Isaac Lapp, and you know it." They took their ice cream cones and went outside to enjoy them in the warm sunshine. The restaurant had dining tables on a deck in the front of the building. They gravitated to a table and sat down. As he ate, Isaac smiled at her.

"Just like old times," Ellen commented.

A flicker in his expression suggested that he liked that she'd remembered.

Isaac smiled at her. "How's your ice cream?" He took a lick of his cone."

"*Gut*. Yours?"

"The same. *Gut* as usual."

The day felt good. The air between her and Isaac was relaxed. Suddenly Ellen remembered why she'd agreed to meet him today. Isaac had something he'd wanted to discuss with her.

"Isaac..."

"Ellen..."

They had spoken at the same time. They laughed but a sudden tension had cropped up between them, as if they'd both recalled that going for ice cream together was no longer a normal occurrence for them.

"Go ahead, Isaac," she invited.

"About what happened…to our friendship," he began. "I'm sorry. We were friends and I didn't listen to you. You tried to tell me what Nancy was like, and I…" He exhaled sharply and looked away a moment. His gray eyes held regret when he turned to face her again. "I didn't listen. As I recall, I wasn't…kind."

Ellen felt her throat tighten as it all came back to her. The last thing she'd expected was an apology from him. It had been a long time, after all. "Why now?" she asked.

He looked sheepish. "I miss you."

She shook her head. "Isaac—"

"I'm sorry, Ellen. I know it won't change anything between us, but I needed you to know that I was wrong and I'm sincerely sorry for what I said…for the way I hurt you."

"You did hurt me," she whispered. Feeling the sudden need to put distance between them as she processed his apology, Ellen stood and walked a few feet away. She didn't look at him. She was afraid if she did, then she'd do or say something she'd regret. She had longed for his apology. It had finally come, but while she appreciated that it had come at all, the words seemed to have arrived too late to make much of a difference.

She turned, stared without seeing. The street came into focus. Several cars passed by. One turned and pulled into the lot, perhaps tempted by the image of an ice cream cone on a sign on the front lawn. Years ago, she and Isaac came here on occasion. The restaurant called the Hungry Hog was enjoyed by locals and tourists alike. Isaac hadn't said a word after he'd apologized. Ellen wondered if she could trust that things would get better, but she had doubts, considering that her feelings for him were stronger than his for her, just as it had been years ago. She could accept his apology, but could things go back to the way they were? She thought not. She wouldn't be hurt by him again.

She wondered how much she really knew about Isaac. She had thought she'd understood him once, but now she wondered. She turned to face him. "What happened at Whittier's Store that night, Isaac? I find it hard to believe that you spray-painted Bob's siding." She kept going, although she saw how he'd closed off his expression. "I don't believe you had anything to do with vandalizing his place, although I believe you made restitution, because that's the way you are. I think someone else did the nasty deed. I don't know why you took the blame or why you paid for the repairs, but I can't see you doing something like that." She shifted on her seat. She had always wondered what had happened, but she couldn't have asked him, because they were no longer friends by that point.

"Tell me what happened, Isaac." She touched his arm. "Tell me. You know you can confide in me."

"Ellen..." This time her name was an agonized whisper. "I'm sorry but I can't talk about it."

"Can't or won't?" She had thought that if he'd open up to her, then she'd know that he was willing to trust her. The fact that he was reluctant told her that despite his apology, nothing between them had really changed.

"I can't." He swallowed hard. "I'm sorry."

She shuddered out a sigh. "I won't ask again, but I will say this—there is no way you did it. You're innocent and I have always believed that and always will. But it hurts me that you still don't trust me enough to tell me."

"Ellen, I care for you, I do, but you want me to tell you about something that doesn't only concern me."

She blinked. "You're protecting someone." She bit her lip. "Nancy?"

"Nay!"

He'd been so quick to defend Nancy that she wondered if he still wasn't over her. Pain radiated through to her heart. She loved him, but she had to keep her distance.

"I am sorry."

She shrugged as if unconcerned. "I should go..." She managed to smile. *"Danki* for the meal and the cone."

"Ellen."

"I can get home by myself. I'll be fine, I promise." She spied Nate Peachy as he drove a pony cart. It had been a while since she'd talked with her friend. "Nate!" she cried. He pulled up on the leathers and stopped the vehicle. She hurried across the road to meet him, ignoring Isaac when he called out to her to come back. She was blinded by tears as she reached Nate. The young man took one look at her and then at Isaac. He grabbed her arm.

"Come with me," Nate said. "I'll take you home." He turned back the way he'd come, pulling her to follow. "Are you *oll recht?"*

She sniffed. "I... I will be."

He flashed Isaac an angry glance. She hadn't told Nate what was wrong; he had figured it out on his own. She suspected that he knew, had always known, how she felt about Isaac. Nate was the kind of friend she felt comfortable with. She could rely on Nate. He'd been there for her when Isaac hadn't been.

Chapter Sixteen

It was visiting Sunday, and Mae and Amos King were hosting. Isaac got up early that morning to do his chores. Since it was the Lord's day, the only thing he needed to do was feed the animals, and for that he was grateful. Since Ellen had left with Nate, he hadn't slept much. His days and nights were filled with her image: the way she looked as she enjoyed her ice cream, her smile when she was amused, the warmth in her blue eyes when she was pleased with something, the intensity of her expression when she'd told him that she believed in him, in his innocence.

He hadn't seen Ellen since the day he'd taken her to lunch. The loss was slowly killing him inside.

As he'd watched Ellen leave with Nate that day, Isaac had realized that it was over. He had lost his chance at making things right. He had apologized but it hadn't made a difference. She wanted something he couldn't give her—the truth.

He swallowed against a painful lump as he recalled how easily Ellen had gone off with Nate. He'd felt jealousy raise its ugly head. He'd wanted to run after her, tell her that he loved her…confess the truth about what happened that night at Whittier's, but he couldn't. It was Henry Yoder's secret, and until his friend came forward with the truth, he had to continue to live with the lie, although it bothered him to do it. This lie was a sin he couldn't confess and he wondered whether or not things would ever change.

He loved Ellen, more than he'd ever loved anyone. He should have been rejoicing at the realization, except he couldn't. He wasn't good for her. He'd made mistakes that couldn't be fixed. He'd hurt her once, and then he'd hurt her again. He was unworthy of her love.

As he fed and watered the horses, Isaac realized that it would be best if he continued to keep his distance from her. She deserved better than him. He wanted her to be happy, even if it was with another man. *Like Nate.*

Isaac closed his eyes and groaned.

Ellen was in high spirits as she dressed for visiting Sunday at the Amos Kings. On Friday, Bob Whittier had brought her a message from the Westmore Clinic. Dr. Westmore wanted to offer her a job—not as a volunteer as she'd requested but as a paid part-time employee. She'd suffered mixed feelings at first. She wanted to accept the position but she had yet to convince her father. As soon as Bob had left, Ellen had sought out her father where he worked in the barn.

"Dat," she called as she entered the dark interior of the structure.

"In here, Ellen," he replied.

She located him by his voice. He was in the back stables, looking over the pair of goats they kept here.

"I need to talk with you."

He rose from a crouch. "What's wrong?"

"Nothing…" She closed her eyes. "*Dat*, I've been offered a paid part-time job." She bit her lip. "At the Westmore children's clinic." She stood, fearing his rebuke. When she had returned from her appointment, she'd placed the brochures from the clinic where her parents could find them. *Dat* had never mentioned seeing them, and she'd never spoken of her visit.

"I see." He eyed her with displeasure.

"Please, *Dat*. I really want to do this—need to do this," she said. "I would have worked there for nothing, but now I've been asked to work and get paid."

He didn't say anything at first, and waiting for his reply, Ellen felt a burning in her stomach. "*Dat*, I didn't take the job. I wouldn't accept it without your permission."

He remained silent, his expression thoughtful. "Why do you want to do this so badly?"

"I feel that the Lord has asked me to do this." She spoke passionately and from the heart. "The clinic is working on ways to help children, *Dat*. Children from the Amish community. I know I can help. I know parents will talk to me. I can help by listening to them and helping the doctor with treatment and care—and with understanding our beliefs."

Her father didn't say a word until she gave him the literature from the clinic. She showed him information about the different types of genetic conditions that the children of Amish parents were sometimes born with. She told him about some of the treatments the children had to endure just to stay alive. And her father asked questions, which she answered as best she could.

"We are fortunate, *Dat*. The Lord blessed us all with

good health. Please give me your permission to work there. It's only for two days a week."

Her father blinked several times as if he was deeply affected by what he'd learned. *Dat* was quiet for a moment. *"Ja,"* he whispered. "You may work there."

She thanked him with tears in her eyes. *"Danki, Dat."*

He managed to smile for her.

"Mam..." Ellen began.

"She'll give her blessing. We talked about it when you first mentioned it. I didn't like it, but your *mudder* had a different opinion." He smiled. "You'd better go and call Dr. Westmore back. Tell him that you'll be happy to accept his offer."

And so she'd called him back. She was to start on this coming Tuesday. Ellen felt lighthearted as well as excited about her new job...as long as she focused on her good fortune rather than her feelings for Isaac.

She would be working with special children and helping their families! Her good humor stayed with her as they rode in their family buggy to the Amos Kings. It didn't dampen immediately when she saw Isaac arrive with his family. Ellen felt her joy dissipate when Isaac glanced at her coldly, then promptly looked away.

It was only after the arrival of the Abram Peachy family that Ellen made an effort to recapture the pleasure of the day, for Nate Peachy, the deacon's son, was happy to see her. In fact, he immediately headed in her direction after spying her in the yard.

"Ellen," he said with a warm smile.

She grinned at him. "Nate."

"'Tis *gut* to see you."

"And you," she said.

"How are you doing?" Nate studied her with male appreciation, which was a balm to her wounded ego.

"I'm...managing." She brightened. "I got a job at the Westmore Clinic." She had told him about it when he'd taken her home after she and Isaac had argued.

"Want to take a walk with me later? You can tell me all about it then."

She nodded. "That would be nice."

"When?" He seemed eager to go, and she felt pleasure in the knowledge.

"After lunch? Or we could sit and enjoy the sun," she suggested.

He appeared pleased by her suggestion. "*Ja*, we could."

Nate found a spot in the warm sun where they could sit on the lawn and enjoy conversation. Ellen felt someone's regard and saw Isaac's eyes on her. When she looked at him, he quickly glanced away. She saw him talking with his younger brothers and a friend. She saw him say something to Daniel, heard him laugh at his brother's reply...and Ellen tried not to feel hurt that he had accepted the end of their friendship so easily.

Instead she concentrated on Nate, who was clearly more interested in her than Isaac Lapp was. They ate the midday meal and then went for a walk afterward. They crossed the street to the swing set in the schoolyard. Ellen settled on a swing and Nate took the one next to her. He kept up a commentary on the proper way to pump one's feet in order to swing higher.

"Try it, Ellen," he said. "Watch me first!"

Ellen watched with amusement as Nate pumped his feet back and forth to make his swing soar. She laughed as she tried it without luck until she watched

Nate again. She was able to duplicate the movement of his feet. She felt the air rush against her skin, the laughter rise in her throat as she swung to and fro in glorious abandonment.

"Fun, *ja*?" Nate asked.

She grinned at him, "*Ja. Danki* for bringing me here."

"My pleasure," he said, sounding as if he meant it.

She felt joy that she could enjoy the simple happiness of riding on a swing. Then suddenly she experienced a strange frisson of sensation at her nape, traveling down to her heels. She looked up and saw Isaac Lapp standing across the road, watching her... watching her with Nate. And she knew a longing for what she couldn't have. *Isaac Lapp's love.* She looked away, determined to enjoy herself with Nate. But her feelings for Isaac remained heavily in her mind.

Ellen woke up the next day after a night's fitful sleep. She still couldn't get Isaac out of her mind. She should have gone over to say *hallo. When he glanced at you and you looked back, he turned away.*

Did it bother Isaac to see her with Nate? She wasn't trying to make him jealous. She'd needed someone to talk to, to care.

She had promised her mother she would go shopping for her today. There were several things she needed, but *Mam* claimed that she was too busy to go.

She felt groggy, disoriented. She went into the bathroom and splashed cold water on her face. It helped to wake her but she thought that she'd feel even better after a strong cup of coffee with breakfast. She dressed

quickly and went downstairs. She found her mother in
the kitchen, working on her shopping list.

"Sleep well?" she asked as she grabbed a mug from
the cabinet and poured herself coffee from the pot on
the stove. To her relief, the brew was still hot.

Mam studied her as Ellen sat down at the kitchen
table across from her. "I slept well enough." Her eyes
narrowed. "You didn't."

"I couldn't sleep."

"It's because of that young man."

Ellen's heart skipped a beat. "Who?"

"Nate Peachy. I saw the two of you yesterday. You
had fun with him."

She managed to smile. "*Ja*, I did." She couldn't tell
her mother who'd actually been on her mind all night
and into the early hours of the morning. It was Isaac,
not Nate, who was constantly in her thoughts.

"I've invited the Peachys over for supper this evening."

Ellen felt a jolt. "You did?"

Mam nodded. "Thought you'd enjoy it."

"I—" She looked down. "I would." Nate Peachy
was easy to spend time with and she had enjoyed herself with him, but she didn't feel for him as she did for
Isaac. She didn't believe she ever would.

"Is something wrong?" *Mam* asked, furrowing her
brow.

"*Nay.*" Ellen gave her a genuine smile. She would
enjoy having the Peachys over. She just hoped that Nate
didn't expect more from her than she could give him.

"*Gut!*" *Mam* scribbled down a few more items.
"Here you go," she said as she handed her the list.

Ellen looked over its contents. "What is all this for?"

She'd read chili powder, a can of mild green chilies, a bag of flour and several other unusual items.

"I thought I'd try a new recipe for our dinner guests tonight."

She looked at her mother with skepticism. "*Mam*, I don't want to change your plans, but do you think that's wise? What if they don't like chili powder and green chilies?"

Mam gave it some thought. "You're right. Give me the list."

Stifling a small smile, Ellen handed it back to her. She watched with satisfaction as her mother scratched off the first two items and added a few more at the bottom.

When she received it back, Ellen perused the list and nodded with satisfaction. "You're going to make chicken and drop dumplings." She was pleased. "They are going to love them. It's your specialty."

Mam beamed at her. "You should be able to get everything I need at Yoder's."

Ellen nodded. She quickly ate a bowl of cereal and finished her coffee. By the time she'd finished, she felt a whole lot better and more awake.

"I'll head over there now," Ellen said as she stood and brought her bowl and cup to the sink, where she washed them. She suddenly realized how quiet it was. "Where are *Dat* and the boys?"

"Your *vadder* went over to Horseshoe Joe's, something about discussing some new crops. Your *bruders* went with him. They wanted to see Peter. They're fond of him. Peter is kind to them."

Ellen agreed. Peter Zook was a kind man who always treated everyone fairly. He lived the life laid out by the *Ordnung* even though he hadn't joined the church yet.

Why couldn't she fall for someone like Peter? Not that she would have a chance, she realized, since Peter was in love with Meg Stoltzfus and had been for a long time. *Peter is like me, loving someone who doesn't feel the same way.*

And she didn't believe that Meg regarded him as a friend. She reacted to Peter as if she thought him more of a nuisance than anything.

The ride to Yoder's General Store was pleasant, although clouds had started to gather in the sky and it looked like it might rain at any moment. Sure enough, by time she parked the buggy and tied up Blackie next to the building, it had begun to drizzle.

Ellen ran into the store, glad to make it inside before the rain fell in earnest. "*Gut* morning, Margaret," she greeted before she turned and saw that it wasn't Margaret behind the counter but her son. "Henry! *Hallo!*"

"*Hallo*, Ellen," Henry said, glancing away as he did so. He didn't seem happy that he had to work in the store this morning.

"How have you been? I haven't seen you in a long time."

"*Ja*, I've been busy." He met her gaze, but there was something off in his expression that bothered her. "Building furniture and things, over in Ephrata."

"So your *mudder* said." She eyed the young man carefully, noting certain changes in him. He had aged since she'd last seen him. He didn't look well, as if he wasn't particularly happy with his life. "I used to see you at singings and sometimes with Isaac."

Henry jerked at the mention of Isaac. Ellen narrowed her gaze. "Your parents have forbidden you to spend time with Isaac, haven't they?" she guessed. "Because of what he did that night at Whittier's Store."

Henry looked uncomfortable, even guilty, as he fiddled with something beneath the counter.

"Henry?"

He shrugged. "I…" He seemed to stand straighter. "Can I help you find something?" he asked, changing the subject.

"I guess I should get shopping, *ja*?" She held up her list. "*Mam* is waiting for these items to fix supper for friends tonight."

He relaxed and seemed relieved. "Let me know if you have trouble finding anything."

As she walked about the store, finding the items she needed to purchase, Ellen pondered the reason for Henry's odd behavior. Now that she gave it some thought, Henry's absence since the store vandalism incident seemed strange. He and Isaac had been friends who had gone on *rumspringa* together. And he avoided his friend? He hadn't agreed that his parents had put a stop to his and Isaac's friendship…which had to mean that there was another reason that Henry stayed away.

Ellen frowned as she grabbed the last item on her mother's shopping list. Henry had looked almost guilty when she'd mentioned Isaac. Ellen knew that Isaac was innocent of the crime. She'd always felt it, known it to be true.

But what about Henry? Was Henry there that night? He used to hang out with Brad Smith and the others. Henry had liked Jessica, if Ellen remembered correctly, who'd been Nancy's friend. Had Henry painted graffiti on the back exterior wall of Bob Whittier's store?

Clutching the items her mother needed, Ellen returned to the front to pay. She set everything on the counter and watched as Henry began to add the price of her items on a paper bag.

He looked up from his math. "That makes a total of $20.42."

Ellen dug the money out of her change purse and silently gave it to him.

He nodded and then put the money into the old cash register and gave her change. Then he turned the bag around so that she could check his math.

"I trust you," she said, turning the bag back around without checking.

He blushed guiltily as if her words had upset him.

"Henry," she said. "You don't seem yourself. What's going on?"

"What do you mean?" he shot back defensively. "Nothing's going on. Why would you ask?" He looked nervous, and Ellen was suspicious. She knew he was lying; she could tell that something was wrong.

She studied him, trying to get a read. She'd speak her mind and suffer the consequences. "You were there the night Bob Whittier's place was spray-painted, weren't you?" She drew in a deep breath before plunging on. "Did you do it, Henry? Is that why you don't come around anymore? Is that why you've been avoiding Isaac since it happened? Isaac took the blame for you, didn't he? And you're ashamed."

Henry turned pale. "I..." He shook his head as if he wanted to deny the truth but couldn't. *"Ja,"* he whispered. "I was there at the store that night." He hesitated. "I was involved."

Ellen felt sympathy as she looked at him. Henry was

clearly suffering as much as Isaac, if not more. Except that Henry was guilty and Isaac was innocent. "You need to come forward and tell the truth."

"Nay!" he gasped. "I can't!" He was shaking his head. "I won't."

"I won't tell anyone, Henry. It's not for me to say. Isaac took the blame for you and he's never said a word. I knew he was innocent, but he wouldn't admit to anything." She eyed him with disappointment coupled with compassion. "The confession must come from you when you're ready." She picked up one grocery bag. Henry had yet to bag the rest of her items. "It's hurting you not to tell. If you confess and tell the elders that you're sorry, then you'll be forgiven. People won't care that you were afraid to speak up. As long as you're sorry and say so."

"I can't," he said, looking sick. "He said he'd kill me if I did."

"Kill you!" she gasped. "Who?"

"Brad Smith."

Ellen shuddered, recalling the two times Brad had tried to intimidate her. "He's not a *gut* person."

Henry bobbed his head. "I would have told the truth, but I was scared."

"But if you did tell the truth, Brad would be arrested and put in jail…"

"Then my parents would hate me," he said, "and so would everyone else."

"And how do you think Isaac feels? He's been regarded as a criminal because he stood up for you, and he never told a soul."

"He must have told you."

"Nay. He didn't. I guessed. You were acting so

strange." She shifted the bag, which had grown heavy as she held it. "Now I know why he wouldn't tell me." And she felt lighter for knowing the truth, for knowing that Isaac's heart was in the right place. "He's been protecting you."

Henry didn't respond. She watched as he put the remainder of her items in a bag with shaking hands. "Henry, think about it. *Ja?*"

He nodded but looked miserable. She feared that he didn't possess the strength to come forward with the truth.

She grabbed the last bag. "It was nice to see you again, Henry," she said politely.

And then she left. Her thoughts were filled with Henry and Isaac and their situation. Isaac had lied to protect his friend, because he had a good heart. But he wouldn't see it that way. He would focus on the actual lie itself, a lie that weighed heavily on his mind because he couldn't confess his sin to the church deacon without getting his friend into serious trouble. And so Isaac struggled with indecision—and felt less of a man because of it. If Henry came forward, Isaac would feel better because everyone would know the truth and he could ask for and be given forgiveness. But he would never confess… The truth would have to come from Henry.

Tears filled Ellen's eyes as she got into her buggy and drove home. She realized that she loved Isaac even more than ever, if it was possible. She wondered if she'd ever get over her love for him.

Nate was coming to supper with the rest of his family. She would talk with him and make him understand that they could be only friends. She'd feared that their relationship had changed. Their friendship had been comfortable. Nate had known about her feelings for Isaac without her telling him, and he'd understood what she'd needed. She didn't want their friendship to change. Nate could never be Isaac.

Tomorrow she would start work at the clinic. It was something to focus on, something good, a worthy task to take her mind off the situation while she offered her attention and help to those who needed it.

But she'd be thinking of Isaac because she thought about him constantly and she knew that wouldn't change.

Chapter Seventeen

Dinner with the Abram Peachys was a boisterous affair with loud conversation and good humor. After enjoying her mother's drop dumplings and chicken along with peas, chowchow, macaroni salad and dried-corn casserole, Ellen found herself walking about the property with Nate Peachy. For some reason, she couldn't bring herself to head toward her grandfather's bench, where she and Isaac had spent times together, talking and enjoying each other's company. It would seem like a betrayal if she brought Nate there to her and Isaac's special place. So she guided him in another direction, toward the right and outside the pasture fence.

The weather had cleared, and the landscape seemed awash with vibrant color. The pasture itself was a bright green. The scents of flowers and the aroma of horse filled the air, and Ellen loved it.

"'Twas nice of your *mudder* to invite us," Nate said.

She turned to him with her lips curved. "She's like that." She hesitated. "Your *dat* seems happy with Charlotte."

He nodded. "He is. Charlotte is *gut* for him. She's

a *gut mudder* to all of us." He grew quiet. "*Dat* loves her."

Ellen was silent a long moment as she struggled over what to say. "Nate—"

"We're friends, Ellen," he said as if he'd anticipated what she wanted to say. "Nothing more. I know you have strong feelings for Isaac."

"I don't know how you knew, but you did." She regarded him with warmth. "What you did for me after Isaac…" She inhaled sharply. "Stepping in to be my friend when I was hurting and needed one. Taking me home. I'll never forget what you did for me, Nate."

He nodded, looking amused. "Nate Peachy at your service," he teased.

"I'm sorry," she mumbled. "I've made you uncomfortable."

"*Nay*, you haven't. We're friends. We enjoy each other's company. Someday I may need a friend." His gaze darkened. "There is someone…although she doesn't know and she's not ready."

Ellen studied his face, saw him blush. "Who?"

"Charlie."

"Stoltzfus?" she asked. He nodded. "She is young. Does she share your feelings?"

"*Nay*, I doubt she even knows who I am."

"Nate, if you like her, why spend time with me? She'll never know who you are if you're not making her aware of you. You need to talk with her every chance you can get. This Sunday after service."

"She's a child."

"Children grow up quickly," she said. Ellen shook her head. "Here I am giving advice when I've made a mess of things for myself."

"You're trying to help," he said. "And I'll give it some thought. You haven't made a mess of things—not with Isaac." He stared at her, and she squirmed uncomfortably. She felt as if he could see into her soul. "Isaac cares for you, but he won't admit it, because he doesn't feel as if he's right for you."

"I should be the one to decide that."

"I agree."

"Isaac feels the need to protect me. He sees me as a friend," she said with a sigh. "I don't want to be just a friend to him."

Nate grabbed hold of her *kapp* string and tugged playfully, like an older brother would do to his younger sister. "You need to let him know how you feel."

"I want to, but I don't want to get hurt again."

"Love is worth the risk of heartache, Ellen. Say you will talk with him."

"I will talk with him."

"Say it again with more confidence."

"I will to talk with him," she said with resolve.

"Perfect." He gave her a warm smile. "We should head back. We don't want our families thinking something that isn't so."

They started to head back when Ellen stopped. "Nate?"

"Ja?"

"Danki."

He nodded with brotherly affection. "I should be thanking you."

She shook her head. "I wish you success…with Charlie."

"I won't wish you success, Ellen. I know that you've already won."

They headed back to join their families. The Peachys left shortly afterward, and Ellen went to bed with much to think about—Isaac, her first day of work at the Westmore Clinic for Special Children… but mostly about Isaac.

She had to make him see himself as she did…as a wonderful man who had stood up for a friend, a man worthy of God and a man who had already won her love.

Isaac felt terrible. He'd lost sleep over the last few nights. Seeing Ellen with Nate Peachy, despite wanting what was best for Ellen, had hurt him. But what else could he do? She deserved the best—and it wasn't him.

He'd arrived home from work about an hour ago. Since he and Daniel were late leaving the job site, *Mam* had supper on the table by the time the two of them had washed up outside and walked in.

Talk was lively around the table, as it usually was in the Lapp household. Isaac worked hard to be included. He didn't want anyone to guess that anything was wrong. He must have been successful, because no one in his family suspected that he was unhappy.

When the meal was over, Isaac escaped the house using the legitimate excuse of caring for the farm animals. The days were getting longer and he was glad that the sun was still out as he walked over to the barn. It was dark in the interior of the structure, however, so it took a minute for his eyes to adjust enough that he could see.

He went to check on the horses first. Someone stepped out from a stall, blocking his way, startling him.

"Isaac." Ellen stood close. He could smell the scent

of her homemade lavender soap mingled with her store-bought shampoo.

His heart continued to hammer hard and his palms grew damp as he recognized her. Joy filled his heart but he quickly tamped it down. He didn't know why Ellen Lapp was in his barn, but he was more than ready to find out.

"What are you doing here, Ellen?" He hated that his tone was brisk, disapproving. He wanted her to be here, but he was afraid to hope…to want…to love.

His brusqueness must have struck her silent, for she'd backed away without a word. *It's for her own good*, he thought.

"I need to talk with you," she said. Her voice trembled, alerting him to the fact that he'd just hurt her, that she had something she wanted to say but was afraid.

He closed his eyes, scolding himself for being all kinds of foolish. "About what?" He gentled his tone. "What do you need to talk about?" He saw relief settle gently on her features. He looked down and realized that she was twisting her hands together anxiously. He edged closer until he could feel the heat from her body, the warmth of her skin. "First tell me why you thought the barn would be a *gut* place to wait for me."

A small smile touched her pretty mouth. "You forget that I found you in our barn when I brought you that pie." She reached up to touch her forehead. "Besides, you like horses—you are *gut* with them. I figured you'd come out to the barn eventually."

"And if I hadn't?"

He saw her swallow hard. "I would have found a way to talk with you alone. I would have knocked on the door and asked for you if it was the only way."

He stared at her, speechless. She looked amused as she arched an eyebrow.

"Can we talk?"

He cracked a smile. "I thought you were," he teased.

Her expression cleared as she shifted closer to him. "I have something to confess and it might make you mad."

He frowned. Dread filled him as he wondered what she had done. "What about?"

"Henry Yoder. I saw him yesterday," she said.

His chest constricted. "That's nice." He swallowed. "How is Henry?" He spoke easily, as if his heart weren't pounding in his chest and his breathing wasn't shallow.

She shrugged. "I don't think he is well. He acted strange, and I finally figured out why."

"Ja?" he replied, keeping his voice light and breezy, although he felt anything but relaxed.

"I accused him of something. I told him that I thought that it was him—and not you—who threw paint all over Bob Whittier's siding. I was right. He admitted it. I suggested that he come forward, and he refused. He said he was scared. Brad apparently threatened him with bodily harm if he told." She reached up to tug nervously on her *kapp* strings.

Isaac felt a constriction in his chest. The pounding of his heart become louder, nearly deafening in his ears. "Ellen—"

"Henry committed the crime and you took blame," she said, eyeing him closely.

He felt himself squirm under her regard. "You sound so certain."

"Henry confessed, but I always knew that you were innocent. I knew what they said about you wasn't true."

He turned away then, unable to look into Ellen's bright eyes. She seemed to regard him as a hero when he was nothing of the sort. He had lied and committed a sin. It was as simple as that.

"Isaac." Ellen's soft voice was in his ear. She had approached while he'd fought his inner demons.

"I'm not a *gut* person, Ellen," he said crossly.

"You're the person I've always known," she whispered, her breath soft against his ear. "The only one I've ever loved."

He jerked, shot her a glance, and what he saw in her blue gaze made him quiver.

"I'm not *gut* enough for you."

"Don't be ridiculous, Isaac."

He stiffened. "I'm not. I'm being reasonable."

"Like you were when I made the mistake of telling you exactly what I thought of Nancy?" She scowled. "I never told you this, Isaac, but while you were seeing her, Nancy came to me and made it clear in no uncertain terms that you were hers, and there was no room in your life for me—your little friend."

"What?"

"She was jealous, although I have no idea why. You were clearly in love with her."

"She didn't love me," he said. "Do you know what she told me when she wanted to break up? That the only reason she agreed to spend time with me was because she was curious. She said she'd been watching television shows about the Amish and she wanted to date one. She thought it would be a lark to date me because of how I was raised." He emitted a growl of displeasure. "I cared for her, but I was just a joke to her. It was her sweetness that first drew me to her, except it was all an act."

"I'm sorry, Isaac."

Ellen stood close to Isaac and felt his lingering pain and disappointment.

"You should leave now," he said. "You'd be wise to leave before I do something and hurt you without meaning to."

He didn't really want her to leave, she realized. His tone told her that he wanted her to stay. "I'm sorry, but I'm staying," she breathed. She touched his forearm, felt his arm muscle contract at her touch. "I'm not going anywhere."

He looked tortured but hopeful. "Ellen…"

She gazed at him, conveying her love for him in her smile. "I care about you, Isaac."

He suddenly stiffened, pulled away. "What about Nate?"

"What about him?"

"He likes you."

She nodded. "*Ja*, he does, but not in the way you think. We're friends. He likes someone else."

"You and Nate are just friends." His gray eyes gleamed when she nodded.

"Nate Peachy is a friend and he took me home after we—"

Isaac looked at her then.

"I don't know what we did. I only know that we need to stop avoiding the issues between us. Nate is a *gut* man, but he's not you. He'll never be you."

He blinked. "Ellen—"

"I care for you, Isaac, more than I've ever cared for anyone. I cared for you before, during and after Nancy. Why do you think I was so devastated when you didn't believe me, when you got mad because I didn't want you to be hurt?" She rubbed her temple against the onset of a headache. "You said that you missed me. Is that true?"

He nodded. "*Ja,* 'tis true."

"*Gut,* because I miss you, too."

He released a shuddering breath. "Ellen, I lied to the authorities and our community. I took the blame for something I didn't do."

"I know." She smirked. "Do you want to go back and do it for real?"

He blinked. Laughed. "I don't believe that's wise. So the truth of what I did doesn't bother you?"

"You were protecting Henry. The truth only makes me love you more." She cradled his jaw with her hand. His skin was warm and there was a stubble of whiskers on his chin. She smiled, imagining how he would look with a beard after they married.

"Ellen…" He closed his eyes as she rubbed her palm from his ear along his jaw to his chin, then up to his other ear. She felt him tremble beneath her fingers.

"Isaac, I want to spend time with you. Can you give me time?" She withdrew her hand and his eyes opened. "I want us to be honest with each other. If you don't feel for me the way I feel about you— Isaac?"

"I love you, Ellen," he said intently. "I would like to spend time with you."

Ellen experienced overwhelming joy.

"But," he went on, "I can't promise you a future."

"I'm only seventeen, Isaac. I'm too young to wed."

She grinned. "Besides, I started my new job at the clinic today."

"How was it?"

"I liked it. It's only for two days a week, which gives me time to do my chores and continue my quilting. And we'll be able to spend some time together."

A light entered Isaac's eyes. Warmth filled his expression. "I'd like that."

She nodded. He reached out then and turned her to fully face him. There was understanding, tenderness and wonder in his beautiful gray eyes. "I'm happy that you like your new job, Ellen. I knew it would be a *gut* fit for you."

"But?" she asked.

"No buts," he whispered as he drew her into his arms. "I am pleased and happy."

She grinned and wrinkled her nose at him.

He laughed, a deep sound that vibrated inside his chest before it burst free and everything felt right and good to Ellen. "You'll come for dinner at my *haus* tomorrow?" she asked.

He seemed uncertain. "We'll be giving your *eldre* the wrong impression." His expression softened as he studied her. "Are you sure you want me to come?"

"*Ja*, I want you come."

He reluctantly agreed. She could tell that he was nervous about the prospect. If he came alone, it would be giving her parents the wrong idea.

"Why don't you bring Joseph and Hannah with you?"

"I don't know about Hannah..."

"Then Daniel and Joseph?"

He nodded as if it solved the problem. "*Ja*, I could bring them."

"*Gut*, then it's settled."

"I'll walk you home."

Her lips twitched. "I have the buggy."

"Then I'll drive you home."

She shook her head. "Then someone will have to drive you back."

"*Nay*, I can walk—"

"Is this the way it's going to be?" she teased. "You always wanting to take me everywhere, worrying about every little thing? 'Tis not dark, Isaac. I'll be fine going home on my own." She gazed at him tenderly. "I will see you tomorrow." She paused. "Are you working?" She was pleased when Isaac shook his head. "Then can we meet tomorrow morning? We can go for a walk, maybe for coffee or tea somewhere."

His features softened. "Nine o'clock?" he asked. There was affection in his gray gaze.

"*Oll recht*. Where?"

"I'll come for you."

She chuckled softly as she shook her head, but she didn't argue. "I'll see you then." She wasn't surprised when he followed her closely as she headed outside.

"*Guten nacht*, Isaac," she murmured.

"*Guten nacht*," Isaac mirrored with tenderness as his fingers caressed her cheek.

Ellen quickly pulled away and climbed into her buggy before she gave in to the urge to linger longer until it was too dark for her to drive home alone. As she left, her heart beat wildly in her chest, and she was warmed by the memory of their conversation.

I love you, Isaac. She hoped that he understood and

believed it. She didn't want to scare him away. She needed him to decide for himself whether or not they were to have a future together. And she prayed and remained hopeful that God had plans that included the two of them together forever.

Chapter Eighteen

Supper at the house with the three Lapp brothers and her family was a noisy, enjoyable affair. Ellen watched with fond amusement as Isaac, Daniel and Joseph teased Will and Elam as they sat down at the table. If there was an air of awkwardness when Isaac and his siblings first arrived, it was gone within minutes of them all sitting down together at the table. Guests were always welcome at *Mam's* table. She didn't question why the Lapp boys had chosen to visit them. Before eating, they all bowed their heads and her father said a prayer to ask for the Lord's blessing of their food. Ellen peeked up to study the occupants at the table and smiled warmly as she encountered Isaac, who was doing the same thing.

Mam had prepared a number of her favorite dishes. There was roast beef and pork sausage and a bowl of chicken potpie. Ellen had helped to prepare the dried-corn casserole and mashed potatoes. She had also made the raisin bread with white frosting. If the way they were consuming their food was any indication, the young men at the table thought the meal good. Ellen smiled as she studied her brothers before her gaze settled on *Mam*. Her mother smiled and nodded. She was enjoying the company of her family and dinner guests along with her food.

As she reached for the bowl of potatoes, Ellen became conscious of her father's gaze on her. She grinned at him, pleased when he relaxed and smiled back. When her two brothers and the three Lapps took turns teasing her, she gasped and rose from her seat in outrage.

Daniel and Joseph Lapp stared at her in stunned horror, clearly believing that they'd somehow offended her.

"I'm sorry, Ellen," Joseph said.

Isaac didn't say a word as he silently studied her, amused. She blinked and tried not to let on that she was pretending. But she had a feeling that somehow he'd known.

"*Ja*, Ellen, we didn't mean anything by the things we said," Daniel said.

"We're sorry, Ellen," Elam apologized, much to Ellen's glee.

She stared at her brothers, frowned as she glanced at each and every male in the kitchen except her father and Isaac, who still hadn't said a word during the exchange.

Ellen burst out laughing. "As if you could hurt my feelings with a little teasing…" She narrowed her gaze. "But be careful. I have a long memory."

Joseph and Daniel chuckled. Elam and Will gazed at her as if she were a stranger. They'd never seen this teasing side of her before. Isaac's lips twitched as if he was holding himself back.

Ellen sat down and set to passing around the brownies she'd made for dessert. Her gaze settled on Isaac, who continued to regard her with amusement and something more. She was infused with warmth at the affection she saw in his gaze. She shot a quick glance toward her mother, who watched them both with curiosity while managing to hide her thoughts.

"Who wants custard pie?" she asked cheerfully after she'd passed around the brownie plate. She looked at the man directly across from her. "Isaac?"

Eyes gleaming, he nodded. *"Ja, danki."*

She frowned at him until his mouth stretched into a grin. She enjoyed having everyone at the table, and the realization that her father wasn't eyeing Isaac as if he were a criminal or worse made things more pleasurable.

The dinner that evening set the tone for the next several days. She and Isaac spent their every free moment together. They weren't blatant about meeting. She assumed her family would accept their friendship as they had in the past.

Isaac wasn't courting her. There was no mention of a future again, so Ellen simply welcomed the time she got to spend in his company. Ellen still sensed that Isaac was troubled by his past. He hadn't made up his mind about whether or not to stay in Happiness or leave. After a week had passed, then two, then a month, Isaac hadn't said anything about his decision, and Ellen began to worry about his leaving. She knew that she would be devastated if he chose to go. With every day, she fell deeper in love with him, and she didn't know how she would go on without him.

One night, they decided to meet in their special spot on her father's farm after they'd eaten supper in their own homes. Ellen gladdened at the sight of Isaac when she found him waiting for her on her grandfather's wooden bench. She hadn't expected him to arrive first and it pleased her immensely that he might have been anxious to see her.

"Isaac," she murmured as she drew close to him.

He stood and she gazed up into his beautiful gray eyes. "*Hallo*, Ellen," he said quietly.

Something different in his demeanor drew her attention. She experienced a cold feeling of dread.

"What's wrong?" she asked worriedly.

"We have to talk."

"About what?" She stared at him. "You made a decision."

He nodded. "Ellen—"

"You're going to leave. You've decided to leave me."

"Ellen—"

"I love you, Isaac. I want you to know that. It's not just about caring—it's about love."

"And I love you. I'll always love you."

Her eyes filled with tears. "But you're leaving." She looked away.

He grasped her shoulders, turned her to face him fully. "Now, why would I do that when I have everything I've ever wanted or needed right here?"

She blinked, saw him watching her with bright eyes. "I don't understand—"

"You. You're everything I've ever wanted."

"I am?" she whispered, filled with emotion.

"I love you, Ellen Mast." He smiled, cupped her cheek. "These last weeks have shown me that I can be happy again. You've made me happy, Ellen." He cocked his head as his lips curved into an affectionate smile. "I want to court you officially. I want to marry you someday. I understand that it can't be soon, at least, not soon enough to suit me, but with your clinic work and our ages, I know 'tis better if we wait. Besides, I have to start saving for a place for us to live."

Ellen's tears flowed unchecked down her cheeks. "Am I dreaming? Or did you just tell me that you want to court me?"

"You're awake and, *ja*, I did." He appeared confident of his decision, of their love. She started to sob loudly.

"Ellen!" he moaned. "What's wrong?"

She lifted her head and allowed him to see her longing and love for him. "Nothing's wrong, Isaac. Everything is right. I love you."

Relief had him sagging a moment with closed eyes. When he opened them again, he pulled her close and hugged her tightly. He loosened his hold but didn't let her go. "I wish—"

"Ja?" she prompted.

Isaac gazed at the woman he loved and wondered why he'd never seen it before, that Ellen Mast was perfect for him in every way. "I wish I could turn back the clock to a time before I hurt you. I wish we could start over."

"We are starting over."

He caressed her cheek. "What did I do to deserve you?" he murmured. She had saved him. He finally felt as if his life was full. He had to accept that after all this time Henry Yoder was never going to come forward with the truth. But it no longer mattered, because Ellen believed in him, and he realized that her belief and trust in him was more than enough for him.

"Are you ever going to kiss me, Isaac?" she asked softly.

He gave a jolt. He'd been longing to kiss her for weeks now, but he hadn't wanted to do anything he shouldn't.

"We're courting now, *ja*?" she said saucily.

He stifled a grin.

"Then?" she prompted.

A tremor coursed through him as he bent to kiss her in a gentle, tender meeting of mouths. He quickly raised his head and stepped back. He saw the dreamy look on her face and felt satisfied.

"Isaac?"

"Ja?" He stepped close once again to reach out and cradle her face with his hands. "I love you."

She sighed happily. *"Gut*, because I love you."

Weeks went by and Ellen enjoyed the warm and fuzzy glow of having an attentive sweetheart. They were courting—not that anyone knew it yet. They weren't ready for marriage, so they kept their meetings private, which was what couples living in an Amish community who were in love did until they were ready to wed.

They found time to be together each day, even on the days when one or both of them worked. Sometimes it was late when they met in their special place. On certain occasions, it was Ellen who arrived first, but more times than not, it was Isaac who waited for her in the dark with some little token of his affection, like a wildflower he'd picked for her or a pretty rock he'd found at the job site. But it was the look in his eyes and the way he reached for her hand when he saw her that was the greatest gift to Ellen. She would never ask for more than Isaac's love. With him, she had everything she ever wanted or needed.

It was on a Friday morning when Isaac suggested they head to Whittier's Store for some licorice, something else they both enjoyed. Inside, Ellen waited by his side as Isaac picked out two boxes of candy. He handed her a box of Good and Plentys. Together they wandered outside to enjoy it in the warm early-summer sun.

"I should have known you were the one for me when I realized that we share the same taste in many foods," Isaac said.

"Truly grounds for a perfect match," she teased.

They sat down on the benches that Bob had added recently on the side of the store away from the parking lot. Ellen enjoyed the burst of candy coating flavor followed by the lovely taste of anise in her mouth.

"Want a soda?" Isaac asked.

She shrugged. "Maybe later. Not now."

Suddenly, Ellen suffered an awful sense of foreboding. Her stomach started to burn, the fire rising up inside her chest, down her neck and along her back even before she heard someone say his name.

"Isaac."

Ellen glanced toward the person who'd spoken, a girl with light brown hair and no makeup but with a face she'd never be able to forget.

"It's me, Isaac," she said as if confirming it. "Nancy."

Isaac appeared stunned as he rose slowly to his feet. "Nancy, what are you doing here?"

Gone were the English girl's dark hair and clothes, strange jewelry and ruby-red lips. The girl before her was a young woman so opposite in appearance from the girl Isaac had fallen for hard that he stared, dumbfounded. Nancy gazed at him like she was happy to see him…

"May I talk with you a minute?" Nancy asked softly.

Isaac glanced at Ellen before looking back. "For a minute," he said.

Nancy's back, Ellen thought. Isaac's reaction made her feel physically ill.

She watched with growing horror as the man she loved walked away to talk privately with the *Englisher*. Stricken, Ellen looked the other way, unable to watch the two of them together.

But then she had to look back. She couldn't help herself. Nancy stood with her arms out while Isaac held on to the girl's hands. They seemed to be speaking urgently, but Ellen couldn't tell what they were saying and she was afraid to guess. Was the girl asking him for forgiveness, pleading with him to give her another chance?

Isaac flashed her a glance. Ellen forced herself to smile and dip her head as if acknowledging his right to talk with the girl. He said something to Nancy, then broke away, heading in her direction. Ellen drew a fortifying breath and managed to gaze at him with unconcern as he drew near.

"I have to go with her. She needs…" He seemed reluctant to continue.

"Oll recht," she said breezily. "I can find my way home."

He shook his head. "I can drop you home on the way."

"Nay," she replied with a smile, although inside she was slowly dying. "I need to shop for a few things."

"Then I'll come back for you."

"No need. I just saw Nate's brother Jacob. I'll get a ride with him."

"I'll meet you as soon as I can."

She shrugged indifferently.

Isaac gazed at her a long moment as if hesitant to leave her. "Ellen…"

"Isaac?" Nancy urged. The girl approached. Ellen narrowed her eyes, but the *Englisher* avoided her gaze.

"I'm coming," he said, then turned to Ellen. "I'll see you later."

Ellen could only nod.

Then she watched as the man she loved with all of her heart left with his former sweetheart.

"When did this start?" Isaac asked the girl on the buggy seat beside him. He'd been shocked to see the bruises on her arms.

"Three years ago, but not as much as now."

He eyed Nancy with horror. "Brad has been hitting you, abusing you, for three years?"

Nancy blinked back tears. "Yes. It's why I asked you not to say anything that night—to take the blame for something you didn't do."

"I didn't take the blame. I just didn't defend myself. And I didn't do it for you." He paused. "I did it for Henry."

She nodded as if she understood. She looked miserable, and after hearing her story, he couldn't help but feel sorry for her. Sorry and nothing more.

I love Ellen. He realized that he'd merely been infatuated with Nancy. Just as she had been curious and interested in him because he was from an Amish household, he had been curious and interested in her, he realized, because she was English and wildly different in dress and attitude.

"Where are we going?" she asked meekly.

He still couldn't believe that this girl without makeup, black hair and dark clothes was Nancy Smith. "To someone who can help you."

"But—"

"He's a *gut* man. He will figure out how to keep you safe." He tensed his jaw. "You weren't kind to Ellen," he said.

She shook her head. "I'm sorry."

"You should be telling her."

"I owe you an apology, too."

"No need. I'm fine." And he was, because he had Ellen's love.

Nancy was silent as Isaac steered the buggy toward Abram Peachy's residence. As deacon, Abram would know what to do. Within minutes, he put on his right battery-operated turn signal and pulled into the dirt drive that lead to Abram's farmhouse.

As he pulled up and parked the buggy near the house, he saw the door to the house open and Abram, Charlotte and three of their six children exit the structure.

"Isaac!" Abram exclaimed with pleasure. "What brings you here?"

Isaac stepped out of the buggy, walked around to the other side. "I have someone who needs your help. She isn't safe at home. I was hoping you could find a safe haven for her." As he spoke, he opened the door and helped Nancy to alight.

Abram and Charlotte, he saw, were eyeing the girl with curiosity yet without censure.

"Are you in need of a safe place to stay?" Abram asked.

She nodded shyly. "Yes, sir."

"Abram." The man smiled. "Charlotte? Why don't you take…"

"Nancy," Isaac supplied, and he saw surprised understanding brighten Abram's features.

"Nancy," he said softly. "Go with my wife. We will help you. You must be hungry. We have plenty to eat. One thing we always have is *gut* food."

After Charlotte had taken the girl inside with soft words for her children to follow, Isaac found himself alone with Abram.

"Her brother hits her," he said. Then he went on to tell Abram exactly what Nancy had told him. "Check her arms, and you'll see what I mean."

Abram nodded. "We'll see that she reaches safety in a *gut* home."

Isaac bowed his head. *"Danki."* He turned to go.

"Isaac!" Abram's voice stopped him.

He turned. *"Ja?"*

"What is this girl to you?"

"Someone I once thought I knew. Now she is simply a stranger who needs help."

Abram nodded as if satisfied. Isaac started to leave and then turned back. "Abram, may I have a word with you?"

The man nodded.

"Privately?"

"*Ja*, you may say what you want and it will go no further unless you want it to."

Then Isaac told him what was on his mind and the good deacon listened carefully while he talked until he had nothing more to say.

Ellen was home, helping her mother with the baking. She felt frozen inside, half-numb, as she recalled Nancy's arrival and the way Isaac had simply left her in favor of the *Englisher*.

What if he changed his mind about loving her now that Nancy was back? she wondered.

Isaac had told her he loved her. She had to trust in his love. Still, it hurt to see him with the girl.

I love you, Isaac. I want you to be happy. She stifled a sob as she rolled and then pounded fresh bread dough.

She'd hoped that he would have come by now. Why had he gone with her? What possible reason would make him urgently leave with the *Englisher*?

"Ellen," *Mam* said, "what's wrong?"

She looked at her mother, managed to smile. "I'm fine."

"*Nay*, you're not, but I won't press. You'll tell me when you're ready."

Ellen nodded, then went back to work, preparing the dough for baking.

A knock on the front door drew her and *Mam's* attention. "I'll get it," her mother said.

Ellen heard talking but couldn't distinguish the owner of the voice or the tone. Then her mother returned to the kitchen, her expression guarded. *"Mam?"*

"You've got a visitor," she said. "You'd best talk with him."

"Him?" Ellen said, feeling a nervous flutter.

"Isaac."

"I don't know—"

"Go talk with him, Ellen. The man is extremely upset. He thinks he's hurt you and he needs to see you."

Ellen raised her eyebrows. "He told you all that?"

Mam shrugged. "Just talk with him before he goes away."

Ellen quickly wiped her hands on a tea towel and hurried toward the front door.

"Isaac," she whispered as soon as she saw him.

He gazed at her with a strange sort of hunger in his eyes. "Ellen, can we talk?"

She glanced quickly over her shoulder, saw they were alone, then nodded. As she stepped outside, she was shocked when he took her hand and clasped it firmly. The warmth of his fingers against her own was nearly her undoing. He was everything to her.

Isaac led her to their special spot.

"Ellen, I'm sorry," he began.

"I understand. Nancy is back and you love her."

He looked stunned. "*Nay!* That's not true! I want you—I love only you."

"I don't understand. You left with her."

"She needed help. I took her to Abram's." His features softened. "I love you, Ellen. And I just said so to Abram."

Ellen caught her breath. "You told the deacon?" She felt the budding warmth of happiness.

He nodded. "I brought Nancy to him for protection." He assisted her onto the wooden bench, then took his seat next to her. Keeping her hand in his, he cradled it against his thigh. "Her brother, Brad—" Ellen shuddered at the name. "He's been beating her for years. I didn't realize it but it makes sense. I guess I should have known."

"Why didn't Nancy leave home before now?" she asked as joy filled the space where her pain had lodged.

"He'd never beat her this badly. You should have seen her arms—I couldn't believe it. She told her mother what he'd done, and the woman didn't believe Nancy. She chose her son over her own daughter."

Ellen gasped, her eyes filling with tears. "That's terrible."

"Ja," he said as he turned, reached out to touch her face with the back of the fingers of his other hand. "I told Abram about you. I told him I didn't know when, but that I planned to marry you, and that…" he blushed "…I thought you felt the same." He was quiet as he continued to caress her cheek while he waited for her response.

"I do want to marry you." She wondered if she could wait to have him as her husband.

"I love you, Ellen."

She felt her heart overflow with love. "Isaac Lapp, you're all I've ever wanted." She closed her eyes briefly. "I thought I'd lost you to Nancy. Again."

"Never," he replied urgently. He gazed at her with love. "I confronted Nancy about the way she treated you." He clamped his teeth together. "She didn't deny it. Said she was sorry. I told her that she should be apologizing to you."

She saw the proof of his love in his expression, naked for her to see. They were meant to be together. She'd prayed and God had answered her prayers, showing her the truth of His love.

"I love you, Isaac."

He beamed at her. "I love you, Ellen."

"Ellen!"

They heard Ellen's mother and rose to head back toward the house. Ellen felt a spring in her step that came with happiness and the wonder of loving and being loved.

As they reached the gate, Isaac stilled. "Your *eldre*."

"My parents will accept you," she said with resolve.

"I hope so. I don't want to be the cause of any more pain for you. If your *mam* and *dat* won't approve of me—"

"The only way you could hurt me is to leave me."

"I don't think I can leave you."

They walked out of the pasture and into the yard to discover her mother by the clothesline, taking down clothes.

Isaac stopped and with a grin picked up Ellen at the waist and spun her around. "I love you," he whispered. As soon as he set her down, she broke away but met his smile with a loving look of her own.

"Mam," she breathed as she felt the first raindrop. She ran to help her mother hurriedly take down her clothes.

"Ach, there you are." She smiled as Ellen unclipped clothespins as fast as her fingers could manage. To her mother—and Ellen's—shock, Isaac joined them, his masculine fingers assisting with rapid speed and skill.

"There, all finished," Isaac said. He reached down to pick up the full laundry basket. "Where would you like these?"

"In the *kiche*," *Mam* said, referring to the kitchen.

He nodded and followed them into the house. He

stepped inside, set down the basket and then reached for Ellen's hand. "Josie," he said, "I'm in love with your *dochter.*"

Josie studied him thoroughly and Ellen was pleased to see him gaze back at her without fear. "Well," *Mam* said, "'tis about time."

Isaac blinked. Ellen gasped. "You're not surprised?" she asked.

A soft smile settled on her mother's mouth. "You two have cared for each other for years. I was wondering if you'd ever get together—so, *ja.* 'Tis about time."

"But *Dat*—"

"What about *Dat*?" her father said as he entered the room from the front of the house. He took one look at his daughter holding hands with Isaac Lapp.

"Oh, *gut*! It finally happened."

"But I thought you disapproved of me," Isaac began.

"For that incident at Whittier's Store? We know you, Isaac. You didn't do it. You may have been protecting someone, but you yourself would never do anything to hurt a friend—and Bob Whittier is a friend."

Ellen was stunned to see Isaac's eyes glisten as if he was emotionally moved and trying to hold back tears.

"See?" Ellen said. "Like me, they never believed in your guilt. And they will come to love you as I do." When Isaac arched an eyebrow with amusement, she blushed. "Well, not as I do, but as a *soohn.*"

"Will we be getting a visit from the deacon?" *Dat* asked.

"You can count on it," Isaac said, much to Ellen's delight.

Epilogue

A year later, on a sunny day during the month of November, Isaac and Ellen stood before their families and the entire church congregation to pledge their love for each other as they wed. Ellen's cousin Mary Ruth had come for their special day. Ellen was glad to see her and took her cousin's ribbing about Isaac good-naturedly.

No one witnessing the event could doubt the bride and groom's love and their commitment to each other.

Although Isaac had remained silent on the subject of Whittier's Store, the truth finally had come out when Henry Yoder confessed his role in the crime to the church elders and then later to Bob Whittier. His confession didn't come immediately; it happened well after Josie and William Mast had given their approval and blessing for Isaac and Ellen's marriage.

During the past year, Ellen had continued her work at the Westmore Clinic. She enjoyed doing her part to help special children and she would continue there into the future, at least for a little while. Now she wanted nothing more than a life with Isaac and to give her husband children—lots of them.

All the members of the Lapp family stood by, watching with love and joy as Isaac wed his beautiful Ellen. Like the Masts, they had always believed in Isaac's innocence, but they had been waiting for him to come to them with the truth. They didn't approve of his taking the blame for Henry, but they understood why Isaac had kept silent about his friend.

As he stood next to his lovely bride, Isaac felt a peace and happiness he'd never expected to feel again.

"Ellen," Isaac whispered as he leaned close before they headed outside to the vehicle that would take them to the William Mast farmhouse, where a wedding feast would be provided for all.

"Ja?" she breathed, looking deeply into his eyes. She would never grow tired of gazing into those gray orbs, of standing at Isaac's side, of feeling the warmth of his touch.

"I love you, Ellen Lapp," he murmured as he dipped his head to brush his lips against her forehead.

Thrilled to hear her new surname, Ellen gazed lovingly at her groom, then leaned close to whisper, "Isaac, my dear husband, I love you even more."

* * * * *

A GROOM FOR GRETA

Anna Schmidt

For Larry

But you delight in sincerity of heart
and in secret you teach me wisdom
—*Psalms* 51:6

Chapter One

Celery Fields, Florida
Summer 1934

Luke Starns hammered the molten iron into shape, the sound of metal on metal ringing in his ears as the hammer struck the rod. He set the half-completed horseshoe on the white-hot fire and wiped his brow with the back of his bare forearm. Then he stretched as he pushed open the single window that offered relief from the shadowy darkness of his blacksmith shop and livery stable. He was hoping for a breeze, but this was Florida, not Ontario. And it was August, steamy and humid, and at four in the afternoon there was no sign of relief from the oppressive heat. He fanned himself with the wide-brimmed straw hat that was one of the unmistakable signs of his Amish heritage.

Business was slow but not nearly as slow as it was in the outside world—the rest of Florida. The economic depression that had gripped the entire United States had taken a huge toll on businesses and lives all across the state. Luke counted himself fortunate that he had skills that were still in demand—although with the growing number of cars and trucks crowding the roads, he wasn't sure how long there would be enough customers to sustain his business.

He thought about taking a break, perhaps getting a dish of ice cream at the parlor next to the bakery. He wasn't exactly dressed for shopping but it was late on a Saturday. Most everyone living in and around the Amish settlement of Celery Fields would have already headed home. As he rolled down the sleeves to his collarless shirt, he heard voices just outside the small window—a man and a woman—the man's voice was stern and serious, the woman's laughter was high-pitched and nervous.

"I can't marry you, Greta Goodloe," the man announced. Luke sighed. Quarrels between Greta and her long-time beau, Josef Bontrager, were so common that most of the townspeople tended to ignore them completely. Luke was inclined to agree that this was probably the best plan. He finished rolling down his sleeves and glanced out the window when he heard the soft plod of horse hooves in the sandy street and saw Bontrager's dark buggy driving away. After that all was quiet.

Wiping his hands—black with the soot of his work—on a rag he kept hanging by the window, he removed his leather apron and checked the front of his homespun cotton shirt. Then he ran his fingers through his damp black hair and reached for his hat. A dish of Jeremiah Troyer's vanilla ice cream was sounding better and better, but he wanted to at least make the effort to look decent before venturing out. His concern was not for himself, but he felt it was just good manners to make the effort for others. He was headed for the door of his shop when he heard a sound.

The two double doors to his blacksmith shop and livery stood fully ajar but there was no one there. At least that he could see. Then he heard the sound again. A soft keening like someone in pain. He moved closer to the door's opening and there framed in the doorway, cast in silhouette by the late afternoon sun at her back, stood a woman—an unwed Amish woman, given the black ties of her prayer *kapp* that peeked out from beneath her bonnet. She was grasping the frame of the doorway.

Fearing that she had been struck ill or perhaps overcome by the heat, Luke rushed forward. On his way he grabbed the shop's one battered chair. "Hold on," he ordered, but before he could reach her, she took two steps forward and then started to crumple to the floor. Luke dropped the chair and caught the woman.

"What's to become of me?" she whispered as she looked up at him from beneath the brim of her bonnet with fathomless sea blue eyes that belonged to only one female in Celery Fields.

Greta Goodloe.

"Are you ill, Greta Goodloe?" he asked, raising his voice in case she might be on the verge of passing out. "Wounded? Have you been in an accident?"

"Oh, he's broken it," she moaned miserably, her voice choking on her sobs.

"Who? What is broken?"

She looked up at him, her eyes widening in what he could only describe as horror. With surprising strength for one so petite, she pushed him away and stood without support for the first time since entering his shop.

She glanced around and seemed stunned to find herself there, but she no longer appeared to be in danger of passing out.

"Sit down," Luke ordered, sliding the chair behind her. "Let me have a look. Is it your…" He ran through the possibilities. She was standing without apparent pain on both legs. Her arms were flailing about like windmills as she apparently tried to regain control of her emotions. "Where is the pain, Greta Goodloe?" he shouted, hoping to break through what was clearly a case of hysteria.

"Right here," she announced, clutching at her chest. "And please stop shouting. Do you want the whole town to witness my…" Fresh tears leaked down her cheeks and she sat down hard in the chair and buried her face in her hands as her entire body shuddered with the force of her crying.

She was awfully young for a heart attack but he seemed to recall that her father had died of one a year or so earlier and her mother had succumbed to heart failure when Greta was but a toddler. If it ran in the family…

"Stay there. I'll go for the doctor."

She was on her feet in an instant and looking mighty healthy for a woman having palpitations. "You will do no such thing," she growled. "You will have the decency to forget that I ever came in here today, that you ever witnessed…" Once again her eyes filled with fresh tears. "My shame," she whispered and sat down on the chair.

Only this time she did not fall to pieces as Luke might have expected. Instead she looked all around the shop, finally settling her gaze on him. Then she drew in a heavy sigh and fixed him with a look that seemed rather harsh, considering he had done nothing more than show her kindness and concern.

"So, Luke Starns, we have a problem. That is, I have a problem—several of them at the moment. But let's begin with addressing the problem before you and me."

"I'm listening," he replied. "I'll help if I can but I'm not sure what…"

"Oh, please do not pretend that you weren't eavesdropping just now," she snapped. "I saw you standing by that window there. You had to have heard and seen every horrible bit of it."

Luke frowned. "And I am telling you that whatever might have taken place between you and Josef Bontrager…"

"There," she interrupted pointing her finger at him, "you admit it. You were watching us. I have not so much as mentioned Josef's name and still you…"

Luke had no time and little patience for her tantrum. "You are speaking in riddles, Greta Goodloe. This is my establishment and if I take a moment from my work to stand at my window that is my right."

"Your window is open as are your doors. Do you honestly expect me to believe that you did not hear my conversation with Josef?"

"I cannot say what you will believe or not. I am telling you that whatever business you had just now with Josef is of no interest to me. And now if you are feeling better I have work to do." He abandoned the idea of ice cream and headed back toward the fire. But given that Greta Goodloe was right there next to him when he turned to pick up his apron, it was evident that this was not yet over.

* * *

He was dismissing her. Greta was certain that the blacksmith had heard and seen everything. When Josef had driven away, she'd seen Luke Starns watching from his window—the window that overlooked the town's main and only street. Her intent in entering the shadowy recesses of his shop had been to confront him and make sure that he did not speak of what he had seen to anyone else. For surely Josef's announcement was some nightmare from which she would awaken any moment.

One minute she and Josef Bontrager—the man she would finally marry after five long years of courtship—were looking at a china teapot in Yoder's Dry Goods. The next they were crossing the street on their way to the lane that led past the blacksmith and livery stables and on to the small house that Greta shared with her older sister, Lydia.

Suddenly Josef had stopped walking and when she had turned back to him, her chatter about plans for their wedding momentarily silenced, Josef had looked down at his dusty boots and said the very last thing she could ever have imagined coming from his mouth.

"I cannot marry you, Greta Goodloe."

At first Greta's mind had raced with any possible cause for Josef's unbelievable declaration. "You mean this autumn?"

Tradition had it that marriages took place in late autumn after the fall harvest. At least that had been the way of things up north where most of the Florida Amish had lived before migrating to Celery Fields. Of course, in Florida late autumn was just when the planting started. The following day at services, Bishop

Troyer would announce all the weddings that would take place that fall.

So Greta and Josef had planned their wedding for September to give themselves plenty of time to travel north for the traditional round of visits with family and friends. They'd be back in time to plant the fields of celery, the cash crop on the large farm that Josef had taken over when his father and brothers decided to move back north.

"I mean I know times have been hard," she had rushed to add, wanting to assure Josef that in spite of his constant worries over financial matters, they would be fine. He was always talking about the depression and how even though business in Celery Fields had not been affected, there could come a time when the community would feel the ravages of the financial disaster sweeping the rest of the country.

"I suppose that we could wait one more year," she added, hoping to find some way to quell his worries. She would be twenty-three by then, almost as old as Lydia was now. But still if Josef thought it best to wait…

Josef's features had been shadowed by the brim of his hat. "This isn't about hard times, Greta." He sucked in air as if he'd been underwater for far too long. "Well, there's that, of course, but what I mean to say, Greta, is that I can't marry you—ever."

"Oh, Josef, is this because you saw me talking to the Hadwells' cousin last week?"

Josef snorted and transferred his gaze from the ground to the sky, still refusing to look directly at her. "You certainly seemed to be enjoying your time with him."

"So, you're jealous." Relief mixed with irritation flooded her veins. This was not the first time that Josef had been upset with her for what he saw as flirting and she saw as simply being herself. "The Hadwells' cousin has gone back home to Indiana," she pointed out.

"There will be others," Josef muttered.

Greta counted to ten. How many times had she reassured this man over the course of their lives together? How many more times would she have to apologize for being herself? She closed her eyes and prayed for guidance—and patience.

"Well," she replied with a smile that felt as if it might actually make her face crack, "if that is your decision…" And with a toss of her head she had continued on across the street. She'd been so certain that Josef would come after her. He always did. He would apologize. She would accept his apology and reassure him that he was the one for her and that would be that.

She had almost reached the blacksmith shop before she realized that Josef was not coming after her. Indeed after a moment she heard the jingle of harness and the creak of buggy wheels headed out of town. He had left her. Her step faltered. Her mind had reeled with the possible options of where she might go. She could have gone to the school where Lydia would be preparing lessons for her students for the coming week. She could have gone to the bakery where her half sister, Pleasant, would also be preparing to close up shop for the day, or to Bishop Troyer's house where his wife, Mildred, would undoubtedly offer her a sympathetic ear and a nice cold glass of lemonade.

That's when she looked up and saw Luke Starns,

the dark mysterious man who had shown up in Celery Fields just a few months earlier, standing at his window. He must have seen and heard everything. In an instant she had retraced her steps, determined to set Luke Starns straight about minding his own business.

But when she had reached the open doorway of Luke's business, she had caught a glimpse of Josef's buggy disappearing in a cloud of dust and the full force of what had just happened had hit her like a blow to her stomach. For one horrible instant she could not seem to breathe and her knees had turned to jam. She had grasped the rough door frame for support and barely noticed as a splinter pierced her thumb.

Now as the blacksmith loomed over her—all six feet and more of him—she sucked at her injured thumb and considered her options.

"Do you have a cut?" Luke asked, nodding toward her hand.

Greta instantly ripped her thumb from her mouth and curled her other fingers around it. "No. It's a splinter—from your doorway," she added as if he had purposefully left the offending object there to wound her.

"Let me look at it," he said as he gently took hold of her hand and coaxed her fingers open. Then he held her hand closer to the light of the fire, examined the wound and frowned.

For her part Greta was taken aback at the contrast of her hand—small and very white—resting on his rougher, larger, burnished palm. He reached for a pail of clear water with a tin dipper resting in it and trickled a little of the cooling water over her thumb. Fascinated in spite of her determination to maintain her focus on the larger problems at hand, Greta watched as with surprising dexterity for one with such thick fingers he worked free the splinter.

"There," he said, and the word came out as if he'd been holding his breath until the deed was done. He released her hand. Filling the dipper with fresh water, he offered it to her. "Drink this."

She did as he asked, more to buy time than because she was thirsty. She found that the absence of his hand holding hers was troubling—as if she had been deprived of something precious. It was a ridiculous idea of course. She was simply missing the absence of Josef's touch. This had nothing to do with Luke Starns, nothing at all.

"Denki," she said, thanking him as she drank the water then handed back the dipper. She waited until he had turned to set the bucket back in its place before adding, "I want to set your mind at ease but first I must know how much you overheard?"

"Bitte?"

"Of the disagreement between Josef and me," she reminded him. When he said nothing, she added, "We seem to have a lot of those these days."

Luke remained silent.

"Nerves, I expect—for both of us," Greta explained, warming to her tale. This earned her a flicker of curiosity from the blacksmith's deep-set eyes.

"The wedding?" she reminded him. *Men. How could they be so incredibly thickheaded about the important events of life?*

She glanced toward the street and across the way she saw her half sister, Pleasant, locking up the bakery for the night. Her conversation with Josef had taken place right out in the open where anyone might have seen or heard—not just Luke Starns. Panicked anew at the thought of others witnessing the scene, Greta made a quick inventory of the businesses along the street. Yoder's Dry Goods where Hilda Yoder was known to keep an eye on everything that might happen in town. But three local women had passed by Josef and Greta as they left the shop. So Hilda would have been busy serving her customers when Josef made his astounding announcement.

The hardware store next door to the blacksmith's? Roger Hadwell and his wife, Gertrude, were known gossips but neither of them had been in evidence when Josef made his stunning pronouncement. Greta breathed a little easier and decided that she only had to worry about the blacksmith. She studied him for a long moment, trying to decide on her best strategy. Charm had always been her most potent weapon for getting herself out of any tight spot. But would charm work on this man?

Luke Starns was not someone she had had the opportunity to get to know. The truth was that she had kept her distance from him. There was something about him that stirred a shyness in her that simply was not there with anyone else. Perhaps it was his looks. Where most of the men in Celery Fields—as well as the women—were fair with white-blond hair and skin that freckled easily, Luke Starns was dark— his hair was as black as the leather apron he wore to do his work. His skin was deeply tanned as if he spent his days outdoors instead of hunched over a roaring fire hammering bridle bits and horseshoes into shape. And his eyes were set deep under a brow of thick black eyebrows and were the most unexpected shade of blue—like cornflowers, Greta had thought the first time she'd seen him at services.

Of course, from the minute he'd arrived in Celery Fields, every woman in town had begun planning a match for him. Theirs was a small community and that meant that the available number of eligible men for every single female in the town was limited. The preferred candidate for Luke Starns was Greta's sister, Lydia. But Lydia had dismissed such idle speculation as she had all hints that this man or that might make a good match for her.

"Don't you want to marry?" Greta had asked.

"Yes, that would be nice. But I will not settle, sister. I'd rather spend my days alone."

Now Greta shuddered in spite of the oppressive heat of the August day. The very idea that in the face of Josef's abandonment she might now spend *her* days alone was beyond her ability to comprehend. How would she survive? What would she do? Lydia had her students who adored her, but Greta—what did she have? Practically her entire life, everyone had simply assumed that one day she would marry Josef, keep house for him in the impressive farmhouse that set on the edge of town, and fill that house with babies.

That had been the plan—until twenty minutes ago.

She felt Luke watching her now. There was not a single reason to think he had any interest in what had happened between Josef and her. *Oh, the sin of conceit,* she thought as she stood up and pressed her hands over her green cotton skirt—the one that Josef had always liked.

"The wedding?" Luke prompted her now.

Greta pasted on a smile that came as naturally to

her as breathing. "I am quite aware that you may believe that what you witnessed between Josef and me earlier was unusual. I assure you that it was not. Josef is having an attack of nerves, nothing more."

He frowned. "*Yah,* you are probably right."

"I am right," she assured him and almost believed it herself. "So there is no need for you to concern yourself with my…"

"Might this mean that Josef Bontrager will not be available to drive you and your sister to services tomorrow then?" he asked.

The idea had not yet occurred to Greta. Oh, the ripples this thing was going to have if Josef didn't come to his senses before morning. She was barely aware that Luke had continued speaking, so caught up was she in the ramifications Josef's fit of pique might have.

"Because if that is the case then I would be pleased to drive you—and Lydia Goodloe. It is on my way."

As she forced her attention back to the blacksmith, Greta bristled. The man had some nerve. "Luke Starns, it has not been yet half an hour since the man I thought for years I would wed has broken with me. And you want me to set all that aside so you can court me in his stead?"

She saw him stiffen with wounded pride. It was a male trait that she was well familiar with. After all, she'd observed it numerous times in Josef.

"*Neh,* Greta Goodloe." He held up both hands as if to ward off such an unpleasant thought.

He didn't have to look quite so repulsed, Greta thought. "Forgive me," she said. "I misunderstood. It has been…"

But Luke did not allow her to finish her apology

before blurting out, "It is not you but your sister that I wish to call upon."

And suddenly the events of the day seemed far too ridiculous to be real. Were the tables to be turned so that Lydia was the one to be courted and wed while Greta spent her days alone? She couldn't help herself. She started to laugh and could not seem to stop.

"Lydia?" Greta finally managed to form the word. "You have finally found your nerve and set your sights on Lydia?"

"I have." Everything about his posture challenged her to dispute his decision.

"My sister is not seeking a match," Greta warned. But the more Greta thought about it, the better the idea seemed to her. Why shouldn't Lydia find happiness even if Greta herself seemed doomed to eternal spinsterhood? After all, everyone in town had speculated that the best possible match for the blacksmith would be Lydia. For months now the local gossips had been waiting for Luke to make his move. Apparently he had finally decided to do so. "On the other hand, perhaps she has not considered every available candidate." She walked around him, studying him carefully. "Would you consider a bargain?"

"A bargain?"

"Yes. I will do what I can to help in your campaign to win my sister's affection. And in return, you will say nothing to anyone about what you observed earlier between Josef and me."

He sighed wearily. "How many times must I say this? I heard nothing. I did see you with Josef outside my window as I have seen the two of you and many other people in town numerous times before. I cannot be responsible for what takes place on the other side of the glass, Greta."

"Yes or no," she challenged. "I can be more influential than you may suspect in whether or not Lydia takes your attentions seriously."

Luke chuckled. "Why, Greta Goodloe, are you threatening me?"

"Not at all. After all, I have no control over what you may do with whatever information you gathered while observing Josef and me earlier." She fought to keep her voice steady. It was very important to her that the whole town should not know the embarrassing circumstances of Josef's sudden decision to call off their engagement. She looked up at Luke, wondering if she could trust this relative stranger to hold his tongue when the gossip began—as it surely would. "Please," she whispered.

"Very well. We have a bargain, Greta. One I fully intend to see that you keep. I will call for you and your sister tomorrow morning and…"

But Greta had lost interest in the conversation as she once again faced the fact that after five years of courtship—on the eve of the announcement of their plans to wed—Josef Bontrager had quit her. She sank down onto the chair and buried her face in her hands as the tears flowed anew with no sign of stopping.

Chapter Two

Luke was willing to admit that his offer to drive the Goodloe sisters to services had been a spur-of-the-moment idea. For a good part of the day, he'd been trying to think of some way that he might approach Lydia Goodloe. He wanted to ask her if he could see her home from the Sunday evening singing that served as an opportunity for the single population of Celery Fields to socialize and court.

Circumstances in his past had forced Luke to make some major changes in his life. The first had been to leave Ontario and move here to Celery Fields where he knew no one—and more to the point, no one knew him. The second was to settle here permanently and that meant taking a wife. Now that his business was established, if not exactly flourishing, and he seemed to have been accepted by others in the community, it was time to marry and start his family. He was twenty-seven years old. By his age his parents had already had him plus three brothers.

Then just as he was planning his strategy for how best to approach Lydia, Greta Goodloe had suddenly appeared in his doorway and the way had seemed clear to him. If he could enlist her aid in courting her sister...

But after interacting with Greta over these last several moments, he was having second thoughts about involving her in his quest. At first the woman had been nearly hysterical. Then she had accused him of eavesdropping—no, spying—on her private conversation with Josef and when he had told her of his intent to court her sister, her mood had once again shifted. She had actually burst out laughing. He certainly saw no cause for such merriment—at his expense.

Now she was back to crying again—crying so hard that she had begun to hiccup. For the life of him Luke would never understand women. Not that he was all that used to being around women in the first place. His mother had died when he was just six and his younger brothers and father had been his world until he'd left the family home in Ontario this last spring. Blacksmithing was his trade, which did not bring him into much contact with the female of the species. That had worked out fine for him so far.

It occurred to him that a woman like Greta—a woman well known for her charm and beauty throughout the community—might logically assume that any man would be attracted to her. That explained her reaction when he'd offered the ride to Sunday services. And Luke had to admit that when he'd first begun to consider the single women of Celery Fields, he had—as any man would—taken notice of Greta Goodloe.

She had a smile that was as filled with sunshine as her golden hair—at least what he could see of her hair bound tightly beneath the covering of her black bonnet. And she was not the least bit shy about spreading the sunshine of that smile around. More than once he'd been working and had heard her musical laughter as she passed by his shop on her way home or to do some shopping at Yoder's.

But he'd quickly learned that she and Josef Bontrager were together. In fact it was the idea that Greta would soon wed, leaving Lydia in her late parents' house alone with no further responsibilities for her sister that had made him take closer notice of the teacher.

From what Luke had observed, Lydia was her younger sister's opposite in just about every way. Greta was petite with a natural beauty. Her sister was attractive but her height and angular features gave her an aura of authority and more than a little intimidation. Luke supposed that suited a schoolteacher who needed to maintain order and control over children of a variety of ages. But away from school she was still wary and withdrawn when it came to socializing with others— especially those she did not know. Greta, on the other hand, was outgoing to the point of being a bit adventurous. Her ready smile and lively eyes reflected an innate curiosity about people. One more reason, Luke had decided, that he should set his sights on the quieter, more steadfast Lydia.

Determined to get on with the matter of pursuing his courtship of Lydia, Luke was beginning to lose patience with the way Greta's mood could change from tears to laughter and back to tears with stunning quickness. But then she buried her face in her hands and her slim shoulders shuddered violently. "How is this possible?" she managed between hiccups.

"I believe that your sister and I would make…"

"Not that," she snapped, the hiccups apparently cured by her sudden fit of temper. She looked off toward the direction that Josef Bontrager had gone as silent tears flowed freely down her cheeks. "Oh, what's to become of me?" she moaned, wrapping her arms around herself.

"I expect you'll do fine," Luke said as he refilled the dipper and handed it to her. "You're young and from what I've observed there isn't an eligible man in town who…"

She looked up at him, her blue eyes wide with horror, her mouth working as if she wanted to say something but could not make her voice work. "You men think that it's… How dare you for one minute…" she stuttered and shoved the dipper into his hand. "Do not plan to call for us tomorrow for services, Luke Starns," she ordered, then turned and stalked off down the lane that led to the house she shared with her sister.

How dare I what? Try to console you? Treat your injured finger? Fetch you water?

"Women," Luke muttered as he strode back inside his shop, hooked the halter of the heavy leather apron over his head and started pounding out the iron that he'd left on the fire.

Through the next half hour as Luke continued his work, Greta's accusations stayed with him as did her tears. Clearly she remained convinced that he had passed judgment over whatever had passed between her and her beau. Still, thinking back on it, he realized that he'd been more aware of the disagreement than he'd fully understood. And the more he thought about the conversation he'd only partially paid attention to while he stood at the window, the harder he struck the iron on the anvil with extra force.

Josef Bontrager was a man given to the kind of bombastic announcements that carried above the normal sounds of a town going about its business. Though his announcement to Greta had come at the time of day when most folks had already gone home, his voice insured that anyone who happened to be nearby would hear what he had to say.

"I can't marry you, Greta."

No wonder the young woman had been so upset. This was no surely ordinary quarrel. The couple's plan to wed within a month was to be announced the following morning at services. If Bontrager meant what he'd said...

"*Guten tag,* Luke." Roger Hadwell stood at the door of the shop, watching Luke pound the iron into shape. "You're working later than usual," he observed.

"*Yah.* Just finishing up here. Have some water." He nodded toward the bucket.

Roger helped himself while Luke made the last two strikes on the molten metal then shoved it into another bucket of water at his feet. Hot iron striking cold water produced the familiar sizzle of steam rising that Luke found somehow calming. "Come sit awhile," he invited. He followed Roger outside to the warped bench he kept ready for just such visits.

Roger owned the hardware business next door and frequently stopped by to exchange bits of news with Luke during the workweek. He was uncustomarily quiet as he sipped water from the dipper. "Did something happen to Greta Goodloe?" he asked finally.

Luke stalled for time. "Why do you ask?"

Roger shrugged. "Me and the wife couldn't help noticing that she stopped by your shop here after Josef drove off—and stayed a good little bit. My wife seemed to think that Greta was upset about something. She and Josef have another spat?"

Luke sent up a silent prayer for forgiveness for the lie he was about to tell. "It's the dust." He nodded toward the street where a hot westerly wind created little flurries of dirt and sand on the street. "Got something in her eye."

"That was it then," Roger said and Luke understood that this was a question.

"That and she'd gotten a splinter. I picked out the splinter and gave her some water. She took a few minutes to catch her breath and went on her way."

They sat watching Jeremiah and Pleasant Troyer pass, their buggy loaded with kids and the week's shopping. Pleasant nodded in greeting as Jeremiah turned the buggy toward home. The town would be pretty much deserted until everyone gathered at the Troyers' place the next day for services and the start of a new week.

"When I saw Greta and Josef earlier," Roger continued, "it looked like they were having words."

I can't marry you, Greta.

What kind of man just blurts out something like that in the middle of town where anybody might see or hear? What kind of man walks away without so much as an explanation for the woman he's professed to love for most of his life?

Luke couldn't imagine treating a woman—or any human being—with such callousness. He didn't know Greta Goodloe very well—really not at all other than seeing her in town or at services—but she seemed a kindhearted person and surely did not deserve such treatment from a man who had professed to love her. He thought about her smile and the way it could bring a special radiance to her features. But she had not been smiling much during the time she had spent in his shop.

He realized now that he'd gotten lost in thought while Roger had continued to speculate on what might have gone on between Greta and Josef. "…wouldn't be human if they didn't have words now and again. Whole town knows that this is hardly the first time. I mean you take a fiery little thing like Greta and put her with a man as fence-straddling as Josef and there are bound to be some times when they don't see eye to eye." He chuckled and stood up. "Wait 'til those two are married and spending all day and night together. Oh, there are gonna be some fireworks then, I'll guarantee it."

Roger was still chuckling to himself after he'd tipped his hat and sauntered back to the hardware store—no doubt to report to his wife that Luke had not had any further information to offer. Luke started inside his shop, but a flash of color caught his eye and he paused to look down the lane toward the house where the Goodloe sisters lived.

In the gathering dusk, Greta was taking down laundry from the clothesline that ran from the house to a palm tree and back again. She yanked free the clothespins and dropped them into a basket at her feet, then snapped the sheet, towel or clothing item hard against the hot westerly breeze and folded it into a precise rectangle before adding it to the pile already in another larger basket.

Luke told himself that he remained where he was watching her until the line was empty because he wanted to be sure that she had recovered from her earlier distress. But the truth was that he could not seem to stop watching her. It was as if Josef's harsh words had pried open a door. Suddenly the beautiful Greta Goodloe might be free to consider other suitors. And there had been a time when a much younger and more foolish Luke would have taken a good deal of pleasure in that news. But he had been different then.

"This is not the sister for you," he told himself sternly as he forced his gaze away from her and headed inside.

Greta saw Luke Starns watching her. She'd also seen Roger Hadwell make his way over to the blacksmith's, observed the two men talking and wondered if Luke had decided that since she had already broken their bargain by refusing his offer of a ride to services, he was free to tell Roger everything. In that case she had made a complete fool of herself confiding in the blacksmith and, no doubt by morning, everyone in town was going to know about it. She would be the subject of whispers and conversations that stopped the moment she entered the room when she and Lydia arrived at services.

Oh, who do you think you're fooling? Sooner or later everyone has to know the whole story.

Well, let people talk. It certainly hadn't been her idea to end her relationship with Josef. And the way he had done it—in the middle of town, with no explanation at all? Of course, she really hadn't waited for

him to explain. On the other hand, he could have followed her. But, oh no, he was too…

What?

Shy?

Proud?

Cowardly. Yes, that explained it. For as long as she'd
known him, Josef had allowed her to have her way
and deep down she had known that even the hint that
she might be attracted to some other boy could have
Josef falling all over himself to win favor with her. On
the other hand, he had made it clear on more than one
occasion that once they married, he would determine
where she went and who she saw and when. Greta
had accepted that, once she married, the man was in
charge. But she had always assumed that after marriage she would be able to find her way around Josef's
jealousies and strict ways the same way she had during their courtship.

She paused for a moment—a clothespin clinched
between her lips—as she looked at Luke Starns. As
usual she had acted in haste—confiding in him without thinking through the possible consequences. She
barely knew the man beyond seeing him at services
and the occasional nod when she passed his shop.

Honest. Trustworthy. These were words she'd heard
applied to the blacksmith. But could she trust him? It
had been evident that he failed to understand the seriousness of what had transpired between Josef and
her—of just how precarious things were. And yet he
had listened and shown concern.

She had to trust someone. Perhaps he and Roger
Hadwell had been discussing business or just passing
the time of day. She would know tomorrow as soon as

she and Lydia arrived at services. If Luke drove Lydia and her to services, as soon as they pulled into the yard of Pleasant's house, there would be one of two reactions. Either the women would be whispering about her and giving her those pitying looks that she could not abide. Or they would be talking about the surprise of seeing Lydia and Luke arrive together, delighted that at long last the romance they had all anticipated had taken its first baby step.

An idea began to take shape in her mind and she smiled softly to herself. She placed the last folded pillowcase on the pile of laundry. Arriving with Luke was definitely the way to go. If he had gossiped, she would know it at once and would then inform him that he was not worthy of Lydia and could certainly not depend on Greta to help him court her. If, on the other hand, he had held his tongue under the pressure of Roger's probing, then she could turn the attention of others to the prospect of a romance between Lydia and the blacksmith and all speculation about what had happened to her would be short-lived.

She hoisted the heavy basket onto one hip and headed back to the house. Somehow she had to get Lydia to agree to let Luke Starns drive them to services and see her home after the singing. While it would be nigh on to scandalous for Luke and Lydia to arrive for services without Greta's company, Sunday evening singings were occasions where single people in the community could openly socialize, even flirt a bit. Of course, in most Amish communities such gatherings were intended as events for young people in the sixteen to twenty age group. And in most Amish communities they attracted additional young people from surrounding Amish towns.

But Celery Fields was the sole Amish community for miles around in Florida and so these social evenings included anyone who was single—regardless of their age. Greta had never seen Luke at a singing in all the time he'd been in Celery Fields but clearly his intention was to be there the following evening. Now if indeed she found that she could trust Luke then all Greta had to do was make sure that he and Lydia were seated across from each other at the long table set up in the barn with the males on one side and the females on the other. And then she could make some excuse as to why she could not ride back to town with them.

Early on Sunday morning Greta heard Lydia stirring. Usually her sister would already have seen to the horse and cow they kept, gathered the eggs, prepared their breakfast and dressed in the lavender dress she reserved for their biweekly services, all before Greta was even out of bed. But not today.

Still smarting from the events of the day before, Greta had not slept well at all and she felt restless and out of sorts as she dressed. Using the blackened pins lined up on her bureau, she anchored her skirt into place. Then she twisted up her hair into a bun and pulled hairpins from between her lips to stab it into submission. Finally she lifted the prayer *kapp* from its resting place on her bedside table and prepared to set it atop the tight bun.

Unfortunately Lydia's answer to Greta's distress the evening before had been to counsel prayer, Scripture and early to bed. There had been no opportunity at all to bring up the subject of Luke Starns. Furthermore, in the middle of the night Greta had realized that because she had rejected Luke's offer to drive them after all, she needed to reverse that decision and hope that he would agree. Thus the urgency of her early morning errand—one that her sister must not observe.

Checking to be sure that Lydia was otherwise occupied, Greta picked up the note she'd prepared the night before and ran down the lane to the blacksmith shop. All was quiet through the little village and she thanked God for that. She crept up the staircase on the side of Luke's shop that led to his living quarters and slipped the envelope under the door. When she heard the distinctive sound of a man clearing his throat from somewhere beyond that door, she ran down the stairs and all the way back to her house.

Luke had found the small white envelope when he'd headed out to hitch up his wagon.

Luke Starns,
Your kind offer to drive my sister and me to
services today is most appreciated. We will be
ready at eight.
Greta Goodloe

Luke couldn't help but smile. So Greta Goodloe had decided to keep her end of their bargain after all. He wondered why. Greta did not strike him as a woman who did anything without a good reason—something that would be of benefit to her. Not that she wasn't devoted to her sister. Their closeness was well-known through Celery Fields and it was seldom that one was seen without the other—even when Josef Bontrager was around.

He reread the note. The implication was that Lydia had agreed to this idea—and that surprised Luke. More than surprised him, it made him suspicious. Had Greta actually gotten Lydia to agree to the plan? He doubted it. But now that he'd been given the opening he'd sought to call upon Lydia, he hardly cared what Greta's motives might be. Of far greater concern was that he return to his room above the shop and make sure that he had done everything he could to make the best possible impression on the schoolteacher.

He changed his shirt for one that he'd been saving for just such an occasion. He ran his thumbs down his suspenders making sure they were straight and without any twists. He brushed his navy wool pants to remove any possible traces of crumbs from his breakfast. Finally he picked up his wide-brimmed straw hat and set it precisely on his head, wishing for the first time in his life that he owned a mirror.

Pure vanity, he thought, chastising himself for such a lapse on the Sabbath of all days. He set his hat more firmly on his thick hair and headed downstairs to hitch up the wagon, thinking that it would be more proper if he had the courting buggy he'd been given when he had turned sixteen and left behind when he moved to Florida.

"Courting buggies are for kids," he muttered to the horses as he fixed them with their bits and harness. "Lydia Goodloe and I are no longer young. And she is a practical woman. She will not mind the wagon."

Outside he took special care hitching the team to the wagon and ran the flat of his hand over the seat to be sure there were no splinters that might catch on the sisters' skirts. He paused as he thought about the splinter he'd removed from Greta's thumb the day before. How vulnerable she had seemed standing there in the reflected light of the fire, licking at her wound like a kitten whose paw had been injured. How very smooth her skin had been especially in contrast to his rough and callused palms. For a moment he was carried back to Ontario—and another young woman whose hands had been as soft as that.

Luke shook off such thoughts. Those days were behind him. He lived here now. His life was here in Celery Fields and if God granted him his prayer, his future was with Lydia Goodloe—not her sister, no matter how pretty and lively she was.

Greta closed the door to her bedroom and sat on her bed, trying to catch her breath before going to share breakfast with Lydia. She was relieved that Lydia had long ago insisted that she would take care of the usual chores and preparing their breakfast on Sunday mornings. She took a minute to steady her breathing as she felt the flush of exertion from having run all the way back after leaving the note for Luke. She hoped she could trust the man.

Trust.

Perhaps Josef had looked to the future and seen a lifetime of uncertainty when it came to trusting her. For it was true—as often as he had declared his love for her, she had never once been able to bring herself to say the words to him. She had simply accepted that she and Josef were meant for one another and she had believed with all her heart that in time she would come to love him as much as she liked him.

Her head reeled with the need to find some logical explanation for his sudden decision to quit her, and then to find an equally agreeable solution to this sudden upheaval. On a morning when she had expected to arrive at services and hear her name linked with Josef's in the announcement of coming nuptials, she must instead wonder how she could possibly endure the day. For endure it she must. Even if Luke found her note and showed up to drive them to services, chatter about a romance between Lydia and Luke would take time to develop. And there was always the possibility that Lydia would refuse to accept the ride.

And what of the added humiliation if Josef had failed to tell Bishop Troyer not to include them when he made the announcement?

"Liddy," she called out, her voice shaking with panic as she flung open the door of her bedroom. "Liddy!"

Chapter Three

Lydia came running down the hall from the kitchen. "What is it? Are you all right?" Greta looked up at her sister with tear-filled eyes and an expression of pure panic. Lydia rushed to her side. "Come, sit. Take a deep breath."

Greta did as her sister instructed. Since their mother's death when Greta was only a toddler, she had relied on Lydia to show her the way through the travails of daily life. "What if…" She drew in a long breath and gasped, "What if Josef has not spoken with Bishop Troyer? What if…"

Lydia frowned, a sure sign that she had not considered this possibility and was even now working through the logistics of how best to handle this latest crisis in Greta's life. "Well, we shall simply have to make certain that the bishop knows what has happened. Therefore, it would be best if we arrived at services as soon as possible."

Greta nodded. "You'll speak with him?"

"Bishop Troyer? Of course, but Greta, he is likely to want to speak with you—and Josef."

Greta groaned.

"Now, sister, it's not necessarily as dire as you may think. As I told you last night," Lydia continued, "I suspect that Josef has simply had a bout of nerves. Marriage is a big step. There is every possibility that after a night's lost sleep he regrets his impulsive action and has not yet figured out how to set things right again."

When Greta had told Lydia the news over supper the evening before, she had taken great comfort and hope from her sister's reassurances. But Lydia might know many things—might even be the smartest person in all of Celery Fields—still when it came to matters of the heart, Lydia had almost no experience and besides, didn't Greta know Josef better than anyone did? Although he had a reputation for being wishy-washy, once he did settle on a plan of action, he could be as stubborn as any other man when it came to changing his mind.

And yet when she heard the snort of a horse and the soft plodding of hooves on the sandy road that ran past their house and on out to the countryside, Greta flew to the window. She could not help but hope that it would be Josef bringing his buggy to collect the two sisters for services as he had done ever since their father had died a year earlier. In that instant she played out the entire scene of how he would come to the door, hat in hand, eyes on the ground. And she would greet him as if nothing had passed between them the day before. The three of them would climb into his buggy and arrive at services as they had every other Sunday.

But when she looked outside there was no buggy. Instead there was a wagon with a matched team of black Percheron horses and climbing down from the driver's seat was none other than the blacksmith, Luke Starns.

"What on earth?" Lydia had followed Greta to the window and was also watching Luke approach the house.

"He's come to drive us to services," Greta said. "He offered," she added with a shrug as Lydia's eyebrows lifted in surprise.

"And you accepted this offer of a ride with a man we barely know?" Lydia asked, her voice the one she used when questioning a student.

"Not right away," Greta stammered. "I mean I thought about it and well, Josef is certainly not going to call for us."

There was a knock at the door. It was five minutes before eight o'clock. "I told him to come at eight," Greta added.

"Come drink your tea and eat something," Lydia said with a resigned sigh. "I'll get the door."

Theirs was a small house and Greta did not really have to eavesdrop to overhear the exchange between Lydia and the blacksmith. She nibbled at a slice of rye bread as her sister greeted Luke.

"You are early, Luke Starns. My sister is just having her breakfast."

Greta frowned. "Oh, Liddy," she whispered to herself. "Show the man a little kindness."

She heard Luke mumble an apology.

"Well, come in out of the heat," Lydia instructed.

While Lydia marched down the hallway to the kitchen, Greta saw that Luke had remained uncertainly by the front door.

"Liddy," Greta hissed, "offer the man some juice."

"We do not have time for juice, Greta." She took a cloth napkin and wiped a crumb from the corner of Greta's mouth. "Now, come along or we'll be late."

Outside, Lydia stood aside, making it clear that she expected Greta to climb up to the wagon's only seat first. "It's going to be another hot day," Greta said, trying to ease the tension that hung over the trio as heavily as the humidity. "Even for August," she added when they were all three seated.

But it was apparent that she could not expect comments from either Lydia or Luke. Both of them were sitting as if someone had placed a board against their backs and they were each staring straight ahead, their mouths tightly set into thin lines. Clearly any attempt Greta might make to start a conversation was useless so she bowed her head and folded her hands in her lap. She might as well put the time to good use—praying that somehow she might get through this day.

At Pleasant's house, where services were to be held, Pleasant's husband, Jeremiah, came forward to welcome them. If he thought it odd that they should arrive with Luke Starns, he gave no sign.

"Is your great uncle inside, Jeremiah?" Lydia asked as he helped her down from the wagon. Jeremiah's uncle was the head of their congregation.

"Yes. Is there a problem? Has something happened?" He was clearly mystified that Lydia's first comment would be to ask the whereabouts of the congregation's bishop without so much as a greeting for him. Greta felt a touch of relief as she realized that at least Jeremiah seemed to have no idea at all that Josef had quit her.

"Greta just needs to ask him a question," Lydia replied with a smile. She waited for Jeremiah to help Greta down then turned to Luke. "Thank you, Luke Starns, for the ride. My sister and I will be staying to help Pleasant prepare the barn for tonight's singing and can find our way home after that."

In spite of her own worries, Greta rolled her eyes heavenward as if seeking God's help. No wonder Lydia had never had a serious beau. She treated every man she met as if he were one of her students. She saw that Luke had been about to say something to Lydia, then thought better of it.

"Are you better?" Greta heard Luke murmur and realized that he was addressing her while Lydia was already halfway across the yard on her way to the large farmhouse.

"I am perfectly fine, Luke." She offered him a tight smile. "And having kept my end of our bargain I trust that..."

"I'm not given to gossip, Greta, but you should prepare yourself because soon enough..."

"Greta." Lydia was expert at delivering an entire lecture with a single word. In two syllables she had effectively reminded Greta that it was the Sabbath, that they were to turn their hearts and minds to God and that the bishop was no doubt awaiting her arrival.

As the two sisters walked toward the house, Greta glanced back over her shoulder toward the barn where Luke was now unhitching the horses while Jeremiah greeted more neighbors. Luke was right, of course. It hardly mattered what he might have said to Roger Hadwell. By the end of today's service everyone would know.

"Let's get this over with," she said as she and Lydia reached the front door of Pleasant's home.

Inside the modest white frame house, the backless wooden benches, transported from house to house for the biweekly services, had been set up in the two large front rooms that were a feature of every Amish home. From down the hall that led to the kitchen, Greta could hear the voices of those women and girls who had already arrived. They would gather there to deliver their contributions for the light meal that would follow the three-hour service. She and Lydia were each carrying a basket that held their contributions for the meal. It was a comfort to realize that the women all seemed to be talking in a normal tone, not whispering as she might have expected.

Pleasant rushed forward to greet them.

"Could you take these?" Lydia asked, handing Pleasant her basket. "Greta needs to speak with Bishop Troyer."

"Of course," Pleasant replied, taking Greta's basket, as well. "Something to do with a certain announcement to be made today?" she asked and she actually winked.

Greta forced a smile as Lydia took her arm. "We won't be long," she assured Pleasant.

"Maybe it would be better if we just told everyone now," Greta murmured. "At least then it would be out in the open." On the other hand, there was still time for Josef to find her, tell her he'd been wrong, beg her forgiveness.

They passed through the front hall separating the rooms where services would be held. They dodged a group of small children racing up the stairs. The younger men and boys tended to linger outside until others took their places for the service.

Glancing around for any sign of Josef, Greta turned toward the hallway that led to a downstairs bedroom, knowing the bishop and other elders always gathered there before the services began. She was about to tell Lydia to go to the kitchen when she practically ran into Josef. Through the open doorway behind him, she could see Bishop Troyer and the two other preachers who would speak that morning. They were all looking at her, their eyes full of pity.

"Guten morgen, Josef," she said brightly as she edged around him in the narrow hallway.

"I have just told them," Josef said without returning her greeting or meeting her eyes.

"Gut," Greta murmured with no further pretense at acting as if anything about this morning was normal.

"Greta?" Bishop Troyer had come to the doorway. "I wonder if I might have a word with you and Josef before services begin?" The other church elders left the room and Bishop Troyer closed the door.

Woodenly Greta sat down on the only chair in the room. Normally she would have remained standing out of respect but the truth was that, upon seeing Josef, her knees had gone weak and she wasn't at all sure that she could maintain her balance without support. Josef stayed close by the door, studying the wide planks of the wooden floor.

"Josef has told me of your decision," he began.

Her decision?

She glanced up at Josef and saw that his cheeks had gone red. "It was my decision, Bishop," he muttered. "Greta…" He shrugged which only infuriated her more.

Greta what? Had no say in the matter?

Bishop Troyer seemed momentarily perplexed. "I see," he murmured. "When you told me that you and Greta would not be marrying this autumn, I just assumed that…"

"It was my decision," Josef repeated.

"The fact is, Bishop, that we won't be marrying at all," Greta added, surprised to hear the words come out of her mouth.

Josef looked up then, his eyes wide with shock. "Well, that is…"

"Isn't that what you told me?" she challenged. She stood up and realized that her anger at the unfairness of the situation had given her strength. "It's for the best, don't you think?" This she directed to the bishop.

The kindly white-haired man who had been the head of their church for as long as Greta could remember looked at her and then at Josef, his brow furrowed with concern. "This is a time for prayer—not haste. You must both ask God to show you His plan for your lives. It is true that you and others have long assumed that His intention was for the two of you to share a life. And that may yet be the way of it. This is not for either of you to decide without first praying on the matter."

"It was not a decision made in haste," Josef replied.

"Then why?" Greta blurted out before the bishop could speak. "Is there someone else?"

Josef looked at her and she saw for the first time the pain that lined his features. "How many times have I asked you that question," he said softly. "I have asked it time and again."

"And time and again I have told you that you are imagining things."

"And yet, not once have you said that you love me, Greta."

It was true and there were no words to deny it. Fortunately she was saved by a soft knock on the door. "Pastor?" she heard one of the other ministers say. "It's time."

Josef opened the door and brushed past the two other preachers waiting in the hallway.

"Come along, child," the bishop said as he led the way down the hall and into the front room where Josef had already taken his seat with the other men. Greta took her place next to Lydia on the first of two benches where the unmarried girls and women were seated.

In spite of the cool reception he'd received from Lydia that morning, Luke was determined to ask to see her home later that evening. If she refused him at least he would know where he stood. It would have complex ramifications, for if Lydia Goodloe turned him down, he might have to think seriously about moving on to another community. But one step at a time. Having settled on his plan, he was free to focus all of his attention on the words of Bishop Troyer—a lesson that seemed directed at him. But, of course, that wasn't possible. He'd taken care to keep his past to himself since his arrival in Celery Fields. But the flicker of panic he felt whenever he thought there was the possibility of others learning of his past was never far from the surface of his emotions.

The lesson came from the twenty-ninth chapter of the book of Genesis. It was the story of Jacob's love for Rachel and how her father, Laban, tricked Jacob into marrying his elder daughter, Leah, instead. Two sisters, the elder less desirable than the younger. And although the minister's sermon was about Laban's deceit, all Luke could think about was the biblical sisters. In the end Jacob had married them both but God had given him children by Leah while the much beloved Rachel remained barren. Had that been God's punishment? And if so, why punish a man like Jacob who had worked years for the privilege of marrying the woman he truly loved?

Luke shifted uncomfortably on the hard wooden bench as he remembered another pair of sisters—this time in Ontario. Their father had also been anxious to see his eldest daughter married and he had set his sights on Luke as the best possible candidate. But Luke was drawn to the man's younger, fairer daughter just as Jacob had been. And just like Jacob the father had tried to trick him into the match with the elder daughter. Only Luke— unlike Jacob—had refused to be drawn into such a plot.

When everything had turned out for the worst, Luke had often wondered if God had punished him for his refusal to even consider courting, much less marrying the older sister. But in that Biblical world multiple wives were allowed—Jacob could marry Leah and the beloved Rachel, as well. Luke did not have that choice. In the end his only real choice had been to leave the community where he had lived his whole life and move to a place where he could start over. Celery Fields had seemed the perfect place.

He glanced over to the bench where Lydia Goodloe sat, her eyes riveted on the pastor, her hands folded piously in her lap, her face intent as she took in the lesson of the sermon. Luke did not love her—how could he? He barely knew her other than to nod politely whenever they crossed paths. Still he had observed that she was a good and steadfast woman. In spite of her strictness, the children who were her students clearly admired her. Yes, Lydia Goodloe would be a wise choice to manage his home and raise his children in the faith of their ancestors. He could do a lot worse than Lydia Goodloe.

But then his gaze was drawn to the sister—Greta. Unlike Lydia, Greta's eyes did not remain fixed on the minister. Instead, she glanced around, out the window, up at the ceiling, at some lint she picked off her dark green cotton dress. Although she sat relatively still, her eyes darted around the room like a butterfly pausing at one flower and then quickly moving on to the next.

It occurred to Luke that if he were successful in his courtship of the elder sister, he would no doubt be expected to take in the younger one, as well. In the absence of her late parents, he and Lydia would be Greta's guardians, at least until she married. He could only pray that Josef Bontrager would reconsider his decision and take Greta for his wife.

Just then Greta's eyes lighted on him for an instant and he saw her scowl before quickly ducking her head and folding her hands in her lap. Likewise, Luke turned his attention back to the minister. As the words of the lesson continued, Luke silently prayed for God's guidance for this treacherous trip he was about to take down the path of courtship. At least this time he had chosen the elder sister with his eyes wide open. In this case there was no father to trick him as

Laban had tricked Jacob or the man in Ontario had tried to deceive Luke.

No. The challenge facing him was to persuade Lydia Goodloe that they could make a nice life together. Convinced that he was up to that challenge, he risked one more look across the aisle at the Goodloe sisters and was unnerved when he realized that his gaze had settled first on Greta before moving on to Lydia.

Chapter Four

Greta squeezed her eyes shut tightly as the service came to an end, praying that God might forgive her for not listening to the lesson for the day. Oh, she had gotten the part about two sisters—one fairer than the other—but then her mind had started to wander. Surely the Lord would understand that she had so many things to consider—so many things to work out. The worst of it would be how best to handle the barely perceptible murmur that would surely spread through the congregation after Bishop Troyer announced the couples planning to marry that fall. That list, of course, no longer included Josef and her. So, soon everyone would know at least a part of the story. She brightened a little as it occurred to her that, like the bishop, most would simply assume that Greta had quit Josef rather than the other way round. Their pity would be directed toward him.

But then her relief collapsed as she realized that this was only a momentary reprieve. Soon enough everyone would know the real story. She glanced over toward the men's section, meaning to see how Josef was handling things but her eyes had settled instead on Luke Starns. The man was watching her and the only way she could describe his expression was one of disapproval. At that very moment, Lydia nudged Greta with her elbow—her signal for Greta to stop fidgeting. Those two were going to make a perfect match, she thought, as she laced her fingers together in silent prayer. It would appear that Luke Starns followed the rules as strictly as her sister.

The announcement of coming nuptials was made and the congregation reacted exactly as Greta had imagined. When the service finally ended, the women moved as one toward the kitchen to lay out the meal while the men and boys began rearranging the benches into tables and seating. She heard Josef's laugh and whipped around to see him stepping aside to allow Esther Yoder to pass by on her way to the kitchen.

Esther was the eldest daughter of the Yoders who owned the dry goods store. She was two years younger than Greta and it was well-known throughout Celery Fields that her mother thought it high time she found herself a husband. From the looks of things she had set her sights on Josef.

Well, she can have him, Greta thought swallowing her bitterness even as Lydia took hold of her elbow and turned her away from the scene.

"Come along, sister."

On their way to the kitchen they crossed paths with Luke, one long black bench under each powerful arm. He looked from Lydia to Greta and then back again. To Greta he seemed rooted to the spot like the giant live oak tree that stood outside his shop and she couldn't help but smile at the ridiculous comparison.

He cleared his throat. "May I speak with you later, Lydia Goodloe?"

Greta thought she had never seen her sister quite so shaken. Her lips were pressed together so tightly that no sound could possibly be expected to come out, so Greta took matters into her own hands.

"We are needed in the kitchen. But if you plan to attend the singing, then there will be time enough to have your say. Excuse us, *bitte.*"

Luke stepped aside and this time it was Greta who guided her sister the rest of the way to the kitchen.

"How could you say such a thing?" Lydia whispered when she had recovered her voice. "I had thought you of all people would wish to skip this evening's singing."

"Of course we must attend the singing, Lydia. Luke Starns wishes to see you home afterward. Will you accept or not?"

Lydia's eyes widened in disbelief. "How do you know such a thing?"

"He told me so."

Further conversation was not possible as they joined the other women in the kitchen. As Greta had feared, the room went silent the minute that she and Lydia entered.

Greta saw her choice plainly—she could pretend that nothing was out of the ordinary or she could address the matter and get it over with. She took stock of the glances flying among the women—lifted eyebrows of speculation and worried frowns of curiosity.

"Well," she said brightly as she picked up the baskets that she and Lydia had brought and began setting out the goods. "It sounds like we're going to have a busy season of weddings here in Celery Fields." She grinned broadly at the three other women whose betrothals had been announced that morning. "Perhaps it's a good thing Josef Bontrager changed his mind about marrying me."

She couldn't help it. Her voice broke on those last words, but she kept her tears in check and continued to place the food from the basket on the table.

Almost as one unit, the women gathered around her. She felt consoling hands placed gently on her shoulder and gratefully accepted the healing power of their murmurs of concern, which comforted her like a soothing balm for her jumbled spirit.

"Perhaps the Lord has another plan for you, Greta," Pleasant said softly. "We sometimes think we know what He has in store for us but then things change."

Of all people, Pleasant knew what she was talking about. Certainly she had thought she would never marry and then she had agreed to marry the widower, Merle Obermeier. He had died soon after, leaving her penniless with his four children from his first marriage to raise. And then Jeremiah Troyer, the bishop's great-nephew, had moved to town, just as the depression was starting, to open—of all things—an ice cream shop.

But the likelihood of some stranger moving into town and making everything all right again for Greta seemed remote at best. With the combination of droughts and deluges that had plagued the fields of celery and other produce crops over the last few seasons, people were beginning to move away from Celery Fields—not settle there. The last person to actually come to town had been Luke Starns.

Luke Starns...and Lydia.

Suddenly Greta saw her opportunity to turn the attention of the women away from her and on to something that would give them far greater pleasure. "You are right, Pleasant. After all, who knows what the Lord has in store for any of us when it comes to matters of the heart." She cast a sideways glance at Lydia, leading the other women to do the same.

As usual Hilda Yoder took charge. "I noticed that the two of you arrived for services with the blacksmith, Luke Starns. Has your horse pulled up lame, Lydia?"

"The blacksmith was kind enough to offer us a ride," Lydia replied as she sliced a loaf of bread.

"Roger tells me that he will definitely be settling here permanently. His business is doing surprisingly well given the fact that there's less call for services like his these days," Gertrude Hadwell, wife of the hardware store owner, said with a sly glance at Lydia. "It's hardly any secret, Lydia, that he has his eye on you."

"Then offering you a ride was the first step," Hilda announced.

"Toward what?" Lydia asked, her cheeks turning a deeper shake of pink than usual.

"Toward courtship, of course. I expect that he'll ask to see you home after tonight's singing? It's no one's business, of course. Such matters are private, but still…"

Lydia lifted her chin, hoisted the platter stacked high with sliced bread and said, "He will have to work up his nerve first, but if he asks I will accept."

Greta was every bit as shocked by this announcement as any of the women in the kitchen. Lydia had always said that she could not be bothered with court-

ship unless she were truly in love. She barely knew
Luke Starns so what could she be thinking?

Luke filled his plate but kept his eyes on Lydia
Goodloe. The truth was that the schoolteacher intim-
idated him the same way his former teacher had back
in Ontario. How on earth was he going to court this
woman? Where would he find the words? And why
did the mere intent to do so feel more like a difficult
task—one he would rather not attend—than something
that would lead to a pleasant conclusion?

Perhaps the best plan was to approach her with the
idea that a match between them was a practical decision. He wanted a family. Her job as teacher of the
community's children might be in jeopardy if families
kept leaving Celery Fields to return north. How would
she and her sister make their way if she lost her position? Would it not be a relief for her to surrender the
burden of trying to make ends meet?

The more Luke thought about it, the more it seemed
to him that this could work out to the mutual benefit of
both parties. And grasping that, his confidence grew.
At least until he spotted Greta. She presented a problem. The idea of living in a house with two women
was not especially appealing. The idea of living there
with the capricious Greta Goodloe was unnerving altogether. Of course Greta might yet marry. But who?

Unless Josef Bontrager changed his mind, who was
there?

"Would you like some pie, Luke?"

Lydia was standing next to him. She was smiling
although somehow her smile did not seem to quite

reach her eyes. In her expression he read something else—something more like resignation.

"Denki." He took the plate and fork. "Did you make this?"

"I did."

Luke speared a bite of the pie and ate it. Without a doubt it was the worst-tasting peach pie he'd ever had. The fruit was hard and undercooked and had none of the enhancement of cinnamon or sugar to help flavor it and the crust was doughy and heavy. He swallowed the lumpy mess and smiled. *"Denki,"* he said again, unwilling to tell a lie especially on the Sabbath.

To his surprise Lydia burst out laughing. "It's horrid, I know." She relieved him of the plate and replaced it with another that she picked up from the spread of desserts on the table. "Try this one. Greta and my half sister, Pleasant, are the bakers in our family. I thought you might want to know that if indeed you are intent on…spending time with me."

And there before him was the opportunity he'd been seeking. In fact it appeared he did not even need to ask—although it would be rude and conceited not to. And the truth was that when she smiled, Lydia Goodloe was not quite so intimidating.

"I will be at tonight's singing," he began. "I understand that you—and your sister—will also be there?"

"We will indeed." Greta Goodloe stepped up next to them, her eyes twinkling mischievously.

Luke swallowed around the lump that seemed to be blocking his ability to speak. *"Das ist gut,"* he murmured and speared another bite of the pie.

"My sister will need a ride home," Greta prompted.

"We both will," Lydia corrected.

Luke had not counted on seeing the two of them home. That was hardly the way things were done. "I would be pleased to drive you—both."

"Then in that case," Lydia said, "we will see you this evening."

Luke watched the two of them move through the gathering, clearing plates and glasses as they went. Within minutes they had both gone back inside the farmhouse where the women would finish packing up the leftover food while the men moved the benches into the barn for the singing. He turned to help with the benches and found himself working next to Josef.

Luke had not liked Bontrager from the day he'd first come into the blacksmith's shop to hire Luke to check the team of giant Belgian horses he used to plow his fields. The man had instantly reminded Luke of the milk toast his father used to make for him and his brothers—soggy. It was an odd word to use in describing another man, but it fit Josef Bontrager as far as Luke was concerned.

For all his booming voice, Josef was timid and indecisive when it came to business. And to Luke's way of thinking, he was penny-wise but pound-foolish as the old saying went. On the one hand he had bought up the land of surrounding farms when those farmers had hit hard times and decided to return to their homes up north. On the other he was dickering over paying the price for a proper shoe for his horse. When Luke had told him that three of the team of four horses would need at least one shoe replaced, Josef had hedged.

"You're certain we couldn't get by one more season?"

Luke had shrugged. "In my opinion you'd be taking a risk but it's your team."

Josef multiplied what Luke had given him as the price for one shoe times the total number that he recommended replacing. He tapped the stubby pencil against the final tally for a long moment and then released a low whistle through his teeth. "That's pretty steep," he said.

"That's my price," Luke replied as he packed up his equipment and climbed onto his horse. "Let me know if you decide to go ahead."

A full two weeks later—after Josef, according to Roger, had gotten at least two other bids—the farmer came to the shop and hired Luke to do the work. By that time all four horses were in need of his wares. And when Josef had hinted that Luke was simply trying to get more money for his work, Luke had told him the price he'd originally quoted would stand. He did this not for the owner, but out of pity for the horse. No, Luke did not much care for Josef Bontrager. And the more he saw of Greta Goodloe, the more he had to wonder what she had ever seen in the man.

Greta felt immeasurably better as she and Lydia worked together later that afternoon laying out the "thin book" version of the centuries-old Amish hymnal, the Ausband. The full version of the hymnal was used for regular services. It was thick—well over five hundred pages and contained the words of hymns passed down through the generations as far back as anyone could remember. The book contained no musical notations—just words. Because most of the hymns had been written during the time of persecution in

Europe when Joseph Amman had broken from the Mennonites but not from the Anabaptist beliefs, the hymns they sang during services tended to be somber and even mournful in tone. By contrast the "thin book" version of the Ausband contained hymns that were lighter and more joyful and far more suitable for the kind of social occasion that the Sunday night singing was.

Greta was actually beginning to look forward to the evening. Her plan appeared to have worked. Instead of everyone buzzing about Josef's breakup with her, they were speculating about what Lydia had been thinking offering Luke Starns that piece of pie and what might the two of them have had to discuss for such an extended time. Just wait until Lydia left with Luke after the singing.

"The blacksmith seems nice," she ventured.

"Hmm." Lydia was noncommittal as always.

"He's very strong. Did you see the way he lifted two benches at once as if they were no more than small branches?"

"He's a blacksmith," Lydia pointed out. "In his line of work one develops strength."

Greta gauged her sister's mood. She seemed indifferent to the conversation, focusing instead on the precise alignment of each songbook. Every now and then she would reach across the long table and straighten a book that Greta had set in place before moving on.

"Still, he's quite handsome. I mean in a dark, brooding sort of way. Do you think perhaps that's the way men are in Ontario?"

"Ontario?" Lydia blinked at her as if she'd heard that single word and nothing else.

"Where he's from," Greta reminded her. "Canada?"

"I know where Ontario is," Lydia replied. "And I know what you are trying to do, Greta."

Greta bit her lip. "I'm just…"

"…trying to take the attention of others away from your current troubles. And that is understandable. Furthermore I am quite willing to help you in that, but do not for one minute think that I am the least bit interested in Luke Starns—at least romantically speaking."

"You don't even know the man," Greta protested. "For all you know he might be…"

"I am sure that he is a good and kind man. From what I have heard from others, he is honest and fair in his business dealings and he seems quite determined to make a life for himself here in Celery Fields. The question I have is why?"

"Why does anyone come here? The weather for one thing. I mean, Ontario?" Greta shivered in spite of the oppression of the heat.

"But alone—no family ties here? At least when Jeremiah Troyer arrived he had connections—his great-uncle and aunt were here and he had visited them in the past."

Greta sighed happily. "Yes, and then Jeremiah set his sights on Pleasant and it was so romantic."

"You're missing the point, Greta. Luke Starns simply…" She seemed lost for the right word. "He simply appeared one day. No one knew him or anything about him for that matter." They had finished their task and as Lydia surveyed their work she added, "And once again you are losing sight of the point of our conversation."

"Which is?"

"Which is, dear sister, that I am going to attend the singing tonight and allow Luke to see us home because it will indeed give people something to talk about other than you and Josef. However, get one thing straight." She pointed her forefinger at Greta the way she often pointed it at students in her classroom. "After tonight you will need to face the fact that there will be gossip and speculation regarding you and Josef and your best path is to ignore it and move forward."

Greta blinked back tears. "With what?"

"Pardon?"

"Move forward with what, Lydia?" Greta snapped peevishly. "You have your teaching. Even before she met Jeremiah, Pleasant had the bakery and the children. What exactly do I have to move forward with?"

And just like that, the misery returned, the misery she had felt once she realized that Josef was not going to come running back to her, not going to beg for her forgiveness, not going to—marry her. "I gave that man all my time—every waking hour was spent thinking about him, what would most please him and now…"

"Do not exaggerate, sister. You have our house to oversee—the cleaning and cooking, the laundry, the upkeep," Lydia scolded. "You and Josef spent a great deal of time together. That's true. Often, I might add, to the neglect of your responsibilities. Our house has not had a good cleaning in months. I think you will find that, if you keep yourself busy and away from the shops, in time you will find your way."

So she was to be a castaway, banished to the house until the talk died away? Greta whirled around to face her sister. "I keep up with the housework just fine. Papa used to say that it was the best-kept house in all of Celery Fields and that Josef was fortunate to have won the heart of one who…"

Lydia was fighting to hide a smile—and failing. "Feeling a little better?" she asked.

It was an old pattern the sisters had established early in their motherless lives—whenever Greta felt sorry for herself, Lydia would turn the tables on her. She would find some fault with Greta, knowing that the criticism would not go unchallenged.

"Yah," Greta admitted. *"Aber…"*

Lydia shushed her. "It's the Sabbath, Greta. Time for us to gather our thoughts and ruminate on the week past and the week to come." As was her habit on Sunday afternoons, Lydia retrieved the Bible she carried with her and walked outside where she sat on a bench under the shade of a tree and began to read.

Greta knew that her sister would spend hours reading scripture and praying before the cold supper they would share with Pleasant and her family. Ever since their father's death a year earlier, Lydia had isolated herself this way on Sunday afternoons. At first Greta had been hurt by what she saw as her sister's abandonment and had roamed the rooms of the house until it was time for Josef to come by so they could go out walking or for a ride in his buggy. But then Lydia had explained that it was Greta's restlessness that had driven her to seek the refuge of her reading.

"You are in constant motion and I need the quiet," she had said. "We each have our way."

It was true. Greta did her best thinking—and praying—on her feet. Sometimes—like today—she would go for a walk. Fallow fields that had once provided enough to support the farmers stretched out as far as she could see. Here and there, those neglected fields were interrupted by a span of freshly plowed and planted fields—land that would yield crops to support the families remaining in the community. She turned her gaze to the distant silo that stood next to the large barn on Josef's farm, marking the otherwise undisturbed horizon. On other Sundays she had waited for him to join her. But not this Sunday…or next…or the ones beyond that…. She turned away from anything that might remind her of Josef. How could he have been so cruel?

A motion outside the barn caught her eye. Luke Starns was taking something from the back of his wagon. Greta frowned. The man ought to have a proper buggy for courting her sister. She glanced to where Lydia sat reading and trying to catch whatever breeze there might be. She doubted that Lydia would care one way or the other about a buggy, but Greta cared for her. Maybe they did things differently in Canada. Greta folded her arms in her apron and continued watching the blacksmith—who seemed totally oblivious to her presence.

He took off the jacket he'd worn during services and placed it on the wagon seat. Then he pushed back the sleeves of his shirt and led one of his team of horses into Jeremiah's barn before returning for the other. As he went about these tasks she could see his suspenders stretch over the muscles of his broad back. She couldn't help thinking that in spite of the years farming and building furniture for the Yoders to sell in their store, Josef was given to the pudginess that had plagued him as a boy.

"Too fond of Pleasant's pies," he had often teased,

patting his oversize stomach. And certainly he was a regular customer at the bakery. Since most of his family had moved north again, he lived alone and at least twice a week he was at the bakery buying a couple dozen of the large glazed doughnuts that were Pleasant's specialty and always a pie—sometimes two.

Greta felt her cheeks flush at the realization that she was actually comparing Josef's physical appearance to Luke's. What was the matter with her? She forced herself to turn away. She needed to concentrate on how best to get Lydia to allow the blacksmith to court her. Her sister could be so stubborn sometimes.

After he'd finished helping Jeremiah and the other men set up the benches for the evening singing, Luke had intended to head to town. But the truth was that once there he'd have little more than an hour before he'd just have to turn around and come back again. And in this heat even if he washed himself and groomed the horses in town, he and his team were bound to be sweat-soaked and dust-covered by the time he returned. No, best to stay here.

Jeremiah wouldn't mind and it would give Luke the time he needed to sort things out properly in his mind. Things that yesterday had seemed fairly straightforward now made little sense. His decision to persuade the schoolteacher that they would make a good match had seemed so simple in theory. In other parts of the country, there were several Amish communities within several miles of each other allowing for a much broader opportunity to get to know others. But in Celery Fields there were no outlying or neighboring

Amish communities and so there were few options for single men and women.

The idea that Lydia might rebuff him had never even entered his thinking. Yet he'd had the distinct feeling earlier that she had agreed to be seen leaving the singing with him tonight for one reason only—to turn the attention of the gossips away from Greta and onto her. On the one hand he admired her loyalty to her sister. On the other the realization that Lydia found such a drastic move necessary only served to remind him that Greta was no longer a detail that he could overlook as he considered the future.

In the time he had spent considering how best to pursue Lydia as his wife, he had never given much thought to Greta. Like everyone else in town, he had assumed she would marry Josef and that would be the end of it. But now...

Now he found himself thinking about how the house he had thought to share with Lydia would also be home to Greta—at least unless Bontrager came to his senses or some other man in the community stepped up to court her. He and both Goodloe sisters would share meals and holidays and outings. She would be there when he came home in the evenings and when he left for his shop in the mornings. It was enough to try and imagine himself settling in with one woman. Two—especially when one of them was the mercurial Greta—was more than he had bargained for. But it was too late to rethink his plan. In a matter of hours the singing would be over and he and the Goodloe sisters would be riding back to town—together—in the dark.

Greta represented a fly in the ointment of his plan. Yet he could not deny that earlier on their way to services, he had been uncomfortably aware of Greta's closeness, positioned as she was between him and Lydia on the high wagon seat. Her shoulder had been only a fraction of an inch from his upper arm. When he had tried to steal a glance at Lydia to see how she might be reacting to the clearly unexpected circumstances of riding to services with him, he had instead found himself looking at Greta—her fair ivory cheek and full pink lips just visible beneath the brim of her bonnet.

Yes, he had a problem. It was obvious to him that Lydia's first and primary concern was going to be caring for her sister. Any interest she might have in him was going to be a distant second. It was also obvious to him that he was spending far too much of his time thinking about Greta Goodloe.

Sometimes Greta loved the fact that Celery Fields was such a small, close-knit community. But as young people began to arrive for the evening singing, she would have happily traded her surroundings for a bustling, impersonal city. The singing was a far livelier occasion than Sunday services. Everyone mixed together, talking and laughing and sharing refreshments. Along with barn raisings, festivals and other community events, this was an approved venue for courtship and for flirtation.

She had been naive to imagine that everyone would be focusing on Luke and Lydia. After all, the idea of a courtship between her sister and the blacksmith was something townspeople had speculated on almost from the moment Luke Starns had arrived in Celery Fields. It was old news whereas Greta's breakup with Josef was fresh fodder for the gossip mill. Everyone would be far more interested in where she—and Josef— might choose to sit.

"Staying for the singing is a terrible idea," she announced as she plopped down next to Lydia on the bench where her sister had spent the afternoon reading.

"But I thought…" Lydia studied her for a long moment. "I see. You are afraid of what people will say about you—and Josef."

"I am not afraid," Greta protested. "It's just that it's so soon and…"

"If we leave then I cannot accept Luke Starns's offer of a ride home," Lydia reminded her.

"Of course you can. In fact it makes more sense than my tagging along. I'll just pretend…"

"No. Either you and I both go home now or we both stay."

Greta could be every bit as stubborn as her sister. She folded her arms across her chest and said, "Then I guess we both go home. We can walk."

"Fine. You will go and tell Luke Starns of the change in plans," Lydia instructed. "Now."

"You should be the one. It's you he wants to see later," Greta argued.

"It was your decision to accept his offer to drive us here for services and it is now your decision to leave before the singing. You owe the blacksmith an explanation—in person."

"Fine," Greta huffed. As the sister of the woman that Luke intended to court, there was no reason for Greta not to be seen talking to Luke. Anyone observing them would assume that she was simply furthering the courtship on her sister's behalf. So Greta made no attempt to hide her destination as she stomped across the yard toward the barn. From inside the barn she could hear the snort of a horse and the deep, soft voice of Luke talking to the animal. She took a moment to close her eyes and pray for the right words and then she walked toward the stall at the far end of the barn.

"Luke Starns," she called out, inching her way forward as her eyes became accustomed to the shadows cast by a late afternoon sun.

He stepped out from the stall, holding a grooming brush in one hand. *"Yah?"*

Greta pasted a smile on her face although she doubted he could really see it. "I'm afraid that... That is my sister..."

Luke turned and continued brushing the horse. "Your sister is having second thoughts," he said flatly. It was not a question.

What it was though was a way out of this entire mess. If she agreed then there would be no further need for explanation. Greta chewed on her lip. But lying was a sin and that would definitely count as a lie.

"I am having second thoughts," she admitted.

The brush rested on the horse's hindquarters for a fraction of a second before Luke once again resumed the rhythmic stroking. "About me and your sister?"

"Oh no," she hurried to assure him. "Not at all."

"Then what?"

"Josef will be here for the singing." It was all the explanation she felt he needed. After all, he knew the whole story.

"Yah. And at least a dozen other people."

"All talking about us—Josef and me."

"That will happen whether or not you are here."

He was right, of course. "But…"

He continued grooming his horse. "It seems to me that this boondoggle is something like a wildfire. If you can contain it before it spreads too far then it'll die down a lot quicker."

The man was speaking in riddles. "And just how do you suggest I do that?"

He put down the brush and turned to face her. "Go to the singing tonight. Tomorrow go about your business—shopping, errands, whatever you would normally do. It's natural that you'd rather hole up in your house there until this thing burns itself out, but that'll take a lot longer than facing things head-on will."

The fact that she knew he was probably right annoyed her. The fact that he thought she would "hole up in their house," when Greta Goodloe had not once in her life backed down from anyone, was just plain insulting. She drew herself up to her full height—a good six inches less than his—and took a step closer to him.

"You don't know the first thing about me, Luke Starns," she challenged and to her fury the man actually chuckled.

"You've got me there. But it seems to me that if you're in favor of us becoming family one day, then it might be a good idea for you and your sister and me to get better acquainted." He went back to brushing the horse. "So what's it going to be, Greta?"

He was daring her and clearly he thought she would not take the dare. Well, she would show him. She would show all of them. "My sister and I will be sitting at the far end of the table. Try to be there in time to take the seat across from her although I suspect most everyone will make sure you have that privilege," she announced and turned on her heel and marched out into the fading sunlight. Behind her she was sure that she heard Luke chuckling again.

Chapter Five

As Greta had predicted, Josef was at the singing. He had taken a seat directly across from the storekeeper's daughter. And Esther Yoder was lapping up this unexpected attention like a cat at a bowl of fresh cream.

With a defiant lift of her chin, Greta turned the beam of her smile on young Caleb Harnischer and took the seat opposite the boy. Caleb looked alarmed and at the same time Lydia jerked her head in the direction of Pleasant's stepdaughter, Bettina Obermeier. The girl had been about to take the place that Greta occupied.

"Sorry," Greta murmured and slid away from Lydia, leaving the space between them free for Bettina. When she recovered from her embarrassment, she glanced up and saw that she was seated across from Cyrus Bontrager—Josef's bachelor uncle. The man was something of a legend in town and not for good reasons. Over his fifty-some years he had attempted to pursue just about every eligible young woman in Celery Fields with no success. When he looked across the table and saw Greta sitting there, his eyes lit up.

A smothered giggle from Esther Yoder told Greta

that she was once again the center of attention. She cast about in desperation for some way to take back control of her situation.

"Aah, Caleb," she asked, turning her attention to the boy who was five years her junior, "how are things at the ice cream shop?" Her voice sounded shrill and nervous even to her own ears, and drew the attention of several people up and down the table, to her horror.

Caleb murmured something in reply but Greta was beyond hearing him. Close to tears from the exhaustion of a sleepless night and the strain of the day, she stood up. "Excuse me," she murmured and started for the door. But Luke stepped around the table at that moment and blocked her way. "Let me pass," she whispered hoarsely.

"No," he murmured back although he was smiling at her. "Stand your ground." It occurred to her that his smile was meant not for her but for the others. The man was covering for her. He had been on his way to take his place next to Caleb and across from Lydia. He glanced at Caleb as if he had simply joined the conversation. "It's amazing that in spite of hard times people still need their treats, right, Caleb?"

The boy grinned at Luke, clearly flattered that this man would engage him in conversation. "We'll have a fresh batch of butter pecan next Saturday," Caleb said. "That's your favorite, right?"

"It is. Do you know everyone's favorite flavor?"

"Just the regulars," Caleb replied shyly.

"And Greta Goodloe? What's her favorite?"

"Chocolate with nuts."

Greta noticed that everyone else seemed to have

fallen back into the normal routine of getting settled onto the benches and greeting their friends.

"And Lydia Goodloe's?" Luke asked as he took his seat across from Greta's sister.

Up and down the table conversation paused as those near enough to overhear nodded knowingly as if they knew they had been right all along in assuming that Luke and Lydia would be together.

"Strawberry," Lydia said and to Greta's amazement her sister gave Luke the most radiant smile. Then she opened her songbook and looked over her shoulder at Greta. "They are about to begin, sister." She nodded toward the empty space next to Bettina and across from Cyrus. Reluctantly Greta took her seat.

The singing seemed as endless as the service that morning. Greta felt as if she were a prisoner in the large barn lit by a line of kerosene lanterns spaced along the table. She could hardly ignore the way that Josef would every once in a while glance at Esther over the top of his songbook and smile. And as the evening wore on, Greta realized that the smiles Josef and Esther were exchanging were far too familiar to be the start of something new. No, those smiles were the smiles of two people who shared a secret.

So there had been someone else, Greta fumed silently and she made no pretense at keeping up with the words the others were singing. A combination of jealousy and guilt overwhelmed her and this time she needed no excuse to leave the table. Without a word she stumbled toward the open doors of the barn and the sanctity of the darkness beyond. She felt all eyes follow her as she hurried away and once outside she gulped in the humid night air and fought against the tears that she simply refused to allow herself to shed.

Cry over Josef Bontrager after everything she had put up with all these years? His moods, his insistence that everything be done to his satisfaction, his constantly trying to change her—mold her into some ideal he held of the perfect wife and mother?

That was it, she realized. All the time that Josef had courted her, he had been trying to change her. He didn't love *her,* she realized. He loved her appearance—took sinful pride in being seen with such a pretty and popular woman. But how many times when he spoke of their future had he reminded her that, once they were married, she would need to temper her curiosity and natural instinct to speak her mind?

And truth be told she had thought she could change him, as well—once they were married. She had imagined that he would become less reserved and more outgoing. She had been certain that the children they would have would soften his strict demeanor. But now, as she walked a distance from the barn to the bench where Lydia had sat earlier, she had to admit that she had been wrong—as wrong about Josef as he had been about her. And in her heart she forgave him for the pain he had caused her and she prayed for God's forgiveness for her own selfishness. "But, heavenly Father, I cannot understand what You have in mind for me."

The darkness gave her the advantage of seeing without being seen and so she studied the gathering in the barn even as she tried to make sense of what God's plan for her could possibly be. She saw Lydia glance anxiously toward the yard a couple times but knew that her sister would not come to find her. Doing so would just call more attention to the situation and Lydia was a little like Josef in that she did not like being noticed by others.

Calmer now, Greta took a moment to consider Luke Starns. She wondered if Lydia had noticed how truly handsome he was. He did not smile readily or often but on the rare occasions when he did, his full lips parted to reveal even, white teeth and just the hint of a dimple in his left cheek. He was broad shouldered and well muscled—the result, as Lydia had suggested, of the work he did. And he was tall. That was good because Lydia was also tall—with dark hair and thick lashes and a smile that she kept mostly to herself.

Greta supposed that they would make a good match—at least they made a handsome pair. But she had now come to realize that outward appearances were far less important than what intentions and secrets might be kept inside. Lydia was right. What did anyone truly know about Luke Starns after all? The man had appeared in town last spring and purchased the livery business from the previous owner who had decided to move back north. He had quickly earned a reputation for honesty and hard work and those two traits had been enough for most people in town to accept him without question. But who was he?

Greta frowned—all thoughts of Josef gone as she focused on the dark stranger who had set his sights on her sister. In the absence of their parents or any other close family beyond Pleasant, surely it was up to her to look out for Lydia's best interests. Before she would condone a match she wanted to make certain that this man was exactly who he presented himself to be. *And what was that?* she wondered and realized that neither she nor Lydia nor anyone else in town had the slightest idea.

The minute he'd seen Greta flee the crowded room, Luke's instinct had been to go after her. But, of course, that would raise eyebrows up and down the table and the last thing she needed right now was more gossip and speculation. He glanced over at Lydia. She kept her eyes lowered but with an almost imperceptible shake of her head seemed to read his thoughts and let him know that it would not do to go after Greta.

Still, he could not seem to help but worry about her, imagining her out there in the dark, heartbroken. She had had a difficult time of things these last two days and his heart went out to her. Greta wasn't like her sister. Lydia was strong willed and pragmatic. And she had a deep abiding faith that whatever might happen, it was God's will and would become clear in due time. Greta did not appear to be quite so blind in her faith and Luke realized that this was a trait that the two of them shared.

He forced his attention back to the singing and the barrel-chested Josef Bontrager seated three men away from him. The man had his head thrown back and eyes tightly closed as he raised his high-pitched—and slightly off-key—tenor in song. It was almost as if he was determined to call attention to himself. Or was he simply trying to drown out the vision of Greta running from the room? Watching him, Luke found himself curling his hands into fists. He had never in his life wanted to strike another human being the way he wanted to strike Josef. He forced his breathing to calm and relaxed the tension in his hands. Was it reasonable for him to feel so protective of the Goodloe woman? If it had been Lydia his reaction might make sense, but Greta?

Of course, in the future, if his plan to court Lydia worked out, Greta would become his sister-in-law. She would be family. And as such his instinct to protect her—especially if she remained unwed—would be normal. It would even be expected. But the venom he was feeling toward his fellow man at the moment seemed anything but brotherly concern. He was about to close his eyes and seek God's forgiveness for his rambling thoughts when a movement outside the double barn doors caught his eye and he saw that Greta Goodloe was standing just out of the pool of light cast by the lanterns. Her arms were folded across her rigid body and if he didn't know better he would think that she was staring not at Bontrager—but at him.

With relief Greta heard the gathering launch into the final song of the evening. *Gott ist die Liebe* was everyone's favorite and seemed a fitting conclusion to a day that had begun with prayer and ended in song. Now everyone would spend the next half hour visiting and enjoying some refreshments before heading home.

In the past she and Josef had often been the center of a lively group of young people, talking and laughing before the two of them headed back to town in Josef's open-topped courting buggy. On such occasions Lydia would either have stayed home from the singing, staying the night with Pleasant or she would find her own way home to allow the courting couple their privacy. If Lydia went home, she would head to her room to pretend to sleep so that the couple could sit on the porch together. It struck Greta that tonight she would be the one to go off to her room and pretend sleep while Luke and Lydia sat together on the porch. Would Luke try to kiss Lydia? She found herself thinking about how his full, soft lips might feel.

"Stop that," she hissed, shocked at such a scandalous thought.

Once everyone had risen from the long table and gathered in small clusters near the entrance to the barn to partake of the refreshments that Pleasant had set out, it was easy to rejoin the group without making herself a spectacle. She slipped back into the gathering and took her place next to Lydia. Blessedly the others were more focused on the pastries and—in some cases— each other as everyone enjoyed this rare opportunity to socialize. Greta nibbled at a cookie, nodding and smiling as the conversation swirled around her.

"Come help Pleasant carry these leftovers back to the house, Greta," Lydia instructed as she wiped the table with a damp cloth. "Then we should be getting home. It's been a long day and I have school tomorrow."

"Where's Luke?"

"I expect he's gone to hitch up his team," Lydia replied, handing Greta an empty platter and nodding toward the house.

Lydia's demeanor had not changed in the slightest. If she was nervous about Luke seeing her home she certainly didn't show it. *How does she do it?* Greta wondered as she carried the metal tray across the yard to the farmhouse. Nothing ever seemed to ruffle Lydia.

Oh how Greta wished she could be as calm and serene as her sister was.

"Tell your sister that I have the wagon ready, Greta Goodloe."

The voice came out of the dark and startled her so much that she dropped the tray. When she bent to retrieve it, Luke was already there and their fingers brushed as he picked it up and handed it to her. "Sorry. I thought you saw me walking across the yard," he said. As the two of them slowly stood upright, Greta was far too aware of how very close their faces were. In the dim lamplight that glowed inside the kitchen and spilled out onto the back porch, she saw that he was studying her and his lips were parted in a half smile.

"What?" she demanded, touching her bonnet that must surely have been knocked askew.

"Nothing. You were looking right at me just before and yet it's as if you didn't see me at all." His voice softened as he added, "What had you so lost in thought that you didn't know I was here?"

"I was just… It's been a puzzling day."

"How so?"

She shot him a look as she clutched the empty tray to her chest. "Now you're making fun of me and that's just cruel, Luke Starns." She marched up the three porch steps but he was there ahead of her, holding open the screen door for her.

"Again I apologize. It's that for a moment back there you looked so…"

"So what?"

"Lost," he said.

The word mirrored her feelings and so overwhelmed her that she felt tears fill her eyes. "You should go and find my sister, Luke. I think I will stay the night here with Pleasant and her family." The minute the words were out Greta knew that this was the best possible decision. She could help Pleasant with the children and her Monday chores and then walk back to town later tomorrow when everyone else would be occupied with their daily routines.

He frowned. "Don't make the mistake of hiding from your fears, Greta," he advised.

Greta laughed. "You are already beginning to sound like an older brother and you have not yet begun the first instance of courting my sister. Can you not see that I am doing you a favor? Now you will have my sister's company all to yourself."

Luke frowned and Greta sighed heavily. "Is this not what you want? My help in your courtship of my sister?"

"Your sister did not agree to be escorted home without you," he replied.

"Well, she will understand that my mind is made up and that she has no other choice but to accept your offer to take her home. Now go."

Greta did not think she had ever been as exhausted as she was in that moment. Honestly, was there no pleasing the male of the species?

Luke held the reins loosely in his right hand as the team plodded along the familiar road. The night was pitch black without moon or stars and Lydia sat stone still beside him. So still that she might have been a piece of the wagon rather than a living, breathing human being. The two of them had not exchanged two words from the moment they had left the Troyers' farm. Even then her words had been for her sister, Greta, and for her half sister, Pleasant. Both of them had assured her that the idea of Greta staying the night was a blessing all around. But it was clear that Lydia remained unconvinced.

It was also evident that her concern was not about finding herself alone with him headed to a house where she would be alone for the night. In the Amish community courtship was a private matter—even among those as young as Caleb and Bettina. Routinely when a boy asked to see a girl home the parents would make it their business to be in bed, leaving the young couple the privacy of the porch where they could sit and talk and plan a future. In fact once a couple began seeing each other, it was assumed that both had already decided that the other had the necessary traits to make a good mate—patience, humility, frugality, hardworking and devoted to their faith. Love did not enter into the decision for many. It was a practical decision—a next step in the routine of their earthly life. Luke had no reason not to believe that this would be the case between Lydia and him.

No. There would be no gossip about Lydia riding home alone with Luke tonight. Now if he had driven her home after services in broad daylight, that would be a different matter altogether. Once he and Lydia had begun their courtship it would be all right for Greta to ride with him in daylight, but not Lydia. Not until the bishop had announced their intention to wed.

Luke realized that he had allowed his thoughts to wander, unable to come up with any topic that might interest Lydia and lead to a conversation between them. They were almost halfway back to town when she cleared her throat and shifted slightly away from him on the wagon seat.

"We must discuss this, Luke," she announced as if they had been talking from the moment they left the farm.

"Bitte?"

"This business," she gritted out, flicking her forefinger back and forth between them. "This…courtship." The way she said the word it sounded as if it was something distasteful.

Luke bristled. He wasn't the smartest man in the community—certainly his book learning was nowhere near hers, but that did not mean that…

"We are too long past our youth to deceive ourselves, you and I," Lydia continued. "I admit that I do not fully know your reasons and I suppose that if we both set our minds to it we could have a satisfactory life together."

"But?" he prompted.

She actually turned toward him. "But why would either of us want such a life?"

"It is what we do, Lydia," he reminded her. "In our tradition we find a mate and if love comes then…"

"But why not marry for love in the first place?"

Luke was stunned. "That's just…" He fumbled for words.

"Not done?" She knotted her hands together in her lap. "Oh, but it is. In Celery Fields there have been two such instances just in the recent past—Hannah and Levi Harnischer were a most unlikely match. And Pleasant and Jeremiah? It seemed impossible and yet look at them. Look at the way they are with each other.

Think how their love has brought such life and happiness to those dear children."

"Celery Fields is a small community, Lydia," he reminded her gently. "It's getting smaller each year as more people leave to return to homes and families up north. As you have already noted, you and I are no longer teenagers. If we are to have a marriage and children, then..."

"It sounds like a business arrangement," she huffed. "And I will have no part of it. I have a good life. I have my teaching and my students. I have no need of a union that is made for the sole purpose that it's the best we can manage."

Luke's hand tightened on the reins. He hardly knew what to say. Certainly he had misjudged this woman with her independent ideas and her sharp words that she seemed unaware could wound another person. "I may not be..." he began softly, then swallowed hard around the fury he was feeling and trying to control. "I would be a good provider, Lydia," he amended.

"Oh, Luke, forgive my thoughtless words. You are much respected throughout the community. But I am not blind, Luke. I saw the way you watched Greta tonight."

"Your sister..."

She interrupted his protest with a raised hand. "Actually I have observed you for some time now."

Luke looked over at her, surprised at this admission.

"Oh, don't look so shocked. It's common knowledge that all of Celery Fields has been planning a match for us. I needed to know exactly what such a match might offer."

"And I offer so little that you want to thrust me off onto your sister?"

"Now you are suffering from wounded pride. I love my sister, Luke. If I am saying that I see you as a good match for her then I am paying you the highest of praise. Rest assured that I never thought or said such a thing about Josef Bontrager."

"Which brings us to the heart of the matter," he argued. "Greta and Josef have been in love for…"

"My sister does not love that man—not in the way she needs to in order to spend the rest of her life under the same roof with him. Josef was a habit—a safe harbor in a community that offers women like my sister few choices. She has never loved him as more than a friend and surrogate brother."

"And what if he comes back to her, apologizes and…"

Lydia actually snorted with laughter. "Open your eyes, Luke. Did you not see the way he was flirting openly with Esther Yoder tonight?"

"Yes, but he could have been doing that just to make Greta jealous." Lydia's lack of a quick comment told him that she was considering this.

"Then there's no time to waste. Greta is most vulnerable at the moment." She turned to him. "It is evident that you are attracted to her, perhaps only now recognizing those feelings because of her break with Josef that makes her available for you to consider seriously."

"I have not once…"

"Please do not attempt to cover your feelings with excuses. I have long ago grown used to the fact that there is something about Greta that draws others to her—men and women and children alike. Why should you be any different?"

"I was going to say, your sister is someone who has a way about her, that's for sure. However, it was not your sister that I set my sights on when I decided to take a wife."

Lydia sighed heavily. "Will you listen to yourself? You speak of choosing a partner for life as if you were in the throes of choosing a horse. 'You' decided?" She practically spit the words at him.

"Well, of course, if you would rather I not…"

"I would rather we all be happy, Luke—you, me and yes, Greta."

"I'm not sure she would appreciate your trying to replace Josef Bontrager in her affections almost before she's had time to get used to the idea that this might indeed be final and not one of his little tantrums."

To his surprise Lydia actually giggled. "He does have a tendency toward the childish behavior, doesn't he?"

Luke smiled. "You know as well as anyone that there is still every possibility that he will come to his senses and beg for her forgiveness."

"All the more reason for you to step in now."

"I do not follow your reasoning and besides…"

Yet another sigh of pure exasperation. "Luke, are you or are you not attracted to my sister?"

"We have already…"

"The truth," she demanded.

"*Yah.* Of course, but not in the way that you may think."

"Or is it not in the way that *you* won't allow yourself to think?"

Luke gritted his teeth. Lydia Goodloe with all her book learning was far too smart for him. She talked in riddles that made him uncomfortable. He fought hard to maintain his temper with her and then thought about years of enduring such probing conversations.

"I will say this only once more, Lydia Goodloe. If you do not wish to be out riding with me then say so and tonight will be the end of it."

For a long moment the only sounds were the night-calling birds, the clop of the horses' hooves on the hard-packed road and his own frustrated breathing. Then Lydia straightened on the wagon seat next to him and said softly, "I have taken care of Greta for most of her life, Luke. She is not only my sister—she is my responsibility. Our parents have died and we have no other siblings—other than Pleasant, our half sister. I only want what is best for Greta."

"And what is that?"

"Greta's attraction to Josef was never about her love for him but rather for the life he represented to her. A home that she could manage, children she could mother and raise—these are the things that my sister has dreamed of her entire life."

"I can see that, but where do I fit into this picture?"

Lydia looked directly at him for the first time since they'd boarded the wagon for the ride to town. "You could give her all of that, Luke Starns. And more importantly, you could give her a great deal more."

Luke met her gaze. "I'm listening."

"I believe that given some time you and Greta could love one another and even if not, you would provide her with the safe haven she needs—the kind of security to be herself that she has known with me all these years. Josef has never been able to accept her for who she is."

"And what about you?"

"I have a good life, Luke. I do not need more. Truly. But I worry about Greta and when she told me about what Josef had done, I realized that perhaps this time I could help her find another way. So I prayed last night and all through the day today for God to show me His will. And it seemed that every time I looked up from my prayers, you were there. I know that you protected her yesterday. I know how inquisitive Roger Hadwell can be. Before you know it, you are telling him things you hadn't planned to reveal. And yet I knew the minute I saw the Hadwells this morning that they had no idea anything had changed until the marriage announcements. They were as stunned as anyone else."

"Your sister suffered a terrible blow yesterday when Bontrager just quit her there in the middle of town, Lydia. It was not my business—much less Roger Hadwell's—to pry into that. I did only what anyone would have done given her state of distress when she entered my shop."

"And you have kept on doing such things. Tonight at the singing? Twice you intervened. Your instinct to protect her is apparent."

Luke sucked in a long breath and let it out slowly. "If you and I were to marry, Lydia, Greta would become my sister, as well. Of course, it would be my…"

"But if we married, Luke," she reminded him gently, "where would your heart be?"

From the day that he'd stepped off the train and settled in Celery Fields, the women in town had been planning a match for him and it was hardly a secret that their choice was Lydia. "You realize that in rejecting me you are going to disappoint all of Celery Fields?"

"They'll recover, especially if you will follow my advice and pursue my sister instead."

In that moment the front wheel of the wagon hit a deep rut and swayed. Lydia instinctively put out her hand to steady herself, clutching Luke's hand in the process. He spoke gently to the team of horses to reassure them but it was not the brush of Lydia's hand—quickly withdrawn—that he found himself recalling. It was the memory of Greta's fingers on his when they both reached for the tray.

Nonsense, he thought, shaking off the memory as he gathered his thoughts.

"Well," Lydia prompted. "What do you think?"

"I have stated this as plainly as I can, Lydia. If you prefer that I not call on you, just say so and we'll have no more of it. I do not need your assistance in seeking a wife."

"No, you don't. But Greta needs precisely such assistance in her quest to find a husband."

They had finally reached the Goodloe house and Luke called for the horses to halt. Lydia was down from the seat before he could make his way around the team to offer help. She stood on the first step that led up to the front door.

"Come and sit," she invited. "We need to work out a plan as soon as possible if you would be interested in a match with Greta," she said. Clearly in Lydia's mind they had both agreed to this incredible plan of hers to secure a groom for her sister.

"Lydia, I barely know your sister." But he followed

her onto the porch and took his place next to her in the weathered wooden swing.

"You know me no better, Luke, and yet you evidently felt you knew me well enough to escort me home this evening. Greta would be a good match for you. Far better than I could ever be. You and I are both of a more serious nature. I thank God every day for the blessing of having Greta in my life. She brings a certain joy to the lives of others that would certainly be missing if it weren't for her. It seems to me that you would be a man in need of her...lightness."

He smiled in the darkness. "Now who is the one speaking as if she were selling a horse?" he teased.

"There is a way that we could manage this so that no one would be the wiser. All of Celery Fields would assume you were courting me, and in the meantime you and Greta..."

Luke stood. "It's clear you want what's best for your sister, Lydia, but give her time to find her own way—her own heart."

"Very well. I will not pursue this any further this evening but I will ask that you think over what I have proposed. Should you decide against the idea, then I would accept that. Either way I want to thank you for the kindness and caring you have shown Greta. It is evident to me that you are a good man, Luke. A man that my sister—and I—can trust to do the right thing. Good night."

Luke waited until Lydia had entered the dark house. After a moment she lit a lamp. And he saw her in silhouette as she took a seat near the window and opened a book. Behind him one of the horses shuddered, setting the harness to jingling in the still heat of the night.

Without climbing back onto the wagon, Luke led the team down the lane to his shop, and all the while he found himself thinking about the impossible idea that Lydia had suggested. Him with the vibrant and fickle Greta?

If ever he'd needed proof that God had a sense of humor, surely this was it. But he admired Lydia for her intense loyalty and love for her sister. And the truth was that he could not stop thinking about Lydia's plan—and how it might just work.

Chapter Six

"What do you mean you rejected Luke Starns?" Greta demanded the following day when the sisters sat down for their evening meal after Lydia had come home from the schoolhouse. "You might at least give the man a chance."

"We are not right for each other, Greta. We are too much the same. There would be no...no..."

Greta had rarely seen her sister at a loss for words. "No what?"

Lydia shrugged and turned her attention to her soup. "No surprise, I suppose."

"You do not like surprises," Greta reminded her. "When I tried to surprise you on your birthday last year you were very cross with me as I recall."

"Greta, shocking someone out of their wits by springing at them from the dark with a cake lit by candles is hardly the same thing as getting to know another person and revealing hidden traits that are not at first evident."

"Don't use your teacher's tone with me," Greta snapped as she stalled for the time that she needed to translate what Lydia had just said. "Besides, isn't getting to know Luke exactly what is required here?" She felt triumphant to have found the chink in her sister's argument.

Lydia sighed. "You must trust my judgment in this, Greta. I know what makes my life content, what gives me pleasure and joy." She continued eating her soup as if they were discussing the weather.

"I don't understand you sometimes, Lydia," Greta groused. "And I have to say that I feel a little sorry for Luke Starns. It is obvious that he has taken some time to work up the nerve to approach you at all and then you reject him after one buggy ride?"

"We rode in a wagon," Lydia corrected, ever the stickler for the details.

"Wagon…buggy. You're missing my point."

Lydia looked at Greta directly. "What is your point, sister?"

"I… You…" Greta drew in a long breath, forcing her jumbled thoughts into some semblance of order and out came the one thing she had not expected. "Are the two of us then to spend the rest of our days here—a couple of spinster sisters?"

To her surprise Lydia laughed. "Oh, Greta, Josef Bontrager is not the only candidate to court you. He has become a habit—one you should be more than happy to quit."

"I was not the one to quit this 'habit' as you may recall."

"No, he was. And I appreciate that you are hurt by his action—his cruelty. But the fact of the matter is that there is a man living right here in Celery Fields that I have come to believe would be the perfect match for you—and you for him."

Greta searched her brain for some logical candidate and found that no one came to mind. "Who?"

"The blacksmith."

"Oh, for goodness' sake, Lydia. I thought we were having a serious discussion about your future here. It is unlike you to make jokes…"

"I am quite serious, Greta." Lydia laid down her soupspoon and gave Greta her full attention. "Knowing that everyone had assumed Luke Starns and I would begin seeing one another, I took some time to study the man these last several months—to learn what I could of him through observation and conversation with others."

"And you decided he was not right for you. That does not mean that you can simply pass him off as if he were a book you'd started and decided you didn't care to finish."

"I am not passing him off, Greta. I had resigned myself to you and Josef marrying although I will admit to praying for God to ease my concerns for your ongoing happiness once the union took place. But now… Oh, sister, do you not see God's hand in all of this?"

It was rare for Lydia to become so impassioned—only when she believed that God was leading them did she exhibit such zeal and enthusiasm. But Luke Starns? And Greta?

"I have prayed long and hard on this and yesterday it seemed to me that God was guiding us in a direction that could not be denied. Just say that you will consider the idea, Greta," Lydia pleaded.

Greta hesitated. She could hardly admit that ever

since she'd gotten past the announcement of coming nuptials and everyone's gasp of surprise not to hear her name called, her thoughts had turned more than once to Luke Starns. She'd told herself that her only interest in the man was in whether or not he could make Lydia happy. But during the night when her thoughts had turned to memories of his smile and the touch of his hand brushing hers, she'd feared that perhaps she was more attracted to Luke than she had allowed herself to admit.

She studied her sister's features for any sign that she was simply giving up before she'd given her own romance a chance to begin. Lydia met her gaze clear-eyed and with the expression of one who knows her own mind. "But what of Luke's feelings in the matter?" Greta asked. "Does he have no say in this?"

"I have spoken to him and he…"

"You what? Lydia, how could you?" The words were a shout in Greta's mind but they came out as a whisper of pure disbelief. "Have you completely taken leave of your usual good sense?"

Lydia pressed her lips together and frowned. "Since the day our dear *Maemm* left this world, Greta, I have been trying to do what I believe is in your best interest, what will give you a life that fulfills the potential that God endowed you with—a spirit filled with joy and happiness that you so brilliantly share with others. You are meant to be a wife and mother—that is so clearly God's plan for you. Luke Starns will make a good husband and father. He will be a mitigating influence on your more capricious disposition and you in return will bring out the lighter side of his nature. The man carries a burden of sadness, Greta. That much is plain to see. And you said yourself that he is pleasant to look at and…"

"What did he say?" Greta had left the table, her supper untouched. She paced back and forth before the windows that looked out over the town and Luke's blacksmith and livery business. "When you spoke of this with him—what was his response?"

"He agreed to…consider the idea." Lydia's voice was not nearly so self-assured as it had been earlier. "Greta, I see now that I may have overstepped, but…"

Greta whirled around to face her sister. "*May* have? Do you have any idea of what you have done, Lydia?"

Lydia stood, picked up her soup bowl and turned toward the sink. "As I have said, I have tried to do what I thought best for you, Greta."

"I am not a child," Greta said. "And I am not one of your students, Lydia. The man I thought I would marry has not been gone but a little over two days and you have already…"

Lydia set down her dishes then faced Greta squarely. "Tell me that you love Josef Bontrager," she challenged. "Tell me that you ever truly felt for that man what a wife should feel for her husband."

The one thing that Greta had never been able to do—at least not convincingly—was tell a lie. She bowed her head for a moment, trying to frame her response. "In time we would have…"

"You have been together for much of your life, Greta. If you cannot summon such feelings now, what difference was a ceremony going to make for either of you?"

Greta felt the need to defend Josef, especially because Lydia's words had a disturbing element of truth to them. "He is a good man. He has been a good friend…"

"He is all of that and more—a good provider, a man of faith. Do you love him? Have you ever truly loved him?"

It took Greta several moments to answer but only because she was reluctant to admit what she had known for some time now. Lydia waited patiently.

"No, but…"

Lydia rested her hands on Greta's shoulders. "And that is my point. You deserve to love and be loved, Greta. You have so much to bring to a marriage and home of your own. Perhaps I have gone too far in speaking with the blacksmith. I see now that it was too soon—that you needed some time. And he may not be the right person at all. But I have prayed for your happiness for so long and last night when you were so upset at the singing I saw something quite unexpected."

"What was that?"

"I saw, sister, that Luke was upset for you."

"Of course. He looks upon me as a future member of his family—or at least he did. He thought that once you and he married we would be as brother and sister." She glanced out the kitchen window at the smoke rising from the chimney of Luke's business. He was still working although it was late in the day and all other shops were already closed. "I have to go and set things right," she announced.

She took down her bonnet from the hook by the front door and jammed it over her prayer *kapp,* not caring whether the pinned-up hair held. "I know you were only trying to help, Lydia, and I am grateful for that, but the idea that Luke Starns would have the slightest interest in me when everyone knows he had set his sights on you is ridiculous. You are understandably nervous about this entire matter of Luke courting you. But to turn the tables and try to convince him…"

"Please don't act in haste. Will you not pray on the matter first, Greta?"

"I will pray as I walk down to town," she called out as she left the house. "I will pray that God will give me the words to set this right again," she added in an undertone as she made her way down the sandy lane to where she could hear the rush of wind as the blacksmith pumped the giant bellows to stoke the fire.

Luke had thought of little else once Lydia Goodloe had laid out her idea that her sister Greta was the woman he should set his sights on. It was almost comical the way things had reversed. Back in Ontario the crafty father had sought a match for his elder daughter. Now the elder sister sought a match for her younger sibling. And in both cases Luke was in the middle of things. What plan did God have for him in all of this?

He pumped the large bellows next to his fire, noting how the exhale of air matched his own huffs of exertion and frustration. All he wanted was to settle down and start a family. That had always been God's plan for men like him—the responsibility to continue the line of the faithful, to do good works and to be a reliable member of the community. Why did that have to be so complicated?

"Luke Starns!"

He startled and nearly dropped the half-formed bridle bit that he'd begun to bend over the anvil. He glanced over his shoulder to find Greta Goodloe standing quite close to him, not more than a foot from the fire itself. She was tapping her foot impatiently and her arms were folded tightly across her body. From her expression he gathered she had been there for some time already.

"Careful of the fire," he said as he turned his attention back to his work.

She rolled her eyes. "I am not a child," she announced. "Although it appears that you and my sister have decided that I am. I am a grown woman and I will decide who I will permit to court me and who I will not."

Slowly Luke laid down the jig that he'd been about to use to break off an errant piece of metal. He glanced at her and fought a smile. The fact was that she looked exactly like a petulant child trying hard to appear grown-up. She was scowling up at him, her blue eyes glittering in the combination of the reflected light of the fire and late afternoon sunlight spilling in through the small window.

"I see you and your sister have discussed the matter," he said, turning again to his work mostly to hide his smile.

"My sister has taken it upon herself to manage my life for many years now."

"How blessed you are to have someone so concerned for your well-being."

She seemed to consider this and loosened the grip she had taken on her body with her folded arms. "Yes, well, she means no harm. Lydia is a good woman," she mused and then seemed to recall where she was and why she had come, "and that is all the more reason that you should see her suggestion that you and I... That we... She is testing you, Luke Starns."

He filed a burr from the bit. "How so?"

Her lips worked but no sound came out. She looked down at her black shoes and for the first time failed to meet his eyes directly. "It would be prideful of me to say so and that is not at all my intention but the fact remains that for all our lives people have thought of Lydia as the smart one and me as..."

Her voice trailed off.

"The pretty one?" Luke guessed.

She nodded once and then met his gaze. "But Lydia does not see her own beauty. She is not only smart. She is kind and caring and when she smiles..."

"She is all of that and more," Luke agreed.

Greta let out a sigh of relief. "Then you see it, as well. Oh, Luke Starns, do not let her put you off. My sister deserves happiness."

"And what about you?" He had not meant to speak his thought aloud and yet there it was. Greta's eyes widened in surprise. "Forgive me, Greta," he hastened to add. "I should not have... We were discussing your sister."

"And you," she reminded him. "So, what do you intend to do about this turn of events, Luke?"

"Do? Your sister made her feelings plain last evening. She does not wish to spend her time with me."

Greta sighed heavily. "She does not know what she wants. The question is are you serious about finding a wife for yourself or not?"

"I am quite serious."

"Then..."

"What I will not do," Luke interrupted her, "is go

after a woman who has declared openly that she has no interest in making a home with me."

Greta frowned, then took several breaths as if preparing to say something. But the silence between them stretched on for a long moment. At one point she turned away and he thought she had decided to leave, but then she paced a few steps and returned. This time she found the words. "And what of her idea that you and I should…" She let the sentence trail off.

Luke set down his file and examined the bit. "That depends," he said slowly.

"On what?" Greta had placed both hands on her hips, a stance so defiant that Luke was tempted once again to laugh.

"On whether or not you are able to put aside your feelings for Josef Bontrager. Your sister believes that your feelings for him were not as strong as they should be for two people planning a life together. Do you agree?"

"Lydia is… I mean… Oh, I don't know," Greta replied. "How can either of you expect me to know what it is that I'm feeling these days? It's too soon."

"Then let me put this a different way. If Josef came to you and asked for your forgiveness and pleaded with you to reconsider, would you?"

She blinked up at him—once, then again, then a third time. And all the while she chewed on her lower lip. He could practically hear her thinking this through. "No," she finally whispered. "I would not."

In his chest Luke felt his heart pounding and he realized that over the months he had been in Celery Fields, he had taken more notice of the beautiful Greta Goodloe than he had allowed himself to admit. He had learned a hard lesson back in Ontario and he had been determined not to make the same mistake twice.

But if she had come to realize that Josef was not for her...

On the other hand, surely the idea that she might be firm in her decision to be rid of Josef did not mean that she was ready for someone new. He cleared his throat. "Then that is an important first step that you have taken toward coming to an understanding of exactly what God's plan may be for you."

"And what comes next?" she moaned.

"In your shoes I think that I would ask God's guidance for moving forward from here."

She seemed to consider this and then accept it with a nod. "And what of you and Lydia?"

Luke sighed. She was like a dog with a fresh bone, worrying the thing to death trying to get at the marrow. "I have taken your sister at her word, Greta. And having done so, I also must pray for guidance."

Greta smiled and with that smile it seemed as if her entire being relaxed. She glanced around the shop, her gaze once again reminding him of that image he'd had during services of the butterfly flitting from one thing to the next until she finally settled her attention on him. To his surprise she plopped herself down on the wooden chair as if settling in for a long visit.

"We're quite a pair, aren't we, Luke Starns?"

"How so?"

"Each of us being so certain that we were on the right path. Neither one of us prepared in the least for the bumps and gullies along the way."

This time when he smiled, he did not try to hide it from her. At the same moment he realized that in the short while since he had first become aware of her presence, he had felt the urge to smile several times. "You will find what you want—what God wants for you," he assured her as he went back to his work.

"And you?" She was nothing if not persistent. Luke could only imagine how her pursuit of a matter to its end must have grated on the fence-straddling Josef Bontrager.

He shrugged and concentrated on completing the bridle bit, more to avoid her eyes than because the work was urgent. She got up and wandered closer to the fire.

"Why do you not have more light in here?" she asked.

The abrupt change in topic was unnerving—as was his awareness of her nearness as she studied the work he was doing. "I need the shadows to distinguish the temperature and pliancy of the metal," he replied.

"How so?"

He took a length of scrap metal and placed it in the fire pit. "See the red? And now orange?"

She nodded.

"It will glow yellow and when it is white, then it will melt. I need to take it from the fire when it is somewhere between the orange and the yellow. We call that 'forging heat'—the point at which the metal can be shaped. Too much light can make it hard to see the change in color."

She was standing so near to him that if either of them moved an inch their sleeves would brush. In the glow of the embers, her face took on a radiance that made his heart beat faster. He took a step away. "You should probably be getting back," he said.

She walked toward the double doors but paused when she reached them. "You know," she said wistfully as she looked out toward the street that was deserted as evening began to settle over the town, "Josef was not simply the man I thought I would marry. From the time we were seven he was like the brother I never had. Oh, we had a half brother—Pleasant's brother. He was Caleb's *Dat,* but he died when I was very little and I never really knew him. So I relied on Josef. Josef and Lydia have always been my two best friends. Now there is just Lydia."

Her voice trailed off as she continued staring out at the street. He watched her for a moment, trying to decide if she might be shedding more tears over Bontrager. But she seemed calm and if not serene, then at least resigned. He wiped his hands on a rag as he walked to where she stood.

"I would be your friend, Greta Goodloe," he said softly.

She turned to him, the fading sunlight on her face. Her expression was one of bewilderment. Then without another word she walked out of the shop and back down the lane to the house she shared with her sister.

"I would be your friend, Greta," Luke repeated in a high falsetto voice that mimicked his own. "No wonder you are not yet wed," he groused as he returned to work.

All the way back to the house, Greta thought not about her own troubles or even about Josef. She found herself thinking about Luke Starns—the gentleness of his words, his offer of friendship. Lydia was right. He was a good man.

"Well?" her sister asked the minute Greta stepped into the kitchen. It was as if Lydia had been holding her breath the entire time Greta was gone.

Greta shrugged. "We talked a bit." She took down a jar of candied orange rind the sisters had put up the previous winter and selected one of the sweets, then held out the jar to Lydia who waved it away impatiently.

"And?" she demanded.

Greta shrugged. "He said that he will not pursue you if that's your wish." She sucked the sugar off the orange rind. "Of course, in my opinion, you are making a huge mistake."

Lydia snorted with derision. "This is hardly a matter for levity, Greta."

"I'm not laughing."

Lydia frowned. "I thought you went there to set matters straight regarding a courtship with you."

"We discussed that, as well—briefly." Greta popped the last of the orange sweet into her mouth and then licked her fingers.

"Well, to what end did you discuss matters?" Lydia asked.

"I told him that I thought you had simply suffered a bout of nerves."

"I have suffered no such thing. I know my mind, sister."

"He seems to have accepted that. It would appear that the two of you are well matched in your determination not to be swayed."

This time the sigh that Lydia released was one of relief. "Well, at least there is that." She focused her attention on Greta. "But my concern is for you—you and your dream of starting a home and family of your own, Greta."

"With Josef."

"So you thought."

"So everyone thought," Greta corrected.

"Even so, it appears that God has given you—and Josef—a new direction. However that does not mean that His intent for your future has changed. Luke would make a fine husband and father. He is a good provider and a solid member of the community. You could not do better."

"Nor could you."

Greta almost laughed when she saw Lydia's mouth working but no sound coming out. Her sister was always at a loss for words on those rare occasions when Greta made a strong logical point. The role of teacher turned student was not a comfortable one for Lydia.

"But I will accept your decision in the matter," she added.

"Gut," Lydia announced, taking charge once more. "Then my decision is that you and Luke Starns will begin seeing one another for the purpose of determining whether or not this is the direction God is leading the two of you." She stopped Greta's protest with a raised hand. "In fact, while you were out, I came up with the perfect plan to give you both the time and privacy you will need to become better acquainted. Should things not work out, no one will be the wiser."

Greta sat on the edge of a kitchen chair, her chin in her hands. There was no sense arguing with Lydia. She would have her say and once she had spoken, Greta would do as she always had. She would go her own way. "I'm listening."

"As of last evening, the whole community thinks that Luke has begun his courtship with me," Lydia began. "That means that should they see you and Luke talking or walking together or riding somewhere together, they will not so much as raise an eyebrow. As my sister—and presumably someone who is helping the romance along—it is perfectly acceptable for you to be seen with Luke."

Greta was completely confused. "So, you are saying that you wish for Luke to court you after all?"

"No," Lydia exclaimed. "Don't you see? Because everyone will assume that he is courting me, you and he will be able to spend time together without any pressure or expectations." She drummed her fingers on the kitchen table as apparently a new wrinkle in her plan came to mind. "Of course, it will be expected that he will come to call on me in the evenings after you have retired for the night, but no matter. It will be dark and the two of you on the porch will look no different to anyone passing by than if I was the one sitting there with Luke. Yes, this will work beautifully."

"Aren't you forgetting one small thing, Lydia?"

"I don't think so. I have gone over this idea thoroughly and…"

"You do not have Luke's agreement—or mine—to pursue this." But even as she said those words, her mind had already begun racing with the possibilities that Lydia's plan could work for her. It would take the attention off her troubles and place the focus on Lydia and Luke. Besides, the limited time that Greta had spent with the man had not been unpleasant. Not at all. And she could possibly coach him in ways to pursue Lydia—ways that would make Lydia fall in love with him.

"Greta, I am asking you to give the idea a try. Where is the harm in that?"

Greta knew her sister well enough to understand that Lydia had made up her mind on this matter and would not be moved. "All right," she said. "If Luke Starns agrees to your plan then I'll do it."

But later that night long after Lydia had gone to sleep, Greta lay awake trying to work through the jumble of thoughts that came with the idea of putting Lydia's plan into action. Finally she threw back the light quilt and went to stand at her open window, hoping to catch a breath of air in the still steamy night.

And that's when she saw the smoke and then a flash of orange—a flame reflected in the window of Luke's shop.

"Fire!" she shrieked as she grabbed her shawl and ran toward the blacksmith's shop.

Chapter Seven

"Fire!" Greta shouted again and pointed to the blacksmith's shop when a sleepy-eyed Lydia stumbled onto the porch, barefoot and confused.

"I'll go to the school and ring the bell," Lydia told her, instantly awake and taking charge as she pulled on her shoes and grabbed her shawl. "You go and make sure that Luke is out and rouse the Hadwells and Yoders and others."

Greta took off, her loosened hair flying out behind her, her bare feet oblivious to the stones and calcified seashells that pocked the sandy lane. The smell of smoke was strong now and from inside the shop she could hear a horse whinny and the crackle of the flames. "Luke," she screamed as she started up the outer stairs that led to his living quarters above the shop.

Before she could reach the door, Luke emerged, hooking his suspenders over his shoulders as he ran down the stairs toward her. "Get back to your house," he ordered. "Go!"

In the background they both heard the clanging of the schoolhouse bell.

"There's a horse," Greta told him.

"I know. There are four of them. I'll take care of that. Just get away from the building now." He wrapped his arm around her and half carried, half propelled her the rest of the way down the stairs.

A buzz of voices coming their way told Greta that the school bell had done its job and those people living in town were up and responding. Roger Hadwell was already handing out buckets from his hardware store. Someone else was pumping water into a horse trough outside the burning building. A bucket line quickly formed—men, women, children all working in unison to fight the flames that now had broken through to the roof.

Seeing that there was nothing she could do to help the others, Greta ran back to the rear of the shop where she'd seen Luke head after he'd told her to go home— as if she could. As if anyone living in Celery Fields would stay in the safety of their own homes when a fellow citizen was in trouble.

He was pulling a terrified horse from the stables, tugging on the rope as the horse dug in its heels and tossed its head, trying to loosen the rag that Luke had tied over its eyes to lessen the animal's panic. Luke had also covered the lower half of his face with a towel and now Greta did the same, pulling the end of her shawl over her mouth and nose as she ran toward the stables. Luke had said there were four horses. He had saved one, but the others must still be inside.

She ignored Luke's muffled shouts as she entered the stables where the fire raged at the front of the building. The rear stable area was filled with acrid smoke that stung her eyes and made her breathing come in labored huffs. She felt her way along the series of stalls, unleashing the remaining three horses and sending them one by one running free from the burning building, certain that Luke would be out there to calm them.

As she stumbled back into the yard of the livery, gasping for air, she saw Luke racing after the terrified horses as they dashed away in all different directions. "No!" he shouted as he chased one and then another to no avail. Then seeing Greta, he turned on her as he pulled down the wet cloth he'd used to cover his face. "What were you thinking?" he demanded as he took hold of her upper arms and stopped just short of shaking her.

"I was thinking we needed to get those animals to safety," she shouted above the din of the gathering crowd and the roar of the fire. Too late now she realized that in letting the animals run free she might have cost Luke a great deal more than the loss of his building and home. The horses were not his. He was providing livery service for their rightful owner. No wonder he was so angry with her. "I didn't think there was time…"

"You could have been overcome," he said, his face very close to hers. "You could have been killed."

It hit her then that what she had taken for anger was not that at all. His first thought had been for her—her safety, her well-being.

"But the horses—you would have lost…" She started to shake uncontrollably as it struck her that he was right. She had put her life at risk to save those animals.

He pulled her close, uncaring of who might take notice as he cradled her head in one large hand against his chest. "Sh-h-h," he said softly. "It's all over now. You're safe."

And as she gave herself over to his embrace of consolation she realized that in all the times that Josef Bontrager had held her, she had never once felt the safety and certainty that she felt now in the arms of Luke Starns. After a moment he stepped away but kept his one hand tangled in the thickness of her loose hair. Slowly he released her and then he took hold of the edges of her shawl and covered her hair and shoulders.

"Better?" he asked.

Greta managed a nod.

Behind her she heard a cry of alarm from the crowd fighting the flames and turned just in time to see one wall of the large structure collapse, sending a shower of sparks into the sky that was just beginning to show the first signs of dawn. She heard a horse's snort and saw that all three of the animals she'd set free had wandered back into the yard where they stood in a row, drinking from the trough in back of the hardware store.

Luke released a shuddering sigh and Greta took hold of his hand as they stood side by side, watching the uncontrollable fire. "You can rebuild," she assured him. "Everyone will help."

He stared at what had been his business and his home and nodded. "You should join the others," he told her as he gently pulled his hand free of hers and she knew that he was thinking of her reputation. Lydia was right. Luke Starns was definitely a man who thought of others before himself.

"You'll need a place to stay," she said.

"Something will turn up and it won't be for long." He smiled at her. "After all, this is Florida. I can sleep under the stars if need be and we can spend every day rebuilding."

She knew he would have no need to sleep outside and that in just a matter of days work would begin on rebuilding for that was the Amish way. Neighbor took care of neighbor. Luke's home and the source of his livelihood might lay in ashes today but it would not be long before he was back in business. The people of Celery Fields would see to that.

"Come on," she said, taking his arm and guiding him toward the main street where the members of the bucket brigade had faced reality and were standing together, waiting for the fire to burn itself out. As Luke approached the gathering, several men patted his shoulder while the women murmured their sympathies. Greta stood aside and let him be drawn into the circle of the townspeople.

"Is he all right?" Lydia asked, coming alongside her.

"He will be," Greta replied and in her heart she realized that she intended to make sure that this was the truth.

In the light of the new day, Luke stood at what had once been the entrance to his business and considered the smoldering remains. Dawn had brought with it a sky that was overcast and one that held the threat of rain. It occurred to him that God would send the showers to smother any embers that might lay hidden beneath the rubble. After that he could start the process of clearing away the rubble left after the fire. Roger had already stopped by to write up the order for the lumber and other supplies that Luke would need.

But as he stared at a thin thread of gray smoke rising from what had once been the stairway that led to his living quarters, he couldn't help but wonder if God had meant him to receive a different message from the fire. It was from the small kitchen at the top of the missing stairway that he had begun his study of Lydia Goodloe. From there he had watched her leave for the schoolhouse on the mornings when school was in session. He had watched her handle whatever chores needed attention outside the house while Greta apparently took charge of the cooking, laundry and cleaning chores. He had watched both sisters sitting on the porch after services or on the Sundays when there were no services reading or waiting—in Greta's case—for Josef Bontrager to come calling.

From time to time he would see Greta. Although he rarely studied her as he did Lydia. In those days he hadn't paid much attention to Greta. But he realized now that he had always been far more aware of the younger Goodloe sister than he had allowed himself to admit. She'd come out to the porch, say something to her sister and then take off walking toward town. Sometimes she would mount the bicycle the sisters owned and head off in the opposite direction toward the main road, toward Sarasota. Once or twice he had seen her return hours later and she would add a large whelk or conch shell to the border around Lydia's vegetable garden.

Today all that had changed. Today he couldn't seem

to focus on anything other than the sheer panic he'd felt when Greta had run into the stables and not reappeared for some time. The way her hair had felt as it tumbled over his hand. The way her small thin body had felt cradled against his. The lightness of her and at the same time a strength that could not be named—or denied. When he'd looked around and seen her running into the stables—into the very heart of the fire— he had acted purely on instinct, running after her. But he'd not gotten three steps before he was stopped by first one horse and then another and another charging him as they ran for safety. And then there she was and seeing her he found that he could breathe again.

When he'd held her and she'd looked up at him, her eyes sparkling with tears brought on by the smoke and perhaps her own realization of the chance she had taken, the urge to kiss her had been almost overwhelming. So much so that he had stepped away. But he had not released his hold on her hair—thick and yet fine as silk, golden with highlights of red like the flames shooting up to the sky behind her.

Lydia was right. He had set his sights on the wrong sister. But how best to convince Greta of that?

"Luke?"

He stiffened at the sound of Greta's voice behind him. He might be clear now about his feelings for her, but she was still too close to Bontrager's betrayal. For that matter she might be in love with Josef. He forced a half smile and looked around. "Thank you again for saving the horses," he said. "And to your sister for raising the alarm."

"It's still a total loss," Greta replied as she considered the pile of charred debris before them. "Have you found a place to stay until you can rebuild?"

"Haven't really thought about it. Something will turn up."

Greta released an exasperated sigh. "That's what you said last night. You're welcome to sleep in the loft of our barn if you like. Lydia said to offer."

Luke's grin widened. "She did, did she?"

"Don't get your hopes up," Greta advised, clearly mistaking his words for a sign that Lydia was softening toward him.

"I wasn't. I was just curious how you might feel about the arrangement."

"People will talk," she said with a shrug. "Lydia doesn't care one bit about what other people think or say but…"

"You do?"

She looked down. "Through no fault of our own, my sister and I have been the topic of gossip these last few days. I would like not to be in that position longer than is necessary."

He wondered if she was thinking about him holding her the night before. He wondered if perhaps someone had seen them and let Greta know that she had been seen in the arms of the man supposedly interested in her sister. "I'm sorry," he murmured. "The last thing I would want is to cause you—or your sister—distress. Tell Lydia that I am grateful for her kind offer but I will make other arrangements."

"*Denki,* Luke." She turned her attention more fully to the ruins before them. Carefully she walked closer, stepping over blackened wood as she reached down to retrieve one of his chisels. "Still warm," she said when she handed it to him.

"But still useable," he replied.

She smiled up at him and for a moment he could not find his breath. The business of being unable to breathe normally whenever Greta Goodloe was around was becoming an alarming habit.

"There must be more," she said. "Let me help you find them."

"Take care," he said as he followed her through the rubble. "There are still some live embers."

"I'll use this to move them," she said, holding up a piece of metal the length of a cane or walking stick. "Found another," she crowed triumphantly, holding up something that caught the sunlight. "We should have a contest to see which of us can find the most."

"We'll find everything when we haul away the debris," he reminded her. "There's no need to…"

"But that would not be nearly so much fun, Luke Starns. Do you not ever consider having a little fun?"

Fun? It sounded like a word from another language to Luke. He had been forced to maintain his focus on weightier matters for so long that solemnity had become a habit. How long had it been since he'd done something just for the pure pleasure of doing it? He moved a charred board with the toe of his boot and quickly uncovered three more small hand tools.

"Three to one," he called out as he set the tools in a pile.

"Unfair," Greta said but she was laughing and the sound was like musical notes. "You know what to look for—the shape and size and all."

"It was your idea," he reminded her as he held up

two nails that he'd forged last week. "There are at least a dozen of these if that helps."

"Found one," she shouted and then quickly dropped the nail and shook her hand. "Hot," she admitted.

"Work in this area," he advised, motioning to the ruins where he stood. "Everything here seems to have cooled off." He had to force himself not to go to her and examine the possible burn to her fingers.

"Here's another—and another," she said as she took his advice and immediately found two more of the nails. "You'd best start searching, Luke, or I am surely going to be the winner."

Luke made a halfhearted attempt to search the ground around his feet, but the truth was that the only thing he could look at was Greta's face hidden by her black bonnet and then turned up to him with that luminous, heart-stopping smile whenever she unearthed a new treasure.

He was considering the possibility that just maybe he might be able to persuade Greta to give her sister's plan a chance when he heard a shout from across the street and looked up to see Hilda Yoder bearing down on both of them.

"Uh-oh," Greta muttered. "We're in for it now, Luke Starns."

Greta straightened to her full height and folded her hands primly in front of her as she waited for Hilda Yoder to make her way from the dry goods store across the street to where Greta and Luke had been searching for things to be salvaged.

"Such levity after such tragedy," Hilda muttered, clicking her tongue in disapproval as she approached them. "Surely, Luke, you find no humor in the loss of your business."

"But I have not lost my business, Hilda," Luke explained. "I have only lost the building that housed it. I will rebuild and be back in business by month's end."

"Still, it hardly seems proper for the street to ring with laughter at a time like this." She frowned at Greta. "Do you not have things to do, Greta Goodloe?"

"Things to do?" Greta decided to play the innocent. She blinked her eyes at Hilda and was aware that Luke was fighting a smile.

"Shopping, ironing—whatever it is you do on a Tuesday morning."

"I had thought that such mundane chores might be postponed in light of our neighbor's loss," Greta replied. "I came to see how Lydia and I might best help Luke recover his losses. Lydia extended an invitation for him to lodge in our barn loft."

Hilda sucked in a breath that said far more than the stream of words she clearly was trying to swallow. But the very idea that two single women might house a single man, albeit in their barn, was clearly news that had shaken Hilda to her very core.

"It is a kind offer," Luke said, "and one that I have refused. I will seek other shelter."

"I should hope so," Hilda muttered.

"Perhaps you and your husband have a spare room?"

Greta had to bite her lip to keep from laughing out loud at the expression that passed over Hilda's face. So Luke Starns had a sense of humor after all. "The storage room at the back of the store," Greta suggested. "It would be perfect—close to everything he needs."

"I suppose that could be arranged," Hilda hedged.

"But there's to be no cooking on the premises. We've had one fire and there's no need to tempt fate by setting the stage for another."

"There, Luke, you see. It's all settled. Hilda and her family will take care of housing for you while Roger Hadwell takes charge of organizing the supplies and labor necessary for you to rebuild as soon as possible. And the women will see to organizing meals to feed the work crews." She clapped her hands together and beamed at them both.

Hilda pursed her lips and glared at Greta. "Then may I suggest that you get on with your piece of this, Greta? The work crews will likely be here first thing tomorrow to begin clearing away this rubble and they will need plenty of water and sustenance if they are to withstand the heat."

"Right you are," Greta said as she turned to head to her house. "I'll get started right away."

"I'll send Esther to help," Hilda called after her.

Greta's step faltered only slightly as the full weight of Josef's betrayal hit her once again. "Yes, please do," she called over her shoulder, but she knew that her voice was too high-pitched to sound sincere. And she knew that, in her way, Hilda had as usual had the last word.

"Oh, why does she have to be so mean-spirited?" Greta fumed later as she and Lydia sat together, each doing a bit of mending before bedtime.

"We may be Amish, but we are none of us angels," Lydia reminded her. "You must include Hilda in your prayers for surely her unpleasant behavior comes from some deep-seated unhappiness."

Greta sighed. "You are too forgiving sometimes,

Lydia. How about the idea that maybe she's just plain mean?"

"There is no such thing as being too forgiving and now I would suggest that you add a prayer asking God to forgive your sharp tongue when it comes to Hilda Yoder."

Lydia was right, of course. Greta's feelings toward Hilda—and Esther—were every bit as intolerant as Hilda's comments to her. "I will pray," she agreed, and then she smothered a giggle. "I do wish you could have seen the look on her face when Luke suggested that he could stay with her."

Lydia concentrated on her needlework, but she was smiling. "It would appear that in the aftermath of Luke's tragedy, you have come to a different opinion of him?"

Greta was surprised to feel herself blushing. "He is more…complicated than I first thought."

"Truly? In what way?"

"He has a lighter side. One we have not been aware of before now. Before he always seemed so solemn and stiff, but today…" Her voice trailed off as she recalled the lighthearted way that she and Luke had challenged each other to find the salvageable pieces of his business. "And how odd that it should be revealed once he has suffered such calamity."

"Perhaps it was not the fire and his losses there that stirred this lighter side of his disposition," Lydia mused. "Perhaps there was another cause—one that was quite unexpected."

"Must you always speak in riddles, Lydia?"

"All right, in plainer language, I am saying that perhaps his interactions with you—of which there have been several in just the last few days—are responsible for his lighter disposition."

Greta was struggling to find the words to tell Lydia how ridiculous that theory was when there was a knock at the door. It was past dark—past the time when someone might come calling unless there were some emergency.

Lydia set aside her mending and carried a lamp with her to the door. As she opened the door and lifted the lamp, Greta was surprised to see Luke standing on their front porch.

"*Guten abend,* Luke Starns," Lydia said and Greta was sure she did not imagine the hint of humor that brought a lilt to her sister's voice.

"I have come to discuss your idea," he announced without bothering with the usual polite greetings. "Could we—you, your sister and I…"

"If you are referencing the suggestion that you and my sister could take advantage of this time when all of Celery Fields believes that it is me you are calling upon to become better acquainted…"

"*Yah,*" Luke said, cutting Lydia off midsentence.

Lydia turned to Greta. "You know, sister, I find that I am suddenly quite weary." She set the lamp back on the table. "Be so kind as to offer our guest a glass of that wonderful lemonade you made this afternoon. *Guten nacht,* Luke… Greta."

And before Greta could say anything, Lydia had entered her room and closed the door with a firm click, leaving Luke standing on the porch and Greta to deal with him.

"A glass of that lemonade would be welcomed," he said softly, "that is if you would ask me to stay."

Without a word she headed for the kitchen as much to gather her wits for this meeting with Luke Starns as to prepare the beverage for him. What could Lydia have been thinking? What was Luke thinking showing up unannounced like this? Had the world gone completely mad? It would seem so. Well, there was nothing to be done but for her to set things right again.

Chapter Eight

While Greta went to get the lemonade, Luke remained standing at the door. He was having serious second thoughts. It had taken him most of the evening to work up the nerve to come here. He should have taken more time to consider his purpose—develop some plan. He had no idea at all what he would say to Greta once she came out to the porch with the lemonade. He had thought it would be the three of them—that there would be the buffer of Lydia's presence to make the entire discussion take on the trappings of a business meeting. Now he was to be alone with Greta.

Greta—who was certainly taking her time getting lemonade for him. He peered into the darkened hall that led to the kitchen, but could see nothing so he sat down heavily in the wooden swing. He leaned forward, his forearms resting on his knees as he debated simply getting up and leaving. Coming here had been a mistake.

The screen door creaked and she backed her way out, holding the door open with her hip as she balanced a tray set with two tall glasses of lemonade and a plate of ginger cookies. Luke sprang to his feet to hold the door and then relieve her of the tray. "You needn't have gone to so much trouble," he said as he looked around for where he might set the tray. Other than the swing, the porch was bare.

"On the step," Greta said as she lifted the glasses and waited for him to set down the tray before handing him one. Their fingers brushed and for an instant her hand shook and the liquid sloshed dangerously close to the lip of the glass before she steadied it. "Please sit while you have your lemonade," she said with a nod toward the swing.

He did as she instructed, grateful to have anyone else making decisions about how this encounter might go now that he had come here with no thought other than to accept Lydia's offer to spend time with Greta. He left plenty of room for her to join him but she settled herself on the top step next to the tray and offered him the plate of cookies.

"Did you make these?" he asked, taking one. Now both hands were filled—one holding the glass and the other the cookie. Luke had never felt so awkward in all his life. He sat back, inadvertently setting the swing in motion and causing the lemonade to spill over his hand and the front of his shirt.

Greta was on her feet at once, using the tea towel that had lined the tray to dab his fingers and shirt, blotting the sticky liquid. Every attempt she made only made things worse as the swing rocked back and forth.

"Hold still," she ordered as she reached to relieve him of the glass and hand him the towel. But as he clumsily tried to assist her, the swing bolted like a skittish horse and she came tumbling onto his lap as the glass flew out of his hand and the rest of the lemonade showered them both.

At first, as he tried to help Greta off his lap, he thought that the gurgling sounds coming from her were a sign of how distressed and embarrassed she was. "I'm sorry for my clumsiness and for upsetting you, Greta Goodloe," he said. "I should not have come."

She raised her face to his then and in the soft amber light from the living room, he saw that she was not upset. She was laughing, her eyes sparkling with a glint of mischief. "Oh, Luke, don't be so serious. It was an accident—one I had as much part in as you did. As the *Englischers* might say, it looks like we have broken the ice—or at least the glass." She nodded toward the broken pieces on the porch floor.

Luke felt the bubble of laughter rising in his throat and before he could stop it, he was chuckling with her as together they bent to pick up the pieces of the glass and set them on the tray. When the deed was done, Greta sat back on the swing next to him and handed him the tea towel. "I don't think it will stain badly— not if you add a little white vinegar when you wash it."

With one foot he pushed the swing into motion as he wiped his hands on the towel. "I'll remember that," he said.

"Who does your laundry anyway?" she asked.

"I do. My mother died when I was just a boy, leaving my brothers and my *Dat* and me. We learned to do for ourselves."

"My *Maemm* also died when I was little. We had Pleasant though and of course, Lydia was older by a few years, so she taught me."

"So, we have this in common. Do you remember your mother?"

"Not much. I was only three. Sometimes I think that it's only the stories I heard about her over the years that I call memories."

"*Yah*. I was older than you, but through the years…"

"Your *Dat* never remarried?"

"No. We kept busy with the farm and the business. Time passed."

"Your father was also a blacksmith?"

"*Yah*. He taught me his trade."

"And your brothers?"

"They took to the farming more. It suited them once they married and started families."

She was quiet then and her silence made him all that more aware of her closeness. She was so small and slim that if they had sat closer there might have been room for a third person on the swing. She smelled of soap and the zest of the lemons she must have sliced for the lemonade. He was beginning to relax and enjoy the quietness of the night, the nearness of Greta Good-loe, when she spoke again.

"You never married, though. Were you not tempted?"

And there it was—the one topic he had dreaded from the day he'd left Ontario. Should he tell her the entire story and accept the fact that once she heard it, she would want nothing more to do with him? Or should he stick to the plan he'd made the day he'd left a letter of farewell for his father and brothers and left Ontario for good? The plan to start fresh and leave the past behind.

"I mean," she added when he said nothing right

away, "there must have been…opportunities. Surely the single women in your community saw…"

He forced a smile and shrugged. "I never gave them a chance," he said with a chuckle. "Growing up without a mother—or sisters—I guess I learned to be on my own."

"Until now. Now your plan is to convince Lydia to marry you."

She stated this with such assurance that he was momentarily taken aback. Had she not understood why he'd come? Had Lydia not spoken with her about this? Of course she had. Greta had come to the wreckage of his business earlier that very day to discuss the matter.

"I no longer wish to marry your sister, Greta. I wish to marry you—if you'll have me." There. It was said. There could be no misunderstanding now. He found he could not look at her as he waited for some response. If she burst out laughing—as he'd noticed she had a tendency to do—he would simply stand up and walk back to the dry goods store where Hilda Yoder had set up a cot for him.

But she did not laugh. In fact she did nothing more than sit there beside him, still as a stone. Then she picked at some bit of string on her apron and he thought perhaps she had at last composed her reply. But she said nothing.

"If you do not wish," he began.

"Are you always so impatient, Luke Starns?" she snapped. "I am well aware that you and my sister think this the best possible plan for all our futures. What I don't understand is why. You had set your sights on Lydia and just like that, when she rejects you, you have turned them on me?"

"You were not…available for me to consider earlier." He chose his words carefully, but clearly not carefully enough for Greta.

She was on her feet in an instant, wheeling around to face him, hands planted on her slim hips. "I am not 'available' now, Luke Starns. I can understand my sister's role in this. She has taken charge of my well-being from the time we were both children, but you? What am I to you?"

Several answers to that question sprang instantly to mind—sunshine, loveliness, laughter and lightness among them. But he said none of those things. Instead his wounded pride overcame his true feelings and he stood, as well, towering over her as he brushed past her on his way to the porch steps.

"If you do not wish to even consider…"

"I did not say that," she replied, stopping him in his tracks.

"You confuse me, Greta Goodloe."

"Gut." There was the hint of a smile in her tone. "For you confuse me, as well."

He fought a smile of his own. Without turning to look back at her, he asked, "And is that a place where we might begin? Perhaps as friends?"

"I have already mistaken friendship for love, Luke. I will not make that mistake again. They are not the same thing." Her voice was so soft and filled with sadness.

"Do not equate me with Josef Bontrager," he warned.

"Josef believed we could build a future together. Now, apparently so do you. I really cannot see much difference. In both cases it would seem that you men decide when it suits you to take a wife—mostly for the purpose of starting a family and perhaps companionship…"

He was back onto the porch, his hands grasping her shoulders in an instant. "Stop it," he ordered. "Your sister is the one who has suggested a match between you and me. She has also plotted out a way for the two of us to become better acquainted without the barrier of gossip and speculation. I have given it considerable thought and it seems to me that this is worth pursuing. Celery Fields is a small community and if, in the end, we only come away with a friendship, doesn't that carry its own reward?"

He eased his hold on her and forced his breathing to steady. And then she did the very last thing he might have expected her to do. She stood on tiptoe and gently kissed his cheek. "You make a good case, Luke Starns. I will sleep on it and give you my answer tomorrow."

And then she was gone, the screen door closing behind her with a soft click and then the front door. Luke stood there for a long moment, his fingers touching the place where she had kissed him, his heart hammering so hard he doubted seriously that he could make it back to the dry goods store. Instead he sat down on the top step and absently picked up a cookie from the plate she'd left behind.

He chewed slowly, savoring the spicy crispness. Greta Goodloe had one thing in her favor for any man considering her as his wife—she made the best ginger cookie that Luke had ever tasted.

In her room Greta undressed and pulled on her ankle-length cotton nightgown. She straightened the gown's long sleeves and then carefully folded her clothes for use the following day. And all the while she was thinking about Luke. She crossed her arms over her chest and held onto her shoulders, remembering how his hands had felt when he'd gripped her there earlier.

For an instant she had thought he might kiss her. More to the point she had hoped that he might. She shook her head at that realization. What kind of woman was she that she could so easily leave all thought of Josef behind and turn to this stranger instead?

But Josef's touch had never aroused in her these feelings. Luke's simple act of placing his hands on her shoulders had provoked turmoil of her heart and mind.

Greta fell to her knees beside her single bed and clasped her fingers tightly together as she bowed her head and prayed for God's guidance. "I am so very confused," she admitted aloud. "About Josef and now Luke and…well, just everything. I want to follow the path You have set for me but I honestly don't understand which turn to take." She unclasped her hands and pounded her fist on the soft mattress. "Help me," she whispered. "Show me the way." And then she thought better of her words. "Show me *Your* way," she amended and quickly added prayers for Lydia and Pleasant and her family and even Josef. "And Luke," she added finally. "He has suffered the loss of his home and business in one event. But more than that he seems to carry a heavy burden of loneliness and sadness. Whatever life he left behind when he came to Celery Fields troubles him still."

Her eyes sprang open as she realized that Luke Starns had not offered her his friendship out of pity.

He had offered it out of his own need to find someone he could talk to and trust. What had he said? Something about friendship being its own reward?

"Oh, Greta Goodloe, you do suffer from the sin of self-importance. Surely God is showing you that it is time—past time—that you stopped thinking always first of your needs and dreams and place your attention on others." At first light she was determined to be up and putting into practice her newly established guide for life. She would serve others, always with an eye to making their lives better—and she would begin with Luke Starns.

"You seem to be in unusually good spirits this morning," Lydia said as she nodded her thanks for the breakfast that Greta had set before her.

Greta understood that this was her sister's way of inquiring about what had happened on the porch after she retired. "Did Luke stay long?" Lydia added.

"I am indeed in good spirits, and no, Luke did not stay long." Greta took her place across from Lydia. She reached across the table and took Lydia's hand as both sisters bowed their heads. After a moment Greta released Lydia's hand and picked up her fork. "After all," she continued as if there had been no interruption, "it is a beautiful day that we have been given. We must be sure to make the most of it."

She saw Lydia arch one eyebrow, her skepticism evident in that subtle gesture. "And how do you intend to do that?"

"I will go first to the bakery and work out an order with Pleasant for the breads, rolls and other baked goods we will need for the raising of Luke's stables and shop. Then I will visit the other women in town to see if I can recommend what to prepare for the men and boys working on the rebuilding."

"Everyone will simply bring what they can," Lydia said. "You know that."

"I do, but so many families have left Celery Fields that there will be fewer sources for the food and baked goods we'll need. I just want to see if I can persuade the women in town to focus on the basics. That way whatever those living in the outlying areas can bring what they like."

"You've given this quite a lot of thought," Lydia said.

"I have. It's taken my mind off…other things. Besides everyone is busy right now and as I mentioned we are shorthanded. Does it not make sense to be more organized under such conditions?"

"It does." Lydia studied her as if she were looking at a complete stranger. "Did Luke say when the rebuilding might begin?"

"No." Greta added a note to the list she had begun. "I should ask Roger Hadwell when the lumber and other supplies will be delivered. Of course, in the meantime there is the work of removing the remains from the fire." She glanced up at Lydia. "Could you let the children—the older ones—out of school early so they might help?"

Lydia set down her coffee cup. "I do not know what has stirred this spirit of goodwill in you, Greta, but I must say that it becomes you."

Greta could not hide her surprise at receiving such praise from Lydia. More often than not, Lydia was gently chiding her for her tendency to dwell too much on her own small problems when there were others suffering around her.

"It's high time I stopped feeling sorry for myself and concentrated on others," Greta announced and then she grinned. "Wouldn't you say so? Oh, that's right, you have said so many times."

Lydia smiled and set aside her napkin as she rose to gather the satchel that held her school supplies. "Let me know when you need the help of the older children and I will excuse them from class," she said as she headed for the door where she paused. "Well, it would seem that the work may go faster than we had thought, Greta. Luke and Roger are already unloading supplies."

Greta ran to the door. "Then there's no time to be wasted," she announced as she reached for her bonnet. "Come on, Lydia, I'll walk partway with you and go first to the bakery."

She was well aware that Luke had paused in the unloading of the beams and other lumber stock to watch as she and Lydia walked down the lane toward town. Halfway along, Lydia took the path to the schoolhouse while Greta continued on her way to her half sister's bakery. As she passed Luke and Roger, both men nodded briefly in her direction and then turned their attention back to their work.

"Heard you saw Lydia Goodloe home from Sunday's singing," Greta heard Roger say as the men transferred the lumber from the wagon and stacked it in a pile near the foundation of Luke's shop.

She strained to catch Luke's reply but could only hear a mumbled response—a response that had Roger chuckling.

"Pleasant?" Greta called out as she entered the bakery.

"Back here."

Greta followed the smells of cinnamon and yeast to the large kitchen where Pleasant prepared the goods that she sold. On one long table were loaves of bread dough rising in their pans. "I am way ahead of you," Pleasant announced as she wiped her hands on her apron. "I thought we'd start with a dozen loaves and then add to it as necessary."

"Pies," Greta began and before she could say more Pleasant pointed to the large wood-burning stove.

"When I saw Roger Hadwell taking in that delivery this morning I knew we would be getting started tomorrow morning once everyone has finished the milking and other chores."

Greta consulted her list. "I thought I would ask the other women in town for side dishes and casseroles."

"I could speak with Hilda Yoder and Esther," Pleasant offered.

Greta sighed. So word had spread about Josef flirting with Esther at the singing. "No. I'll do that. How many men do you think will come to help?" She was determined to change the subject, determined to turn Pleasant's pitying look away.

Pleasant shrugged. "Jeremiah and I were just talking about that last evening. It's hard to believe how the community has shrunk these last months. And it's been a while since there's been any call for raising a new barn or house or shop at all."

"Maybe some of Luke's customers from Sarasota will come to help," Greta said. "He's built a good business with them."

"He has at that, but the *Englisch* have a way of thinking that once they've paid for a service there's no need to do more. I wouldn't count on that if I were Luke."

"I didn't say he was counting on it," Greta said, knowing she sounded peevish.

"How are things going between Lydia and him?"

"She hasn't really said." It wasn't a lie. Indeed Lydia had told Greta nothing about her conversation and the ride home from the singing with Luke. "I expect he's going to have other things to think about for a while."

Pleasant laid a pie pastry over the dish, pressed it into place and crimped the edges, all the while her lips were working with no sound coming out. "What do you think about a match between those two?" she finally asked.

Greta could not have been more surprised at the question. In general Pleasant had always viewed Greta as far too flighty to try and hold a serious conversation with.

"I don't know," she replied, trying to gauge Pleasant's mood. "They are both…"

"Serious to the point of being almost solemn, even grim. I was in a marriage like that before Jeremiah came into my life. I would not wish that for Lydia."

"You disapprove of Luke Starns?"

"Not at all. He's… Well, the truth is that he's far too much like me and like Lydia. Where will they find the laughter and the lightness that is so very very important in a marriage?"

"Luke is nothing like Merle Obermeier," Greta said softly. Everyone in Celery Fields had been well aware, when Pleasant had married the widower, that the man's sole purpose had been to find a mother for his four children. He had not loved Pleasant; in fact there were rumors that he had been quite cruel to her before his sudden death left her alone to manage a farm that was deeply in debt and four small children who had now lost both their parents. That's when Pleasant had returned to the bakery and that's when Jeremiah Troyer had come into her life.

"No, he is nothing at all like Merle was, but you cannot deny that he has a certain somberness about him, bordering on sadness. Does Lydia even care for the man? I mean in a romantic way of speaking?"

"Surely it's too soon for either of them to know," Greta protested, suddenly afraid that Pleasant might make her feelings known to Lydia—and Luke—and disrupt Lydia's plan for Greta and Luke to become better acquainted. For an instant she considered revealing Lydia's idea to Pleasant but then thought better of it. The fewer people who knew about it, the easier things would be when it did not work out.

"You mark my words," Pleasant said, continuing to line pie pans with pastry, "those two will either make each other miserable or they will come to their senses and understand that going their separate ways makes more sense—for both of them."

"I'm sure Lydia will find her way," Greta said, always loyal to her elder sister.

"He's awfully good-looking," Pleasant mused and then she giggled.

"Why, Pleasant Troyer, wait until I let Jeremiah know that you said such a thing."

"You didn't let me finish. Luke is very good-looking in that dark, mysterious way he has, but he can't hold a candle to Jeremiah. Now there's one fine-look-ing man."

Greta considered the differences between Luke and her half brother-in-law and found that, in her book, there certainly was no contest. Luke Starns won every time. But she wasn't about to say so to Pleasant. "Have to go," she said as she headed out and crossed the street to the dry goods store. But not before she glanced over to the hardware store, saw that Luke was nowhere in sight and felt a twinge of disappointment rise in her chest.

Chapter Nine

Over the next several days, Luke spent every hour of daylight clearing away the remains of his destroyed building. Lydia sent the older boys from the school to help him in the afternoons and Greta provided cookies and lemonade. Finally the day came that the framework for the shop, livery and his living quarters would be raised. Luke was awake well before dawn wondering how many men would come to help. How many were left to come? And of those, how many were able-bodied and young enough to manage climbing the scaffolding and straddling the beams as the building took shape?

He stepped out the back entrance to the dry goods store where he'd spent the last couple nights sleeping on a cot. He splashed water over his face and neck. It was going to be a hot day. The haze that hung heavy over the town was a sign that by noon the temperature was likely to be well into the eighties and the humidity would be even higher. He was glad of the wide flat brim of his hat as he set it in place.

As had become his habit he glanced toward the

Goodloe sisters' house. Now that his shop was gone, he had a clear vision of the place from the porch of the dry goods store. He wondered what Greta was doing. The evening before, he and several others in town had helped her and Lydia set up long rows of tables in the Goodloe barn. That's where the workers would take their meals. He'd been touched by Greta's assumption that there would be a host of men ready to go to work and in need of sustenance as the rebuilding progressed.

She had that way about her—a way that refused to believe that everything wouldn't work out for the best. In spite of her near hysteria when Josef Bontrager had broken off with her, Luke had begun to understand that her reaction was less about being heartbroken and more about being embarrassed. Bontrager was sure to show up today and Luke couldn't help but wonder how Greta would handle that. For that matter he had to consider how he would handle working alongside the man. Bontrager was known for his carpentry skills and he would be a valuable member of the crew. It was going to be important for Luke to set aside his personal feelings toward the man.

He'd taken to having his breakfast—a hard roll and a cup of coffee—at the bakery since the fire. He liked Pleasant Troyer, although her disposition was nothing like her given name. Pleasant was known for stating her mind and most of the time Luke found that refreshing. Unfortunately that was not the case on this particular morning. She seemed determined to ferret out information about his past.

"Quite a difference in weather I'd guess between September here and what you were used to back in

Canada." She set the roll in front of him and slid a dish of orange marmalade across the table.

"We could already have some cold weather by this time of year, that's certain," Luke replied as he poured fresh cream into his coffee and stirred it slowly.

"You had a shop back there, as well?"

"It was my *Dat*'s business."

"But you left there to come here." The statement rang with the unasked question: *Why?*

Luke took the last bite of his roll and licked his fingers. He smiled at Pleasant. "Like you said, the weather. Got to go." He left coins on the table to pay for the roll and coffee and escaped, but not before he saw the scowl that wrinkled Pleasant's forehead.

He heard the creak of wagon wheels and the plod of horses and looked up to see several dozen men parking their vehicles along the main street. As they stepped down from their wagons or buggies, they reached for their tools—aprons that held a variety of nails, toolboxes loaded with hammers, saws, tape measures and T squares. They talked in low voices as they gathered in small groups, each group assembling around one man that they had selected as their leader. In one group that leader was Josef Bontrager and Luke was grateful that the man had come to help.

From the opposite end of the street came the sound of several motorized vehicles and Luke saw trucks loaded with men—some that he recognized as his *Englischer* customers from Sarasota— pull up next to the hardware store.

Luke was unexpectedly moved by the arrival of these non-Amish men because he was well aware that many of them had lost their jobs when businesses in

Sarasota went under and others were trying to make ends meet by working two jobs at low wages. And yet they had set their own worries aside to come and help him.

Overall there were far too many men to count but Luke would guess there were at least fifty or sixty of them. With this many skilled laborers, they would have a good start on rebuilding his shop by sundown.

"You gonna stand there gawking all day, Starns, or put us to work?" one of the *Englischers* teased.

Within an hour the work was underway. By sundown the frame of the building would be in place. Greta and the other women had transformed the Goodloe barn into a feast of casseroles, cold cuts, salads, baked goods and cool lemonade. At noon several men took their plates and moved down the line cafeteria-style. Luke couldn't help but notice how the *Englischers* were suddenly shy with the women around. "Thank you, ma'am," they would murmur without looking up or smiling.

The men would eat in shifts so that the work could continue until dark forced them to stop. Luke saw Greta moving among this first shift, refilling their glasses from a large tin pitcher of water, its sides sweating as the ice melted in the noonday heat. He saw that she was coming to the group of Amish men where Josef was sitting and wondered what she would do. Her smile never wavered as she bantered with the men and refilled Josef's glass. Luke felt such respect for her at that moment. Bontrager barely acknowledged her, maintaining a running conversation with another man until Greta had turned away.

But then Luke saw the way Josef's gaze followed

her. Was the man having second thoughts? And if so, what would Greta do about that?

"Back to work," somebody called out and as one the men rose, set aside their plates and glasses and returned to the building. Luke turned to set down his plate and found Greta standing not two feet away, her face wreathed in a smile.

"It's going so well," she exclaimed. "Look how many men came from Sarasota to help—and on a workday for them."

"I have Jeremiah to thank for that," Luke admitted, having learned that Pleasant's husband had let it be known among the men he worked with at the local ice plant that their help would be welcomed.

"And your customers came, as well," she reminded him. "You'll be back in business in no time at all, Luke."

The way she said it Luke felt certain that she was right. That was the thing about Greta. She always seemed to see the positive in life. The way she was smiling up at him now made him feel like he could do just about anything he set his mind to doing.

"Luke Starns, we cannot work if we do not know what you want," Josef Bontrager said. He had returned to the barn and was standing there, hands on hips as he glared at Luke.

"Coming," Luke said and handed Greta his plate and glass. His good spirits plummeted when he realized that her smile had faded and her eyes were on Josef, not him. "Fool," he muttered to himself as he strode away from the Goodloe barn into the hot and steamy afternoon.

* * *

The men took another break in the late afternoon. By that time Greta and the other women had cleared away all the leftover food and washed and dried the dishes. Most of the women left shortly after the lunch had been served. There were chores to be done and children in need of their naps. As the sun moved lower in the western sky, Greta and Pleasant's stepdaughter, Bettina, moved among the workers, offering them cookies and cold milk. Greta was all too aware that Josef's gaze followed her wherever she went. If she spent too much time lingering over conversation with any one of the men—even the married ones—that gaze became a glare. More disturbing than that was the fact that Luke Starns also seemed to be watching her—and he appeared to be no more pleased than Josef was with her behavior.

Well, let them gawk all they wanted. Greta was so very tired of trying to live up to somebody else's ideal of how she should conduct herself. She liked people. She found the sheer variety and diversity of them a source of endless fascination. Wasn't it amazing how God had given each of his creatures their very own unique qualities? If Josef—and Luke, for that matter—chose to view her behavior as inappropriate, that was hardly her problem. Josef had made his choice and as for Luke—well, if he wanted to be her friend, or more than that—then he would just have to accept her for the way she was. After all, that's what true friends did.

"Greta?" Josef had come alongside her and was handing her his water glass. "Would it be all right if I called on you this evening?"

The very last thing that Greta had expected was

this. Calling on her after dark meant—well, it meant that he wanted to pick up again with courting her. Didn't it?

She eyed him carefully. "Why?"

Josef chuckled nervously. "Do I truly need a reason?"

"Truly you do," Greta replied.

"Do not make me plead with you." In an instant Josef's tone had gone from a chuckle to an order.

"I am not making you do anything, Josef. Lydia has…" She fumbled for some excuse.

Josef frowned. "Of course. I had heard that the blacksmith was calling on her," he said. "Perhaps tomorrow?" He walked away without waiting for her to answer. She realized that he simply assumed that sooner or later she would agree to see him.

Using Luke and Lydia as her excuse had not been at all what Greta was about to say but since Josef's assumption had ended this awkward conversation Greta was thankful. Thankful that was until she saw Luke staring at her from across the yard and then turned to find Esther Yoder glaring at her, as well. So many people looking at her—all of them seemingly unhappy. Well, Josef had approached her. For once in her life she could not be accused of flirting. She picked up the last of the dishes and headed for the barn.

As Luke watched Greta and Josef it occurred to him that he might just be walking right into the situation that had gotten his heart broken back in Ontario. It occurred to him that Greta Goodloe might have agreed to Lydia's idea to make Josef jealous. If that was her plan then it appeared to be working. Josef Bontrager had been unable to take his eyes off Greta all through the lunch break in spite of Esther Yoder and her mother hovering around him, making sure that he had second helpings and a large piece of shoofly pie. By late afternoon the man had clearly found his courage to approach Greta.

Luke was not given to jumping to conclusions. He reminded himself that he had no knowledge of the conversation that had passed between Greta and Josef. As he set in place the large heavy-notched beams that formed the support for the roof for his business, he went over every detail of what he had observed. Josef's approach. Greta's polite smile—or had that smile been one of expectation? Did she still have feelings for the man? How could she not? It had been less than a week since their break.

He was a fool on a fool's mission. Perhaps God did not intend for him to marry at all. Certainly the signs pointed toward that. The business in Ontario. Lydia's outright refusal to even consider a courtship. Had he become so desperate to marry that he had fallen into the trap once again of being someone's pawn in a game he did not wish to play? Was Greta's intention to use him to win back Josef?

"Well, we'll just see about that," he grumbled to himself as he dropped the last beam into place and signaled to Roger Hadwell at the other end of the log that it was secure. He scrambled down the scaffolding and stood with the rest of the crew to consider the day's work. The frame was in place for the building and the roof. Where that morning there had been nothing but barren ground, there now rose a skeleton of fresh-hewn wood and the men standing around him had done it all.

"I'd say that's a good day's work, Luke," one of his customers from Sarasota announced. "By the end of next week at this rate I expect you'll be in business." The man clapped Luke on the back as he and his friends headed for their trucks and drove away.

Luke glanced toward the Goodloe house and saw Lydia coming home from her day at school. He wanted to thank her for letting the older boys come help with the work but he knew approaching her now would cause tongues to wag. Everyone assumed that they were courting—that much was evident by the sly comments some of the other men had made in his presence throughout the day. He saw Lydia pause for a moment and gaze at the structure. She called out something to the cluster of men nearest to her and kept on walking. Greta was nowhere in sight.

"Shall we offer a prayer of thanksgiving?" Bishop Troyer asked and all of the men gathered around the church leader as he offered up a prayer thanking God for the blessings of the day.

As soon as the prayer circle ended, those men that had remained for the whole day headed for home— some in their wagons or buggies and others walking, all promising to return the following day after chores to continue the work. Luke stood in the middle of town and watched them go and for the first time since coming to Celery Fields he felt like one of them. He was no longer a stranger in this community. His decision to rebuild his business, when it would have been just as understandable—given the dwindling population and customer base—for him to leave Celery Fields and start over somewhere else, had secured him a place among the others as one of their own.

"Luke?"

He was surprised to see the bishop's wife coming his way. Mildred Troyer was a spry woman of indeterminate age and always ready with a kind word and a smile. She was much beloved by everyone in town and she had made Luke feel welcome from the day he'd first arrived. Now she handed him a package wrapped in brown paper and tied with string.

"I thought you might have use for these," she said. "I had to guess at the size but used our nephew Jeremiah's measurements. It seems to me that you and he are about the same size. If they won't do, you just bring them right back to me and we can alter them."

Luke loosened the string and pulled back one edge of the paper to reveal a stack of clothing—two shirts and a pair of trousers. Every bit of clothing he owned other than what he'd been wearing had been lost in the fire. He'd been making do with washing out his one shirt every night before he went to sleep and carefully brushing the day's dirt from his pants.

"Can't have you calling on Lydia Goodloe in clothing you've spent the day working under this hot sun in," Mildred teased with a twinkle in her bright blue eyes.

"Thank you. I never expected…"

Mildred patted his hand. "It's just neighbors helping neighbors," she assured him and then she went to join her husband for the short walk home.

Luke watched them go—two people who had spent more of their life together than they had with anyone else. They walked side by side, exchanging bits of conversation. They would share their supper and then sit for a while. The bishop would probably read or work on his next sermon while Mildred did some mending or quilting. Then they would go to bed—to the bed they had shared for so many years and through good and bad times.

Luke wanted that life. He wanted that one person he could trust to be there through everything. He wanted to know that at the end of his workday he would go home to that kind of comfort and companionship. He turned his attention back to the Goodloe house. A thin stream of smoke rose from the kitchen chimney. Greta was preparing supper for herself and Lydia. She must be almost as exhausted as he was for she'd been up early organizing the meals for the workers, making sure everyone was fed, clearing away and washing the used dishes.

He closed his eyes and pictured her in that kitchen, her laughter like music as she went about her cooking. He thought about her hands—hands he had held in his when he had removed that splinter—hands that knew how to work but that were still smooth and as soft as a baby's cheek. And from there it was an easy leap to thinking about children—his children—their children.

He shook himself free of his revelry and headed back to the dry goods store with his bundle of clothing. The women in town were taking turns feeding him, leaving a tin bucket with a cold supper for him in the evenings. They would do that anonymously for it was not the way of the Amish to seek recognition or praise for their good deeds. Sure enough, waiting on the back stoop of the dry goods store was a picnic hamper so filled with food that the top would not close all the way.

He sat on the step and opened it, suddenly ravenous. Inside were three pieces of fried chicken wrapped in waxed paper, a bowl of cabbage slaw, another of three-bean salad, and on top of it all a generous serving of chocolate cake. Sitting next to the basket was a thermos filled with sweet iced tea. Luke leaned against one of the posts that supported the covered stoop and began pulling the chicken apart with his fingers. Whoever his benefactor was tonight, she was the best cook in all of Celery Fields—at least as far as he'd been able to judge.

He thought about the women that had come that morning with their husbands, carrying their baskets of food up to the Goodloe barn to be set out for the workers. He mentally ran through the dishes the women had served as the men moved down the line filling their plates. There had been the chicken and the side dishes and of course, the bread, but that chocolate cake had not been served at noon. For dessert there had been a variety of pies, but no cake. As he savored every bite he thought that he would give a lot to know who had baked that cake for him.

And then he remembered. At the lunch served after services the previous week, when he'd tasted Lydia's terrible peach pie, Lydia had said something about Greta's chocolate cake. "If you like that pie," she'd commented as he savored the piece of pie she replaced her own with, "just wait until you taste Greta's triple chocolate cake."

"Triple chocolate?" Luke had asked.

"Chocolate cake, chocolate cream filling and chocolate butter frosting," Lydia had explained, ticking off each item on her fingers. "My sister has a weakness for chocolate."

Luke studied the remains of his piece of the cake. Was it possible that with everything else she'd had to do today, Greta Goodloe had also prepared supper for him? And if this was indeed her chocolate cake, then why had she not served it at the lunch? Was there some message in the fact that she had reserved a piece for him?

"One way to find out," he said as he packed up the remains of his picnic and drank the last of the tea. Normally he would simply leave the container and dishes from his supper on the stoop and the following day it would be replaced by that day's meal. He could only assume that the women somehow had figured out how to return the previous day's dishes to their rightful owner. Tonight though, he intended to be the one to return the used dishes—and if he was right about their owner, then just maybe she would offer him a second piece of that cake.

Greta had told herself that she was simply overtired. That's why she had gone out to the porch to sit awhile after Lydia had retired for the night. It certainly wasn't because she expected Luke to come calling. The man had barely said ten words to her all day. And between the fire and the days spent preparing to rebuild, courting was surely the last thing on Luke's mind. And besides, who knew what the rules for courting were where he came from? Amish communities could differ greatly in the manner in which the people conducted themselves. Maybe in Canada…

The house was dark but there was a moon and light enough for her to see the stark silhouette of Luke's new building. *Courting.* Were they actually going forward with Lydia's plan? Had Luke agreed? Had she?

"*Guten abend,* Greta Goodloe."

She had been unaware of him coming up the path, so lost had she been in thoughts of the day just past and her confusion about what she wanted in all of this.

"May I sit with you?"

"*Yah,*" she said, her voice barely a whisper as she made room for him on the weathered porch swing.

He set down the basket that had held his dinner. "I would hope there's some of that chocolate cake left," he said and in spite of the darkness she heard the lilt of lightheartedness in his tone.

His teasing gave her confidence. "What makes you think we have chocolate cake to offer?"

He chuckled as he settled next to her, filling the space so completely that there was less than an inch between his shoulder and hers. "Your sister once told me that you made the best chocolate cake in all of Celery Fields. I just assumed that the piece I had tonight for my supper was from your hand. I could not imagine a more delicious cake, but if I have guessed wrong then perhaps one day…"

She jabbed him with her elbow. "Stop teasing me. The cake was mine although there are any number of women in Celery Fields that might have given you its equal."

"Somehow I doubt that." Luke pushed the swing into motion and the two of them sat in silence for a long moment, all hint of lightheartedness replaced by their shared realization that they were here side by side in the dark.

"Tell me about the seashells," he said finally. "I saw you return with one for the garden the other day. Where do you find them?"

"In the bay."

"The bay?"

She studied him, trying to see if he was still teasing her. "The bay between the mainland and the barrier islands—the keys that separate the mainland from the Gulf of Mexico."

"You go there? Alone?"

"Sometimes. I like going there. It's very quiet and peaceful. There are wonderful birds and of course, the shells—some of them are still occupied and it makes me laugh to see them scuttling around in the shallows."

"I would like to see that."

An idea came to her. "We could go—the two of us. Everyone thinks that you are calling on Lydia so if you and I went down to the shore together, no one would be surprised. It's perfectly normal for you to be seen with me as Lydia's sister. Do you want to go there one day?" Suddenly her mind was filled with the image of Luke walking with her through the shallow waters of the bay, examining the sea life, watching the birds. It was an image that filled her with joy. "Perhaps this Sunday afternoon?"

Luke's hesitation gave her pause. As usual she had rushed in with a plan not fully considered. How did she know he was even interested in courting her at all? Perhaps he still had his thoughts set on Liddy. "Forgive me, Luke. Sometimes I…"

"I would like to walk at the shore with you, Greta. I would like that very much."

The warmth that swelled in Greta's chest spread to her lips as they parted in a smile of delight. "You could fish there, as well. Many of the men and boys from Celery Fields fish there."

Luke laughed. "I'm afraid I'm not much of a fisherman, Greta."

"Then we will simply wade in the water and study the sea life and perhaps be fortunate enough to find an unoccupied seashell to add to Liddy's collection."

"How is it Lydia's collection when it would seem that you are the collector?"

"It's something I do to help her. She likes taking the different shells to the school to show her students and they make a lovely border for our kitchen garden. Liddy can name every single shell. She is so very smart about such things."

"But does she make the community's best chocolate cake?" Luke asked.

Now it was Greta's turn to laugh. "You are still determined to have a second piece, are you?"

"I am—and a third tomorrow if there is any left."

Greta stood up. "Very well. Wait here and I will cut you a slice, but after that…"

He caught her hand as she turned toward the door. "And will you sit with me while I eat the cake, Greta?" He ran his thumb over hers.

"I will," she agreed and as she gently pulled free of his touch and entered the house, her heart sang with what she could only define as giddiness. She liked Luke Starns—she liked him a great deal.

* * *

Luke found himself smiling broadly as he leaned against the porch swing, his arms spread across the back of it. He listened to the sounds of Greta in the kitchen—taking out a dish and cutlery, uncovering the cake, pouring a glass of milk or water to wash down the cake—and he found that he liked those sounds very much. More than that he liked the image of Greta Goodloe in the kitchen preparing something just for him.

He closed his eyes and thought about how his life had changed in only a matter of days—the fire and then the way the community had come together to help him rebuild. The business with Lydia and now calling on Greta. He thought about how sitting so close with her on the swing he had been more aware than ever of the sheer life force that seemed to radiate from her petite frame and touch everything around her with its energy and power. In all of his life Luke had never felt so alive as he did in the presence of Greta Goodloe.

He closed his eyes and prayed silently that he truly understood God's plan for his life and, if that plan included the possibility of a life spent with Greta, then God had surely blessed him. He heard her come onto the porch, the screen door closing with a soft thud behind her. He made room for her next to him on the swing and held out his hand to take the plate she offered.

In the light from the window he saw that she was smiling and he thought that he had never in his life seen a woman so very beautiful as Greta Goodloe was. *"Das ist gut,"* he managed around a large bite of the cake.

"So happy not to disappoint you," Greta replied as she set a glass of milk on the floor near him and sat down next to him. She sighed heavily. "Do you truly wish to do this?" she asked.

Aware that they were no longer discussing the merits of her chocolate cake, he set the plate next to the glass of milk and gave her his full attention. "Do you? I saw you talking to Josef earlier today and…"

"It is unlikely that I will be able to avoid talking to Josef now and again," she snapped irritably.

"I did not mean it as an accusation."

She pushed herself more firmly back onto the swing and folded her arms. "He asked to call on me."

Luke was confused. "I thought that he and Esther Yoder—that…"

"Josef is a man who has difficulty choosing what he truly wants."

Luke took a moment to consider this. "But surely, in the matter of choosing a wife…"

"He's always afraid that there might be something better—someone better."

"Then he is a fool."

"And are you any different, Luke Starns? You set your sights on Lydia and yet here we sit. What about that is so very different than Josef deciding to consider Esther?"

Any comparison between him and Josef Bontrager was insulting in Luke's mind and his lips hardened into a straight line as he stood up. "Thank you for the cake—for the supper tonight, Greta. I can see that your sister and I have not given you the time you need to consider whether or not your feelings for Josef…"

"Please do not try and hide your wounded pride

under the veil of pretending that this has anything to do with my feelings for Josef. I will admit that I am still reeling from the events of the last several days, but I know my mind, Luke Starns."

Luke bristled. "This is not a matter of wounded pride," he protested.

"Then what?"

"I like you," he blurted. "Your sister saw before I did that I noticed you long before Josef quit you. In time I think that perhaps we could…that I could come to…" He ran his hand through his thick hair as he struggled to find the words. "The fact is, Greta, that…"

She was standing next to him now and in the lamp-light he saw that she was smiling. "The fact is, Luke Starns, that you are seriously seeking a wife. My sister has spurned you and you have turned to me—also spurned. We make quite a pair."

Under the light of her smile and her softened tone, he felt all of the tension drain from him. "We do at that," he admitted.

And suddenly they were both laughing—laughing so hard at the ridiculous situation in which they found themselves that they were unaware of a buggy passing the house on its way out of town.

Chapter Ten

Over the next two weeks, Greta and the other women once again set out the lunch for the men as they finished construction of the outer walls, laid the floor for the hay loft and framed out new living quarters for Luke. As soon as the last shingle was in place on the roof, the men would go back to their farms and businesses and jobs in town and Luke would work alone with the occasional help of neighbors as they had time. There would be no further need to organize meals for the crews of neighbors and customers from Sarasota. Once the last dish had been washed after the last shift of men taking their noonday meal before returning to work, the other women gathered their belongings and headed for home, leaving Greta alone to finish cleaning up.

She stretched her back as she stood at the kitchen door of the house that her father had built before she was born and watched the men working. By sunset the roof would be complete. Within another week Luke would be back in business. She saw Luke walking across the high roof as easily as if he were walking on firm ground. He carried a stack of shingles and she heard the sound of his laughter as he set them down and began to work next to Roger Hadwell.

She also saw Josef glance to where Luke was working. He'd been about to start up one of the ladders leading to the roof, but then he had turned toward Luke and back to where Greta watched from her porch and stepped away from the ladder. He'd set down his hammer, wiped his hands on a cloth before drinking a dipper of water and starting across the yard toward her.

Greta steeled herself for the confrontation that was bound to come. It was clear to her that Josef had changed his mind about pursuing Esther Yoder. Pleasant had confided that news to her earlier when Greta had wondered what might be keeping Esther and Hilda from coming to help serve the workers.

"He quit her just last evening," Pleasant told her. "She is devastated, of course, and Hilda is furious."

Greta sighed as she watched Josef approach. So, he had changed his mind after all. Well, he was too late. The realization struck her like a bolt of lightning as she realized that her mind was made up. The idea that she needed to make a choice between Josef and Luke was no longer a matter of concern. Of course there was no way of knowing whether or not things would work out with Luke in the end. But for now she was more certain than she had been of anything in a very long time that it was God's plan for her to give a courtship with Luke the time necessary to see where it would lead.

"Did you need some more lemonade, Josef?" she asked when he reached the foot of the porch steps.

"I need to know why Luke Starns was sitting—

laughing—with you and not your sister on your porch the other evening."

Greta's heart beat a staccato rhythm as she tried to come up with some plausible answer that would not jeopardize Liddy's plan to give Greta and Luke the time they needed to get better acquainted. "You must have…"

"It was not your sister's laughter I heard—only yours, Greta—and his. Lydia was nowhere in sight."

"She was inside," Greta replied. It was not a lie. "Were you spying on my sister and me, Josef Bontrager?"

"I was driving by on my way home—a fact you might have taken note of were you not so engaged with the blacksmith. I have to wonder what Lydia thinks of your spending time with him?"

"She thinks that it is fine," Greta said. "Not that it is any of your business. This is a private matter, Josef."

"He is not courting Lydia. He is calling on you." The way Josef's eyes widened Greta understood that he had finally worked out the details to their logical conclusion.

"Again, this is none of your…"

"You will not deny it?"

"I will not discuss it."

"Because denying it would be a lie and you do not lie, Greta."

Before she could form a reply, Josef had turned on his heel and stalked off. She watched as he returned to the construction site, packed up his tools, offered some explanation to Bishop Troyer and then drove away.

Once again Greta felt her chest tighten with the certain knowledge that by morning everyone in Celery Fields would know that Luke was calling on her and not Lydia. Once again she would be the topic of speculation and gossip. Oh, why did life have to be so very complicated?

After Greta told him later that Josef had uncovered their secret, Luke decided to take a ride out to the Bontrager farm. His plan was unclear. He knew only that Greta had been more than a little upset and he wanted to protect Greta from becoming the topic of fresh gossip in the community. She'd been through enough and through no fault of her own. What was Bontrager's problem? Hadn't he been the one to quit Greta? Hadn't he been the one to make it no secret that he had turned his attention toward the Yoders' daughter?

The Bontrager farm was an impressive expanse of plowed fields laid out like a patchwork quilt around a large white farmhouse, a whitewashed barn and other outbuildings. The property lay along a rushing stream and was surrounded by a split-rail fence. When Luke saw what Greta would not have, his heart went out to her. He thought about how she would have thrived in this place, turning the house into a home, the large yard into a playground for the children, the kitchen garden into her own private store of herbs and vegetables.

Forcing himself to contain the rising irritation he felt with Josef Bontrager for being such a fool, he tied his horse to a hitching post and walked up the path that led to the front door.

"He's not there," a voice shouted.

Luke turned to see Josef's Uncle Cyrus standing

in the doorway to the barn, a piece of straw dangling from the corner of his mouth.

Luke retraced his steps since it was obvious that the older man had no intention of moving toward him. "Any idea when he'll be back?"

Cyrus shrugged. "I expect it'll be some time— maybe a couple weeks. He left this morning. Asked me to watch over things 'til he returned. Something about needing to make a visit up north."

"I hope no one in the family has taken ill," Luke said and meant it.

"Nobody I know of and I do keep up with all of them wherever they are." Cyrus's tone was defensive. He squinted at Luke. "He owe you money or something?"

"No. I just… It can wait until he gets back." Suddenly a thought had come to Luke that made his heart race with excitement. With Josef gone—possibly for several days or even a couple weeks—he and Greta would have the time they needed to discover whether or not they were right for each other unencumbered by her concerns about Josef exposing them. Luke headed back across the yard to where his horse was tied up.

"Kind of sudden his leaving," Josef's uncle remarked and Luke realized that the man had followed him. "Seemed kind of upset about something."

"He probably just had a lot on his mind and wanted to be sure this place was looked after," Luke offered as he mounted his horse.

"Could be. More likely it's something to do with the Goodloe woman. He thinks he made a mistake there."

"Well, it was his decision," Luke said through gritted teeth.

"*Yah,* that's true. I expect that he was thinking that as a practical matter a union with the Yoder girl made more sense—financially speaking. After all, these are hard times for everybody and Josef has got himself a big nut to crack running this place. The Yoders—as everybody knows—have a real steady business. Secure."

Luke understood what the man was saying. Joining forces with the Yoders made more sense financially speaking than marrying Greta who had no dowry at all.

"But the heart knows," the older man continued, "and that boy's heart has always been set on Greta Goodloe." He shook his head as he turned and ambled toward the barn. "I'll let Josef know you came around once he gets back."

Luke nodded and turned his horse toward town. He could not wait for evening when he could walk up to the Goodloe house and tell Greta what he'd learned. He wondered if she would see it as the opportunity that he did. Only time would tell—and thanks to Josef Bontrager's sudden decision to take a trip, they now had that time.

"I hope nothing's gone wrong with his family," Greta said that evening when Luke told her about Josef's trip. "Maybe somebody's sick."

"I asked, but I didn't get the idea that it was anything like that," Luke told her. "His uncle certainly would have known if somebody in the family had taken ill, don't you think?"

"I suppose. But then where could he have gone? I mean to just take off like that?"

"Maybe he needed some time to sort things out.

Seems to be common knowledge that he's regretting his decision to quit you."

Greta considered this as she and Luke sat side by side on the porch swing, the lamp in the window casting a pale golden light over them.

"Are you regretting his decision, Greta?" Luke asked and she realized that his voice had softened to the point where it was barely above a whisper.

"It was his decision," she said firmly.

"But he might have changed his mind and that's not an answer."

Greta had to wonder if all men were like this—always questioning what her feelings might be, what they were going to be in the future. Josef had done that repeatedly, taking every conversation she had with any male and turning it in his mind into a flirtation or abandonment of him. "What are you asking me, Luke Starns?" she demanded irritably. To her further annoyance the man actually grinned. "What's so amusing?" She sounded like Lydia now—Lydia would say something like that.

"Which question do you want me to answer?"

"Both."

"All right. Second answer first—I was smiling because when you get your dander up you are a little like a spoiled child."

"I seem to have to repeatedly remind you that I am not a child," Greta snapped. "I am a grown woman—grown up enough to have been jilted once and now maybe yet again."

"I have no intention of jilting you, Greta."

She noticed that any hint of amusement had disappeared from his tone. "Then what?"

"When I learned that Josef had gone away for a while, it seemed to me that perhaps God was giving us this opportunity."

"What opportunity?"

"To become better acquainted without the shadow of Josef Bontrager hanging over us. To consider whether or not your sister is right in her estimation that we could make a good union and to do it all before Josef returns. That way if things between us do not work out, you know that Josef…"

"Don't you dare say that he would be willing to take me back as if I were some flawed piece of farm equipment or something."

Luke surprised her by taking her hand between his larger ones. "Listen to me, Greta, and hear me clearly. There is not a flaw in you that I can see. If things do not work out for us it will be because you found flaw with me—that you realized that a union with me would not make you happy."

She studied him, his features now fully revealed in the lamplight and realized that he was serious. "And how will we know this?"

He ducked his head for a moment and his thick, dark hair fell across his forehead. Greta had to resist the urge to brush it back with her fingers. When he looked up he was smiling and that smile had a way of making her heart beat a lot faster than was normal. "I suggest that we could start by thinking we might wed, then we could spend these evenings talking about what being married to each other might look like."

"What it might look like? I don't understand."

"You know, we could imagine how we would be together, what we would do, what we would talk about, what things we share in common and how we may differ."

"And then?"

He tossed his head like a horse clearing the errant strands of hair. "I don't know. I mean I just came up with the idea this afternoon after I learned that Josef had gone away. Don't you see? It's like God is giving us the time we need to figure this all out."

It gave her comfort to see in his expression and hear in his voice that he was as confused about this entire business as she was. But like Lydia he had laid out a plan—one that just might work—while she had come up with nothing at all.

"Very well," she said, pulling her hands free of his and sitting back in the swing so that they were side by side but no longer facing each other. "How do we begin?"

There was a moment of silence that stretched on for long enough that she glanced his way and saw that he was smiling—yet again. Then he stood up and held out both hands to her.

"What?" she demanded as she came to her feet and realized the two of them were fully concealed in darkness now.

"Well, I was thinking that in courting it's sometimes getting that first kiss out of the way that can break the ice, so to speak. You know, it sets both parties more at their ease not having to think about when or even if it will happen."

"You wish to kiss me?"

"Very, very much," Luke said huskily as he drew her closer. "If you would agree."

His mouth was no more than a whisper's distance

from her own and she realized that she had raised onto her toes to meet him halfway. "I think that would be a good start," she said.

"Das ist gut," Luke murmured as his lips skimmed hers.

Greta and Josef had kissed, of course. After all, they had been a couple for most of their teen years. But Josef's wet, almost desperate kisses were nothing at all like Luke's full lips touching her face. His kiss darted and teased as his lips met her lips and then skittered to her cheeks and onto her eyelids, squeezed shut to savor the experience. And just when she thought that her knees might buckle with the sheer pleasure of being in his arms, he tightened his embrace and kissed her fully on the mouth for what seemed an eternity and yet was over in an instant.

"Das ist sehr gut," he whispered as he pulled her to him, her hands trapped against the broadness of his chest. His mouth now rested close to her ear and his breath came in audible gasps as if he had just run a very long way to reach this place.

Beneath her hand she could feel the steady thumping of his heart. It reminded her of that day in his shop when she had watched him pounding out the bridle bit. She snaked her hand between them until she had freed it enough to comb her fingers through his hair.

"Again," she said and smiled when she heard the rumble of his laughter. She looked up at him. *"Bitte?"*

A shudder ran through his entire body as he cupped her jaw in his palm and tilted her face to his. This time when he lowered his lips to hers, there were no teasing forays onto her cheeks and eyelids. Instead their mouths collided in a burst of warmth and need that

Greta realized was exactly the kiss that she had imagined sharing with the man she would marry. A lifetime in Luke's arms? She did not even need to think twice about it.

When he pulled back a little, she actually whimpered in protest. "I think that we have done a good job of getting that first kiss—and the second—out of the way," he said, "and now we can go forward with truly getting to know each other and deciding if there's a future for us."

"If you kiss me once again," Greta teased as she stroked his cheek, "I think there may be no need for discussion."

His laughter rang out in the silence of the night as he set her back on the swing and collected his hat. "We will discuss," he said as he bent and kissed her cheek in a purely brotherly—and disappointing—way. "I want you to be very, very sure of whatever decision you make." He walked back toward his shop then and as he went Greta heard him humming softly to himself.

Greta sat on the swing alone for a long time after Luke left. She repeatedly ran her tongue lightly over her lips, tasting the kisses she'd shared with him, remembering the way she had fit so perfectly in the curve of his arms. She relished the realization that while his kiss had nearly been her undoing, her kiss had caused that shudder of pleasure she felt rocket through his chest and shoulders.

But she reminded herself sternly that a few shared kisses were not a solid foundation for a lifetime spent together. Luke was right. They barely knew one another and if she didn't want to make the same mistake she had made with Josef—a man she had known perhaps too well—she was going to have to do something to remedy that.

"A frolic," she said aloud. "It's the perfect solution."

Frolics were events where the entire community came together to complete some project—sometimes frolics involved only the women when they gathered for a quilting bee, for example. But she had to come up with something that would involve the entire community—male and female.

Lydia agreed when Greta presented her with the idea the following morning. "The schoolhouse could use a fresh coat of whitewash and a good cleaning," she suggested. "I'll send word home with the children today. We can plan it for a week from Saturday."

Greta frowned. "But then how will Luke know?"

Lydia's eyes twinkled mischievously. "Well, we will have to order the whitewash from Roger Hadwell and it seems to me that he does enjoy spreading news of all sorts."

"He does at that," Greta agreed and giggled. "I'll go and order the whitewash this morning."

As it turned out there was no need to rely upon Roger to tell Luke about the frolic for when Greta walked into town she saw the two men sitting outside Luke's shop.

"*Guten morgen,* Greta," Roger called out as she came around the corner of the livery.

"And to you," she replied, but it was all she could do to keep her eyes on Roger when all she really wanted to do was look at Luke. Was it possible that she was so very fickle that she could so easily be drawn to this dark stranger when it had been just a week and a half since Josef quit her?

She focused her attention on Luke's hands, the fingers long and thick, and could think only of how those palms had felt cradling her cheeks the evening before. "I…" Her voice failed her. She felt a fire ignite in her cheeks as if he had touched her now. She cleared her throat. "Liddy is announcing a frolic to clean and whitewash the schoolhouse a week from Saturday," she said, spilling out the words in one breath lest she lose her voice once again.

Roger pushed himself to his feet. "Whitewash, you say? I think there might just be some leftover from when we last painted the house." He headed for his store. "Coming?" he asked when Greta did not make a move to follow him.

"Yah," she said and glanced at Luke for the first time since encountering the two men. "In a minute," she added, her eyes locked on his. She realized that he seemed to be as nervous as she was about this encounter in broad daylight. "Lydia was wondering, Luke Starns," she began in a voice that even she realized was too loud, "would you have the time to come and help? I don't know if you have frolics where you're from back in Canada, but…"

Roger had paused on his way back to the hardware store and was studying her curiously.

"We do have frolics," Luke said softly. "I'll be there."

Three simple words, accompanied by a smile that set her heart to racing, was a promise she could count on.

"Denki," she murmured softly, but inside she was singing as she followed Roger to the hardware store.

Chapter Eleven

News of the frolic to clean and paint the schoolhouse spread quickly. Lydia reported that she could hardly keep the children's mind on their lessons because they were so excited about the event. For the citizens of Celery Fields—as indeed for all people of the Amish faith—work was rarely if ever considered drudgery. Greta had sometimes marveled at the way *Englischers* complained about having to take on the simplest tasks. More than once she had been helping Pleasant in the bakery and served a visitor from Sarasota who sighed happily over the fact that "At least I don't have to bother baking bread or making dessert for my family. I don't know how you can do it day after day in this heat."

For Greta the woman's comment had come as a complete mystery. She could not wait for the day when she could bake and prepare meals and keep house for her husband and their brood of children. She had been preparing the meals and managing the house for her father and Lydia for years now and in the process she had earned a reputation throughout the town as an accomplished cook. Unlike the *Englischers,* who tended to spread compliments around like so much chicken feed, those of Amish faith did not believe in receiving or giving compliments. That would lead down the path of prideful ways. Thinking well of oneself or of something done well was a sin. But Greta could tell by the way the other women of Celery Fields were always glad to see her arriving at some function with her basket, or how the men belched with satisfaction after enjoying one of her cakes, that God had blessed her with the gifts to do everything associated with managing well a home and family.

On the Saturday of the frolic, she smiled as she waited for the chunks of bittersweet chocolate to melt on the wood stove and thought about the night that Luke had come asking for a second helping of her chocolate cake. Then she closed her eyes as she relived, for perhaps the hundredth time, the taste of his lips on hers. She thought about little else these days other than Luke Starns. When would she see him again? What was he thinking about as he went about his work or lay alone in his restored upstairs apartment at night? And most of all she wondered when he might kiss her again.

Her nose told her that the chocolate was burning and she opened her eyes with a start and grabbed for the pan with her apron-wrapped hand. There was nothing so sweet as the scent of chocolate warming on the stove and nothing so rank as the odor of that same chocolate burnt to a tarry mess. She dropped the pan in the sink and pumped water into it, making a face as the combination of cold water on the hot ingredients only intensified the acrid smell.

"That's what you get, Greta Goodloe," she chastised herself, "for daydreaming and not minding the task before you. Now it's ruined and you'll have to start again and there's no time to get the cake made and properly baked before…"

"Greta?"

Luke stood in the kitchen doorway, filling the space with his broad shoulders. "Who are you talking to?" He glanced around.

"Myself," she admitted. "I was baking a cake for the frolic and I got…" Her eyes focused on his mouth—a mouth that seemed to be fighting a smile—and she found that she was having trouble breathing much less finishing a thought or sentence.

He wrinkled his nose as the odor of the burnt chocolate hit him. "I just came from the schoolhouse and from what I could see there are more than enough sweets there already." He crossed the room and took her hand in his. "You didn't burn yourself, did you?" He was frowning and running his thumb over her palm.

Greta felt the color rise to her cheeks and she knew that she should pull her hand away. She was far too aware that the only burning going on at the moment was the heat she felt with Luke being so near. "Why did you come?" she asked, her voice catching in midsentence.

"Lydia sent me to tell you to be sure and remember to bring…" His eyes locked on hers and she realized that he had also lost his train of thought.

With a will of its own her head tilted up and her eyes fluttered shut as she fought to steady her breathing.

"Greta," he whispered, his lips so very close that

she felt his breath tickle the strands of her hair that had worked their way free of her bun in the hot kitchen. "Do you think of me?"

"Constantly," she admitted. "And you?"

He chuckled. "I can't work. I can't sleep for thinking about you—about us."

Greta fought a smile of pleasure and opened her eyes. "Me, too," she agreed.

But then all trace of his smile vanished and he stepped away. "It's important that you take plenty of time in this matter, Greta. You have suffered a great disappointment and…"

Oh, why did he have to spoil everything by bringing up the past? What was it about men that they had to always dwell on the realities of a matter? She turned away and began scrubbing the pan. "Of course, you're right," she said, her voice far too bright to be sincere. "Now what was it that Lydia did not want me to forget?"

"The extra cleaning rags," Luke said, his expression one of pure confusion at her sudden change in topic and conduct.

"They are there on the back porch. You can take them with you now."

"I had thought we might—that is, no one would think anything of it if you and I were to walk down to the schoolhouse together."

"And that's important to you, isn't it? That others not question your actions?"

He waited a long moment before he said anything, then quietly he said, "I thought such things were of concern to you, Greta."

Greta paused in her scrubbing, aware that he had

turned away and started for the door. She so wanted to stop him, to call him back, to rest her cheek against his chest and beg his forgiveness for her foul mood. "I'm sorry, Luke," she murmured but he was already gone, walking past the kitchen window with the basket of rags and an expression that looked like the coming of a storm.

"I'm sorry," she repeated and was struck by the difference in her apology to Luke from the ones she had offered to Josef over the years whenever something she said or did upset him. With Josef her apologies had been more a matter of habit—automatic in the knowledge that, whether she felt she had wronged him or not, this was the way to end whatever argument or disagreement they might be having. But with Luke the apology had come straight from her heart, from her understanding that her words had been hurtful and her change in attitude confusing for him.

She stood at the window with the scalded pot in one hand and a hunk of steel wool in the other and watched Luke until he was out of sight. And when she could no longer see him she felt such a sense of loss that she let the pot and steel wool fall from her slack hands as she ran from the house to catch up to him.

"Luke! Wait!"

His heart hammered with relief as he turned to watch her run toward him. He savored the moment of Greta Goodloe running across the fallow field to him. The strings of her black bonnet had come undone and flew out behind her as she clutched at her bonnet with one hand and gathered the skirt of her dress and apron in the other to prevent herself from tripping. In his mind he was already years into the future and now she was wearing the white starched prayer covering of a married woman. She was running to him as his wife.

While he waited for her to catch up to him, he prayed that the dream of a union between them one day might be so and he vowed that soon he would find the right time to tell her everything that had happened in his past. Somehow in his heart he was sure that she would understand why he had made the choices he had made.

"Forgive me," she gasped when she reached him at last.

"There is nothing to forgive," he replied as he set down the basket and tried to tie the ribbons of her bonnet into a bow.

She looked up at him, the sun full on her face and he thought that he had never seen a woman more beautiful than Greta. "My fingers are too thick," he said huskily.

"I think your fingers are fine, although probably better for other tasks," she said as she took over the tying of the bow herself while he picked up the basket of rags and waited for her to finish. "I did not mean…"

"Sh-h-h. It's past."

She fell into step with him and side by side they walked the rest of the way to the schoolhouse. There seemed to be no need for further conversation and for that Luke was grateful, for he found that whenever he was around Greta he had trouble making his voice work or even coming up with the words he might say to her.

"Ah, here they are," Lydia said as soon as she spotted them. Her eyes flickered toward a small group of women that included Hilda Yoder who was scowling at them with disapproval.

"We have had to stop our work waiting for those clean rags, Luke Starns," Hilda chided. "What took you so long?"

Greta took the basket of cleaning rags from Luke and handed it to Lydia. "I ruined the cake and Luke was kind enough to help me clear the mess," she announced and in the background Luke heard several of the men groan.

"No matter," Lydia told her. "We have plenty." Then she clapped her hands together as she might if she were settling her students in for the day and began giving out assignments. "If you boys there would set up the ladders. The siding will need scraping before we can paint. Start on the north side and complete that so the men can begin the painting while you move on around the building." Next she pointed to the place where the desks had been set out into the yard along with the bookcases—empty of their books. "And Bettina, take your friends and the younger children and set to work polishing the desks and bookcases. Then you will need to dust every book, pound the chalk from the erasers and wash the chalkboard."

"Esther," Hilda called out. "Go with Bettina and the others."

Without question or comment the children ran to the shade of the large banyan tree and set to work, their excited chatter filling the heavy air that hung over the now empty school. Without the need for instruction, several of the men set to work climbing the ladders the boys had put in place and scraping the outer walls of the building while the women went inside to scrub the inner walls, wash the windows and polish the floor.

Around noon, Lydia sounded the bell and everyone gathered for the meal of cold cuts, cheeses, salads and desserts arrayed on boards set on sawhorses outside the schoolhouse. Like Sunday evening singings, frolics were acknowledged as occasions when males and females were allowed to socialize openly. With no comment from their elders, the older teens and young adults who were not yet married gathered in small groups to enjoy their lunch. Luke filled his plate and then took a seat on the ground next to Greta and Lydia.

He saw Hilda Yoder make some comment to Gertrude Hadwell as they looked his way. Both women nodded knowingly and smiled broadly at Lydia as they passed by on their way to sit with their husbands. Clearly they had no idea that it was Greta Goodloe being courted—not her sister. He glanced at Lydia and Greta and the three of them collapsed into laughter, drawing the attention of the two older women—as well as their frowns of censure. But Luke didn't care. For the first time in a very long time he felt a part of a community—a part of a family. Should he and Greta marry someday, then they would share many afternoons like this one with Lydia and Pleasant and Jeremiah and their children.

"Bettina is a good influence on Caleb Harnischer," Lydia said as she bit into a sandwich and nodded toward the teenagers. "He has become a far better student since taking up with her." She smiled as she glanced at Greta. "I have to say that I have noted some changes for the better in my sister recently, as well, Luke."

Luke sneaked a peek at Greta and grinned. Her cheeks were a rosy red and she was frowning. "In what ways would you say that she has changed, Lydia?"

"Oh, she is far more content these days and I hardly ever have to remind her to attend her chores and…"

"You have never had to remind me about chores, Lydia," Greta fumed.

Lydia lifted one eyebrow as she continued eating.

"At least not often. Most of the time you simply instruct out of habit, unaware that I have every intention of getting to whatever chore you may see."

Lydia turned her attention back to Luke. "You also seem in better spirits. With the disaster of the fire and your loss of business for those few weeks, it would be understandable for you to be a bit down in the dumps."

Now it was Luke's turn to flush. "My spirits have been uplifted by the kindness of my neighbors," he replied softly.

"That's it then?" Lydia pressed and he saw that she was fighting a smile.

"That's a good part of it. The rest I will keep to myself for now."

This brought a laugh from Lydia as she got to her feet and clapped her hands. "Back to work," she called and Greta was on her feet at once, collecting the used dishes from the others and organizing the washing up.

On her way back to the schoolhouse, Lydia paused and screened her eyes from the sun with her hand as she looked up at Luke. "I want to thank you."

"For?"

Lydia nodded toward Greta. "Whatever happens between you and my sister, you have seen her through a very difficult time. I would ask one more favor of you, though."

"Anything," Luke said and meant it. For when it came to Greta Goodloe he would happily move mountains if she needed him to do so.

"Do not hurt her," Lydia said. "If you find that you cannot love her—that she is not for you, then find a way to quit her so that she suffers no public humiliation."

"I have no intention of bringing Greta any pain at all if I can help it," Luke said quietly. "The truth is that you were wise to suggest we become better acquainted for I have come to see that…"

"Lydia Goodloe?" Hilda Yoder was standing by the entrance to the school, her hands on her ample hips and a scowl on her face as she watched Lydia and Luke closely. "The sun will not stay out forever," she reminded them. "And there is still a great deal of work to be done."

"Coming, Hilda," Lydia called, but before she turned away she looked up at Luke. "Just be very sure of your feelings, Luke."

"I will," he promised as she walked away. *I already am,* he thought.

As the work continued amid lively chatter and general high spirits, Luke was aware of the frequent lilt of Greta's laughter wafting out from the open windows to where he worked. He found it comforting somehow— the nearness of her.

All around him the men shared news they had heard about the state of the world outside Celery Fields. Mostly they talked about the man who had been elected President of the United States a year earlier.

Franklin Delano Roosevelt was from a wealthy New York family and yet according to what several of the men had heard, he was focusing much of his attention on those that had suffered so much loss over the last few years. Luke heard the term *New Deal* and wondered why such a plan might be necessary. If neighbors worked together and took care of each other in hard times, as his neighbors had helped him after the fire and as they were all pitching in together now, there should be no need for a "new deal." He did not understand the ways of outsiders.

Above him the school bell clanged and he glanced up to see Greta balancing herself on the edge of the cupola as she reached to polish the large brass bell.

"Get down from there," he ordered, his fear that she might fall leaving a bitter taste in his mouth.

"Oh, Luke, don't worry. I have done this at least a dozen times—since Lydia and I were students here ourselves."

"You were smaller then and had more space to work and…"

She paused in her polishing and studied him. "Why, Luke Starns, I do believe that you are seriously concerned for my safety."

He saw a couple of the men working nearby glance his way, their interest suddenly on what was happening in their world rather than the world of outsiders.

"As I would be concerned for anyone taking such a risk, Greta Goodloe," he replied, turning his attention back to his scraping. "But as you say, you have done this many times and after all I am new to all this."

He heard the men chuckle as they returned to their work and conversation. That's when he looked up at

Greta, his eyes pleading with her to move to a safer position.

At first she gave him a teasing smile, but then as she read his expression, her eyes softened and she eased herself back inside the cupola. Seeing her on safer ground, he heaved a sigh of pure relief and found that he could breathe normally again. And once again it occured to him that breathing normally whenever he was anywhere near Greta—and sometimes even when he wasn't—was becoming more and more difficult.

As the day and the work progressed, Greta's thoughts seemed more fixed on the future than on the present—a future that it surprised her to realize definitely included Luke Starns. Surely it was far too soon for her to have such reflections that ran the gamut from what it would be like to be married to him to imagining sharing a home with him all the way to envisioning the children they would have. And yet she thought about all of those things and more. Where would they live? With more and more trucks and automobiles on the road would there be enough call for his blacksmithing skills and the use of the livery to sustain them? And what of Luke's family? He never spoke of them. All she knew was that his mother had died when he was young and his father and three brothers still lived in Ontario. The brothers were married and presumably had children.

If she married Luke she would be coming into a much larger family than the one that she and Lydia had in Florida. She imagined summer holidays spent in Canada away from the oppressive Florida heat. And of course, Luke's family would all come south to escape the harsh winters—many Amish families were doing that these days. They would hire a driver to bring them or come on the train or bus. This was allowed even though operating or owning any motorized vehicle of their own was not. She envisioned riding to Canada on the train with Luke after their wedding. Tradition had it that newly married Amish couples took several weeks to visit friends and family following the ceremony. Along the way they would receive gifts to help them set up their household. The idea made Greta smile as she completed the polishing of the bell and took her bucket and rags outside to start washing one of the school's tall windows. Slowly she polished the same area over and over again with the newspaper she'd soaked in a white vinegar solution once she'd cleaned away the surface dirt and grime.

"You're going to work your way right through the glass if you keep polishing that same spot," Luke teased. He had moved his ladder closer to where she was working and was painting the trim above her. "And I'm not sure I can mend a cut as easily as I removed that splinter."

Greta felt a rush of pleasure at his nearness. "Liddy likes for the windows to sparkle. She says the cleaner they are, the more light the children have to do their work by and that makes them better students."

"She certainly has a way with those youngsters," Luke agreed. He lowered his voice. "May I come by to see you tonight, Greta?"

But before Greta could reply, they were interrupted.

"You missed a spot way up there, Luke Starns," Esther Yoder shouted, coming alongside Greta before she could respond and pointing to a place that Luke hadn't gotten to yet. She giggled and glanced up at him. "Perhaps you need some help? I could hold the paint bucket while you reach those cornices."

Greta's mouth fell open. Esther Yoder was openly flirting with Luke when she knew—or thought she knew—that he was already courting Liddy. Of course he wasn't courting Liddy at all. He was courting her. Or at least that's what she'd thought until now when she looked up and saw Luke grinning down at Esther. He was giving the Yoder daughter that very same heart-stopping smile that he'd given Greta numerous times these last several days.

"Now, Esther, what would your mother say if I had you climb onto this ladder next to me?" he asked.

Esther's giggle turned into something more resembling a cackle. "My mother is not here, Luke. She's working inside."

The brazenness of Esther's invitation was downright shocking. The way Luke seemed to be eating it up was infuriating. "Luke," Greta said, intentionally keeping her tone sweet and adding a friendly smile for Esther's benefit, "if you've finished there, I think Lydia could use some help inside reaching the cobwebs that have gathered in the corners of that high ceiling." Greta fought to hold her composure despite her annoyance as she squinted up at him.

But when he turned the same smile that he'd offered Esther on her, Greta could tolerate no more. She gathered her bucket and newspaper and with a toss of her head went inside to find Lydia. "Never mind. I can ask one of the other men. I can see that you're still busy here." What could she have been thinking? Luke Starns was just like every other man she'd ever met—easily won over by sweet talk. Well, she would show him.

"Sister?" Lydia came clear across the room to meet her. "What has happened?"

"It's nothing," Greta assured her.

"But you're so flushed. Are you ill? Perhaps too much sun?" She pressed the back of her hand to Greta's cheek and it was all that Greta could do not to lean into the solace of her sister's touch. "Is it Luke?" Liddy asked, her voice barely audible in the din of chatter from the half-dozen other people busy working inside the small schoolroom.

Greta nodded. "He's no different than…"

"Now stop that," Lydia chided, still keeping her voice low. She glanced toward the window and evidently surmised the problem when she saw Esther still standing at the foot of Luke's ladder, gazing adoringly up at him and giggling at something he'd just said.

"First Josef and now Luke," Greta murmured. "Why does that woman dislike me so?"

"Be careful that you not suffer the sin of pride, sister," Lydia warned. "Besides, how can you think that Esther wishes to harm you by flirting with Luke? Let's remember that Josef has recently quit her, as well, and like it or not Luke Starns is one of the—if not the only—single man in the community that most women would set their eye on. Besides, wouldn't it make more sense if I were the one upset by Esther's actions?"

"*Yah,* I suppose, but…"

"I would remind you that, in all the years you spent with Josef, not once did I ever see you upset when some other girl caught his eye. But Luke Starns seems to have caused you great distress when I expect that all he was doing was being kind."

"He smiled at her," Greta argued.

Lydia laughed. "As he is prone to do these days— ever since he started coming around and calling on you, I might add. God gave the man a wonderful smile, Greta. Would you deny him the use of it?"

"*Neh,* but…"

Lydia squeezed Greta's hand. It was a warning that almost came too late as Hilda Yoder was suddenly there beside them. "Is something wrong, Greta?" she asked.

"Nothing at all," Greta replied. "I've finished with the windows so Lydia and I were just going over the list of chores yet to be done." She turned to her sister. "The cobwebs, right? I'll get to them right away." She picked up a broom and wrapped the bristles with a clean rag.

"Oh, Greta, you are far too slight to reach the corners," Hilda huffed. She glanced toward the doorway. "You there, Luke Starns, come here and make yourself useful." She took the broom from Greta and handed it off to Luke. "Greta can show you where to reach." Then she smiled. "Or perhaps you would rather Lydia Goodloe instruct you?"

Greta almost laughed when she saw the sly look that Hilda gave Lydia. As if she knew a secret. But then the older woman's face collapsed into the more familiar grimace that she usually wore. "Esther," she called out when she spotted her daughter lingering near the doorway, her eyes on Luke. "I thought I sent you to make sure the young ones are doing a proper job polishing the desks. What are you doing in here?"

Esther mumbled an excuse and scurried back outside, her mother on her heels still lecturing her.

"That was close," Lydia said with a sigh. "Do you think you two can work together without causing trouble?"

"I..." Greta started to protest but Lydia was already halfway across the room, calling out to Caleb Harnischer to stop visiting with Bettina and get back to work.

"Want to show me where those cobwebs are hiding?" Luke asked as he scanned the rafters above them. "And while we're at it maybe you can tell me what just happened outside there? I thought we were..."

"We can talk about it tonight," Greta said primly as she led the way to the back of the room. "There," she pointed to a web that stretched across one corner.

Luke raised the broom and swiped at it until it was gone. The fact that he was smiling only irritated Greta more.

"Do you truly take such pleasure in removing cobwebs?" she asked as she continued to point and he continued to swipe, smiling the whole time.

"No. What I take pleasure in is knowing that even though you seem to be more than a little upset with me—for reasons I can't quite figure out—you're still going to let me come calling tonight."

"We have things to talk about that cannot be discussed here," she reminded him.

"Do I get a hint?"

"Just one—Esther Yoder."

"You think that..." he sputtered, drawing the attention of others.

"Hush," she hissed as she pointed to a far corner

that forced him away from the prying eyes of the others.

"You can't be jealous." He had lowered his voice again and then he flashed that maddening grin of his. "Because that might mean that you care, Greta. It might mean that you care a great deal."

"And what if I do?"

He studied her for a long moment, his tone softening into something far more serious than the banter he'd been exchanging with her before. "I want you to be very sure," he said. "Because the fact is that I care about you—more than I would have thought possible."

She felt her mouth go slack in response to her surprise at such a declaration. "What are you saying?"

"I'm saying that when I come calling tonight, I'm hoping that we might do more than just talk," he said softly and as he then turned back to his work he was chuckling.

Suddenly Greta found that she was the one fighting a smile as she scanned the corners, praying to discover even more cobwebs so that she could stay close to Luke for the remainder of the afternoon. But in her mind she wasn't seeing the dark corners of the schoolhouse. She was seeing the two of them sitting together on the porch swing, in the shadows of the night, and Luke kissing her.

Chapter Twelve

"You must be very tired, sister," Lydia commented later that evening after she had declared the work on the schoolhouse complete and sent everyone home.

"Not so very," Greta replied absently as she paced from the window of one of their two front rooms to the other across the hall.

"Are you expecting someone?" Lydia asked, not looking up from her mending.

"Luke mentioned that he might come by."

"And you agreed? I thought that you were annoyed with Luke," Lydia said.

Greta plopped down in the upholstered chair on the other side of the fireplace that they used to heat the front rooms on those rare days when the Florida weather turned chilly. "Oh, Liddy, I don't know what I feel for him. I keep telling myself that it's only been a few weeks. How is it possible that in such a short time I might have come to…" She waved her hands in frustration then clasped them tightly around her knees as if it were necessary for her to hold herself together.

"To what? I have no understanding of my feelings when it comes to that man but these last few days…"

"Have you considered the idea that perhaps you are in love with Luke Starns?" Lydia said, her voice as calm as if she had simply asked Greta if she intended to make chicken or beef for their supper.

"How could I love him?" Greta protested. "Surely it's far too soon."

"God does not work on our timetables, sister," Lydia reminded her. "If it is His will for you and Luke to be together, then why wait?"

"But how can I be certain?" Greta moaned.

Lydia lightly tapped the place on her chest where her heart beat. "You must pray for guidance and when the time is right then you will know it here."

They both looked up at the sounds of footsteps on the porch. After a moment the swing creaked and Lydia folded her mending. "It has been a long but fruitful day and I find that I am very tired, Greta." She kissed her sister's forehead as she passed her on the way to her room. "Let God guide you," she said softly.

"Easy for you to say," Greta mumbled as she remained sitting in the chair by the unlit fireplace. Then as she had done her whole life, she followed her sister's advice. She squeezed her eyes closed and prayed silently.

After a long moment she heard Luke quietly calling to her through the open window. "Greta, will you not come out?"

"*Yah,* coming."

Slowly she walked to the door and out onto the porch where she was surprised to see Luke standing rather than sitting on the swing. He took a step toward her and held out his arms and she did not hesitate to walk directly into his embrace.

"I am sorry for upsetting you earlier today," he said as he folded his arms around her, creating a kind of safe cocoon that Greta found she never wanted to leave.

Was this feeling of coming home God's answer? Was He showing her that Luke was the man she would spend her life with? Lydia had advised prayer and then listening to her heart, and while her prayer had been brief and interrupted by Luke's presence, there was no denying what her heart was telling her in this moment. "It's so late," she murmured. "I thought you might be too weary."

"Come and sit with me. I want to tell you something," Luke said as he led the way back to the swing.

He sounded so very serious that Greta feared that he might have decided to quit her as Josef had done. But if that were the case, would he have come at all? And would he now be holding both her hands between his own as he sat forward on the swing so that he could face her?

The lamp from the front room cast its glow on her features while Luke's face remained in shadow. "What is it?" she asked and the tremor in her voice gave away her nervousness.

He cleared his throat, revealing his own unease. "I know that the time we have spent together has not been long," he began. "And it would be wrong of me to ask this without acknowledging that."

He sounded as if he were delivering a speech, one he had practiced many times.

Greta's heart sank.

"But," he continued after drawing in a deep breath, "I have come to a decision."

"I see," Greta whispered. "Perhaps Lydia should be present for this?"

He seemed surprised by the suggestion. "Why would..."

"If you are quitting me, then Lydia must know for others will surely..."

"I am not quitting you, Greta. I love you. I am asking you to—when you are ready and certain—to become my wife."

Greta's mouth fell open but no sound came out so Luke rushed forward. "As I have said, I realize that our time together has been brief and you may not yet be ready to make such a decision—such a commitment. But I have prayed much on this matter and I truly believe that God is leading me in this. You should take the time you need—days, weeks, even months if necessary—to be very certain of your answer. I will wait. For I know without a doubt that you are the reason I came to Celery Fields. God was leading me to you and even if you see matters otherwise and refuse me, then..."

Greta laid her finger on his lips to quiet his ramblings. "I accept," she said. "I would marry you, Luke Starns." She slipped her hands from his and cupped the smooth skin of his jaw. "I will be your wife."

"You are certain?"

Greta laughed. "Are you?"

"Yah," he replied, his voice husky as he moved closer. "I am very, very certain."

In the past he had kissed her or she had kissed him but this time their kiss was shared, each meeting the other's lips with all the fervor of the decision they had just made. Greta's heart sang with the pure joy of realizing that everything she had ever dreamed of for herself would now be true, including a life with a man who truly cared for her—loved her. She and Luke would marry and settle together in a home of their own where they would raise a family and live—God willing—many years together. She thought that her heart might fly right out of her body, so truly happy was she.

But when Luke pulled away from the kiss, he seemed once again to be struggling to find the words he wanted to say to her.

"I love you, Luke," she said softly. She had never uttered those words before and yet they seemed so very right and true now. "I have never found a way to speak those words with—anyone else, but I find them coming so easily now. I love you with all my heart."

"There are things you must yet know," Luke said and she did not like the way his voice had taken on a tone of warning. "If we are to be together then you must know everything about my past about my family…"

"Sh-h-h," she whispered. "There will be time enough for us to each learn all that has brought each of us to this moment. Whatever is past should remain there. I want only for us to look ahead. Oh, Luke, we are going to be so very happy. Please don't spoil this moment with worries about the past."

"But it is only right that…"

"Whatever it is that you are burdened with from your days in Ontario, it does not matter. If you love me, then that is everything I need. We will build a life— here." He said nothing and as they sat in silence for several long minutes Greta could not quell her fears. "Luke? Tell me that you are not having doubts."

Luke pulled her closer and kissed her forehead. "No doubts. Never any doubts."

Greta settled against him. "Then you will go and see Levi Harnischer first thing tomorrow?" Levi was the deacon of their congregation and as such it was his role to receive the man's request to wed and then to visit the family of the proposed bride to be sure that her parents—or in Greta's case, Lydia—and the bride were in agreement.

"Are you saying that you do not wish to wait—to be certain?"

"I am already certain." She giggled happily. "Levi will be surprised that it is me you wish to marry," she warned. "Everyone thinks that you and Lydia..."

Luke chuckled as he sat back and pulled her to him, his arm resting around her shoulders. *"Yah,* no doubt there will be many surprised people." He sighed with pleasure and gently rocked the swing.

Greta thought she had never before felt so protected nor so certain of what lay ahead for her. "Let's go tell Lydia," she suggested.

"It is late and she will be sleeping. Besides, we have much we need to discuss before we share our news with others—even with Lydia."

"But she will know something has changed the minute she sees my face for I will not be able to contain my happiness, Luke." She grabbed his hand and pulled him to his feet. "Come on. We can talk about whatever serious matters you think we must discuss tomorrow."

"Greta, you don't understand. Please, you must listen to..."

"Liddy!" she shouted, allowing the screen door to slam with a bang behind them as she and Luke entered the house.

As Greta had expected, Lydia came running from her room, wrapping her shawl around her, her bare feet padding on the wood floors. "What's happened now?" she asked and then froze in the archway that led from the front room to the bedrooms when she saw Luke standing next to Greta.

"God has spoken," Greta announced.

"Sister!" With a single word Lydia warned against any blasphemy but then she looked from Greta to Luke and back again. "You are to marry?"

"We are," Luke replied, "with your agreement."

"Luke is going to see Levi tomorrow morning first thing," Greta gushed. "And then Levi will come here tomorrow evening and then… Oh, Liddy, we have so much to do. Do you think we should tell Pleasant? I mean she is family, as well, and…"

"It's to be soon then?" For the first time Lydia seemed to have some concern. "The wedding?"

"Why would we wait?" Greta asked, fighting to keep her tone light in the face of her sister's unexpected doubt.

But Luke placed his hand on her shoulder. "Lydia is right to question the suddenness of our decision, Greta." He stepped forward and faced Lydia directly. "I can only tell you, Lydia Goodloe, that in a very short time I have come to love your sister more than I would have thought myself capable of loving anyone. I find that there is hardly an hour that passes when she is not in my thoughts and I promise you that I will do everything I can to see that she is well cared for and happy."

Greta watched as Lydia worried her lower lip, a sure sign that she was not completely convinced. "This was your idea, Liddy," she reminded her. "It has worked out as you prayed. Can you not be happy for us?"

Lydia looked from Greta to Luke and then she walked forward, extending one hand to each of them until the trio had formed a little circle there in the front room. "I am happy for you, Greta. And as for you, Luke, it will be good to have a brother."

"And I will have a sister," he replied.

"We must write to your father and brothers at once," Greta said, pulling free of the circle as she hurried to the desk and pulled out writing paper and a pen.

"There will be time enough for that," Lydia said. "Right now, we should all get some rest."

"Your sister is right, Greta," Luke said as he gently relieved her of the pen and placed it back on the desk. "I will speak to Levi tomorrow—today," he added as they all glanced at the tall clock standing in the front hallway that was just striking midnight. "*Guten nacht,* Lydia."

"*Guten nacht,* Luke," Lydia replied as she drew her shawl around her and headed back down the hall. "Do not be out there seeing Luke off for too long, sister," she warned, but there was a lilt to her voice that told Greta that Lydia did not really care if the happy couple stayed on the porch until dawn.

As soon as Liddy's door closed with a soft click, Greta gave a soft cry of pure joy and flung herself into Luke's arms. "I love you. I love you. I love you," she said, punctuating each declaration with a kiss and filled with the joy of knowing without a doubt that she had discerned God's plan for her life—and this time she had gotten it right.

In the face of Greta's euphoria, Luke decided to postpone the conversation he knew they would need to have about his past. Surely he would be able to make her understand why he had left his home in Ontario to move to Celery Fields. Surely she would see that he had really had no choice. And in the meantime it gave him great pleasure to see her so happy. So early the following morning he drove out to the Harnischer farm and stood in the barn, speaking with Levi Harnischer—the deacon of their congregation. As Luke had expected, Levi Harnischer was taken aback when he heard of Luke's intention to marry Greta.

"You are already the nervous bridegroom," Levi teased. "You mean to say that it is Lydia Goodloe that..."

"I have not mistaken my words, Levi. It is Greta Goodloe whom I wish to wed," Luke said firmly. Then he told Levi how Lydia had come up with the plan to allow Greta and Luke the time they might need to get better acquainted while everyone in Celery Fields thought that Lydia was the object of his affections. "After Josef Bontrager quit Greta, I believe that Lydia was somewhat relieved but that she also felt an urgency to take some action to turn her sister's head in a new direction. She thought that Josef might realize his mistake and try to win Greta back."

"As he has," Levi noted. "So, it is Lydia who set this plan in place?"

"Yah. But she did so with Greta's full agreement."

"And you also agreed?"

"Not at first. But then I prayed on the matter and it seemed that with Josef quitting Greta perhaps there was a message in the timing of things. I cannot deny that when I first came to Celery Fields I was drawn to Greta, but she was with Josef and so I turned my attention to Lydia."

"And she rejected you?"

"She did, as she seems inclined to reject the very notion of marriage for her at all. You should understand that Lydia was quite worried about Greta. She made it clear that she did not necessarily expect the match between Greta and me to be one of true love, but rather one in which her sister could achieve the life that she had always aspired to live."

"And do you love her—Greta?"

"More than I would have thought possible."

"And what of her feelings for you?"

"She has said that she loves me in return." *Repeatedly,* Luke thought, and could not seem to hide the smile that tugged at the corners of his mouth.

"And all of this has come to pass in what—a matter of a few weeks?"

"A little longer than that," Luke protested but he knew that he was splitting hairs. It had been a courtship of what some would see as a shockingly short duration. "I am not some teenager just coming from his *Rumspringa,* Levi. And Greta herself is past her twentieth birthday already."

Levi stroked his beard, still dark like his hair but with hints of gray. "When is this marriage to take place?"

"As soon as possible." Luke saw the startled glance

that Levi gave him and hastened to add, "We are both anxious to begin our life together."

"I see. You are asking me then to serve as the *Schtecklimann*—the go-between for brokering this marriage?"

"We wish to do everything properly," Luke said, "although Greta—and Lydia—have already given their consent. But in the absence of living parents, I had thought that you might call on Lydia and Greta for their assurance that they are in agreement with this plan. Perhaps their half sister Pleasant should be there, as well?"

"I would think so. Pleasant was like a mother to both those girls for some years." He finished tossing clean hay onto the floor of the stable stalls and turned to face Luke. "All right, I will call on the sisters tomorrow and unless there is something that would prevent this union, I will report to Bishop Troyer and he can publish your intent at our next service."

"Das ist gut." Luke tried hard to ignore the dread he felt at the deacon's words about something preventing the union. Once again, he vowed to himself and God that he would tell Greta the story of his past the very next day.

But as they sat together on her front porch the following evening with a steady rain falling, Greta was anxious to tell him every last detail of the meeting that she and Lydia and Pleasant had had with Levi earlier that night. By tradition, the deacon had arrived after dark. "I suppose that's in case the parents—or in this case, Lydia—deny permission. That way no one loses face since presumably no one else is aware of the courtship—although that's unlikely in a place as small as Celery Fields." She was babbling, but it was born of her excitement and happiness so she hurried on to tell him the rest. "It was all so very serious," she said with a mock grimace. "As if Levi needed to assure himself that I—that we—knew what we were doing."

"He was just doing his job as *Schtecklimann*," Luke reminded her. "It's all part of the tradition."

"I know. It's meaningless—no more than a formality passed down through the generations. I mean what was he going to do? Tell me not to marry you?"

"That would not be his place."

"Anyway, once he had gone through the ritual and Lydia and Pleasant had assured him that they approved, he did seem genuinely happy for us. Oh, Luke, we have so much planning to do. I mean if our intent is to be published this next Sunday, there is no time to waste."

Luke chuckled and stretched his arm across the back of the swing. She leaned her head against his shoulder. "I am pretty sure that Bishop Troyer and the others are well practiced at this, Greta."

"I'm not talking about the announcement itself—there's the ceremony to plan. We'll need to allow time for friends and relatives from out-of-town to arrive. But even so, we need to set a date for just a few weeks from now if we are to make the journey north to visit friends and family and still be back in time for the harvest season."

In the days when they were first getting to know one another, Luke had explained to her how he was busiest during the planting and harvest seasons. Those were the times when the horseshoes and equipment his neighbors used for plowing and harvesting their crops were more likely to need a repair. This year, whatever business he could take in during the harvest season would be especially important since the fire that had destroyed Luke's business had come at the very height of the planting season, severely limiting his ability to serve his customers.

Greta continued to chatter on about plans for the ceremony and the meal that would follow, but Luke listened only to the lilt of her voice so filled with joy and excitement. He felt such power in realizing that he was the cause of her elation. He was relishing the picture she painted with her planning right up until the moment when she began speaking about their wedding trip.

"Do you honestly think that we can travel all the way to Canada and still be back in time?" she asked. "How long does the train take? And what of the cost?"

"Canada?"

"To see your family, of course. Unless you think they might be able to come here for the ceremony. But you mentioned that your father's health has not been good so perhaps it's best if we go there. I can't wait to meet your father and brothers. Do you think they'll like me? And what about the wives?"

Luke swallowed. The time had come. In truth the time had passed when he should have told Greta exactly why he had left Canada and moved to Celery Fields. "Greta, we cannot include my family in this."

"Why on earth not?" She smiled uncertainly. "Oh, do they do things differently there? I mean is the tradition of a wedding trip not part of…"

Luke closed his eyes against the understanding that the moment he had dreaded for days was at hand. He had allowed himself to be swayed by Greta's assurances that there was nothing he could tell her that could possibly change her feelings for him. Yet all the while he had known that indeed there was something.

"Listen to me," he said sternly. "When I was living in Canada, Greta, there was a woman—two women…" He felt Greta stiffen as if she were preparing herself for bad news. "I had passed my *Rumspringa*—my running around time—and my *Dat* was urging me to settle down. All my brothers were married already with families of their own and my father was getting along in years. He was already in poor health and it was important to him to see us all settled. He had promised my mother."

"Did you love these women?" Her voice was dull and carried no hint of her usual enthusiasm.

"Not really—I never thought about the need for love to be a part of choosing a wife, Greta. It was something to be done at a certain stage of life. Admittedly I thought that perhaps the younger one…that in time…"

"What happened?"

"The young woman's father had other ideas. Like Laban with Jacob, he wanted his elder daughter to marry first."

"These were sisters?"

"Yah."

"Like Lydia and me." Her voice was thin as if her vocal cords were stretched too tight and she did not look at him.

"In some ways, yes. Certainly the elder one was like Lydia in that she had made up her mind that she would not marry. But her father had other ideas and like the story of Laban and his daughters, he was intent on seeing her married."

"But you and the younger sister…"

"There was nothing there, either," Luke said softly. "I see that now. At the time I thought that she and I could make a life but that was all there was to it. It was plain that she hoped her sister would agree to their father's plan."

Greta edged away from him on the pretense of reaching for a dry leaf that had blown onto the porch.

Luke felt such a sense of panic that it was all he could do not to grab her by the shoulders and force her to face him—to hear him out. "Greta, I am asking you to believe me when I say that even then—before I ever knew you existed—I did not feel for her anything close to what I feel whenever I look at you."

"Did you kiss her?"

"No. Her father would not permit the courtship."

"But you would have?"

"I don't know. I suppose. That's not the point, Greta. The point is that I did not marry either of them."

"If your only purpose was to seek a wife, why not the elder one?"

Luke had never imagined that this would be so very difficult. "Because I understood that marrying was not something that she wanted. Unfortunately her father would not listen to reason. In the end there was an accident involving the elder sister. She did not survive."

"Oh, Luke, how horrible. But then the father—surely he would want his younger daughter— I mean, in time…"

Luke shook his head. "There is more," he said, his

throat closing around the words making it nearly impossible for him to speak.

"That's enough," Greta said softly as she sat forward, pulling away from him and folding her arms protectively over her chest. "I don't need to know anything more. I am sorry for the loss of this woman and for what her family must have suffered but, Luke, this is our time—our happy time." She turned to him and in the lamplight he saw her eyes go wide with pleading. "Can we not just let the past go?"

And once again, against his better judgment, Luke agreed. But as she settled back into the curve of his arm and he rested his cheek on her fair hair, he realized that he had allowed himself to set aside his past. A past he had hoped to put behind him by coming to Celery Fields. But that was not possible—not now. Before their intent to wed was published, he had to find a time to tell Lydia the whole story. If Lydia still accepted him as a proper husband for Greta in spite of his past, then they would go forward. If not, he would seek the promise of Levi and Bishop Troyer to say nothing of the plan to wed Greta so that she would not have to suffer the pity of others yet again. Then he would make Greta hear him out so that she would understand once and for all why he would not tarnish her good name with his past and why he would leave Celery Fields for good.

Chapter Thirteen

On Monday evening before the Sunday that the union between Luke and Greta was to be published at services, Lydia and Greta were at supper discussing the plans for the wedding when there was a knock at the front door.

"That will be Luke," Lydia said. "He has asked to speak with me privately."

Before Greta could question her, Lydia went to the door and Greta could not have been more surprised to hear her sister exclaim, "Why, Josef Bontrager, you're back from your travels. Come in and share our supper."

Greta took that as her cue to set another place at the small kitchen table. She offered up a quick prayer to keep her high spirits and excitement about the coming wedding in check so as not to wound Josef. "Hello, Josef," she said when he entered the kitchen. "Did you have a good trip?"

She waited until he sat down and then filled his glass with sweet tea before taking her own place next to him and offering him a helping of the meat loaf and mashed potatoes that she had made. The sisters sat in silence while Josef bowed his head in a brief prayer.

"I was not traveling for pleasure," Josef stated as if she had somehow accused him of frivolity. He snapped open his napkin and tucked it into the neck of his shirt.

"Business then," Lydia said and offered him the bread.

He helped himself to two thick slices and reached for the butter. "I am afraid that I have returned with some news, Greta. News that will no doubt wound you in the telling but that will nevertheless save you from making a mistake that could…"

Greta set aside her fork and folded her hands in her lap. She was all too familiar with this side of Josef. He liked to deliver bad news preceded by a lecture. "Just tell us what you came to say, Josef."

He ignored her request and continued to set the stage for his news. "It would seem that things between you and the blacksmith have moved forward at a faster pace than I would have hoped, Greta."

"What makes you say such a thing?" Greta asked, casting a worried look at Lydia.

"My Uncle Cyrus went to see Levi Harnischer the other evening but he was away. Hannah said he had come to town. My uncle saw Levi's buggy parked outside your house and as the deacon was leaving Cyrus heard him say that he would tell the bishop to publish the news."

"Your uncle spied on us," Greta said flatly, not in the least surprised that Cyrus Bontrager would stoop to such tactics.

"Oh, Josef," Lydia entreated, "you really must accept that Greta has…"

"So now you know the news. It's true, Josef. Bishop Troyer will publish our intent to wed at services next Sunday."

"You cannot allow this," Josef exclaimed, turning to Lydia.

"It is not for you to decide…" Lydia protested but Greta interrupted her.

"Let him say what he has come to say, Liddy." Her fists were clenched now and she was having trouble breathing. The panic she had felt that day weeks earlier when Josef had quit her was back. Only this time it was ten times worse. She focused all of her attention on Josef. "Just tell us why you have come here, Josef."

Josef helped himself to the meatloaf and mashed potatoes that Greta had prepared for her supper with Lydia. "Luke Starns is under the *Bann*," he said as he scooped food onto his plate without looking at either sister.

Lydia glanced at Greta and smiled uncertainly. Greta focused all of her attention on her plate.

"He was excommunicated by his church in Ontario," Josef continued, stuffing his mouth with the food as if he had not eaten in days. "And that is why he left there and started up his business here. That is also why he had no letter from his bishop to present when he joined our congregation. He has deceived you, Greta. He has deceived all of us, allowing us to do business with him and welcome him into the fold of our community when all along he knew…"

"Surely there is some explanation," Lydia challenged. "What were the circumstances?"

"I will say only that the circumstances were not dissimilar to the situation here in that they involved two sisters." He paused to take a long drink of his tea before adding, "One of them ended up dead and the circumstances surrounding that death were at the very root of Luke's being cast out."

"You are accusing Luke of murder?" Greta was outraged.

"I am not accusing Luke of anything. He stands accused by his own congregation and shunned by his own family. Some say her death was an accident but, by and large, most believe that she died by her own hand. All are convinced that she died of a broken heart when Luke rejected her."

"Without knowing all of the circumstances, you cannot hold him responsible for a decision made by another," Lydia argued but her voice shook and Greta saw that she had been completely unnerved by Josef's news.

Josef took a bite of his bread—bread that Greta wanted to rip from his hand. How could he drop such news on them and go on calmly eating his supper? He was enjoying this. She wanted to tell him that she already knew about the sisters in Ontario, that she already knew that the elder one had died—although it was true that Luke had failed to tell her the details. On the other hand, she had not asked—had not wanted to know of anything so sad in the face of her own joy.

"Liddy is right," she argued, determined to defend Luke. "If this woman did not die by his actions, then of what could he be accused?"

"Arrogance in his refusal to accept the accusation made by the woman's father and to make any amends or seek any forgiveness." He sopped up the last of the sauce on his plate with the crust of bread. "I have already spoken to Bishop Troyer and presented him with a letter that the bishop in Ontario asked me to bring back with me. A letter insisting that our congregation uphold the *Bann* on Luke or risk creating disunity within the larger church."

"Why have you done this?" Greta whispered, her hands shaking so hard now that all she could do to still them was to knit her fingers together.

For the first time since his arrival, Josef turned all of his attention to her. He set his fork on the plate and pulled the napkin from his shirt, wiping his mouth with it before explaining. "Can you not see that I did it for you, Greta? It was for you that I left my farm with the fields barely plowed and traveled to Canada. It was for you that I sought to learn the truth about this man—to save you from possibly becoming his next victim. We have long known that the circumstances that brought Luke here were never fully revealed and…"

"You did not do any of this for me, Josef Bontrager. You did it for you—out of your sense of wounded pride that I had moved forward with my life after you quit me."

"I had hoped, of course, that you and I could find our way back to each other—that is still my hope. But even in the absence of that I could not allow…"

A strength born of outrage roiled through Greta, bringing her to her feet. He could not *allow?* He was not her father or brother and certainly not her husband. He had no right to decide what was best for her. "I must go," she said tightly even as she took down her bonnet and tied it in place.

"Greta, wait," Lydia called after her.

But Greta was already halfway across the yard that

separated their house from Luke's shop. He would still
be working and not yet aware of the doom that Josef
Bontrager had brought back with him from his trip to
Ontario. For the moment she had every reason to believe that Luke was still as happy and excited about
their future as she had been just before Josef showed
up on their doorstep.

She knew she was too late the minute she rounded
the corner of the shop and saw Levi Harnischer's
buggy parked outside. Levi rarely came to town on
a weekday unless he had business to attend to in his
role as deacon of their congregation. And although
there was the possibility that he had come to town
on other business, that was unlikely at this late hour.
Greta slowed her step as she edged her way toward
the open double doors. She heard the murmur of male
voices, surprisingly calm if the conversation was what
she thought it must be.

She peered around the frame of the door and saw
Luke sitting on the chair he had offered her that day
that now seemed so very long ago. He was holding a
paper while Levi and Bishop Troyer stood quietly by.
He handed the letter back to the bishop and stood up.
Although she could not make out his words without
moving further inside the shop and revealing her presence, Greta could tell by his gestures that Luke was
telling the two church elders the story.

It was a story that he had tried to tell her, she realized. They were to be married and she understood now
that before the news was made public he had wanted
to make sure that she knew about his past—all of it.
She realized that in trying to tell her about the sisters,
he had wanted to see if perhaps she would be will-

ing to forgive him. Now the entire business would be made public—as was right, she understood. But allowing everyone to learn of Luke's past could destroy their happiness.

For if the people of Celery Fields knew that he had left Canada under the *Bann,* then they would have had no choice but to honor that. No one in Celery Fields could do business with Luke or invite him to join them in their homes or sit down for a meal with him. And what was she to do? She who loved him more than she had ever thought she could love a man?

She jumped as she felt a hand on her shoulder and turned to find Lydia standing next to her.

"Come home, sister," Lydia pleaded. "It is out of our hands now."

"Josef?"

"I sent him home."

Greta nodded and gave herself over to her sister's steadfast strength and comfort as she had all her life— as she no doubt would need to for the remainder of her days. Once again there would be no publication of her coming wedding at services, no happy exclamations of surprise from the other women, no moments of doubt as others tried to decide if this was good news or if they should pity Lydia. There would be instead the shocking revelation that this man, that all of Celery Fields had taken into their homes and hearts, had deceived them all by keeping a secret that in their world was unforgivable.

Luke was trying to explain the circumstances alluded to in his former bishop's letter when he saw a flash of movement at the door of his shop. *Greta.*

There was no reason she would have come to him at this time of day. They had made plans for him to come to the house after dark, where they would sit together as they had through so many evenings now planning their future. No, Bontrager had gotten to her. He must have gone straight there after delivering the letter to Bishop Troyer.

Every fiber of his being wanted to go to her, to hold her and tell her that they would find their way through this. But then he saw Lydia take Greta away and he knew that to involve her in any way was to do her irreparable harm. She would be forgiven for associating with him while everyone assumed that she had no knowledge of his past, but if she had anything to do with him now…

"Luke?" Levi placed a hand on his shoulder.

From the moment the bishop and Levi had entered his shop, the two men had talked to him in tones that spoke of the seriousness of the situation and yet their kindness toward him was evident. He understood that they hoped—as had his family and friends back in Ontario—to find a way to resolve things so that he could be reinstated into the good graces of the church.

"I will seek the congregation's forgiveness for not revealing my past," Luke said.

There was a silence that Bishop Troyer and Levi filled with the exchange of worried looks. "I'm afraid, Luke, that seeking our forgiveness will not be enough. You must resolve this business with your former congregation in Ontario."

"Don't you think I tried to do that?" Luke said. "But the deacon there is the woman's father and in his understandable grief he would not hear of anything less than my admission that I had caused her to take her life. It was a lie, Bishop Troyer. And to my dying day I will never believe that Dorie took her own life."

"That is the story," Levi said, pointing to the paper they had shown Luke.

"That is *their* story. Dorie often walked along the river when she needed to think or work something out. The rains had made the path slippery and soggy. I believe that the bank gave way and she was washed into the swift current."

"And that may have been the way of it," Josef Bontrager announced, stepping out from the shadows at the back of the shop and coming forward. "But the fact remains, Luke Starns, that this woman felt the need to think on that day because you had rejected her. She would not have been there had it not been for your cruelty in quitting her for her sister."

Luke clenched his fists at his sides and forced his voice to remain calm. "Everyone knew that it was Dorie's father who wanted the match between us. Dorie had stated her intention to remain unwed, but her father would not hear of it. What Dorie overheard that day was her father offering to pay me in land and cash if I would agree to marry her."

"How can you possibly know what this woman overheard?" Josef sneered.

"Because I spoke with her later that same day and she told me. I asked her to come with me so that together we could talk with her father but she refused, saying that she needed some time to think. That was the last that I or anyone else saw of her until her body was found the following morning."

"So you say."

"So says the entire congregation," Luke replied. "Every person voted in favor of my reinstatement save that Dorie's father. As you are well aware the vote must be unanimous and so I was excommunicated. I lost everything."

"But surely you can recognize that the disunity your actions created within the community…"

"What actions?" Luke challenged. "Somebody tell me what I did wrong and I will own it, but I cannot admit to something that I did not do nor can I seek forgiveness if I have no knowledge of what the accusations are."

Levi held up the letter. "You were charged with arrogance, Luke."

Luke drew in a breath to steady himself. It was all happening again. "Because I would not admit to something I did not do, I was accused of arrogance. Was I to surrender to the lie that I had caused the woman to take her life when it was not true and everyone knew that?"

"There is, in the *Ordnung,* the requirement that we be submissive to the greater good of the community," Josef reminded him.

"I…" Luke threw up his hands in a gesture of surrender. What was the point? In trying to defend himself he could be accused of arrogance again for in their faith a man did not put himself above the whole—the community. "What do you wish me to do?" he asked the bishop, turning his back on Josef and any more pronouncements that he might decide to make.

"On Sunday following the service we will publicize this entire matter to the congregation. I will advise that we take the next two weeks to pray for guidance and at the following service I will bring my recommendation for their vote. Until then we will abide by the situation as it is stated in this letter. And," he added, turning to face Josef directly, "we will not speak of this matter to anyone outside this building until that is all in place."

"But at the very least for those two weeks, Luke Starns, you will be…"

"Meidung," Luke murmured. "Shunned."

Levi placed his hand on Luke's forearm. "Of course, you may continue to conduct your business and reside in the community. However…"

"I know how this works, Levi," Luke said gently for he understood that the other man was only trying to be as clear as possible without being cruel. "I endured that punishment for months before I decided to leave Ontario and come here. To this day I have not heard from my father or brothers, although I write to them regularly."

Bishop Troyer grasped Luke's shoulder briefly and then walked away. "I find that I am quite weary, Levi," he said. "Would you be so kind as to drive me home?"

"Yah," Levi murmured. "Coming, Josef?" he asked but Luke gratefully understood that this was not a question but an instruction to the man who had managed to destroy any chance Luke might have had for happiness.

"Greta will try and see you," Josef said in a low voice as he hesitated before following the others outside. "I will do my best to console her but…"

Luke stood toe to toe with the shorter, heavier man. "You stay away from her," he ordered.

"Or what?" Josef challenged but a thin line of sweat

trickled down his temples and Luke saw that the man was afraid of him.

Luke stepped away, effectively releasing Josef without ever having touched him. "Just stay away until this is settled. She will need time."

Josef looked at him, his eyes squinting with curiosity. "You would give up so easily?"

"I would protect the woman I love from gossip and scandal," Luke replied and turned back to his work, taking out all his frustration at this latest turn of events by pounding out a hot piece of iron on the anvil. Behind him he heard Josef's footsteps moving quickly away.

When all three men were gone, Luke moved to the small window and stood for a long time, staring out at the deserted street. The sun was almost set now and he knew that, in houses all around Celery Fields, families would be gathering for their evening prayers.

He took off his leather apron and hung it on the hook then walked outside and down the street toward the old Obermeier house at the far end of town. He had bought the property earlier that week from Pleasant. It had been the home of her first husband and the place where his four children had been born. It had been Pleasant's home after his death while she ran the bakery and raised the children until Jeremiah Troyer came to town. For the last couple years, it had sat vacant and neglected and Pleasant had been happy to hear that Luke wanted to live there.

"Alone?" she had asked with a twinkle in her eye.

"For now," he had replied and been unable to stifle the half smile that tugged at his mouth whenever he thought about the life he was going to build with Greta.

He had asked that Pleasant not speak of the transaction to anyone else. "The house is to be a gift," he told her, knowing that he needn't say more, for having been with Lydia and Greta when Levi called to seek their approval of Luke's proposal, Pleasant now knew the whole story.

In preparation for getting the house refurbished and ready for Greta, he had gathered all of the supplies he would need and stored them in the abandoned chicken coop behind the house. His plan had been that once the announcement of their upcoming wedding had been publicized at services, he would spend every spare hour working to ready the house for their wedding night.

Now it hardly mattered when he worked on the property. Now there was no longer any reason to keep the surprise for Greta. For now there would be no wedding, no house for them to share, no future with the only woman he had ever truly loved. He had told Bontrager that he wanted to protect Greta from gossip and scandal. But in truth, by not admitting to his past when he had first come to Celery Fields, by not insisting that she hear him out—all of it—before she agreed to marry him, he had brought her the very pain that he had sought to avoid.

Luke climbed the front steps and sat down on the weather-warped boards of the porch. He buried his face in his hands as he prayed for God's guidance. And when he looked up and looked over the town that he had come to think of as home, he saw one lamp burning. It stood where it had stood every night since he and Greta Goodloe had first started keeping company and to his eyes it was like a beacon drawing him to her.

* * *

Greta did not know whether or not he would come but she was determined to stay on the porch swing until dawn in case he did. Lydia had refused to make any comment on the story that Josef brought them about Luke or on the few details that Greta was able to offer based on her conversations with Luke.

"I will pray on the matter," she had said. "I suggest you do the same. There must be some explanation beyond what Josef has been able to uncover," she had added as she went to her room, her Bible grasped firmly in her hands.

It occurred to Greta that Lydia had come to care for Luke a great deal—and the feeling was reciprocated. Oh, it was nothing remotely romantic. The two of them interacted as if they were already family—favorite cousins or sometimes even sister and brother. Lately when Luke came calling, Lydia would join them on the porch for part of the evening and the conversation would often turn to the difficulties each faced at work. Enrollment at the school was down now that so many families had moved north and Lydia worried that the elders might be forced to close the school altogether. Meanwhile Luke's non-Amish customers—who were an important part of his business—had fallen on hard times. Many had lost their jobs or businesses and could not afford his services.

Greta preferred to focus her attention on happier topics but she was glad that Lydia took an interest in Luke's business, as he did in her teaching. One day he had even gone to the school to speak to the students about the work he did. That evening Lydia had come home beaming and at supper she had announced to

Greta that one day Luke was going to make a fine father. "And you'll make a fine mother," she'd added with a smile.

But again Josef had spoiled things for her—for all of them. If only he had never gone to Ontario. She sat on the porch swing, pushing it into motion with her bare foot, and wondered why she wasn't more upset with Luke. After all, Josef was simply delivering the news. Of course it was news that he had set out to discover, but there could be little question that there was at least some truth to the tale he had brought back with him from his travels north.

Still, Luke had kept things from her. How often had she asked him about his life before he came to Celery Fields? Now she remembered how early on when they first began keeping company he had avoided her questions and she had allowed it. He had always turned the subject back to her and she had allowed that, as well. Yet she could not deny that of late when he had tried to tell her about his past—about the events that had led up to his coming to Celery Fields—she had begged him not to speak of such things. "You are so very shallow, Greta Goodloe," she muttered angrily as she pushed the swing even harder.

"Careful there." Luke's voice came out of the dark and it took a moment for her to realize that he was standing in the shadow of the large oak tree next to the porch. "Wouldn't want you to go flying off that swing." His voice held none of the teasing she might have expected from such a comment. Indeed, he sounded sad and defeated. She longed to put her arms around him and tell him everything was going to work out for them. But she didn't know that. In fact it seemed more likely that things would not work out at all for them.

"Come and sit with me," she invited, fighting to keep her voice light when what she really wanted to do was cry out to him for answers. What would they do now? Why had he kept these things from her? Why hadn't he insisted that she listen? What had really happened back in his hometown?

"I shouldn't. If somebody saw us…"

"I don't care about that," she fumed, unable to hide her bad mood a second longer. She was so very tired of worrying about what other people might think. She needed to understand what *she* thought. That very morning she had thought that she was in love with this man, that they would be married and that by this time next year they might have that first baby. And like the sand castles the tourists' children built on the beach, all those plans and dreams had been swept away. Now what?

The silence that stretched between them at first made her think that Luke had perhaps gone home. But then she heard his step on the crushed calcified shells that lined the path leading up to the porch. She practically leaped from the swing and flung herself into his arms, burying her face against his chest, needing to hear the strong beat of his heart against her cheek. "Tell me that Josef made the whole thing up," she begged.

He wrapped his arms around her and rested his face against her hair. "You know better. Josef is an honorable man and even though he acted out of his deep caring for you, he would not lie to win favor with you."

It felt as if her heart had paused in its beating. She

felt as if she could not find her next breath. "It's true then that you were placed under the *Bann?*"

"*Yah.* I was. I am."

"Then I will join you in that," she said firmly. Never had she been more certain of anything in her life.

Luke held her by her shoulders and moved her away from him so that she was looking up at him. "You will do no such thing," he said, his voice almost a growl. And he pulled her back against him. "I love you too much to let you throw your life away, Greta."

"Don't you understand that without you I have no life?"

"You don't know what you're saying."

She shoved away from him and returned to the swing, folding her arms across the bib of her apron as she glared at him. "Luke. I know exactly what I'm saying."

He did not move but remained standing on the top step of the porch. "No, I don't think you've thought this through. You'd lose everything—and you have a great deal to lose. Lydia—your family, this community that has been home for all of your life…if you had to leave all of that, never to see them or speak with them again?"

"I don't care," she muttered, but of course, she did care. Never to be able to see or speak with Lydia ever again? And what about Pleasant and her children—the children from her first marriage that Greta had come to love as if they were her very own? The twins from Pleasant's marriage to Jeremiah that Greta had rocked and made crib quilts for?

"You do care," Luke said. "You know that you do."

"But what about us?" She was very close to tears

now. Then suddenly it hit her. "You're going away again, aren't you?" In the beat of hesitation he took before he sat down next to her on the swing, she had her answer. "No!" she cried.

Once again he wrapped her in his arms and held her close. "Let's not get ahead of ourselves, Greta. There is one possibility that things might work out for us. If I agree to go back and seek forgiveness from the congregation in Ontario, then if the bishop there agrees to lift the *Bann,* I could come back and…"

"But you didn't do anything wrong," Greta protested. "Even Josef said that there were many who believed that…"

"What exactly did Josef tell you?"

"He told me the gist of it and after I left to find you, he told Lydia more of the details. There was a man who lived in your town and he had two daughters. As you told me, you had thought to court the younger one but the father wanted to be sure his elder daughter found a good husband." She paused and looked up at him, trying to read his expression in the dim light. "Josef told Lydia that the father offered you a large piece of land, a house and a great deal of money if you would marry the elder daughter."

"He did and I refused."

"Then he said the woman killed herself by jumping into the river, knowing it was far too cold to survive and also knowing that she could not swim."

"Josef has spoken the facts, Greta—at least those that he knows. That is more or less what happened. The father—the deacon in the congregation—accused me of causing her death by breaking her heart, but there is one more part to the story—a part that the deacon never tells."

"Tell me."

"Her name was Dorie—the woman who drowned that day. She had heard her father make his offer to me. It was his offer that broke her heart."

"How can you know that?"

"Because she told me so. She came to my shop later that same day—it was just about dusk. She told me what she had overheard and she said that she was no more interested in a union with me than I was with her. She would not be bartered like one of her father's cows was the way she put it." His voice cracked on this last statement and Greta cupped his face with her hands. "Let me finish," he said.

"Yes, tell me everything and then maybe…"

"I offered to come with her so that we could both talk to her father, but she refused, saying that she wanted to take a walk along the river—as she often did—because she needed to think. Did she jump or slip? It had rained for days and the river bank would have been sodden and the puddles would have turned to black ice as the sun set. I have gone over it all a thousand times and I have no answer. If only I had insisted on seeing her home. I offered but she actually laughed and said that she thought the two of us had caused enough gossip for one lifetime. That's the way she said it—for one lifetime."

"What about the younger sister—the one you were in love with?"

He tightened his embrace. "I have already told you that I was never in love with her, Greta. You are the only woman I have ever loved. I need for you to believe that whatever may happen."

"But you had thought to marry her…"

"My brothers had all taken wives. *Dat* wanted to see us all settled. I thought perhaps she was a good choice. Our families had been neighbors."

"Did she love you?"

"I doubt it. I was several years older than she was. Rumor had it that she had set her sights on the bishop's youngest son."

"What happened after her sister died?"

"Nothing really. Her father forbade her having anything to do with me. I think she was relieved in one way and of course in time she came to believe what many others in town believed—that Dorie had jumped to her death because I rejected her."

"I'm sorry for Dorie," Greta said softly.

"You would have liked her. The truth of the matter is that if her father hadn't interfered, in time I probably would have chosen her on my own. We were a good match in age and temperament. But then I would never have come here—never met you—never known what true happiness can be."

He kissed her and it was not like the kisses they had shared before. This kiss held the taste of finality and she clung to him even as he gently pulled away.

"Just always remember that I love you, Greta Goodloe," he whispered and then he was gone, trudging down the lane to his shop without once looking back at her.

Everything in Greta's heart told her to run after him. Everything in her head told her that to do so would only make matters worse.

Chapter Fourteen

In the days between his Monday meeting with Levi and Bishop Troyer and Sunday, Luke first decided that he would spend his time working on the interior of his living quarters at the livery. But Roger Hadwell and others kept stopping by, offering to help or bringing a hot meal their wives had made for him and he did not like knowing that, if they knew what was coming on Sunday, they would not be offering such neighborly kindness. Besides, every time he looked out his window or stood at his door, he found himself looking straight at the Goodloe house.

So after a day of this, he spent the rest of the week calling on his customers in town, driving his wagon from farm to farm or house to house, offering to shoe a horse or repair some bit of hardware at no charge.

Finally the day he had dreaded arrived. On Sunday he did not attend the services—held this time at Josef's farm. Early on Sunday morning he saw Lydia hitch up the buggy that she and Greta sometimes used for visiting or shopping. She led the horse around to the side of their house and after some time Luke saw

Greta come out and join her sister for the ride to services. By the time they came back, he knew that everyone would know why, for the first time in weeks, the Goodloe sisters had arrived for services alone and Luke had not come at all.

At first Luke had thought the shunning would not bother him one way or another. After all he had been shunned before. And yet there was something at once familiar and at the same time strange about being shunned by his friends and neighbors in Celery Fields. In Ontario his father and brothers and their families had all taken part in shunning him—as was right within the guidelines of their faith. At family events he sat separate from everyone else to take his meals. Even when it was just his father and him sitting down for supper, Luke sat at a separate table and the two men did not exchange so much as a single word.

He had thought that being shunned in Celery Fields might be easier in some ways. After all he already took his meals alone—separate from others. And he still had his *Englischer* customers who continued to patronize him, oblivious to the ways of the Amish. Business was slow and his days were long and silent. He had time on his hands that he spent completing the work on his upstairs rooms, sure now that he would need to make his home there instead of with Greta in the Obermeier house. He did not allow himself to think about how he was going to get through the days and weeks and years ahead without her.

One day he drove his wagon into Sarasota, intent on shopping for essentials such as pots and dishes that had not survived the fire. He ignored the curious stares of other shoppers as he drove down Main Street, navigating his team around the motorized vehicles that crowded the street. He found a place large enough to leave his wagon and team and climbed down to walk the half block to the hardware store. He knew and trusted the owner there. The man had sent him a good deal of business and had shown up to help with the rebuilding of his shop and livery. And while he would prefer doing business with Roger Hadwell or even the Yoders, he no longer had that choice.

Determined to make quick work of his errand, Luke reached for the doorknob even as he fumbled in his pocket for the shopping list he'd made that morning. The door flew open and he found himself looking straight into the eyes of Lydia Goodloe. For one long moment they stood there staring at each other. Lydia's mouth worked nervously as if she were fighting to hold back words, then she hurried past him without a word.

He stood in the doorway, watching her as she dodged other shoppers on her way to the bicycle that Luke had often seen Greta take to the beach. She dropped her shopping satchel into the large front basket before peddling toward him and on past the hardware without so much as a glance in his direction.

"Must be my day for the Amish," Jacob Olsen boomed from inside the store. "What can I do for you, Luke?"

Luke handed the proprietor his list, determined to make his purchases and leave as soon as possible. But his curiosity got the better of him as he waited for Jacob to gather the goods, then wrap and box them. "Does Lydia Goodloe come here to shop then?"

Jacob chuckled. "Only when Roger Hadwell runs

out of stuff like the wallpaper paste she likes using for school projects."

"Wallpaper paste," Luke muttered.

"Yep, she can get pretty annoyed with Roger when he forgets to stock up although, if you ask me, she enjoys the excuse to come into town here now and again. For certain that pretty little sister of hers will find any reason to come here or head down to the bay." He chuckled and then licked the stub of a pencil as he figured the total. "You and Miss Goodloe have a spat, did you?"

Luke's expression must have mirrored the shock he felt at the unexpected question for Jacob hastened to add, "Thought I heard some time back that you and the schoolteacher were…"

"Neh," Luke said as he handed over payment for the goods.

"My mistake." The clang of the cash register's bell was doubled by the jangle of the bells mounted above the front door. Both men glanced up to see the new customer. Both men's eyes widened in surprise when they saw Lydia standing in the doorway.

"Did you forget something, Miss Goodloe?" Jacob asked, coming from around the counter and walking up the long aisle to where she stood.

Luke felt rooted to the spot, his hand on the box of goods he'd just purchased, his eyes darting around the store for some other exit that would save Lydia from having to openly shun him twice in one day.

"I… That is… I wondered if perhaps you might have something to recommend for cleaning seashells, Mr. Olsen? My sister is an avid collector and since I'm in town already, I thought perhaps you might know of something that makes the job easier. I know there are many of the tourists who collect when they are in town and…"

In all the time he'd known Lydia Goodloe, Luke did not think he had ever heard her string so many words together without so much as pausing for a breath.

"As a matter of fact," she continued, focusing all of her attention on Jacob, "my sister is at the bay right now and I thought that perhaps when she got home later I could surprise her." Luke found the way she had raised her voice and the emphasis she was placing on specific words mystifying. *At the bay right now. Surprise her.*

Jacob held up a small brush. "This stiff bristle brush can do a good job of removing the barnacles and such without damaging the luster of the shell itself." He scurried down another aisle and returned with some small instruments. "These nut picks are good for the tighter places."

"I can see how they would do the job," Lydia said as she appeared to study the small tools Jacob held. "I'll take both the brush and the picks," she announced as she moved toward the counter, her eyes still avoiding any contact with Luke. She moved past him as if he weren't even there. "As I mentioned, Greta is even now at the bay. She's taken to spending several hours there in the afternoons and early evenings. The sunsets are something she especially enjoys."

"She stays there 'til dusk? How does she get back to Celery Fields?" Jacob had wrapped the brush and tools and made the necessary change while continuing the conversation.

For the first time since she'd returned to the store,

Lydia's gaze flicked toward Luke, but then she turned her attention back to collecting her packages. "She usually has the bicycle but I needed it today so she walked. I do worry about her especially since those Amish who go there to fish always leave well before sunset. That and the fact that there are so many motorized vehicles on the road, but she insisted on going."

"She'll be all right," Jacob assured her. "I hope these work out for her and if not, you tell her to stop by and we can see what else might be available."

"I appreciate that, Mr. Olsen. Good day to you."

Lydia turned and seemed once again about to sweep past Luke as if he were no more than one of the brooms and mops that Jacob had stacked in a barrel near the counter. But in the instant when they were side by side, she ducked her head as if to avoid any eye contact with him and he distinctly heard her whisper, "Go to her. She needs you."

Surely he had been mistaken. The very idea that Lydia Goodloe of all people might go against the *Ordnung* and actually speak to him was unthinkable. And yet after the evenings he'd spent with Greta, he understood the deep bond the two sisters shared. It was not out of the question that either sister would risk everything if faced with the choice of protecting or comforting the other. Lydia had given him a direct order. *Go to her.* Further she had provided him with Greta's whereabouts and the assurance that it would be safe for him to go there.

She needs you.

All that week Greta had made it her habit to complete her chores as quickly as possible and then bicycle to the bay—the one place where she felt she could think. The bay was the one place where she did not have to see Luke moving in and out of his shop, dealing with the few customers who still came to him from Sarasota. The one place where she did not have to deliberately stay on the other side of the street to avoid the possibility of passing by him.

The bay had long been her refuge. Her father had brought her there often, once he realized that she enjoyed coming along whenever he went fishing there. He would wade out into the deeper water while she roamed the sandbar and shallow water closer to shore. After his death a year earlier she had started coming alone. Odd, she thought now, that not once had she ever thought of asking Josef to come with her. Odd, that all she could think about lately was sharing the spot with Luke.

As the announcement of their plans to wed drew closer, she had thought about all the times they would share here. He would learn to fish—and perhaps teach their sons to fish, as well. She and the girls would look for shells and she would teach them to respect the precious life forms that inhabited the conchs and whelks and other species making their home in the calm, warm waters of the bay.

She stubbed her toe and gave a little cry of surprise mingled with pain. She'd left her shoes on the grass near the narrow sand strip where it was easiest to enter the water. She knew better than not to pay attention to where she was walking. Many of the shells had razor sharp edges and others were round and smooth and slippery enough to cause her to lose her balance. She hopped on one foot for a few seconds until the initial shot of pain waned, then bent to find the culprit.

Buried deep in the muck with only its spiraled end partially exposed was a lightening whelk that, given the width of its exposed end, was possibly the largest specimen she had ever seen. Gently she tugged at it and knew it still held its tenant when it resisted her pull. She bent down, uncaring that the hem of her skirt was getting soaked, and pushed away the wet sand until the length of it was exposed. It had to be nearly twelve inches in length. With great care she urged it to release its hold and when it came free with a sucking sound that made her smile, she needed both hands to support the weight of it. With care and wonder she turned it over in time to see the slick black foot of the sea animal slide back inside the shelter of the shell and close the hard aperture or door that kept out intruders like her.

The outside rim of the shell was a pearly opalescent white that caught the late afternoon sun and turned it into rainbows of color. Greta ran her thumb over the shell, marveling at how the exposed part that she had stubbed her toe on was rough and barnacle covered, while this underside was so beautiful that it brought tears to her eyes. Reluctantly she turned the whelk over again and set it precisely into the indented spot it had occupied before she'd disturbed it.

"Sorry," she whispered, "but thank you for being there and for reminding me that even when something appears so worn and scarred on the one side, it might just be protecting something perfect and precious underneath." She stayed there for several long minutes, watching over the whelk as it settled itself more firmly into the sand. It would not be there tomorrow or even an hour from now, she knew.

Many times she had followed the trails of various species left behind like footprints in the sand, hoping to come upon the creature itself. But usually the trail eventually disappeared—not unlike the footprints she was leaving as she moved on across the damp sandbar toward the beds of clamshells that marked the place where an inland bayou emptied into the bay. Not unlike the joys of her life had disappeared, she thought now, unable to stem the roil of bitterness and disappointment that rose in her throat like nausea.

"I know that it is not my place to question You, Heavenly Father," she said aloud as she walked. "But I am so very confused. What is it that You want of me? And Luke? He is a good man—kind and caring of others. Please take this burden from him—from us both."

But she knew that such a thing was unlikely. Lydia had learned from Hannah Harnischer, whose husband Levi was the church deacon, that to go against the ruling of another congregation—even one in Canada—was simply not done. "Of course, there is always the possibility that Bishop Troyer will consider the fact that Luke has already suffered mightily in all of this," Lydia had hastened to add, no doubt aware of the pain that her news was causing Greta.

"It hardly matters, Liddy," Greta had told her. "Even if the bishop recommends leniency, the congregation still must vote unanimously to accept his ruling and we both know that Josef will never vote in favor of such a thing."

The way that Liddy had looked down before forcing a half smile and murmuring something about trusting in God had told Greta that she was right. And so her task when she came to the bay was to pray for guidance. What plan did God have in mind for her? And because she had never believed that God was either cruel or vengeful she knew that indeed there had to be some purpose in all that had happened.

She stared out toward the horizon where the sun was beginning to tinge the clouds with pinks and lavenders. Soon it would be dusk. She should start for home. Liddy would worry, especially since Greta did not have their bicycle for transportation. The walk home would take some time and if she didn't start right away it would be well after dark when Greta arrived.

But still she lingered, searching for answers that refused to come and grieving for all that she and Luke might have shared.

Luke was in such a rush to follow Lydia's instructions that he almost forgot to take the box of goods that Jacob had packed for him. And he did not miss the odd look followed by the sly grin as Jacob called him back to remind him.

"I expect you can still catch up to her," Jacob said with a chuckle and a nod toward the street where Lydia Goodloe was peddling past on her bicycle.

Luke set the box of pans and dishes into the back of his wagon, taking care to pad the box with some old horse blankets to keep them from sliding around. Instead of turning the wagon north toward Celery Fields at the end of Main Street, he turned south and followed the road as it curved along the bay, his eyes peeled for any sign of Greta. He passed fishermen on their way home for the day as well as women from town pushing baby prams. Several drivers honked their car horns at him as they impatiently sped past him, causing his team to shy and stumble.

Realizing that he'd be better off on foot, Luke found a place to leave his wagon and team and retraced his steps along the calm waters of Sarasota Bay. He had nearly given up when he spotted a movement near the bend where the street curved east and there she was, not twenty yards from where he stood. Her head was bowed as she studied the clear water that covered her ankles and feet and soaked the hem of her dress. Her bonnet obscured her face but he would know her form and movements anywhere.

He took a moment to pull off his shoes and socks and set them next to hers on the narrow patch of sand that could not be called a beach. Then he waded into the water, surprised at its warmth and at the soft sandy muck that instantly covered his feet. He uttered a grunt as he pulled his feet free and Greta looked around.

"You do not need to say anything or even look at me," he said as he worked his way closer to her much as he might have approached a skittish horse. But instead of shying away she splashed her way through the shallow water until she was standing within a breath of him. He had to clench his fists to keep from pulling her into his arms.

He needn't have bothered trying to restrain himself for after only an instant she flung herself against him, her arms wrapped around his waist as she pressed her cheek to his chest. "Oh, Luke, what are we going to do?"

Instinctively he completed the circle of their embrace and rested his cheek against the top of her bonnet. "We will do whatever God wills," he told her.

She looked up at him and her expression was one of such fury that he was taken aback.

"And what if God wills it that…" She seemed incapable of finishing her thought.

"Then His will be done," Luke said. "You know that's the way of it. It is not for us to decide or to know what the future holds, Greta."

"But I love you," she fumed.

"Enough to let me go?"

Now she stepped away from him. "You are leaving?"

"I may have to, Greta. I cannot sustain a business in a community where I am shunned."

"You could find another way to make our living— farming. If we farmed then we could live away from town and…"

Luke pulled her to him again, aware of the last rays of sun streaking the sky behind her. "Sh-h-h," he coaxed. "Think how hard it would be for you to live so near to Lydia and the rest of your family and yet never be able to visit or share in their joys. Think how lonely life would become for you. In time you would rightly come to resent making such a choice."

"Never."

"Do not say that, Greta. It is because you cannot know the toll such a decision might take that you must trust in God to lead you in the right way. At this moment I know it seems like everything is going wrong but you have to trust me. I have traveled this road before. It led me to you at a time when I thought that my life was doomed."

"And then why would God bring us both such happiness only to snatch it away again?"

Her logic was simplistic and yet he had no answer for her, nothing he could say that would ease her pain and stress. The truth was that in the still darkness of the night he had asked himself—and God—that very same question. And maybe in that doubt lay the answer. "Greta, I do not have the solution to this struggle we face but I have faith that God does. If we are patient in time…"

"We don't have time," she argued. "The vote is to be taken on Sunday and even if Bishop Troyer recommends forgiveness and leniency…"

Luke pressed his finger to her lips. "Walk with me," he invited as he took her hand and stepped onto a sandbar that had formed close to the shoreline. "Let's enjoy the sunset together."

Together they followed the line of the sandbar until they were standing several feet from the shore, water surrounding them, the sounds of the town settling in for the evening behind them. Luke stared at the lines of vermilion and orange that stretched out across the horizon as the fiery ball of the sun appeared to sink into the water. He put his arm around Greta's shoulder and drew her closer. "There was a time when I stood on the banks of a rushing river, Greta, knowing that Dorie had died there. The day was waning and it had been a day of storms and darkness. But as I stood there I looked up and on the horizon I saw a single ray of light breaking through the layers of thunderclouds. I clung to that ray of light then, Greta, as you must cling to this beautiful sunset today."

He looked down at her and saw that she was frowning.

"Promise me, Greta," he urged. "Promise me that whatever happens you will not lose faith."

"I promise—I will not lose faith. But I also will not lose hope."

He framed her earnest face with his palms and kissed her, knowing that this might be his last chance. Her response to his lips meeting hers was almost more than he could bear, but after a long moment he tore himself away. "We have to go."

"I know," Greta sighed. "I am later than usual and Lydia will be worried."

"Your sister knows you are with me," Luke admitted. "She sent me to find you."

Greta shook her head and smiled her first smile since he had found her. "She is always watching out for me."

"And that is why I know that whatever happens, you will be all right." He laced his fingers in hers and led the way back to where they had left their shoes. Greta stooped to wipe his feet dry with the skirt of her apron. When he reached for his socks, she took them from him and tugged first one and then the other onto his feet, then did the same with his shoes.

All the while the looks they exchanged said plainly that they were performing the sacred ritual of the washing of the feet. In services men washed the feet of other men and women washed the feet of other women, but it felt absolutely right and proper that Luke and Greta should be performing this ritual together. When she had finished, she sat on the grass while he rubbed her feet dry and brushed away the last remnants of sand with his hands, then seeing that she had worn no stockings, he placed first one shoe and then the other on her feet.

And in the tradition of their faith, once the ritual was completed they clasped hands and kissed each other lightly.

"Da Herr sei mit uns," Luke murmured.

"The Lord be with us," Greta repeated then added, "Amen, in Peace."

"Amen, zum vreda," Luke repeated as he silently prayed that it would be so.

Chapter Fifteen

There was hardly a place left to park their buggy when Greta and Lydia arrived at Levi Harnischer's farm for services. The crowded yard was certainly no surprise. Everyone knew that on this day Luke's future in Celery Fields would be decided. For two long weeks Greta's thoughts had seesawed between wishing this day would come and dreading that it ever would. For today Bishop Troyer would make his recommendation to the congregation regarding Luke's fate. Then the congregation would vote as to whether or not they would accept that recommendation. The vote had to be unanimous and therein lay the problem.

If Bishop Troyer should recommend leniency, Greta knew that there was no possible way that Josef would vote in favor of forgiving Luke and accepting him back into the Celery Fields congregation. For the hundredth time she considered the idea of standing with Luke either way, thus assuring that if the vote went against him then she, too, would be shunned and placed under the *Bann*. But they could go somewhere new—start over…

As if reading her thoughts, Lydia leaned close. "Do not act rashly, sister," she said softly. "Whatever the day brings you must accept that this is God's will and He alone can determine the course your life must take going forward."

"I am not thinking of myself," Greta grumbled. "I am thinking of Luke."

Lydia lifted one skeptical eyebrow, then led the way inside the farmhouse where a hush fell over the women gathered in the front hall. By now everyone knew that it was Greta that Luke had courted all these weeks. It was Greta who would be heartbroken—again. Like clusters of sea grass along the shore, they parted to allow the two sisters to pass on their way to the kitchen—where yet another silence surrounded them. They set the baskets of food they'd brought for the meal after services and then without a word Lydia led the way into the front room where they took their places on the bench reserved for the unmarried females.

They had arrived late—Greta's fault. She had dawdled longer than usual over dressing that morning and then she had burned their breakfast and insisted on making a second round of food. Lydia had not protested and Greta was grateful that her sister seemed to understand her need to avoid arriving for services a minute sooner than absolutely necessary.

Slowly and silently the room filled. There were so many people present that it became necessary to press closer together on the narrow benches and Greta found herself pinned between Lydia on one side and Esther Yoder on the other. Across the aisle and at the far end of a row sat Josef. He was positioned closest to the door. If only she could come up with some way to get him out the door before Bishop Troyer announced his recommendation and the vote was called. She squeezed her eyes shut to stem the wave of rage she felt toward Josef. He had ruined her future with his meddling and for what? Hadn't he been the one to quit her?

She felt Lydia's nudge and opened her eyes as the congregation stood for the singing of the first hymn. The service had begun. In just three hours, it would be over and then…

Her heart hammered and her knees seemed to hold no strength for standing. She wavered and Lydia glanced her way—as did Esther. "Are you all right, Greta?" Esther asked in a tone that oozed concern but came from a mouth that was fighting a smirk.

"I am fine." Greta straightened, locking her knees to maintain her posture. She had less than three hours now to come up with some plan, some way to save Luke, for she knew that he would never allow her to stand with him if the decision went against him. She heard nothing of the sermons delivered first by the second minister and then by Bishop Troyer. Three hours passed and she was still no closer to coming up with a plausible strategy. She made her lips move during the singing of the final hymn but no sound came out as she gripped her side of the *Ausband* that she was sharing with Lydia. Instead she silently repeated the same phrase again and again—*Help me please!*

Finally the service ended and Bishop Troyer stepped to the front of the room. He stood for a moment as quiet settled over the congregation. Everyone knew what was coming and the tension in the crowded room was palpable. Bishop Troyer cleared his throat, then bowed his head in silent prayer. Everyone else in the room followed suit. After what seemed an eternity, he cleared his throat again and there was a general rustling of bodies as everyone turned their attention to him.

"We have before us today a most serious business," he began. "Luke Starns came to us nearly a year ago. He bought a business and has served his customers fairly and well these last months. He has attended services without fail and made himself available to serve others in need. He has in short made every effort to be a good neighbor and friend to everyone living here in Celery Fields—as we have been to him in return, for he has been as a brother."

Greta saw a few men nod involuntarily and took hope from the action. But Josef's scowl only deepened as he leaned forward as if to stop the bishop's praise of Luke.

"The charges against Luke Starns in his former community are not to be taken lightly," Bishop Troyer continued. "I have spoken with him at length about this matter and he has requested the opportunity to come before you today to have his say before I offer you my recommendation for his future with this congregation."

There was a gasp of surprise and Josef was practically halfway out of his seat when Luke entered the room from the small bedroom where he'd obviously been waiting. He looked worn and exhausted, the lines around his eyes and mouth more pronounced than Greta recalled. He stood before the bishop for a moment and then turned to face the congregation. He glanced around and for a brief moment his gaze settled on her. She gave him what she hoped was an expression that mirrored her firm belief in him and her determination to stand with him no matter what.

The flicker of a smile skated across his lips but it was gone before it could blossom as he focused his attention on the rest of the congregation. He straightened to his full height and allowed his eyes to skim over every member of the congregation before speaking. Everyone leaned forward to catch every word.

"You have all by now heard some version of my situation in Ontario," he began, his voice raspy as if he badly needed a drink of water. Bishop Troyer moved a step closer to him, but Luke just kept talking. "I have explained to the bishop and deacon and other leaders of this congregation what happened there and why in the end I acted as I did. I am deeply grateful for their willingness to hear me and for the way you—" He raised his hand and gestured toward those seated before him. "The way you have held me in your thoughts and prayers during these difficult days. I want you to know that whatever comes of this, the community of Celery Fields will always be a place that I think of as my home. I have come here today to seek your forgiveness. I have wronged you—especially some of you..." His eyes darted toward Greta then back to the others. "I ask your forgiveness for not revealing the circumstances that brought me to Celery Fields. I ask your forgiveness for placing this entire community in a difficult position as it relates to the *Ordnung* and this congregation's relationship with the greater church. I ask your forgiveness for my arrogance in thinking that I could manage the business of my past alone. And I assure you that whatever the outcome may be, I accept that as my doing and no one else's. God's will be done."

He sat down then, his shoulders hunched tensely, his hands clenched together. Greta had never wanted to go to him more than she did in that moment. She wanted to wrap her arms around those broad shoulders and assure him that everything would work out. God would see to it. But as a low murmur made its way across the room, Bishop Troyer raised his hands and said, "I am prepared to offer my recommendation for the vote of this congregation. Before I do, let us all bow our heads once more in silent prayer as we seek God's guidance in this matter."

Greta bowed her head but she kept her eyes riveted on Josef. He sat upright, his eyes focused coldly on Luke, his arms folded across his chest in a gesture so completely devoid of forgiveness that Greta felt physically ill. Bile rose in her throat as beads of sweat lined her upper lip and forehead.

She stood up and let out a low moan as she clutched her stomach. "I need some air," she whispered as she clamored over Esther Yoder and headed for the door. She was aware that Lydia had followed her as she ran from the house and out onto the porch. But far more important was the fact that Josef had followed her, as well. As she clung to a post that supported the covering over the porch, he came to her.

"Greta?"

"I'll be all right," she assured him. "It was just so very close in there and…"

Josef took hold of her elbow and led her to a chair. Lydia came running from the kitchen with a glass of water.

"This has been too much for her," Lydia said, her

words directed at Josef. "What is your purpose in all of this, Josef Bontrager?"

"I care for your sister," Josef snapped defiantly. "A great deal."

"You have an odd way of showing that care," Lydia groused as she used a handkerchief to wipe the perspiration from Greta's brow.

"No more arguing," Greta said softly as she heard the low murmur of Bishop Troyer's voice and knew the vote was imminent. And in that moment she knew that she must allow whatever was about to happen without her interfering. She had no doubt that Josef would stay with her even if that meant that he would miss the vote. And if the bishop recommended leniency, as he seemed inclined to do given the way he had allowed Luke to address the congregation, then Josef's absence gave Luke the best possible chance to have things turn out in his favor and therefore to turn out well for them. But she found that she could not tamper with whatever course God had set for Luke. She would place her faith in His will.

"They are about to take the vote, Josef. You should go back inside," she said softly. "I will be fine and Lydia is here. Go on." Josef straightened and looked at her for a long moment. She met his gaze and knew that he understood what she was doing. "Luke's fate— and mine—are in your hands, Josef," she said softly. "Isn't that what you wanted?"

"No," he protested. "I only wanted to be sure you would be happy—that you would not cast your lot with a man who…"

"Makes me happier than I have ever dreamed possible?"

Josef looked out toward the horizon where the sky had darkened and a thunderstorm threatened. "I wanted to be that person," he admitted. Then he looked back at her. "But I never was, was I? I mean we were good friends—the best of friends but…"

"We are and ever shall be the very best of friends, Josef. Now please go," Greta urged. *Before I change my mind and do whatever it takes to keep you here.* She turned away as she felt the tears she'd held in check all morning start to spill. She buried her face in Lydia's apron as her sister wrapped her arms around her, crooning to her that all would be well. And when she looked up to protest that idea, she saw that Josef had gone back inside and through the open window she heard Bishop Troyer clear his throat and then call for the vote.

She clutched Lydia's apron in her fists as the tears leaked down her cheeks and onto her dress. From inside she heard a chorus of Ayes.

"And those against the recommendation for forgiveness and reinstatement?" the bishop said.

Greta held her breath.

There was no sound except the rumble of distant thunder.

"Then we are agreed," Bishop Troyer said softly.

And then even as there was an outpouring of relief and warm greetings for Luke inside the house, the skies opened up and released a downpour. The storm that had seemed so ominous just minutes earlier now seemed to release all of the fear and tension that Greta had been holding in check these last weeks. It was over. Truly over.

She looked up at Lydia who was beaming at her. "Feeling a little better, are we?" she teased.

Greta laughed and then she saw Luke standing in the doorway and uncaring of protocol or rules, she ran to him, stopping just short of embracing him. Instead she touched his cheek. "It is at an end?" she asked, her voice seeking his assurance.

"Neh," he said, "For us it is just the beginning." And then he grinned at her and before she could say anything more the two of them were swept back inside the house in a circle of friends and family as everyone hurried to set out the meal they would all share.

Chapter Sixteen

Greta awoke on her wedding day to find Lydia preparing their breakfast. Set on the table by Greta's plate was a small covered jar. "Oh, Liddy, it's some of Pleasant's starter for sourdough, isn't it?"

Lydia smiled. "Pleasant brought it by yesterday."

The tradition of a mother giving her daughter a jar of the base for making the traditional bread the way she'd been given a jar on her wedding day was an old one. Greta had often thought about her mother as she baked bread for herself and Lydia through the years. But their mother had been so young when she died and in truth their older half sister had been their only true mother for all of their childhood.

"Pleasant and I set it to ripen at the bakery so you wouldn't accidentally see it at her house."

Greta hugged Lydia tight. "It's the very best wedding present, Liddy. Thank you."

Lydia pulled back and studied Greta closely. "Are you ready, Greta?"

Mistaking her sister's concern as that of asking about the preparations, Greta laughed. "I think so.

I'm glad we decided on setting up the food in the barn. The house is bound to be stifling by noon and…"

"I'm asking if you are sure, Greta," Lydia said softly as she touched Greta's cheek. "Is Luke Starns the man you wish to spend the rest of your days with?"

"Oh, yes," Greta said without hesitation. "I love him so very much that sometimes my heart hurts from the fullness of that love."

Lydia smiled. "Then let's get you married."

Together the sisters walked through the small farmhouse that they had shared their whole lives. Some of the larger pieces of furniture had been moved down to Luke's shop to make room for the benches and extra seating that would accommodate the guests for the ceremony. There was little doubt that every Amish family that lived within ten miles of Celery Fields would be there along with many families from further north—as far away as Ontario—that would travel south to celebrate the occasion. In the kitchen they could hardly find space to set a single dish, so filled were the counters with the variety of cakes that Pleasant had created for the occasion.

Towering above the others was the wedding cake— a four-layer confection with each layer being nearly six inches thick. Pleasant had piled on white frosting, covered the confection with shredded coconut and studded the entire cake with tiny silver candies. To either side of the main cake was a smaller cake frosted and decorated with the words "Best Wishes" on one and "Good Luck" on the other. These three cakes would make up what was known as the "wedding corner"— the place where Greta and Luke and the members of their wedding party would sit for the meal following the ceremony.

"Did Luke bring the dishes?" Greta asked. Tradition held that the groom provided the dishes for the wedding party's meal as a gift to his bride.

"He did, but he made me promise not to set them out until after the ceremony."

"Is he afraid I'll change my mind?" Greta asked. She had meant the comment to sound light and teasing but her voice caught.

"Not at all," Lydia reassured her. "He wants to surprise you is all."

"Well, I have a surprise for him, as well," Greta said.

"Hello," someone called out from the back porch.

"It's Pleasant and the others!" Greta cried and ran to greet the women who had arrived early to finish the preparations for the big day. "Now we can make the Nothings and finish decorating the tables."

Nothings, a traditional pastry for weddings, were nothing more than round concave saucer-sized pieces of dough, deep-fried and sprinkled with powdered sugar. They were stacked around the cakes in the wedding corner and on the larger table that held the cakes and pies for the guests. In addition to the piles of Nothings, each table for guests held a glass vase filled with stalks of celery. It was an old tradition, as well, but seemed especially applicable to their community of Celery Fields.

"Oh, it's going to be such a wonderful day," Greta squealed as she ran from house to barn and back again, checking to be sure everything was just exactly as she had always imagined it would be.

"You have been planning this wedding day from the time you were five," Pleasant said, laughing at her half sister as Greta traded one bunch of celery for another with more foliage. "Why wouldn't everything be perfect?"

Greta grinned. "There are always surprises," she reminded Pleasant.

"Yes, well, in your case I think we've had all the surprises we can take."

All of the women joined in the laughter that followed as they worked in happy concert to prepare everything for Greta's wedding day.

Because others had been steadily arriving all morning, the kitchen rang with laughter and excited chatter of the women. On the porch several young girls gathered in clusters, whispering and giggling together. In the yard the men and boys stood around sharing stories about the coming growing season or the price of crops while the younger children raced around, infected by the excitement of the day.

"You keep looking out that window as if you are expecting someone," Pleasant said.

"I had hoped…" Greta's voice trailed off and then a moment later she let out a whoop of excitement as she raced out to the porch and pointed to a wagon pulling up to Luke's shop.

Luke had just finished dressing when he heard the creak of wagon wheels outside and realized that the vehicle was not following the lane that ran up to the Goodloe house as every other wagon or buggy had that morning. This one had instead stopped in front of his shop.

Figuring that it was one of his *Englischer* customers with some emergency, Luke sighed and headed down to his shop. After all, business was business and these days he could not afford to turn anyone away. He just hoped that he could persuade whoever it was to let him get married first before he fixed whatever was broken.

He walked through the livery part of his business to the blacksmith shop in front and pulled open one of the large double doors.

"Guten..."

The rest of his greeting lodged in his throat as he saw his father being helped down from the wagon by his three brothers. The four men of his family lined up and faced him. Behind them, still in the wagon, were his sisters-in-law and at least a dozen children and all of them seemed to be holding their breath.

"Son," his father said huskily and Luke stumbled forward to embrace the elderly man.

There was a moment of hushed respectful silence and then one of the children asked, "Are we going to stay?"

"Yah," Luke's father said before anyone else could answer. He touched Luke's cheek. "We are going to stay."

And then everyone was climbing down from the wagon and Luke was greeting his brothers and their wives and the nieces and nephews he had not seen in months and two new ones that he had not met at all.

"How did... Why..."

"We had a letter—two," his brother told him. "One from your bishop and another from Greta Goodloe."

"Greta wrote to you?"

"Yah," his youngest brother replied with a laugh.

"She made a good case, brother—for you and for us moving down here where as she said 'it hardly ever snows.'"

Everyone laughed at that and Luke realized that they already liked Greta even before they'd had a chance to meet her. Then his father took hold of his arm.

"Your bishop wrote to our bishop, Luke. It has been decided that while you are still under the *Bann* back home, you have made your amends with the community here. Since you would not be able to come to us under those conditions, we decided to come here."

"To stay?"

"We'll see," his father said, glancing around and seeming to find the town to his liking. "After the wedding, we can decide."

"You are still planning to get married today, aren't you?" his eldest brother teased.

Luke looked up toward the Goodloe house and saw that Greta had come out onto the porch and was watching the reunion from that safe distance. The way she had knotted the skirt of her apron in one hand told him that she was worried things might not go as planned. "Come and meet Greta and her sister," Luke said and as he helped his father back onto the wagon and then led the team of horses up the lane, Greta came running to meet them.

By the time everyone had been introduced and Pleasant had insisted on feeding all of Luke's family, it was time for Greta to get dressed. Lydia and Pleasant would serve as her attendants and they followed her to her bedroom to help her get ready. Her dress—

a deep green with a white apron and *kapp*—hung on a peg. Today she would exchange the black *kapp* she had worn all her life for the white prayer covering of a married woman. When she died—hopefully years hence—she would be buried in this same dress.

There was a lot of excited chatter as the women helped her bundle her thick hair into a smooth knot and held the dress while she pinned it into place with the series of black straight pins laid out on her bureau. Then came the apron and last of all the starched prayer *kapp*.

There was no mirror but when Greta turned she could see in the eyes of her sisters that she looked beautiful.

"Oh, Greta," Lydia whispered as tears welled up in her eyes. "You look like Mama." It was the most loving thing that Lydia could have said. Greta had little memory of their mother but Lydia had often told her stories about how beautiful their mother was, how kind and giving and admired she was.

"I only hope I can live up to her legacy," she told Lydia.

"You already have," Pleasant assured her. "Now, let's go get you married."

As she stepped out into the narrow hallway, Greta saw Luke standing in the front room with his brothers, talking quietly to Bishop Troyer. He was dressed in a black suit and as tradition dictated, for the first and only time in his life he was wearing a tie. As if he had sensed her presence, he looked up and the smile that lit his face was the only sign she needed that he was as anxious as she was for their life together to begin.

Lydia placed a hand on Greta's waist and guided

her toward the front row of benches where she sat with Luke and his brothers as well as Lydia and Pleasant. They were the bridal party and now that they were in place the guests would begin to take their seats in the rows of benches behind them. At the stroke of nine in the morning the singing began and Bishop Troyer and the other ministers for the day left the room with Greta and Luke following them.

In Lydia's bedroom, the couple sat next to each other on Lydia's bed while Bishop Troyer instructed them on the duties of marriage and all the while Greta could hear the singing from the front room. She thought she had never heard anything so beautiful in her life. Now as Luke took her hand and together they followed the ministers back into the front room, Greta felt a kind of serenity come over her. Usually she was restless and distracted during services, but not today. Throughout the three-hour service she sat as still as a stone, her fingers woven together with Luke's as the bishop told the stories of marriages from the Old Testament—from Adam and Eve to Isaac and Rebekah.

Finally Bishop Troyer called Luke and Greta to come forward. He smiled at them and without benefit of notes he began the marriage ceremony.

"You have heard the ordinance of Christian wedlock presented," he intoned. "Are you now willing to enter wedlock together as God has ordained and commanded?"

"Yes," Luke and Greta chorused.

He turned to Luke. "Are you confident that this, our sister, is ordained of God to be your wedded wife?"

Luke's response was immediate and rang out clearly in the silent room. "Yes."

Bishop Troyer turned to Greta. "Are you confident that this, our brother, is ordained of God to be your wedded husband?"

The memory of all that she and Luke had had to endure over these last months ran through Greta's mind like a rush of wind before a storm. But then she looked up at him and saw in his eyes the calm and peace of certainty. "Yes," she replied.

"Do you also promise your wedded wife, before the Lord and his church, that you will nevermore depart from her, but will care for her and cherish her, if bodily sickness comes to her, or in any circumstances which a Christian husband is responsible to care for, until the dear God will again separate you from each other?"

"Yes."

He repeated the question to Greta and she had to physically restrain herself from cupping Luke's cheek as she replied, "I promise."

The bishop then placed his hand over Luke and Greta's joined hands and intoned, "So then I may say with Raguel, the God of Abraham, the God of Isaac and the God of Jacob be with you and help you together and fulfill His blessing abundantly upon you, through Jesus Christ. Amen."

And so they were married. There were no exclamations of congratulations as the couple made their way from the house to the barn where they took their place in the wedding corner. Luke sat to Greta's right and when all the guests had gathered, the bishop gave the signal for silent prayer. Beneath the table Luke held fast to Greta's hand as they bowed their heads. And then as if a signal had been given, every head lifted and the room exploded with conversation and laughter all interrupted by the occasional song. The festivities continued on through the afternoon and well into the evening. And through it all Greta was aware of only one person—Luke, her husband.

While tradition held that the couple spend their first night in the home of the bride's parents, Luke had asked Lydia if it would be all right with her for him to take Greta to the home he'd prepared for them instead.

"Of course," Lydia replied. "If *Maemm und Dat* were still alive, they would want to follow tradition, but in this case I think everyone will understand. Besides we need the extra space. Your father will stay here with your brother Ivan and his family while all the rest go to stay with Pleasant and Jeremiah. It's all arranged."

"Denki," Luke said, unable to disguise the relief he felt that Lydia—as usual—had taken charge of everything and left him and Greta with nothing to think about except starting their life together.

So when the last guest had gone home and all of the food and tables and chairs had been put away, he took Greta's arm and led her outside. "Come take a ride with me," he said.

She did not protest but looked up at him the way she had looked at him throughout the long day—as if she were certain that he could do anything. She did giggle a little when he helped her into Jeremiah's open-topped buggy. "Why, Luke Starns, don't tell me that at long last you have bought yourself a proper courting buggy," she teased.

"I borrowed it from Jeremiah—or rather from Caleb. It's his buggy and I don't think he was very pleased with having to loan it to me tonight. I'm pretty sure he had his heart set on seeing Bettina home."

Greta snuggled close to him and sighed. "I expect there will be a wedding there within the next year," she said and yawned as she let her head rest on Luke's shoulder. But when he called for the horse to stop barely five minutes after they'd left Lydia's house, Greta sat up and looked around. "Why are we stopping here?" Greta asked sleepily when she realized that Luke had pulled up the buggy to the old Obermeier place. "I don't like this place."

"Truly?" Luke pretended to consider the large old ramshackle house that had sat forlorn and unoccupied at the far end of the main street ever since Pleasant and Jeremiah had married. "I was thinking it would make a good place for us to live—right here in town, close to my place of business and Lydia."

Greta shuddered, fighting an obvious case of nerves as he came around the buggy and helped her down.

"Let's just go have a look."

They walked up the front path together. "I suppose it could work," Greta said hesitantly. "Perhaps after we return from our trip I could invite the other women for a frolic to help me get it fixed up properly."

"I thought we might stay here tonight," Luke said, barely able to keep the smile he was trying to hide in check when she gasped audibly and turned to face him.

"Tonight? But…"

"Sure. It's pretty crowded at your sister's place and…"

"But, Luke, there are bound to be cobwebs and what about furniture—where would we sleep?"

"I thought perhaps we might sleep up there," he

said, pointing to an upstairs window where a lamp glowed.

"Someone is here," she whispered. "The front door is open."

"*Yah.* Others have been here getting things ready," Luke explained.

He held open the screen door and waited for her to enter first. The scent of lemon oil rose from the wood-planked floors and the banister that led to the second floor. The place was spotless and completely furnished. They might have lived there already for years and just be coming home from a visit with friends, Greta thought.

"Oh, Luke, is it truly to be our home?"

Now he laughed out loud. "I thought you didn't like this place."

"I didn't but, oh, Luke, look at it." She clapped her hands together in delight and spun around, trying to take in everything at once. She grabbed his hand and pulled him down the hall. "I want to see the kitchen," she exclaimed.

Luke followed her willingly and stood quietly in the doorway as she examined the dishes—already washed after their use for the wedding and stored on the open shelves—and a few pots and pans polished to a high shine and hanging from hooks overhead. He was well aware that they would be adding to the collection as they visited Greta's extended family in the Midwest.

"It's everything I ever dreamed it would be," she murmured, running her hand lightly over the table that dominated the center of the large room. "We can fit half a dozen children around this table at least."

Luke chuckled and came to her, lifting her so that

she was sitting on the counter near the window. "In the morning look out this window and you'll see the kitchen garden that Liddy planted for you."

She cupped his face in her hands. "You have made me so very happy," she said softly.

With great care and tenderness he removed her prayer covering and set it aside, and then he pulled out the pins that held her hair, freeing it to fall over her shoulders and down her back. Using his fingers he combed through the curls that sprang back to life after being confined for hours. "Your curls are like you," he teased, "oh so properly controlled when necessary but set free to have their own way, they scatter like the shorebirds taking flight."

"Now you listen to me," she said with mock sternness, "I have taken to heart my responsibilities now that we are married. Please don't worry that I will…"

He buried his face in the masses of her long hair that he held in his hands and shook his head. Then he raised his face to hers. "I love you as you are, Greta. I want your lightheartedness to fill these rooms like sunlight. I want to come home at the end of every day knowing that here waiting for me is my wife with her laughter that is like music and her smile that takes away all my weariness and worries."

"And on those days when I may not be smiling or laughing?"

"Then I will come home and hold you and care for you until the lightness and the laughter return," he promised.

"I am sometimes given to tears," she warned, stroking her fingers through his thick hair.

He laughed. "I well remember that. After all, on

our first real meeting it was your tears that stirred the embers of my attraction to you." But then he saw her face lit by the full moon and her beauty took his breath away. "You are my wife, Greta, and never has God blessed a man more."

Greta flung her arms around his neck. "You know what I wish? I wish this day would never end."

"It is only the first of many days, Greta. Days that we will fill with laughter and tears and memories and, if God grants it, the blessing of children."

"Oh, you want children, do you, Luke Starns?" she teased.

"Well, we do have that large table we need to fill." But he knew that he sounded less than absolutely certain about their future. "You do want children, don't you?"

"I do," she replied and as she placed her lips on his, she added, "And if those chairs are to ever get filled, we'd best get started, don't you think?"

With a roar of laughter, Luke scooped her high in his arms and carried her up the stairs to the large bedroom that overlooked the main street of Celery Fields. And as she settled under the light cotton quilt with Luke for their first night as husband and wife, Greta gave thanks and also begged God's forgiveness for ever doubting that His intent all along had been to bring this stranger from Ontario to Florida—and into her life.

* * * * *

WE HOPE YOU ENJOYED THESE **LOVE INSPIRED**® AND **LOVE INSPIRED**® **HISTORICAL** BOOKS.

Whether you love heart-pounding suspense, historically rich stories or contemporary heartfelt romances, Love Inspired® Books has it all!

Look for new titles available every month from Love Inspired®, Love Inspired® Suspense and Love Inspired® Historical.

Love Inspired®

www.LoveInspired.com

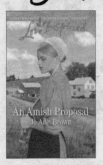

Love Inspired®

Save $1.00

on the purchase of any
Love Inspired®,
Love Inspired® Suspense or
Love Inspired® Historical book.

Available wherever books are sold,
including most bookstores, supermarkets,
drugstores and discount stores.

Save $1.00

**on the purchase of any Love Inspired®, Love Inspired® Suspense
or Love Inspired® Historical book.**

Coupon valid until February 28, 2018. Redeemable at participating retail outlets in
the U.S. and Canada only. Limit one coupon per customer.

52615320

5 65373 00076 2   (8100)0 12325

LIINCICOUP1117R

SPECIAL EXCERPT FROM

All Miranda Morgan wants for Christmas is to be a good mom to the twins she's been named guardian of—but their brooding cowboy godfather, Simon West, isn't sure she's ready. Can they learn to trust in each other and become a real family for the holidays?

Read on for a sneak peek of
TEXAS CHRISTMAS TWINS
by Deb Kastner,
part of the CHRISTMAS TWINS miniseries.

"I brought you up here because I have a couple of dogs I'd especially like to introduce to Harper and Hudson," he said.

She flashed him a surprised look. He couldn't possibly think that with all she had going on, she'd want to adopt a couple of dogs, or even one.

"I appreciate what you do here," she said, trying to buffer her next words. "But I want to make it clear up front that I have no intention of adopting a dog. They're cute and all, but I've already got my hands full with the twins as it is."

"Oh, no," Simon said, raising his free hand, palm out. "You misunderstand me. I'm not pulling some sneaky stunt on you to try to get you to adopt a dog. It's just that—well, maybe it would be easier to show you than to try to explain."

"Zig! Zag! Come here, boys." Two identical small white dogs dashed to Simon's side, their full attention on him.

Miranda looked from one dog to the other and a light bulb went off in her head.

"Twins!" she exclaimed.

LIEXP1117

Simon laughed.

"Not exactly. They're littermates."

He helped an overexcited Harper pet one of the dogs and, taking Simon's lead, Miranda helped Hudson scratch the ears of the other.

"Soft fur, see, Harper?" Simon said. "This is a doggy."

"Gentle, gentle," Miranda added when Hudson tried to grab a handful of the white dog's fur.

"Zig and Zag are Westies—West Highland white terriers."

Zig licked Hudson's fist and he giggled. Both dogs seemed to like the babies, and the twins were clearly taken with the dogs.

But she'd meant what she'd said earlier—no dogs allowed. At the moment, suffering cuteness overload, she even had to give herself a stern mental reminder.

She cast her eyes up to make sure Simon understood her very emphatic message, but he was busy helping Harper interact with Zag.

When he finally looked up, their eyes met and locked. A slow smile spread across his lips and appreciation filled his gaze. For a moment, Miranda experienced something she hadn't felt this strongly since, well, since high school—the reel of her stomach in time with a quickened pulse and a shortness of breath.

Either she was having an asthma attack, or else—

She was absolutely not going to go there.

Don't miss
TEXAS CHRISTMAS TWINS
by Deb Kastner, available December 2017 wherever
Love Inspired® books and ebooks are sold.

www.LoveInspired.com

Earn points from all your Harlequin book purchases from wherever you shop.

Turn your points into *FREE BOOKS* of your choice
OR
EXCLUSIVE GIFTS from your favorite authors or series.

Join for FREE today at
www.HarlequinMyRewards.com.

Harlequin My Rewards is a free program (no fees) without any commitments or obligations.

MYR17

Love Inspired®

Inspirational Romance to Warm Your Heart and Soul

Join our social communities to connect with other readers who share your love!

Sign up for the Love Inspired newsletter at **www.LoveInspired.com** to be the first to find out about upcoming titles, special promotions and exclusive content.

CONNECT WITH US AT:

Harlequin.com/Community

 Facebook.com/LoveInspiredBooks

Twitter.com/LoveInspiredBks

LISOCIAL2017